Thrilling Acclaim for *A Noise Downstairs*

"Linwood Barclay's novels—as intelligent as Michael Connelly's, as compelling as Harlan Coben's—never fail to astonish. *A Noise Downstairs*, his best work yet, is a cobra of a story: smooth, slippery, unnerving . . . and likely to strike when you least expect it. I devoured this book."　　　—A. J. Finn, #1 *New York Times* bestselling author of *The Woman in the Window*

"Vintage Barclay—*A Noise Downstairs* is an utterly compelling read with a twist you won't see coming. I loved it!"
　　　　　—Shari Lapena, *New York Times* bestselling author of *A Stranger in the House* and *The Couple Next Door*

"[Barclay] does a masterful job of layering on the mysteries until we're almost frantically turning the pages, impatient to find out what the hell is going on. A beautifully executed thriller."
　　　　　　　　　　　　　　　　　—*Booklist* (starred review)

"Prepared to be blindsided by an ending you didn't see coming. Barclay's nerve-wracking tale will have readers scared to close their eyes at night."　　　　　　　　　　　　—*Library Journal*

"[A] fast-paced psychological thriller. . . . Barclay carefully conceals hidden motives and secret lives until the startling conclusion. Harlan Coben fans will find much to like."　　—*Publishers Weekly*

"[A] twisty psychological tale. . . . A satisfying and clever novel. The large cast and the story's many moving parts perfectly set the reader up for the final climactic twist."　　　　　　　—*Mystery Scene*

Also by Linwood Barclay

A
NOISE
DOWNSTAIRS

A
NOISE
DOWNSTAIRS

a novel

LINWOOD
BARCLAY

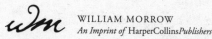

WILLIAM MORROW
An Imprint of HarperCollinsPublishers

A NOISE DOWNSTAIRS. Copyright © 2018 by NJSB Entertainment Inc. All rights reserved. Printed in the United States of America. No part of this book may be used or reproduced in any manner whatsoever without written permission except in the case of brief quotations embodied in critical articles and reviews. For information, address HarperCollins Publishers, 195 Broadway, New York, NY 10007.

HarperCollins books may be purchased for educational, business, or sales promotional use. For information, please email the Special Markets Department at SPsales@harper collins.com.

A hardcover edition of this book was published in 2018 by William Morrow, an imprint of HarperCollins Publishers.

FIRST WILLIAM MORROW PAPERBACK EDITION PUBLISHED 2019.

The Library of Congress has catalogued a previous edition as follows:

Names: Barclay, Linwood–author.
Title: A noise downstairs : a novel / Linwood Barclay.
Description: First edition. | New York : William Morrow, 2018. |
Identifiers: LCCN 2017048396 (print) | LCCN 2017055851 (ebook) | ISBN 9780062678270 (E-book) | ISBN 9780062678256 (hardcover) | ISBN 9780062678263 (softcover) | ISBN 9780062845641 (large print) | ISBN 9780062849465 (audio)
Subjects: LCSH: Psychological fiction. | BISAC: FICTION / Suspense. | GSAFD: Suspense fiction.
Classification: LCC PR9199.3.B37135 (ebook) | LCC PR9199.3.B37135 N65 2018 (print) | DDC 813/.54—dc23
LC record available at https://lccn.loc.gov/2017048396

ISBN 978-0-06-267826-3 (pbk.)

19 20 21 22 23 RS/LSC 10 9 8 7 6 5 4 3 2 1

For Neetha

A NOISE DOWNSTAIRS

Prologue

Driving along the Post Road late that early October night, Paul Davis was pretty sure the car driving erratically in front of him belonged to his colleague Kenneth Hoffman. The ancient, dark blue Volvo station wagon was a fixture around West Haven College, a cliché on wheels of what a stereotypical professor drove.

It was just after eleven, and Paul wondered whether Kenneth—always Kenneth, never Ken—knew his left taillight was cracked, white light bleeding through the red plastic lens. Hadn't he mentioned something the other day, about someone backing into him in the faculty parking lot and not leaving a note under the windshield wiper?

A busted taillight was the kind of thing that undoubtedly would annoy Kenneth. The car's lack of back-end symmetry, the automotive equivalent of an unbalanced equation, would definitely irk Kenneth, a math and physics professor.

The way the Volvo was straying toward the center line, then jerking suddenly back into its own lane, worried Paul that something might be wrong with Kenneth. Was he nodding off at the wheel, then waking up to find himself headed for the opposite shoulder? Was he coming home from someplace where he'd had too much to drink?

If Paul were a cop, he'd hit the lights, whoop the siren, pull him over.

But Paul was not a cop, and Kenneth was not some random motorist. He was a colleague. No, more than that. Kenneth was a friend. A mentor. Paul didn't have a set of lights atop his car, or a siren. But maybe he could, somehow, pull Kenneth over. Get his attention. Get him to stop long enough for Paul to make sure he was fit to drive. And if he wasn't, give him a lift home.

It was the least Paul could do. Even if Kenneth wasn't the close friend he once was.

When Paul first arrived at West Haven, Kenneth had taken an almost fatherly interest in him. They'd discovered, at a faculty meet and greet, that they had a shared, and not particularly cerebral, interest. They loved 1950s science fiction movies. *Forbidden Planet, Destination Moon, Earth vs. the Flying Saucers, The Day the Earth Stood Still. The Attack of the 50 Foot Woman*, they agreed, was nothing short of a masterpiece. Once they'd bonded over the geekiest of subjects, Kenneth offered Paul a West Haven crash course.

The politics of academia would come over time, but what a new guy really needed to know was how to get a good parking spot. Who was *the* person to connect with in payroll if they screwed up your monthly deposit? What day did you avoid the dining hall? (Tuesday, as it turned out. Liver.)

Paul came to realize, over the coming years, he was something of an exception for Kenneth. The man was more likely to offer his orientation services to new female hires, and from what Paul heard, it was more intensive.

There were a lot of sides to Kenneth, and Paul still wasn't sure he knew all of them.

But whatever his misgivings about Kenneth, they weren't enough to let the man drive his station wagon into the ditch and kill himself. And it would be *just* himself. As far as Paul could see, there was no one in the passenger seat next to Kenneth.

The car had traveled nearly a mile now without drifting into the other lane, so maybe, Paul thought, Kenneth had things under control. But there was an element of distraction to the man's driving. He'd be doing the speed limit, then the brake lights would flash—including the busted one—and the car would slow. But then, it would pick up speed. A quarter mile later, it would slow again. Kenneth appeared to be making frequent glances to the right, as though hunting for a house number.

It was an odd area to be looking for one. There were no houses. This stretch of the Post Road was almost entirely commercial.

What was Kenneth up to, exactly?

Not that driving around Milford an hour before midnight had to mean someone was up to something. After all, Paul was out on the road, too, and if he'd gone straight home after attending a student theatrical production at West Haven he'd be there by now. But here he was, driving aimlessly, thinking.

About Charlotte.

He'd invited her to come along. Although Paul was not involved in the production, several of his students were, and he felt obliged to be supportive. Charlotte, a real estate agent, begged off. She had a house to show that evening. And frankly, waiting while a prospective buyer checked the number of bedrooms held the promise of more excitement than waiting for Godot.

Even if his wife hadn't had to work, Paul would have been surprised if she'd joined him. Lately, they'd been more like roommates who shared a space rather than partners who shared a life. Charlotte was distant, preoccupied. It's just work, she'd say, when he tried to figure out what might be troubling her. Could it be Josh, he wondered? Did she resent it when his son came for the weekend? No, that couldn't be it. She liked Josh, had gone out of her way to make him feel welcome and—

Hello.

Kenneth had his blinker on.

He steered the Volvo wagon into an industrial park that ran at right angles to the main road. A long row of businesses, every one of them no doubt closed for the last five hours or more.

If Kenneth was impaired, or sleepy, he might still have enough sense to get off the road and sleep it off. Maybe he was going to use his phone. Call a taxi. Either way, Paul was thinking it was less urgent for him to intervene.

Still, Paul slowed and pulled over to the side of the road just beyond where Kenneth had turned in. The Volvo drove around to the back of the building, brake lights flashing. It stopped a few feet from a Dumpster.

Why go around the back? Paul wondered. What was Kenneth up to? He killed his headlights, turned off the engine, and watched.

In Paul's overactive imagination, the words *drug deal* came up in lights. But there was nothing in Kenneth's character to suggest such a thing.

And, in fact, Kenneth didn't appear to be meeting anyone. There was no other car, no suspicious person materializing out of the darkness. Kenneth got out, the dome light coming on inside. He slammed the door shut, circled around the back until he was at the front passenger door, and opened it. Kenneth bent over to pick up something.

Paul could not make out what it was. Dark—although everything looked pretty dark—and about the size of a computer printer, but irregularly shaped. Heavy, judging by the way Kenneth leaned back slightly for balance as he carried it the few steps over to the Dumpster. He raised the item over the lip and dropped it in.

"What the hell?" Paul said under his breath.

Kenneth closed the passenger-side door, went back around to the driver's side, and got in behind the wheel.

Paul slunk down in his seat as the Volvo turned around and came back out onto the road. Kenneth drove right past him and continued in the same direction. Paul watched the Volvo's taillights recede into the distance.

He turned and looked to the Dumpster, torn between checking to see what Kenneth had tossed into it, and continuing to follow his friend. When he'd first spotted Kenneth, Paul had been worried about him. Now, add curious.

Whatever was in that Dumpster would, in all likelihood, still be there in a few hours.

Paul keyed the ignition, turned on his lights, and threw the car back into drive.

The Volvo was heading north out of Milford. Beyond the houses and grocery stores and countless other industrial parks and down winding country roads canopied by towering trees. At one point, they passed a police car parked on the shoulder, but they were both cruising along under the limit.

Paul began to wonder whether Kenneth had any real destination in mind. The Volvo's brake lights would flash as he neared a turnoff, but then the car would speed up until the next one. Kenneth, again, appeared to be looking for something.

Suddenly, it appeared Kenneth had found it.

The car pulled well off the pavement. The lights died. Paul, about a tenth of a mile back, could see no reason why Kenneth had stopped there. There was no driveway, no nearby home that Paul could make out.

Paul briefly considered driving right on by, but then thought, *Fuck this cloak-and-dagger shit. I need to see if he's okay.*

So Paul hit the blinker and edged his car onto the shoulder, coming to a stop behind the Volvo wagon just as Kenneth was getting out. His door was open, the car's interior bathed in weak light.

Kenneth froze. He had the look of an inmate heading for the wall, caught in the guard tower spotlight.

Paul quickly powered down his window and stuck his head out.

"Kenneth! It's me!"

Kenneth squinted.

"It's Paul! Paul Davis!"

It took a second for Kenneth to process that. Once he had, he walked briskly toward Paul's car, using his hand as a visor to shield his eyes from Paul's headlights. As Paul started to get out of the car, leaving the engine and headlights on, Kenneth shouted, "Jesus, Paul, what are you doing here?"

Paul didn't like the sound of his voice. Agitated, on edge. He met Kenneth halfway between the two cars.

"I was pretty sure that was your car. Thought you might be having some trouble."

No need to mention he'd been following him for miles.

"I'm fine, no problem," Kenneth said, clipping his words. He twitched oddly, as though he wanted to look back at his car but was forcing himself not to.

"Were you following me?" he asked.

"Not—no, not really," Paul said.

Kenneth saw something in the hesitation. "How long?"

"What?"

"How long were you following me?"

"I really wasn't—"

Paul stopped. Something in the back of the Volvo had caught his eye. Between the headlights of his car, and the Volvo's dome light, it was possible to see what looked like mounds of clear plastic sheeting bunched up above the bottom of the tailgate window.

"It's nothing," Kenneth said quickly.

"I didn't ask," Paul said, taking a step closer to the Volvo.

"Paul, get in your car and go home. I'm fine. Really."

Paul only then noticed the dark smudges on Kenneth's hands, splotches of something on his shirt and jeans.

"Jesus, are you hurt?"

"I'm okay."

"That looks like blood."

When Paul moved toward the Volvo, Kenneth grabbed for his arm, but Paul shook him off. Paul was a good fifteen years younger than Kenneth, and regular matches in the college's squash courts had kept him in reasonably good shape.

Paul got to the tailgate and looked through the glass.

"Jesus fucking Christ!" he said, suddenly cupping his hand over his mouth. Paul thought he might be sick.

Kenneth, standing behind him, said, "Let . . . let me explain."

Paul took a step back, looked at Kenneth wide-eyed. "How . . . who is . . . who *are* they?"

Kenneth struggled for words. "Paul—"

"Open it," Paul said.

"What?"

"Open it!" he said, pointing to the tailgate.

Kenneth moved in front of him and reached for the tailgate latch. Another interior light came on, affording an even better look at the two bodies running lengthwise, both wrapped in that plastic, heads to the tailgate, feet up against the back of the front seats. The rear seats had been folded down to accommodate them, as if they were sheets of plywood from Home Depot.

While their facial features were heavily distorted by the opaque wrapping, and the blood, it was clear enough that they were both female.

Adults. Two women.

Paul stared, stunned, his mouth open. His earlier feeling that he would be sick had been displaced by shock.

"I was looking for a place," Kenneth said calmly.

"A what?"

"I hadn't found a good spot yet. I'd been thinking in those woods there, before, well, before you came along."

Paul noticed, at that point, the shovel next to the body of the woman on the left.

"I'm going to turn off the car," Kenneth said. "It's not good for the environment."

Paul suspected Kenneth would hop in and make a run for it. With the tailgate open, if he floored it, the bodies might slide right out onto the shoulder. But Kenneth was true to his word. He leaned into the car, turned the key to the off position. The engine died.

Paul wondered who the two women could be. He felt numb, that this could not be happening.

A name came into his head. He didn't know why, exactly, but it did.

Charlotte.

Kenneth rejoined him at the back of the car. Did the man seem calmer? Was it relief at being caught? Paul gave him another look, but his eyes were drawn back to the bodies.

"Who are they?" Paul said, his voice shaking. "Tell me who they are." He couldn't look at them any longer, and turned away.

"I'm sorry about this," Kenneth said.

Paul turned. "You're *sorry* about—"

He saw the shovel Kenneth wielded, club-like, for no more than a tenth of a second before it connected with his skull.

Then everything went black.

Eight Months Later

One

The old man in the back of the SUV could have been taken for dead. He was slumped down in the leather seat, the top of his nearly bald, liver-spotted head propped up against the window of the driver's-side back door.

Paul got up close to the Lincoln—it was that model the movie star drove in all those laughably pretentious commercials—and peered through the glass.

He was a small, thin man. As if sensing that he was being watched, he moved his head. The man slowly sat up, turned, blinked several times, and looked out at Paul with a puzzled expression.

"How you doing today?" Paul asked.

The man slowly nodded, then slipped back down in the seat and rested his head once more against the glass.

Paul carried on the rest of the way up the driveway to a door at the side of the two-story, Cape Cod–style, cedar shake–shingled house on Carrington Avenue. There was a separate entrance at the back end of the driveway. There was a small bronze plaque next to it that read, simply, ANNA WHITE, PH.D. He buzzed, then let himself in and took a seat in the waiting room, big enough for only two cushioned chairs.

He sifted through a pile of magazines. He had to hand it to Dr. White. In the three months he'd been coming to see her, the magazines—there were copies of *Time* and *The New Yorker* and *Golf Digest* and *Golf Monthly*, so maybe his therapist was an avid golfer—were always turning over. If there was a fault to be found, it was that she wasn't scanning the covers closely enough. Was it a good idea, in a therapist's office, to offer as reading material a newsmagazine with the headline "Paranoia: *Should* You Be Scared?"

But that was the one he opened. He was about to turn to the article when the door to Dr. White's office opened.

"Paul," she said, smiling. "Come on in."

"Your dad's in your car again."

She sighed. "It's okay. He thinks we're going to go visit my mother at the home. He's comfortable out there. Please, come in."

Still clutching the magazine, he got up and walked into the doctor's office. It wasn't like a regular doctor's space, of course. No examining table with a sheet of paper on it, no weigh scale, no eye chart, no cutaway illustration of the human body. But there were brown leather chairs, a glass-and-wood desk that looked like something out of the Herman Miller catalog with little on it but an open, silver laptop. There was a wall of bookshelves, restful paintings of the ocean or maybe Long Island Sound, and even a window with a view of one of Milford's downtown parks.

He dropped into his usual leather chair as the doctor settled into one kitty-corner to him. She was wearing a knee-length skirt, and as she crossed her legs Paul made an effort not to look. Dr. White— early forties, brown hair to her shoulders, eyes to match, well packaged—was an attractive woman, but Paul had read about that so-called transference stuff, where patients fall in love with their therapists. Not only was that not going to happen, he told himself, he wasn't about to give the impression it might.

He was here to get help. Plain and simple. He didn't need another relationship to complicate the ones he already had.

"Stealing a magazine?" she asked.

"Oh, no," he said, flashing the cover. "There was an article I wanted to read."

"Oh, God," she said, frowning. "That might not have been the best one to put out there."

Paul managed a grin. "The headline *did* catch my eye. Otherwise, I might have tried a golf magazine. Even though I don't play."

"Those are my father's," she said. "He's eighty-three, and he still gets out on the course, occasionally, if I can go with him. And he loves the driving range. He can still whack a bucket of balls like nobody's business. A lot less chance of getting lost when you don't actually head out onto the course." She extended a hand and Paul gave her the magazine. She took another glance at the headline as she tossed it onto a nearby coffee table.

"How's the head?" she asked.

"Physically, or mentally?"

"I was thinking, physically?" She smiled. "For now."

"Dr. Jones says I'm improving the way I should be, but with a head injury like I had, we have to watch for any effects for up to a year. And I'm still having some, no doubt about it."

"Such as?"

"The headaches, of course. And I forget things now and then. Sometimes, I walk into a room, and I have no idea why I'm there. Not only that, but I might not even remember getting there. One minute, I'm in the bedroom, the next I'm down in the kitchen, and I've got no idea how it happened. And I haven't gone back to squash. Can't run the risk of getting hit in the head with a racket or running into the wall. I'm kind of itching to get back to it, though. Maybe soon. I'll just take it easy."

Anna White nodded. "Okay."

"Sleeping is still, well, you know."

"We'll get to that."

"My balance is getting pretty good again. And I can concentrate pretty well when reading. That took a while. It looks like I'll be back to teaching in a couple of months, in September."

"Have you been to the campus at all since the incident?"

Paul nodded. "A couple of times, kind of easing into it. Did one lecture for a summer class—one I'd given before so I didn't have to write it from scratch. Had one tutorial with some kids, got a good discussion going. But that's about it."

"The college has been very patient."

"Well, yes. I think they would have been anyway, but considering it was a member of their own faculty who tried to kill me . . . they've been accommodating, for sure." He paused, ran his hand lightly over his left temple, where the shovel had hit him. "I always tell myself it could have been worse."

"Yes."

"I could have ended up in the Volvo with Jill and Catherine."

Anna nodded solemnly. "As bad as things are, they can always be worse."

"I guess."

"Okay, so we've dealt with the physical. Now let's get to my area of expertise. How's your mood been lately?"

"Up and down."

"Are you still seeing him, Paul?"

"Kenneth?"

"Yes, Kenneth."

Paul shrugged. "In my dreams, of course."

"And?"

Paul hesitated, as though embarrassed. "Sometimes . . . just around."

"Have you seen him since we spoke the other day?"

"I was picking up a few things at Walgreens and I was sure I saw him in the checkout line. I could feel a kind of panic attack overwhelming me. So I just left, didn't buy the things I had in my basket. Got in the car and drove the hell away fast as I could."

"Did you honestly believe it was him?"

Slowly, Paul said, "No. I knew it couldn't be."

"Because?" She leaned her head toward him.

"Because Kenneth is in prison."

"For two counts of murder and one of attempted murder," Anna said. "Would have been three if that policeman hadn't come by when he did."

"I know." Paul rubbed his hands together. It had been more than just luck that a cop came. The officer in that cruiser he and Kenneth had driven past had decided to go looking for that Volvo with a busted taillight.

Anna leaned forward onto her knees. "In time, this will get better. I promise you."

"What about the nightmares?" he asked.

"They're persisting?"

"Yes. I had one two nights ago. Charlotte had to wake me."

"Tell me about it."

Paul swallowed. He needed a moment. "I was finding it hard to see. Everything was foggy, but then I realized I was all wrapped up in plastic sheeting. I tried to move it away but I couldn't. And then I could see something through the plastic. A face."

"Kenneth Hoffman?"

Paul shook his head. "You'd think so. He's been in most of them. What I saw on the other side was myself, screaming at me to come out. It's like I was simultaneously in the plastic and outside it, but mostly in, and feeling like I couldn't breathe. I was trying to push my way out. It's a new variation on my usual nightmare. Sometimes I think Charlotte's one of the two women in the back of that car. I have this vague recollection, before I blacked out, of being terrified Kenneth had killed Charlotte."

"Why did you think that?"

He shrugged. "She hadn't come with me to the play. My mind just went there."

"Sure."

"Anyway, thank God Charlotte's there when I have the nightmares, waking me up. The last one, my arms were flailing about in front of me as I tried to escape the plastic."

"Are you able to get back to sleep after?"

"Sometimes, but I'm afraid to. I figure the nightmare's just on pause." He closed his eyes briefly, as though checking to see whether the images that had come to him in the night were still there. When he opened them, he said, "And I guess it was four nights ago, I dreamed I was sitting at the table with them."

"With?"

"You know. Jill Foster and Catherine Lamb. At Kenneth's house. We were all taking turns typing our apologies. The women, they had these ghoulish grins, blood draining from the slits in their throats, actually laughing at me because the typewriter was now in front of me and I don't know what to write and they're saying, 'We're all done! We're all done!' And you know how, in a dream, you can't actually see words clearly? They're all a-jumble?"

"Yes," Anna White said.

"So that's why it's so frustrating. I know I have to type something or Kenneth, standing there at the end of the table, looking like fucking Nosferatu—excuse me—will kill me. But then, I know he's going to kill me anyway." Paul's hands were starting to shake.

Anna reached across and touched the back of one. "Let's stop for a second."

"Yeah, sure."

"We'll switch gears for a bit. How are things with Charlotte?"

Paul shrugged. "I guess they're okay."

"That doesn't sound terribly positive."

"No, really, things are better. She's been very supportive, although having to watch me go through all this has to get her down at times. You know, before all this happened, things weren't exactly a hundred percent. I think Charlotte was going through something, almost a kind of reassessment of her life. You know, ten years ago, is this where she would have imagined herself being? Selling real estate in Milford? Not that there's anything wrong with that, you know? I think her dreams were a little different when she was younger. But my nearly getting killed, maybe that had a way of refocusing things. They're better now."

"And your son? Josh?"

Paul frowned. "It hit him hard when it happened, of course. Thinking your dad might die, that's not easy for a nine-year-old kid. But I wasn't in the hospital long, and while I had some recovering to do—and still am—it was clear I wasn't going to drop dead right away. And he splits his time between his mom and me. So he's not necessarily around when I wake up screaming in the night."

Paul tried to laugh. Anna allowed herself a smile. They were both quiet a moment. Anna sensed that Paul was working up to something, so she waited.

Finally, he said, "I wanted to bounce something off you."

"Sure."

"I talked about this with Charlotte, and she thinks maybe it's a good idea, but she said I should get your input."

"I'm all ears."

"It's pretty obvious that I'm . . . what's the word? Haunted? I guess I'm haunted by what Kenneth did."

"I might have used the word *traumatized*, but yes."

"I mean, not just because he nearly killed me. That'd be enough. But I *knew* him. He took me under his wing when I arrived at West Haven. He was my friend. We had drinks together, shared our thoughts, connected, you know? Fellow sci-fi nerds. How could I not have seen that under all that, he was a monster?"

"Monsters can be very good at disguising themselves."

Paul shook his head. "Then again, there were many times when I wondered whether I knew him at all, even before this. Remember Walter Mitty?"

"From the James Thurber story?"

Paul nodded. "A boring, ordinary man who imagines himself in various heroic roles. Kenneth presented as a drab professor with some secret life as a ladies' man. Except with him, the secret life wasn't imaginary. It was for real. He had this underlying charm that women—well, some women—found hard to resist. But he didn't advertise it to the rest of us. He didn't brag about his latest sexual conquest."

"So he never told you about women he was seeing?"

"No, but there was talk. We all knew. Whenever there was a faculty event, and he'd bring his wife, Gabriella, all you could think was, is she the only one in the room who doesn't know?"

"Did you know his son?"

"Len," Paul said, nodding. "Kenneth loved that boy. He was kind of—I don't know the politically correct way to put this—but he was a bit slow. It's not like he was somewhere on the spectrum or anything, but definitely not future college material. But Kenneth would bring him out on campus so he could hang out for hours in the library looking at art books. Kenneth'd gather a stack of books for Len so he could turn through them page by page. He liked looking at the pictures."

Paul gave Anna a look of bafflement. "How do I square that with what he did? Killing two women? And the *way* he did it. Making them apologize to him before slitting their . . . I can't get my head around it."

"It's hard, I know. So, you wanted to bounce something off me."

He paused. "Instead of trying to put all of this behind me, I want to confront it. I want to know more. I want to know *everything*. About what happened to me. About Kenneth. I want to talk to the people whose lives he touched. And not just in a bad way. The good, too. I want to understand all the different Kenneths. If it's possible, I'd like to actually talk to him, if they'll let me into the prison to see him. And if *he'll* see me, of course. I guess what I'm searching for is the answer to a bigger question."

Anna tented her fingers. "Which is?"

"Was Kenneth evil? *Is* Kenneth evil?"

"I could just say yes and save you the trouble." She took in a long breath, then let it out slowly. "I could go either way on this. Do you honestly think it will help?"

Paul took a moment before answering.

"If I can look into the eyes of evil in the real world, maybe I won't have to run from it in my sleep."

Two

———

Anna followed Paul Davis out the door. He continued up the driveway to his own car when Anna stopped to open the back door of her Lincoln SUV, careful not to let her father fall out.

"Come on in, Dad."

"Oh, hi, Joanie. Must have nodded off."

"It's Anna, Dad. Not Mom."

"Oh, right. We should get going. Joanie will be going to lunch soon."

"She's not at Guildwood anymore, Dad," she said gently. "I'm going to get you some coffee. There's still half a pot."

"Coffee," he said. "That sounds good."

He turned his legs out the door, then ever so carefully slid off the seat until his feet touched the ground, like some slow-motion parachutist.

"Ta da," he said. He looked down, saw that the laces on one of his shoes were loose. "For my next act, I will tie my shoelaces."

"When we get inside," Anna said, closing the car door and walking with her father back into the house. Once inside, her father chose to sit in one of the two waiting room chairs so that he could deal with his shoe promptly.

"I'll go get you a coffee, then you can go upstairs and watch your shows," she said.

He gave her a small salute. "Righty-o."

Instead of going through the door into her office, Anna took the route that led back into the main house. She went to the kitchen, got a clean mug from the cupboard, and filled it from the coffee-maker.

She heard, faintly, the side door open and close again. She hoped her father hadn't decided to take up residence in the car again. Then it occurred to her that her next client might have arrived.

"Shit," she said under her breath. Anna did not want her father engaging in conversation with her clients, particularly the one who was now due. In her rush to return to her office, she fumbled looping her finger into the handle of the coffee cup and knocked it to the floor.

"For fuck's sake," she said. Anna grabbed a roll of paper towels off the spindle, got to her knees, and mopped up the mess. Once she cleaned the floor and tossed the sodden towels, she poured another cup of coffee and went back to the office.

She found her father chatting with a thin man in his late twenties who had settled into the other chair and was leaning forward, elbows on knees, listening intently to Anna's dad. When Anna walked in, he smiled.

"Hi," he said nervously to Anna. "Just talking to your dad here."

Anna forced a smile. "That's nice, Gavin. Why don't you head in?"

Gavin shook the old man's hand. "Nice to meet you, Frank."

"You bet, Gavin." Frank White tipped his head toward his daughter. "She'll get you sorted out, don't you worry."

"I hope so," Gavin said.

Gavin went into Anna's office as she handed her father his coffee. She looked down at his feet.

"You didn't do up your shoelaces," she said.

Frank shrugged, standing. "I'll be fine. He seems like a nice fella."

You have no idea, Anna thought.

"Are you going to watch TV in your room?"

"I think so. Maybe work on the machine a bit."

"Dad, you already did, like, an *hour* of rowing this morning."

"Oh, right."

She accompanied him as he went into the main part of the house and walked to the bottom of the stairs. She looked at the coffee he was holding, his untied shoelaces, and that flight of stairs, and could imagine the disaster that was waiting to happen.

"Hang on, Dad," she said.

Anna knelt down and quickly tied his shoes. "You don't have to do that," he protested.

"It's no problem," she said. "I don't want you tripping on the stairs. Hand me your coffee."

"For Christ's sake, I'm not an invalid," he said angrily.

Anna sighed. "Okay."

But she stood there and watched as he ascended the stairs, one hand still gripping the coffee mug, the other on the railing. When he'd reached the second floor he turned and looked down at her.

"Ta da!" he said again.

Anna gave him a sad smile, then went back through the house to her office. She found Gavin standing around the back of her desk where her closed laptop sat, admiring the books on her shelves, running his finger along the spines. Gavin wore a pair of faded jeans, sneakers, and a tight-fitting black T-shirt. In addition to being thin, he was scruffy haired and no taller than five-six. From the back, he could have been mistaken for someone in his early to mid teens, not a man who'd soon turn thirty.

"Mr. Hitchens," she said formally. "Please take a seat."

He spun around innocently, then dropped into the same chair Paul Davis had been in moments earlier. "Your father's nice," he said. "He told me he used to work in animation. *And* he said"— Gavin grinned—"that it's time you found yourself a man. But don't worry, I don't think he was looking at me as a prospect."

"Gavin, we need to talk about—"

"But he called you Joanie. Is that your middle name?"

"That was my mother's name," Anna White said reluctantly.

She did not like revealing personal details to clients. And that was especially true of Gavin Hitchens.

"Oh," he said. "I see. Is your mother . . ."

"She passed away several years ago. Gavin, there are certain ground rules here." She grabbed a file sitting on her desk next to the computer. "You are here specifically to talk with me. Not my father, not any of my other clients. Just me. There need to be boundaries."

Gavin nodded solemnly, like a scolded dog. "Of course."

Anna glanced at some notes tucked into the file. "Why don't we pick up where we left off last time."

"I don't remember where that was," Gavin said.

"We were talking about empathy."

"Oh, right, yes." He nodded agreeably. "I've been thinking about that a lot. I know you think I don't feel it, but that's not true."

"I've never said that," Anna replied. "But your actions suggest a lack of it."

"I told you, I've never hurt anyone."

"But you have, Gavin. You can hurt people without physically harming them."

The young man shrugged and looked away.

"Emotional distress can be scarring," she said.

Gavin said nothing.

"And the truth is, someone *could* have been hurt by the things you did. There can be consequences you can't predict. Like what you did with Mrs. Walker's cat."

"Nothing happened. Not even to the cat."

"She could have fallen. She's eighty-five, Gavin. You locked her cat in the attic. She heard him up there, dragged a ladder up from the basement, and climbed it to the top to open the attic access panel to rescue him. It's a wonder she didn't break her neck."

Gavin lowered his head and mumbled, "Maybe it wasn't me."

"Gavin. Please. They weren't able to prove you did that, not like with the phone call, but all the evidence suggests you did it. If we're going to be able to work together, we have to be honest with each other. You get that, don't you?"

"Of course," he said, looking suitably admonished and continuing to avoid her gaze. His eyes misted.

"You're right, I did the cat thing. And the phone call. I know I need help. It's why I agreed to come here and see you. I don't want to do these things. I want to get better. I want to understand why I do what I do and be a better person."

"Gavin, you were *ordered* to see me. It was part of the sentencing. It kept you out of jail."

His shoulders fell. "Yeah, I know, but I didn't fight it. I heard you were really good, that you could fix me. I'm happy to come here as often as it takes to make me a better person."

"I don't fix people, Gavin. I try to help them so they can fix themselves."

"Okay, sure, I get that. It has to come from within." He nodded his understanding. "So how do I do that?"

Anna took a breath. "Ask yourself why."

"Why?"

"Why would you hide a lonely old woman's cat? Why phone a still-grieving father claiming to be his son who died in Iraq?" Anna paused, then asked, "What would make a person do something like that?"

Gavin considered the question for several seconds. "I know," he said slowly, "how those actions might be viewed as cruel or inappropriate."

Anna leaned forward, elbows on her knees. "Gavin, look at me."

"What?"

"I need you to look at me."

"Yeah, sure," he said, allowing Anna to fix her eyes on his. "What is it?"

"Are there any other incidents you haven't shared with me?"

"No," he said.

"Any that you've contemplated but haven't done?"

Gavin kept his eyes locked on hers. "No," he said. Then he smiled. "I'm here to get better."

Three

Driving home, Paul was pleased Dr. White did not actively discourage his idea of delving more into the Kenneth Hoffman business, rather than retreating from it. He'd come to believe that the nightmares rooted in his near-death experience—"near-death" in the most literal sense, since he had almost died—would persist as long as he allowed the event to consume him.

There needed to be a way to turn that horrific night into something that did not own him. Paul could not let his life be defined by finding two dead women in the back of a car, followed by a blow to the head. Yes, it was horrendous. It was traumatic.

But there needed to be a way for him to move forward.

Maybe there was a way to apply what he did for a living to the situation. Paul taught English literature. He'd studied everything from Sophocles to Shakespeare, Chaucer to Chandler, but more recently, his course on some of the giants of twentieth-century popular fiction, Nora Roberts, Lawrence Sanders, Stephen King, Danielle Steel, Mario Puzo, had proved to be the biggest hit with students, sometimes to the chagrin of his colleagues and the department head. His point was, just because something was embraced in large numbers did not necessarily make it lowbrow. These writers could tell a story.

That was how Paul thought he could approach the Hoffman business. He would take a step back from it, attempt to view it with a measure of detachment, then analyze it as a story. With a beginning, a middle, and an end.

Paul knew much of the middle and the end. He had, literally, walked into the middle of it.

What he needed to do now was find out more about the beginning.

Who was Kenneth Hoffman, really? A respected professor? A loving father? A philandering husband? A sadistic killer? Was it possible to be all these things? And if so, was the capacity to kill in all of us, waiting to break out? Was it possible that—

Shit.

Paul was home.

Sitting in his car, in the driveway, the engine running.

He had no memory of actually driving here.

He could recall getting into the car after he left Anna White's office. He remembered putting the key in the Subaru's ignition, starting the car. He could even recall seeing her next client arrive, a young guy, late twenties, heading in.

But after that, nothing. Nothing until he pulled into the driveway.

Do not panic. This is not a big deal.

Of course it wasn't. He'd been deep in thought on his way home. He'd gone on autopilot. Hadn't this sort of thing happened even before the attack? Hadn't Charlotte teased him more than once about being the classic absentminded professor, his head somewhere else while she was talking to him? His first wife, Hailey, too. They'd both accused him of being off in his own world at times.

That's all it was. No reason to think he was losing his marbles. He was unquestionably on the mend. The neurologist he was seeing was sure of that. The MRIs hadn't turned up anything alarming. Sure, he'd still have the odd headache, suffer the occasional memory loss. But he was improving, no doubt about it.

Paul turned off the car and opened the door. He felt slightly light-headed as he got out, placing one hand on the roof of the car for a moment and closing his eyes, steadying himself.

When he opened them, he felt balanced. Felt—

"I'm sorry about this."

Suddenly, his temple throbbed where Kenneth had struck him with the shovel. He relived the pain, reheard those last words from his would-be killer.

They'd sounded so real.

As if Kenneth were here with him right now, standing next to him in front of his home. Paul felt a chill run the length of his spine as he struggled to get Kenneth's voice out of his head.

Not exactly a sign that my idea is a good one, Paul thought.

No, he told himself. This was *exactly* why he needed to know more. He needed a Kenneth *exorcism*. Grab him by the throat and get him the fuck out of his head.

Paul closed the car door and held on to the keys as he approached the front door. Charlotte's car was not here, and this was not a week Josh was living with them, so he'd have the house to himself, at least for a while. Charlotte was rarely home in the late morning, although as a real estate agent her schedule was erratic. But if she wasn't showing a place to a prospective buyer, or meeting with someone wanting to put their place on the market, she was getting caught up on the paperwork in the office she shared with half a dozen other agents. One of them was Bill Myers, whom Paul had known since before Charlotte joined the agency. Back when Charlotte was getting started, Paul had asked Bill to put in a word with his fellow agents about adding her to the team. He'd pulled some strings, and Charlotte was set.

And working at the real estate agency had given Charlotte the inside track when the house they were now living in came on the market. They were on Milford's Point Beach Drive, which ran right along Long Island Sound. The back of the house looked out over a beautiful stretch of waterfront. They loved the fresh sea air and the never-ending music of the incoming waves.

The house was on three levels, the bottom mostly garage, laundry room, and storage. The middle level was made up of the kitchen and living room areas, and the bedrooms were on top. Both the living room and the master bedroom featured small balconies with views of the beach and beyond.

The property had suffered a lot of damage when Hurricane Sandy stormed ashore back in 2012. The owner had sunk a fortune into rebuilding the place before deciding he no longer wanted to live there. This had been shortly after Paul and Charlotte got married, and the timing was right to move from their small apartment into something nicer. So long as the polar ice caps didn't melt *too* quickly, this would be a great spot for the foreseeable future.

Paul unlocked the front door and climbed the stairs with slow deliberation. Going up, or coming down, could sometimes make him woozy. Given that he'd felt a bit off getting out of the car, he took his time. But when he reached the top, and tossed his keys onto the kitchen island, he felt good.

Good enough for a cold one.

He opened the refrigerator, reached for a bottle of beer, and twisted off the cap. As he tilted his head back for a long draw he caught sight of the wall clock, which read 11:47 A.M. Okay, maybe a little early, but what the hell.

He had work to do.

At one end of the kitchen, on the street side of the house, was a small room the original owners had designed as an oversize pantry— it was no bigger than six by six feet—but which Paul had turned into, as he had often called it, "the world's tiniest think tank."

He'd cut twelve inches off a seven-foot door that had been left in the garage by the previous owner after the reno, mounted it on the far wall as a desk, added some supports underneath, and filled with books the shelves lining two of the other walls that had been intended for canned goods and cereal boxes. By removing a few shelves he'd managed to carve out enough space to hang a framed, original poster for the film *Plan 9 from Outer Space*. He'd found it in a movie memorabilia store in London years ago. As there was no window, he'd lined the wall at the back of the desk with cork, allowing him to hang articles and calendars and favorite *New Yorker* cartoons where he could see them.

Centered on the desk was his laptop. Also taking up space were a printer and several cardboard business boxes filled with lesson plans, lectures, bills, and other files.

Paul dropped himself into the wheeled office chair and set the beer next to the laptop. He tapped a key to bring the screen to life, entered his password.

He stared at the computer for the better part of five minutes. He thought back to when he was six years old and his parents started taking him to a community pool in the summer. It wasn't heated, and Paul couldn't deal with getting in at the shallow end and slowly walking toward the deeper part, the cold water working its way incrementally up his body. It was torture. He took the "ripping off the Band-Aid approach," which was to stand at the edge and jump in, getting his entire body wet at once. The only problem was, the rest of his family could be ready to go home before he'd taken the plunge.

Paul was standing at the edge of the pool again.

He knew what he had to do.

He needed to *understand* what had happened to him. And where there were holes in the story, he'd attempt to fill them in with what *might* have happened. Weren't there photo programs like that? Where the image was grainy or indistinct, the computer would figure out what was probably there and patch it?

What did Kenneth say to these women before he'd reached his decision to kill them? What were their intimate moments like? What lies did Kenneth come up with when questioned by his wife, Gabriella?

Even a partly imagined story would be better than no story at all.

Paul opened a browser.

Into the search field he entered the words "Kenneth Hoffman."

"Okay, you son of a bitch," he said. "Let's get to know each other a little better."

Paul hit ENTER.

Four

Paul thought the best way to begin was with news accounts of the double murder. He'd read many of them before but never with quite the intensity he wanted to devote to them now. He recalled that when Kenneth was sentenced, one of the papers had carried a long feature summing up the entire story. It didn't take long to find it.

The *New Haven Star* carried it. Paul remembered that he had given an interview to the reporter. The story ran with the headline "A Scandal in Academia: 'Apology Killer' gets life in double murder."

He leaned in closer to the laptop screen and began to read:

BY GWEN STAINTON

There are some things even tenure can't protect you from.

So it was that yesterday, longtime West Haven College professor Kenneth Hoffman—the so-called Apology Killer—was sentenced to life in prison for the brutal murders of Jill Foster and Catherine Lamb, and the attempted murder of colleague and friend Paul Davis, bringing to a close not only one of the state's most grisly homicide cases, but also perhaps the most bizarre scandal of academia in New England history.

A lengthy trial might have brought out more details, but Hoffman waived his right to one and pleaded guilty to all charges. It was not difficult to imagine why he might have made that decision. When Hoffman was arrested, he was in the process of disposing of the bodies of the two women, and had just knocked Davis unconscious, striking him in the head with a shovel.

Had he not been discovered by a Milford police officer who'd decided to go after Hoffman's car—it had a broken taillight—Hoffman most likely would have buried all three in the woods. He was in the process of finding a suitable location when police happened upon him.

Paul reached for his beer. *Look at the words. Read them. Don't look away. The man was going to make sure I was dead and then he was going to put me in a grave.*

The point of the exercise was to face this head-on, he told himself. No shying away. It occurred to him, for not the first time, that whoever'd bumped into Hoffman's car in the faculty parking lot and broken that light had effectively saved his life.

After conducting extensive interviews with court and police officials, friends and family of Hoffman and his victims, as well as people from the West Haven College community, the *Star* has been able to put together a more detailed, if no less puzzling, picture of what happened.

Kenneth Hoffman, 53, husband to Gabriella, 49, father to Leonard, 21, was a longtime member of the WHC staff. While his areas of expertise were math and physics, he was perhaps even more skilled in one other area.

Fooling around.

West Haven College was, and remains, a close-knit community, and affairs in academia are hardly unheard of. Hoffman could have taught a course in them. From all accounts, Hoffman did not present as a so-called ladies' man. He was a much-praised professor, admired by his students, and his affairs with college employees, or their spouses, were conducted with the utmost discretion.

There is no evidence he had a sexual relationship with a student. Hoffman seemed to understand behavior of that sort could land him in serious, professional trouble. Nor was he ever the subject of a sexual harassment complaint.

And yet, people knew. Or at least suspected.

"Yeah," Paul said under his breath. He could remember going to Kenneth's office one time, and as he arrived the door opened and a woman came out, tears streaming down her cheeks. You might see a student emerge crying from a meeting with a professor, especially if the prof had found proof of plagiarism, but this woman was a colleague, not a student.

When Paul came in he couldn't help but ask, "What happened?"

Kenneth had been unable to hide his look of discomfort. He struggled for an answer, and the best he could come up with was, "Some sort of personal issue."

Paul, at first, thought he'd heard "personnel" and asked, "Jesus, is she being fired?"

Kenneth blinked, baffled. "If they were going to fire anybody, it'd be . . ."

He never finished the sentence.

Paul read on:

While Hoffman had a pattern of one affair at a time, his statement after his arrest made clear he was seeing Jill Foster and Catherine Lamb simultaneously, although neither knew about the other.

Also apparently in the dark was Hoffman's wife, Gabriella.

Interviews with various sources suggest Gabriella was aware of some of her husband's acts of infidelity over the years, but she did not know he was juggling two mistresses in the last few months.

Jill Foster, assistant vice president of student development and campus life, was married to Harold Foster, assistant manager of the Milford Savings & Loan office in downtown Milford. Catherine Lamb, a senior sales manager at JCPenney, was the spouse of Gilford Lamb, director of the college's human resources department.

After his arrest, Hoffman admitted to police he'd become increasingly obsessive, and possessive, where the women were concerned. He wanted them all to himself, to the point of telling them they were forbidden to continue having sexual relations with their own husbands. It was a demand they'd each found impossible to accept, and no doubt, rather difficult for Hoffman to enforce. But just the same, they'd asked him how they were to explain that to their spouses. Hoffman told investigators he felt that for them to be sexually involved with anyone but him amounted to betrayal.

In what one Milford detective called the understatement of the year, Hoffman told them, "Perhaps I was being unreasonable."

"Maybe just a little," Paul said, moving the story farther up the screen.

But it was during this period of "being unreasonable" that Hoffman set a trap for them both.

He invited them one night to his home when his wife and son were out for an extensive driving lesson. (Leonard wanted to work on his skills to improve his chances of getting a job that involved operating a truck.) Both of the women probably expected a private romantic rendezvous and were undoubtedly surprised to discover each other. They were acquainted through college functions and must have wondered if they had been called there for some other reason.

Posing as the perfect host, Hoffman offered the women glasses of wine, which they accepted. The wine, however, had been drugged, and soon Foster and Lamb were unconscious. When they awoke, they found themselves bound to kitchen chairs, an old-fashioned Underwood typewriter on the table before them.

Hoffman demanded written apologies from them for—as he himself described it later to investigators—their "immoral, licentious, whore-like behavior."

With one hand freed by Hoffman, Jill Foster typed: "i am so sorry for the heartache i have brought to your life please forgive me."

When Hoffman released Catherine Lamb's hand, she wrote: "i am so ashamed of what i have done i deserve whatever happens to me."

"Sounds like you dictated what you wanted them to say," Paul said under his breath, shaking his head.

Hoffman took the two sheets of paper from the typewriter, put them in a drawer in the kitchen, and returned with a single steak knife that he used to slit the women's throats.

Hoffman then wrapped the women in sheets of plastic, loaded them in the back of his Volvo. He also placed into the front passenger seat of the car the antique typewriter, which had the victims' blood on it.

North of Milford, he pulled over, thinking he might have found a wooded area suitable for disposing of the bodies. West Haven College colleague Paul Davis spotted his car and pulled over. When Davis saw the bodies in the back of the station wagon, Hoffman tried to kill him with the shovel he'd brought to dig his victims' graves.

"If the police had not come along when they did," Davis said in an interview, "I wouldn't be here now."

Davis could not explain what made Hoffman, a former mentor, commit such a heinous crime.

"I guess there are things we just never know about people, even those closest to us," Davis said.

His comments were echoed by Angelique Rogers, 48, a West Haven College political science professor who went public about an affair she'd had with Kenneth Hoffman four years earlier.

"She was the one," Paul said to himself. "She was the one coming out of his office."

"I can't stop wondering, all this time later, how close I came to meeting the same fate as Jill and Catherine," Rogers said. "Did Kenneth think I had betrayed him at some level, too, by not leaving my husband?" She said Hoffman had not made the same demands of her that he reportedly had of the two women he killed.

(Rogers and her husband have since divorced. She still teaches at West Haven.)

Hoffman himself seemed at a loss to explain his actions.

When asked how he could have slit the throats of the two women, Hoffman reportedly shrugged and said, "Who knows why anyone does anything?"

Paul read the story through a second time. It raised as many questions as it answered. Why did Hoffman make such strange demands of the two women? Expecting them to stop having sex with their own husbands? Seriously? Why invite them to the house together, allow them to meet each other? Okay, they might have already known one another through college functions, but why put them together like that, at his house? What was the point? He must have known from the beginning what he was going to do, but why kill both of them? What had snapped in Kenneth's mind?

And a minor question the story failed to address was that typewriter. The reporter mentioned that Kenneth put it in the car, but not what he had done with it.

At least, where that question was concerned, Paul had a pretty good idea. His memory of events that night had taken time to come back to him, but while recovering in Milford Hospital he did tell the police about Kenneth's side trip into that industrial plaza to throw something into a Dumpster.

He never heard anything more about it after that. He supposed if the police had found it, they would have used it in building their case against Hoffman, had he not confessed and pleaded guilty. But it was more likely that by the time Paul remembered what he'd seen, the Dumpster had been emptied and the typewriter was in a landfill somewhere.

"I'm sorry about this."

Kenneth's voice, in his head, again.

"No, you're not," Paul said. "You never were. Not for a goddamn minute. The only thing you're sorry about is that you got caught."

Paul heard the front door open downstairs.

"Paul?"

Charlotte was home. It wasn't unusual for her to pop by through the day, especially if her evening was going to be taken up with showings.

"Up here!" he shouted. "In the think tank!"

He heard her walking up the steps. No, not walking. More like running.

"Paul?" she said again, her voice on edge.

Paul got up out of the computer chair and went back into the kitchen in time to see his wife reach the top of the stairs.

"Is everything okay?" he asked.

"Who's that guy parked across the street, watching the house?" she asked.

Five

After lunch, Anna White sat at her desk, opened her laptop, and made some notes from her three Friday morning sessions.

Her first visitor was a retired X-ray technician who was having a hard time getting over the death of her dog. It had darted out into traffic, and the woman blamed herself. Anna understood why that was making it difficult for the woman to move on. Anna's second client of the day, Paul Davis, was making some headway. Anna was not yet entirely sold on his idea of writing about Kenneth Hoffman, but he might be onto something. She wasn't going to tell him not to do it. If Paul believed the exercise would help his recovery, she wasn't going to discourage him.

And then there was Gavin Hitchens.

She had her work cut out for her where he was concerned.

He said he wanted to get better, and she wanted to believe that was true, but she had her doubts. She knew the young man was not being entirely open with her. She didn't know that he was outright lying to her, but he was definitely holding things back.

At least he wasn't denying the basic facts about what had gotten him into trouble.

Sitting in a coffee shop, he'd taken from the table next to him the unwatched cell phone of a distracted babysitter and used it to call the father of a soldier who'd died in Iraq. Gavin claimed to be the dead son. Told the dad he'd faked his death so he wouldn't have to return and face the father he hated so much.

Gavin didn't even know the man. He'd seen his name in a newspaper story. He thought it would be fun.

What he hadn't counted on was the surveillance camera.

When the call was traced back to the woman who owned the phone, she swore she hadn't made it. Besides, the caller had been male. She knew she'd been at the coffee shop at the time. Police recovered security camera footage that showed Gavin grabbing the woman's phone when she wasn't looking, then tucking it back under her purse when he was done with the call.

Gavin had tried to dismiss his actions as a "prank," but the authorities didn't see it that way. A look into Gavin's history revealed other, possible "pranks." Sneaking into an elderly woman's home and hiding her cat in the attic was one.

Anna had been trying to get Gavin to search within himself to understand why he perpetrated such cruel hoaxes. He'd been quick to blame a sadistic, unloving father.

Gavin had spun a pretty good tale of abuse and belittling. His father had mocked him for things he was good at (high school theater, sketching, playing the flute) and ridiculed him for things he was not (football, baseball, pretty much anything sports related). His nicknames for Gavin included "flower fucker" and "Janice." Gavin's dad figured if you didn't know how to rebuild an engine block or throw a left hook at somebody in a bar, you were some kind of cocksucking faggot. (Putting that flute in his mouth, Gavin's father maintained, was a clue.)

"I don't know why he hated me so much," Gavin had said in one of their earlier sessions. "Maybe he had low self-esteem. He could have been haunted by how he was mistreated by his own father."

When patients started tossing around phrases like "low self-esteem," Anna suspected them of trying a little too hard.

But Gavin's story didn't end with his childhood.

At nineteen, he left home. Four years later, his mother killed herself after downing a bottle of sleeping pills. Three years after that, Gavin's father was diagnosed with liver cancer, and leaned on his son to move back home and look after him.

Gavin conceded to Anna that he saw it as an opportunity to exact some revenge.

He'd hide his father's reading glasses. Put his pills in a different medicine cabinet. Leave his slippers out on the deck when it rained. Change appliance settings so that when his father made toast it came out burned. Unplug the heating pad Dad sat on as he watched TV.

One time, he added laxative to the old man's soup, and removed the toilet paper from his father's bathroom.

"I know it was wrong," Gavin told her sheepishly. "I think maybe, after he died, I couldn't stop. I had to find others to torment."

Maybe there *was* something to all this business with his father, Anna thought, assuming the story he told was true. She had checked some of the details—the mother's suicide, the father's liver cancer—and they'd turned out to be true. But the story seemed a little too pat, Gavin's excuse too convenient.

It was also possible Gavin had perpetrated those "pranks"—the ones she knew about and the ones she didn't—not because of a miserable father but because at his core, there was something just not right with him.

It was entirely possible Gavin wasn't wired right. Maybe taking pleasure in the pain of others was part of his DNA. It could be that he just got off on finding people's weaknesses and exploiting them.

Sometimes, the reasons were elusive. People were who they were.

She wondered if there might be a way to find out more about his teenage years, if there were things he might have done that no one had—

Hang on, Anna thought.

When she'd sat down to make these notes, she'd had to open her laptop.

But I left my laptop open.

And then she remembered that she'd found Gavin behind her desk, supposedly looking at the books on the shelves, when she'd come into her office.

Six

P aul went immediately to the window that looked down onto the street. He peered through the blinds.

"Where?" he asked. "What car?"

Charlotte dumped her purse onto a chair and rushed over to join him. She looked between the slats.

"It was right—"

"There's no car there," Paul said. "Where was it exactly?"

"Right there. Right across the street. It's gone. It must have taken off."

"Who was he?"

Charlotte stepped back from the window "I don't know. Just some guy. I didn't get much of a look. The windows were tinted."

"What kind of car was it?"

Charlotte sighed. "It was kind of boxy. It was like the car you said you saw out there the other day."

Paul looked at her. "What are you talking about?"

Charlotte raised her eyebrows. "What was it? Saturday? When you said there was someone on the street watching us?"

"I . . . don't . . . Saturday?"

She nodded. "I was sitting right there." She pointed to one of four stools tucked under the kitchen island. "You were looking out the window wondering about a car. A station wagon. You said some guy got out, stood there for a second, and pointed right at you. Shouted your name."

Paul moved slowly back into the kitchen, turned, and leaned

against the counter. He ran a hand over his chin. "I don't have any memory of that."

Charlotte approached him slowly. "Okay."

"When I told you this, did you see him?"

She shook her head. "I got to the window fast as I could, but there was no car there. But I couldn't help but remember that when I saw that car, right now."

"But that guy didn't get out?"

"No."

"Was he looking at the house?"

"Actually, not so much." She shrugged. "It could have been anybody. I shouldn't even have mentioned it." She shook her head. "God, you're starting to make *me* paranoid."

Paul visibly winced.

"I'm sorry, I shouldn't have said that," she said. "I totally take it back. It was—"

"Don't worry about it, really."

They said nothing for several moments. It was Charlotte who broke the silence with a tentative question. "How did it go today with Dr. White?"

Paul nodded slowly. "It was okay."

"You told her you're still having the nightmares?"

"Yeah. And I told her about my idea of facing this whole thing head-on."

Charlotte pulled out a stool and sat down. "What did she say?"

"She didn't try to talk me out of it. I told her you were on board with it."

"Did you tell her it was my idea?"

Paul frowned. "I didn't. I'm sorry. I should have given you credit."

She waved a hand. "Doesn't matter. I'm just glad she didn't shoot it down. If she had, maybe *that's* when you'd have told her it was my idea."

That brought a smile. "Anyway, when I got home, I actually got started."

Charlotte looked into his office off the kitchen, saw the open laptop. "That's great."

"I'm starting by reading all the news accounts of the trial. I want to know everything, including the things I forgot afterward. And anything I can't learn, I'm going to . . ."

"Going to what?"

"You know how, in *American Pastoral*, Philip Roth has his alter ego character, Nathan Zuckerman, write about this guy's life—he calls him 'the Swede'—and he starts with what he knows, but then when he gets to the parts he doesn't know, he imagines them? To fill in the narrative blanks?"

Charlotte looked at him and smiled. "Only you would use an example like that to try and explain something. I've never read that book."

"Okay, forget that part. And anyway, I'm no Philip Roth. But what I want to do is, write about this. The parts I know, and even the parts I don't know. Not to actually be published. I don't even know that I would want it to be published, assuming any publisher even cared. I'm thinking that writing it would be a kind of catharsis, I guess. I want to try to understand it, and I think that might be the way to do it. Imagine myself in Kenneth's head, what he said to those women, what they said to him."

"I'm not so sure in Kenneth's head is a place you want to be."

"I said, *imagine*." Paul saw hesitation in Charlotte's eyes. "What?"

"I know it was my idea, but now I'm wondering if it's such a good one. Maybe this is a really dumb thing to do."

"No, it's good," Paul said. "It feels right."

Charlotte went slowly from side to side. "You have to be sure."

"I am," he said. "I . . . think I am."

She slid off the stool, walked over to him, slipped her arms around him, and placed her head on his chest.

"If there's anything I can do to help, just ask. I have to admit, I'm alternately repulsed and fascinated by Hoffman. That someone can present as friendly, as someone who cares about you, but can actually be plotting against you. He didn't come across that way when I met him."

"You met Kenneth?" Paul asked.

She stepped back from him. "You know. From that faculty event we went to a couple of years ago, when I thought he was coming on to me? How smooth he was? He wanted to read me a poem he'd written that afternoon, about how a woman is exquisitely composed of the most beautiful curves to be found in nature. I thought it'd be creepy, but God, it was actually pretty good, but then, I've never been much of a judge of poetry."

"I don't—when did you tell me this?"

Charlotte shrugged. "I don't know. More than once. Around the time it happened, and then, you know, since . . ."

"You'd think I'd remember something like that, I mean, if it involved you."

"Anyway, it's not like I got a case of the vapors and started going 'Ah do declare, Mistah Hoffman, you are getting my knickahs in a twist.'" She laughed and tried to get her husband to see the humor in it. But Paul looked troubled.

"I'm sorry. It worries me when I can't remember things."

Her face turned sympathetic and she wrapped her arms around him. "Don't worry about that," she whispered. "It's nothing." She squeezed him. "I nearly lost you."

He placed his palms on her back. "But I'm here."

"I feel . . . like I can't forgive myself."

Paul tried to put some space between them to look into her face, but she held him tight. "What are you talking about?"

"Before . . . before it happened, I wasn't a good wife to you. I—"

"No, that's not—"

"Just listen to me. I know I was distant, that I wasn't . . . loving.

I wasn't there for you the way I should have been. I could offer all kinds of excuses, that I was all wrapped up with myself, wondering about my choices in life, whether my life was going the way I'd imagined it when I was younger and—"

"You don't have to do this," Paul said.

"All I was thinking about was me. I wasn't thinking about *us*. And then that horrible thing happened to you, and I realized . . ."

She pressed her head harder against his chest. He could feel her body tremble beneath his palms as she struggled not to cry.

"I realized I couldn't just wait around to receive what I thought was owed me. I realized that I had to give, that I hadn't been giving to you. Does that make any sense at all?"

"I think so."

She tilted her head up. Tears had made glistening, narrow tracks down her cheeks. She wiped them away before managing a smile.

"Josh'll be here in a couple of days. Maybe, while we still have the house to ourselves . . ."

He smiled. "I hear you."

She gave him a quick kiss, broke free, and said, "How about a drink?"

He'd already had a prenoon beer, but what the hell. "Sure."

As she headed for the refrigerator she said, "I picked up a little something for you the other day."

"What?" he asked.

"You'll have to wait and see," she said.

He was about to press for details, but his phone alerted him to a text message. He dug it out of his pocket. It was from Hillary Denton, the dean of faculty at West Haven College, and read:

Sure, any time you want to come in I'm available.

Under his breath, he said, "What the hell are you talking about?" He scrolled up to look at the previous message.

Charlotte had the refrigerator open and was saying, "Did you get the vodka?"

Hillary's text had clearly been a reply to a message from him that read:

Can we talk sometime about my return in September?

Paul stared at the message. He had no memory of sending it.

"Earth to Paul," Charlotte said. "I asked you to pick up a couple of bottles of vodka? The mandarin flavor? I mentioned it last night?"

Paul looked up from his phone. "What?"

"Doesn't matter," Charlotte said. "Beer's fine. You want a beer?"

The drive home. The man in the car. Vodka. A text message to the dean.

Paul wondered what else might have slipped his mind he didn't even know about yet.

Seven

G avin was breathing so shallowly he was hardly breathing at all.
He didn't want to wake her.

She was sleeping peacefully in her bed. Her name was Eleanor
Snyder and, according to Dr. White's notes, she was sixty-six, wid-
owed, and retired from her job as an X-ray technician.

Gavin had very little trouble getting into her Westfield Road
home. It was a small, story-and-a-half place shaped something like
a barn. He'd waited in the bushes across the street for the upstairs
lights to be killed, then gave Eleanor another half hour to nod off.

He crossed the darkened street and peered through the window
next to the front door, looking for the telltale red glow of a security
system panel. He saw none. He then tried the front door, but Eleanor had at least been cautious enough to lock it before she retired
for the night. Gavin walked around the house until he found an
accessible basement window.

Gavin crawled through and dropped down to the floor. He'd
brought along a half-filled garbage bag, knotted at the top with a
red, plastic drawstring. He worked his way quietly to the first floor,
then found the stairs to the second. He took each step carefully.
There was always one that creaked.

And sure enough, one did.

That was when he froze, held his breath, and listened. If Eleanor Snyder heard that creaky step, she'd get up and check it out.
But Gavin heard no rustling of covers, no footsteps. What he could
make out was soft, rhythmic snoring.

He followed the snores.

And now here he was, standing next to Eleanor Snyder's bed, looking down at her. There was enough light filtering in through the blinds to make out her flowered nightie, a copy of the latest Grisham on the bedside table. If only all the people whose homes he snuck into wore eye masks and stuffed those little plugs into their ears.

Could she be dreaming? And if so, was she dreaming about Bixby?

Bixby was not her late husband. Aaron had been her husband's name. Bixby had been her little schnauzer.

According to Dr. White's notes, after Aaron died, Eleanor funneled all her love—and grief—into that pooch. Bixby got her through those difficult times. It was Bixby who got her back out into the world.

Eleanor walked him around the neighborhood three or four times a day. Bixby didn't just keep her sane. He kept her in shape. She'd bought one of those extra long leashes that extended and retracted with the push of a button. That gave Bixby freedom to run in short bursts, which Eleanor was no longer up to.

She blamed herself for what happened. It wasn't really the driver's fault.

There was no way the driver of the Honda Accord could see that slender leash running horizontally out into the street, or that tiny dog that didn't even come up to her front bumper.

That had been six months ago.

Eleanor, so said the notes, could not forgive herself.

Gavin watched Eleanor breathe in and out. He'd tied the drawstring on the garbage bag too tight to loosen it, so he made an opening by ripping apart the plastic. Once he'd made a large enough hole, he reached in and took something out. He wadded up the empty bag and stuffed it into the back pocket of his jeans.

Gavin looked about the room for what he needed. It occurred to him to check the back of the bedroom door.

With a gloved hand, he moved the door three-quarters of the way closed. A bathrobe hung from a simple coat hook.

Perfect.

Gavin removed the robe from the hook, let it fall noiselessly to the floor, then replaced it with the item he had brought.

He slipped out of the room, closing the door behind him, thereby ensuring that the first thing Eleanor Snyder would see when she woke up was the surprise he'd left for her.

A small, dead dog. Hanging by its collar.

Eight

Anna White woke to a repetitive mechanical sound, something metallic sliding back and forth, as well as a television at very low volume. She threw back the covers, slipped on a robe, and went out into the second-floor hallway. She pushed open the door two down from hers, not worried about disturbing anyone.

"Morning, Dad," Anna said.

Her father, wearing blue pajamas and slippers, glanced her way and nodded. He was on a rowing machine, his hands firmly gripping the handles, sliding back, pulling his arms, gliding forward, then repeating the motion. Before him, atop the dresser, was a flat-screen television on which Wile E. Coyote was trying, once again, to catch the Road Runner.

Frank White's eyes were glued to the screen. He grinned. "It's coming. Where the truck comes out of the tunnel that the coyote painted. It's simply surreal. Ha! There it is!"

The coyote was flattened.

He cackled, looked Anna's way again. "Wish to hell I'd worked on that one." He saw something in her eyes and said, "Did I wake you?"

"It's fine," she said.

"Chuck Jones was a genius, Joanie," he said, looking back at the TV. "I ever tell you what I told Walt when I met him?"

"Yes, Dad," Anna said. She could not be bothered to correct him about calling her by her mother's name. "Shall I put on the coffee?"

"Sure," he said, continuing to row. "I said to him, I said, 'Walt, even Pepé Le Pew could have kicked Mickey's ass.'"

"I know, Dad," she said, and headed down to the kitchen to start the day.

Frank White, Anna had to admit, was something else. Well into his eighties, he was in better shape than she was, at least physically. His arms were roped with muscle and, at 120 pounds, there wasn't an ounce of fat on the man.

If only he were half as fit mentally.

His short-term memory was slipping away, but his recollections of years past, particularly those youthful ones he spent in California working as an animator at Warner Bros., were rich with detail. He'd retired from that world nearly thirty years ago, at which point Frank and Anna's mother, Joan, returned to Connecticut.

They filled their first fifteen years back with gardening and travel and socializing, but then Joan's health began to fail. It was a slow decline, ending in an extended period in a nursing home and finally a chronic care ward. She'd been dead three years now, and Frank had taken it hard.

Anna insisted her father move in with her.

It was not pure altruism on her part. She'd been on her own after she and her husband, Jack, split up two years before her mother's death. She'd taken back her name and thrown herself into her work, but she'd soon found herself spread thin. Having her father around could actually make her life a lot easier.

During the last few years of Joan's life, Frank had taken over the running of the household. Did the grocery shopping, made the meals, did the laundry, cleaned the house, kept track of the bills and the finances.

Anna made it clear to her father that taking him in was not some act of charity. He could look after *her*. She was so busy with her clients, local charitable causes, plus being on the Milford Arts Council, it would be a relief not to have to worry about domestic duties.

It was rocky at first. Even if Frank had not been grieving, it would have taken them a while to work into a groove. That took about six months. After that, things went great. Frank even had time to go back to golf, bought a rowing machine, renewed a long forgotten interest in gourmet cooking, all while Anna made a living for the two of them by counseling the confused, depressed, and troubled of the world. Well, of Milford and environs, anyway. Frank encouraged Anna to get back out into circulation, find herself a new husband, maybe even have kids—"It's not too late! Almost, but not quite!"—and when she did, he promised her, he'd find a place of his own.

She wouldn't hear of it. Anna liked her life. Maybe she didn't care about a husband and kids. She had her career, she had her dad, she had her house.

It was a stable, safe life.

But then, sixteen months ago, things slowly started to unravel.

Frank had a minor fender bender that could have been much worse—he backed into a Ford Explorer at the Walmart in Stratford, narrowly missing a woman pushing a four-month-old in a stroller. He became confused behind the wheel. One day, at the Stamford Town Center, he spent four hours trying to find his car in the parking garage. He'd walked past it, Anna figured later, at least a dozen times. He confessed to her later that he'd been looking for the Dodge Charger he'd owned in the late 1960s.

He lost credit cards. One day, he headed out of the house without a shirt on.

More recently, he'd been calling her Joanie, and other times, when he realized who she really was, he asked to be taken to the nursing home to visit his wife. He'd get in the back of Anna's car, expecting to be taken there. So now, Anna was not only back where she was before her father moved in—running a household as well as doing her job—but taking care of her dad as well.

"Such is life," she'd say to herself.

And yet, in the midst of this, there could be moments of great clarity. Frank was often his best first thing in the morning. When he showed up in the kitchen, Anna put a mug of coffee in front of him as he sat down.

"That cartoon channel runs some of the best Warner Bros. stuff in the morning. They had so much more of an edge than that wholesome stuff Disney was doing back then. Wit and sophistication. Cartoons for adults."

Frank reached over to the counter for a pen and notepad that sat by the phone. He did some doodling with one hand, drank from the mug with the other.

"Lots of customers today?" he asked her. He never called them clients or patients.

"It's the weekend, Dad. But I wanted to talk to you about something."

"What's that?"

"It's not a good idea for you to be chatting with the people who come to see me."

Frank looked puzzled. "When do I do that?"

"Not often, it's true. But the other day, you were talking to this one patient. Gavin?"

Frank struggled to remember. "Uh, maybe."

"You were about to tie up your shoes?"

"If you say so, Joanie."

"It's just . . . he's not the kind of person you want to become familiar with."

"Why's that?"

She had been giving a lot of thought to Gavin ever since she'd found her laptop closed. Maybe she was mistaken. Maybe she *had* closed it before he'd arrived for his appointment, but she hadn't been wrong about seeing him behind her desk. Had he been looking in her computer and, when he'd heard her coming, closed it, out of reflex? And only remembered it had been open when it was too late to do anything about it?

She shook her head, ignoring her father's question. "It's just best if you do not engage with my clients."

Still doodling, he said, "Speaking of engaged."

"Dad."

"Come on, sweetheart, we need to talk about this. I'm dragging you down. We can't go on like this. I moved in to help you, and now you're the one helping me."

"Everything's fine here."

"Remember that cartoon where Bugs Bunny's up against Blacque Jacque Shellacque?"

"Uh . . ."

"Anyway, Jacque wants Bugs's bag of gold, but Bugs gives him a bag of gunpowder with a hole cut out of the bottom. The gunpowder leaves a trail, which Bugs lights, and blows up Jacque."

"I don't remember that one."

"Well, it doesn't matter. The thing is, my mind is that bag of gunpowder. A little leaking out every day. Pretty soon that bag'll be empty. You need to find a place for me. You need to start looking."

"Stop it, Dad."

He tore off the sheet of paper he'd been doodling on and handed it to his daughter. "There you go."

It was a poodle, done cartoon-style, with a face that looked remarkably like Anna's. Frank smiled, waiting for her approval.

"That's quite something," she said. "But my tail doesn't look like that."

Frank stared out the window for several seconds, then turned back to look at her. "I think I might hit some balls around in the backyard."

And we're out, Anna thought.

But wait.

He patted her hand and smiled. "What point is there in keeping me around now?"

She felt a constriction in her throat. "Because I love you, Dad."

"You need to get over that," he said, pushing back his chair. He grabbed his mug and left the kitchen.

Anna sat there, picked up the drawing of her as a poodle, looked at it, then got up and went to the counter. She opened a drawer and tucked the sketch in with several hundred others.

Nine

P aul stopped doing some online research when he heard the front door open and his son, Josh, shout: "Dad!"

Paul exited his office and headed for the top of the stairs in time to meet his son. He knew better than to expect a huge hug. Josh, backpack slung over his shoulder, gave his father the briefest of embraces and ran to the fridge.

"How was the train?" Paul asked.

Josh found a can of Pepsi, popped it, and said, "It was good. Mom went right down to the platform with me to watch me get on." He rolled his eyes. "I'm not a kid. I'm almost ten. I've taken the train before."

"She can't help it. She's a mom."

Josh shrugged, then said, "Charlotte got you something. She wouldn't let me put my bag in the trunk when she picked me up in case I saw it."

Charlotte had reached the top of the stairs. "No blabbing!"

"I don't even know what it is," Josh said, taking a drink.

"Just one of those a day," Paul said, pointing to the can. "You don't need all that sugar."

Josh displayed the can. "It's diet."

"Oh," Paul said, then to Charlotte, "What did you get me? Is this the thing you mentioned the other day?"

She smiled devilishly. "I want you and Josh to take a walk. Go down to the beach. Give me five."

Paul exchanged glances with Josh. "I guess we're getting kicked out."

Paul and Josh descended the steps, went out the front door, and rounded the house to reach the beach. The wind coming in off the sound was crisp and cool, but the midday sun cut the need for a jacket. It was early June, and the temperatures had been below average for this time of year. The water would have to warm up a lot before Josh would want to go in.

"How's your mom?" Paul asked.

"Fine."

"And Walter?"

Josh's stepfather.

Josh looked for a stone to throw into the water. "He's okay." He paused. "I like it in the city. There's tons to do."

"Okay," Paul said. It wasn't that he wanted his son to be miserable in Manhattan with his mother and stepdad. He wanted nothing but happiness for the boy. But it pained him some to think Josh had to endure the boring Connecticut suburbs to spend time with him.

"Walter's always getting free tickets to stuff, like baseball games and shows and stuff. In fact . . ."

"In fact what?"

Josh glanced up warily at his father. "Walter got tickets to tomorrow afternoon's Knicks game."

"Great. I hope he and your mom have fun."

"But so, like, they're going to pick me up tomorrow morning. I'd have taken the train but Walter's got some client in Darien he wants to see in person before heading back. So I'm just here for one night. Maybe I wasn't supposed to tell you. Mom talked it over with Charlotte. She's probably going to tell you after she gives you your surprise."

"Maybe *that's* the surprise," Paul said grimly. He shook his head slowly, feeling the irritation build. This definitely should have been discussed with him. He was expecting to spend the entire weekend with his son. But he didn't want to take his anger out on Josh. He patted him on the back and said, "We'll sort it out."

"But I can go, right?" Josh asked. "I've only been to one other NBA game and I really liked it."

Paul suddenly felt very tired. He glanced at his watch. "I think it's been five minutes," he said.

WHEN THEY GOT BACK TO THE KITCHEN, PAUL IMMEDIATELY NOTICED his office door was closed. Charlotte stood before it, a smug look on her face, but it broke when she saw Paul's expression.

"What?" she asked. "You don't look happy."

"Did you know Josh was going back tomorrow?" he asked.

"Hailey mentioned it when she emailed me about when Josh's train would arrive."

"You couldn't have told me?"

She crossed her arms and waited a beat. "Maybe this isn't a good time."

Josh's face fell. "We're not doing the surprise?"

Charlotte stared at Paul. "It's your dad's call."

Paul looked at Josh, quickly sized up the disappointment in his face, and tamped down the anger he'd been feeling. "Sorry," he said. "Surprise me."

"Is it in there?" Josh asked. He looked ready to charge into the small study.

"Stay right there, buster," Charlotte said. Her look softened as she said to her husband, "I wanted to get something to inspire you as you . . ." She looked at Josh and decided against getting into all the details. "I wanted to celebrate your moving forward."

Paul smiled with curiosity. "Okay."

She aimed her thumb at the door. "Go on in."

Josh said, "Can I open it?"

"Yeah, okay," Paul said. To Charlotte: "Should I close my eyes?"

She shook her head.

Josh turned the knob and pushed the door open.

Sitting on the desk, beside the closed laptop and hidden beneath a tea towel adorned with Christmas trees, was something the size of a football helmet, although far less rounded.

"So it's a Christmas present," Paul said.

Charlotte shrugged. "It was the biggest dish towel I had, and it was too awkward to wrap properly. Take a guess."

Paul grinned. "I got nuthin'."

Josh had squeezed himself in front of his father, wanting to reach out and pull the towel away, but knowing he had to let his dad do it.

"Here goes," Paul said, grabbing the corner of the towel and flicking it back like a magician whipping out a tablecloth from a fully set dining room table.

Josh said, "What *is* it?"

"Oh, my God," Paul said. "It's amazing."

"You like it?" Charlotte said, putting her palms together, as though praying, the tips of her fingers touching her chin. "Seriously?"

"I love it."

For a second time, Josh asked, "What *is* it?"

"That," Paul told him, mussing his hair, "is a typewriter."

"A what?"

"You must have needed a crane to bring it in here," Paul said, running his fingers along the base of the machine. "It looks like it weighs a ton."

Charlotte did her best Muscle Beach pose. "Strrrong vooman. Like ox."

Paul dropped his butt into the computer chair and gave the antique a thorough examination.

"This is so funny," he said. "I was just thinking about one of these old typewriters."

"Seriously?" Charlotte asked. "I'm like a mind reader. Why were—"

Paul shook his head to suggest it didn't matter. Besides, he was too busy inspecting the machine to reply.

It was an Underwood. The name was stenciled onto the black metal just above the keys and, in much bigger letters, across the back shelf that would prop up a sheet of paper, had one been rolled in. The machine was almost entirely black, except for the keypad—Paul wondered if that was strictly a computer term—but anyway, all those keys, marked with letters and numbers and punctuation marks, each one perfectly ringed in silver.

"What does it *do*?" Josh asked.

Above the keys, a semicircular opening that afforded a view of the—Paul wasn't even sure what they were called, those perfectly arrayed metal arms that struck paper as one pounded on the keys. But there was a kind of beauty in how they were arranged, like the inside of a very tiny opera house. Those keys were the people, the paper the stage.

"It writes things," Paul said.

"How?"

"Grab a sheet of paper from the printer."

Charlotte said, "I tried it. There's still some ink in the ribbon, but I don't know if you can even buy typewriter ribbons anymore."

"Ribbons?" Josh said, handing a sheet of paper to his father.

"Okay," he said, taking the sheet and inserting it into the back of the machine. He twisted the roller at the end of the cylinder, feeding the paper into the typewriter until it appeared on the other side, just above where the keys would hit it.

"I don't get this at all," Josh said.

"Watch," Paul said. "I'm going to type your name."

He raised his two index fingers over the keys.

Chit chit chit chit.

"God, I love that sound," Paul said.

Josh watched, open-mouthed, as JOSH appeared, faintly, on the sheet of paper. "Whoa," he said as his father pulled the sheet out and handed it to him. "That's cool. But I still don't get it."

"This is what we used before computers," Paul said. "When we wanted to write something, we used this. And you didn't have to print out what you wrote, because you *were* printing it as you wrote it, one letter at a time."

Josh studied the machine. "But how does it go onto the Net? Where do you see stuff? Where's the screen?"

Charlotte laughed. Josh looked at her, not getting the joke.

Paul struggled to explain. "You know how if you want to write something on the computer, like, you use Word or whatever. That's what you would use this for. But that's all it did. You didn't surf the Web with it. There *was* no Web. You didn't figure out your mortgage on it, you didn't use it to read the *Huffington Post* or watch a show or look at cat videos or—"

"But what does it *do*?" Josh asked.

"This machine does one thing and one thing only. It lets you write stuff."

Josh was unable to conceal his disappointment. "So it's kind of useless, then. How old is it?"

Paul shook his head. "I've got no idea."

Charlotte said, "I looked all over it for a date and couldn't find one. But I'm guessing maybe the nineteen thirties, forties?"

Paul shook his head in wonder. "Who knows. But it's older than any of us in this room, that's for sure."

"Even Charlotte?" Josh asked.

"Josh!" Paul said, and shot his wife a look of apology.

"I'll get you for that," she said, giving the boy a grin.

Paul asked Charlotte, "What made you . . . why did you get this?"

She smiled. "I told you, I wanted to inspire you. How many times have we been in an antique shop and you've stopped and looked adoringly at one of these? I know you love these old gadgets."

His eyes misted. "When I was a kid, we had a typewriter like this, well, it was a Royal, not an Underwood. But just like this, it weighed about as much as a Volkswagen."

"I can attest to that," Charlotte said. "I think there's more steel in that thing than in our stove."

Paul continued. "I liked to write stories, but writing them out by hand took so long. When I was ten, before every house had a computer, I asked my dad to show me how to use the typewriter. I got the world's fastest lesson. Your fingers go here, this one hits this key, this one hits *that* key, and so on. I remember him holding his hands over mine."

He put a hand over his mouth, took a moment to compose himself.

"Anyway, that was it. That was my lesson. Been typing ever since." He smiled wistfully. "All the bad habits I learned at that age, I still have." He ran his hand over the top of the typewriter. "Just think of all the things that may have been written on this. School essays, love notes, maybe letters from a mother to her soldier son fighting somewhere in France or Germany, if she wasn't into handwriting. A machine like this, it has a *soul*, you know?"

"What does that mean?" Josh asked.

Paul struggled to find a way to explain. He turned his son so he was standing directly in front of him.

"You know how—how do I put this—you see things with your eyes"—he pointed to Josh's—"and you take them in, and they're just *there*. Like, watching a bus go by or something like that. But other times, you see things, and you *feel* them in here." He placed his palm on the boy's chest. "Like, a beautiful sunset. Or an eagle, or even when you hear a magnificent piece of music."

Josh stared blankly. "I like buses," he said.

Paul looked at Charlotte with amused dismay.

She smiled. "I wasn't thinking you'd actually write on it. It's not exactly easy to do cut-and-paste with scissors and a bottle of glue. And you could wear out what's left of that ribbon and never get any replacements. I thought of it more like a work of art. Like I said, it's meant to inspire." She cast her eye about the tiny room. "If you can find any place for it."

"Oh, I've got a spot for it. And I like your idea. I'm already inspired. And considering what I've been researching lately, you could have hardly found something more appropriate."

Josh got into the chair and began tapping away madly at the keys. *Chit chit. Chit. Chit chit chit.*

"I love you," Paul said, putting his lips to Charlotte's.

"Right back at ya."

Chit chit chit. Ding!

"Whoa!" Josh said. "What was that?"

"You have to hit the carriage return."

"The what?"

Paul reached around his son to hit the lever on the left side of the machine to move the cylinder back to the right. Josh resumed typing.

Chit chit chit chit.

"Where did you find it again?" Paul asked.

"Someone selling their house had a garage sale to clear out their stuff. Less stuff to pack, right? I stopped because, you know, you never know what you might find, and if they haven't found a new place yet, they might just need an agent, so I thought I might hand out my card. And then I spotted this little beauty and immediately thought of you."

"Well, I'm glad you—"

"*Ow!*"

They both turned to see Josh's right hand deep into the heart of the typewriter. His fingers were entangled in a collection of keys fighting to get to the ribbon.

"Everything's stuck!" he cried, looking at the antique as though it were a dog that had bit him.

"Hang on, hang on," Paul said. "The letters got jammed. It's not a big deal. Just let me carefully pull apart those—"

"It hurts!" Josh said. Before Paul could help him, Josh jerked his arm back to free himself. Blood spurted from the index finger of his right hand. The skin was torn on the side, just back of the nail.

"Shit!" Paul said as blood dripped onto the keys and the top of his desk.

"Why did it do that?" Josh asked.

"If you hit too many keys too fast—"

But Josh wasn't interested. He'd turned to Charlotte, who had grabbed a handful of tissues from a box on the desk and was wrapping them around her stepson's finger. "Come into the kitchen. We'll get you fixed up."

Paul watched as they left his cramped office, then at the blood-spattered typewriter.

Josh could be heard saying to his stepmother, "That thing sucks. You should have got him a new computer instead."

Ten

Bill Myers dropped by that evening with a folder full of real estate flyers that Charlotte had forgotten to bring home with her for an open house she was holding the following afternoon.

Paul went down and answered the door to let him in.

"How's it going?" Paul said.

"Good. Can you give these to Charlotte?"

"No problem. Come on in, have a cold one."

Bill hesitated, then said, "What the hell."

Bill was in his early forties, a full head of blond hair morphing into gray. When Paul first met him, back when they both attended UConn—the University of Connecticut—up in Storrs, east of Hartford, Bill was the classic jock and looked the part. Six-foot, lean, one of those classic chiseled jaws. Nearly twenty years later, he wasn't the athlete he once was but remained trim, keeping himself in shape by running five miles most days.

While always friends, they'd barely kept in touch—Christmas cards, the odd email, maybe meeting up for a drink every couple of years—but had renewed their connection since Charlotte joined the real estate agency where Bill worked. Up until Hoffman's attack on Paul, there had been a weekly squash game, and whenever Bill had a new girlfriend he wanted them to meet, the four of them would plan a dinner out.

Paul took two beers from the fridge and guided Bill through the living room to the balcony that looked onto Long Island Sound.

"Charlotte's upstairs, getting ready to head out tonight," Paul said as they sat down on modern Adirondack chairs. He tossed his bottle cap into an empty coffee can he kept nearby. "This one couple, she's shown them at least twenty places, but they want to go back one last time and see some house in Devon just off Naugatuck."

"I know it," Bill said. "Been on the market thirteen months. Handyman's dream. Someone should buy it for the lot, tear the place, and start over."

"Josh and I are gonna watch a movie. How's your weekend looking? Out with Rachel?"

Bill shook his head. "That's kind of cooled off. She thinks a guy who's been married once before is not a good prospect."

"I can't imagine why."

Bill grunted.

The glass door slid back and Josh stepped out.

"Hey, pal," Bill said, gripping the boy's shoulder and giving him a small shake. He spotted Josh's finger and said, "What'd you do there?"

"A typewriter bit me," he said.

Bill raised a puzzled eyebrow. Paul said, "A surprise from Charlotte. An old Underwood. Josh got his finger caught in it."

Bill nodded. "Okay. Old typewriters are becoming a thing. Not that I'd want to use one. I'm a fan of find-and-replace."

"We talking about women now?"

Josh chuckled.

The door slid open again and this time it was Charlotte. "Hey, Bill," she said as Josh scurried back into the house.

Bill turned around in his chair. "Left those flyers for your thing tomorrow on the counter."

"Thanks." She gave Paul an apologetic look. "I hope I won't be too late."

Paul smiled ruefully. "No problem."

Charlotte withdrew, sliding the glass door into the closed position.

"Uh, good-bye," Bill said.

Paul felt obliged to offer an apology. "She's got a lot on her mind. Me, mostly."

"How's it going with the shrink?"

The term brought a sigh from Paul. "Okay."

"Good. 'Cause we don't want you doing anything stupid."

Paul narrowed his eyes. "Christ, I'm not going to kill myself."

Bill leaned back in his chair and raised his palms as though under attack. "Sorry. It's just, you've kind of been on edge. Depressed, the nightmares, forgetting shit. Like the other day, I returned your call, and you're all 'What, I never called you' except you did."

Paul bristled. "Okay, yeah, I admit, the last eight months have not been the best. But I'm working through it. I've got a plan."

"Okay, great, that's all I wanted to hear." He smiled. "What you need is to get that head of yours fixed up so I can beat your ass again at squash. I'm suffering from the withdrawal of humiliating you."

"Fuck off."

Bill grinned. "Truth hurts, man." He paused. "So what's the plan?"

Paul hesitated. "I want to find out what makes Kenneth Hoffman tick."

Bill eyed him amusedly. "I can help you with that."

"Oh, yeah?"

"Yeah. He's a fuckin' psycho."

———

LATER, AFTER BILL HAD LEFT, JOSH HURRIEDLY SLID OPEN THE BALcony door and said breathlessly to his father, "Don't you hear that?"

Paul, who'd been turning the pages of *The New Yorker*, taking in nothing more than the cartoons, said, "Hear what?"

Josh gave him a *"duh?"* look. So Paul listened. The sound had been there the entire time. He'd just been unaware of it. Music. Well, not really music. It was an endlessly repeating jingle.

Dee dee, diddly-dee, dee dee, dee-da, dee-da, dee da dee.

"Ice cream?" Josh said. "The ice cream truck?"

"Right!" he said, springing out of his chair. "I have to get my wallet."

Josh produced it in his upraised right hand.

By the time they hit the street, the truck was only half a block away. It was an old, rusted blue-and-white panel van with rudimentary drawings of ice-cream cones and sundaes and the words THE TASTEE TRUCK painted on the sides. Josh waved a hand to make sure the driver didn't miss them. The truck slowed with a rusty screeching of brakes at the end of the driveway.

"Whatcha want?" Paul asked as Josh scanned the menu board with wonder.

"Chocolate-coated cone," he said.

The driver moved from behind the wheel to the open bay on the side and asked, in a low monotone, "Yeah?"

Paul suddenly found himself unable to speak.

The ice cream man, not much older than twenty, looked like he ate a lot of what he sold. Thick, pudgy arms; a round face with soft, pimpled cheeks; hair cut so close to his head he was almost shaved bald. He was probably six feet tall, but looked even taller, towering over them from the serving window.

The name tag pinned to his ice cream–smeared apron read LEN.

Len asked, slowly, "What do you want?"

"Dad?" Josh said.

"Uh, two cones. Mediums," Paul said. "Dipped in chocolate."

"Okay," Len said.

Paul briefly turned and looked away while Len grabbed two empty cones, held them beneath the soft ice cream dispenser, pulled down on the bar, then gently waved each cone to create a swirling effect. Then he dipped them in melted chocolate, which instantly froze into a shell.

"Mister?" Len said.

Paul turned back. Len looked at him blankly as he leaned over and handed him the cones. Paul gave one off to Josh, then dug into his pocket for his wallet. Paul handed Len a ten.

"One second," Len said, going into a green metal cash box for change.

"Just keep it," Paul said, and led Josh away from the truck.

Len offered no thanks, returned to the driver's seat, and steered the Tastee Truck farther down the street, the jingle heralding his presence to the neighborhood.

"I haven't seen that guy before," Paul said.

"Yeah, he's new this summer," Josh said. "There was a different guy last year."

"I don't think he knew who I was."

"What are you talking about?" Josh asked.

"Never mind," Paul said. "Let's go back and watch a movie."

––––––––

JOSH HAD LONG WANTED TO SEE THE BATMAN FLICKS, WHICH PAUL felt were a bit too mature and intense for a boy of nine, not counting the Adam West version. All the ones made this century—well, they didn't call him the Dark Knight for nothing—were violent and bleak and occasionally disturbing. But Paul was able to call up the 1989 one starring Michael Keaton, which, while bleak enough, was tamer than the more recent versions.

Josh was very quiet during the part where young Bruce Wayne's parents were murdered in the alley behind a theater.

"I don't think we should ever go out to a movie," he said, leaning into his father on the couch as the final credits rolled.

"It's okay," Paul said, mentally kicking himself for forgetting that central part of the crime fighter's backstory. "We don't live in Gotham City. We live in Milford."

"Bad things happen here," he said. "A bad thing happened to you."

He gave his son a squeeze. "I know."

"I hope I don't get nightmares," he said.

Paul grinned. "You and me both, pal."

Charlotte texted to report that she'd be late. Her clients had decided to put in an offer. Paul said he would say good night for her when he put Josh to bed. As he sat on the edge, about to turn off Josh's bedside table lamp, the boy said, "I'm sorry about tomorrow."

"That's okay."

"I don't even care that much about basketball. But a lot of my friends do, and I wanted to be able to tell them I went to a game."

"It's okay. The next weekend, when you're here longer, we'll do something special."

Josh reached for an iPhone and earbuds next to the bed.

"What are you listening to these days to help you get to sleep?" Paul asked.

"The Beatles."

"Seriously?"

Josh nodded. "They're pretty good. One of them's about a walrus."

"Don't strangle yourself on the cords after you fall asleep."

Josh put a bud into each ear, tapped the phone's screen. Paul leaned in, kissed his son's forehead, turned off the light, slipped out of the room, and closed the door.

As he came down the stairs to the kitchen he heard the front door open. Seconds later, a weary Charlotte appeared.

"Nightcap?" he said, opening the fridge.

"No, thanks," she said. "I just want to go to bed."

"Was the offer accepted?"

She shook her head, exhausted. "We spent nearly two hours on it, sorting out a closing date, inclusions, everything. And then, at the last minute, they got cold feet."

He smiled sympathetically. "Run you a tub?"

She shook her head. "The second my head hits that pillow, I'm dead. How's Josh?"

"We watched *Batman*." He grimaced. "The part where Bruce

Wayne's parents die hit a little too close to home." He hesitated. "A weird thing happened."

"What?"

"We went out to the ice cream truck. Kenneth Hoffman's son was driving it."

"That's Hoffman's son? I've bought ice cream for Josh from him, too."

"It just felt . . . strange. I don't think he had any idea it was me. Not that he necessarily should have." He looked down. "I tell myself I want to face this business head-on, but then I see Hoffman's son and I can't look him in the eye."

"Coming to terms with what Kenneth did doesn't mean you have to confront his boy. What do they say about the sins of the father shall not be visited upon the son?"

Paul grinned. "Actually, I think it's the other way around."

Charlotte rolled her eyes. "You get my point."

"I do."

Charlotte sighed, then trudged upstairs. By the time Paul had tidied the kitchen and climbed the stairs to the bedroom, Charlotte was under the covers making soft breathing noises.

Paul slipped under the covers stealthily, taking care not to wake Charlotte. He reached over to the lamp and plunged the room into darkness.

In seconds, he was asleep.

———————

IT WAS JUST AFTER TWO IN THE MORNING WHEN HE HEARD THE sounds.

He became aware of them while he was still asleep, so when he first opened his eyes, and heard nothing, he thought he must have been dreaming.

There was nothing.

But then he heard it again.

Chit chit. Chit chit chit. Chit. Chit chit.

He immediately knew the sound. It was a new one to the household but instantly recognizable. One floor down, someone was playing with the antique typewriter in his cramped office.

He gently ran his hand across the sheet until he felt Charlotte there. So, it wasn't her. As if that would have made any sense, her getting up in the middle of the night to mess about with her gift to him.

That left Josh.

Paul squinted at the clock radio on the table beside him. It was 2:03 A.M. Why the hell would Josh go down and play with the typewriter now? Or at all, given that he'd hurt himself on it and professed to hate the thing.

Paul gently pulled back the covers, put his feet down to the floor, and stood. Wearing only his boxers, he walked out of the bedroom and into the hall, not turning on any lights.

Chit chit.

He went straight past Josh's closed door and down the stairs, keeping his hand on the railing. It wasn't just because of the dark; he was not fully awake and slightly woozy. When he reached the kitchen, the various digital lights on the stove, microwave, and toaster cast enough light that he could see where he was going.

The door to his small study was closed, and there was no sliver of light at the base. He turned the knob, pushed open the door far enough to reach around and flip the light switch, then pushed the door open all the way.

Josh was not there.

No one was there. The chair was empty.

But the typewriter was there.

There was no paper in it. The single sheet with *Josh* typed on it remained on the desk.

Paul stared at the scene for several seconds, then glanced back into the kitchen. The way he figured it, Josh must have heard him coming, ducked out, hid behind the kitchen island, then scooted back upstairs the second Paul stepped into his office.

Sure enough, when Paul went back upstairs and peeked into Josh's room, the boy was under the covers, eyes closed, buds tucked into his ears.

The little bugger.

Paul smiled to himself. He'd conduct a proper interrogation in the morning.

Eleven

Paul had been in his office for an hour, on his third cup of coffee and researching online what made supposedly good people do bad things, when Josh, still in his pajamas, came padding down the stairs to the kitchen.

Paul closed the laptop, came out, went to the fridge, and got out a container of milk. "Cheerios?" he asked his son.

Josh muttered something that sounded like a yes and sat at the table. Paul put a bowl of cereal in front of him, splashed on some milk, and grabbed a spoon from the cutlery drawer. Josh stared sleepily into the bowl as he scooped a spoonful of cereal and shoved it into his mouth.

"How are you this morning?" Paul asked, glancing at the wall clock. It was half past ten.

Josh made a noise that was little more than a soft grunt.

"You really slept in," his father said.

Josh glanced for a second at his father. Paul noticed there was still some sleep in the corner of his eyes. "It's Sunday."

"True enough. But you seem a little more tired than usual."

"I had bad dreams," Josh said, going back to his cereal. "We shouldn't have watched that movie."

"Sorry. I should have picked something else, but the thing is, almost any movie can remind us of something bad that's happened to us."

Charlotte appeared, both hands to one ear, attaching an earring. "Hey, you two," she said.

"Heading out already?" Paul said. "I thought your open house was at two."

"It is. But I have to make sure the house is presentable. Last time I was there the master bedroom floor was littered with laundry and there were half a dozen dog turds in the yard. And I want to pick up some frozen bread, put it in the oven."

Josh perked up. "Why?"

"Old real estate trick. Make the house smell nice."

She pulled out the glass carafe from the coffeemaker and frowned when she found it nearly empty.

"Sorry," Paul said. "I already went through a pot. I was up kind of early. Couldn't sleep." He tipped his head toward the study. "Thought I'd get back to it."

"How's it going?"

Paul shrugged. He slipped into a chair across from his son. Josh yawned, looked at the wall clock, and rested his spoon in the bowl. "I gotta get ready. Mom and Walter will be here soon."

He started to push back his chair but was stopped when Paul reached out and gently grabbed his wrist.

"So you want to tell me what you were up to in the middle of the night?"

"Huh?" Josh said.

"I heard you. Around two in the morning."

"What's this?" Charlotte said, putting a new filter into the coffeemaker and spooning in some ground coffee.

Paul said, "I thought you hated that typewriter, but you got up in the middle of the night to play with it."

"What?"

"I know what I heard," Paul said. "I know it wasn't Charlotte, because she was in the bed right next to me."

"It wasn't me," Josh said. "Why would I play with that stupid typewriter?"

"Come on, pal. You're not in trouble, except maybe for not being truthful with me now."

"I'm not lying," he said.

Paul gave him a look of disappointment. "Okay, Josh."

Charlotte, pouring water into the coffee machine, said, "I don't understand. You heard the typewriter in the night?"

"Yup," Paul said.

Charlotte gave him a quizzical look. "And it's somehow a big deal if Josh was messing around with it? It's built like a tank. He can't break it."

"It wasn't me," Josh said again. "I'm glad Mom is coming." He got up from the table and fled up the stairs to his room.

Charlotte gave her husband a look.

"What?" Paul said.

"Has it occurred to you that maybe you dreamed it? You heard some *tap tap tapping* in your sleep?"

Doubt crept across Paul's face.

"Okay, the first time I heard it, I was in bed, probably half-asleep."

"There you go."

Hesitantly, he added, "But then I got up and heard it again when I was going down the hall."

Charlotte slowly shook her head. "Your mind plays funny tricks on you when you're half-awake, or half-asleep, that time of night. Maybe you heard something else. Some kind of house noise. A ticking radiator or something."

"This house doesn't have rads."

"Whatever." While the coffee brewed she took a seat at the table. "Look, you've been under an enormous strain lately. Don't take it out on Josh."

Paul ran a hand over his mouth and shook his head.

The doorbell rang.

Paul tipped his head back and shouted to the upper floor, "Josh! Your mom's here!"

"Early, as always," Charlotte said, returning to the coffee machine. "Walter's always in a hurry."

The doorbell rang again.

"Hold your horses," Paul said under his breath.

Then, from the front door one floor below: "Hello?"

Paul and Charlotte exchanged glances. "Did you lock the door when you came in last night?" Paul asked her quietly.

Charlotte grimaced. "I thought I had. Does Hailey have a key?"

Paul shook his head. "Josh does. Maybe she made a copy." He got out of the chair and reached the top of the stairs as Hailey appeared. Five-ten, short blond hair, jeans with artfully arranged threadbare patches, bracelets jangling from each wrist, hoop earrings the size of coasters. She gave Paul's wife a cold stare and said, "Charlotte."

"Hailey."

Paul nodded a silent hello to his ex, then called a second time for Josh. "Coming!" the boy shouted.

Outside, a horn honked.

"Jesus," Hailey said.

"Walter in a bit of a hurry?" Paul asked.

"When isn't he? There's not a damn thing he doesn't do in a hurry."

Charlotte snickered. Hailey, realizing her comment invited more than one interpretation, tried to recover. "Just getting out of the city was a nightmare. Even on a Sunday morning. We were stuck on the FDR for forty minutes. You know Walter and traffic. He totally loses it. And 95 was no picnic, either."

Hailey sighed then regarded her former husband with what seemed genuine concern. "How are you doing?"

"Okay," he said.

"Back to a hundred percent?"

"Getting there."

Hailey smiled. "That's good."

Josh came thumping down the steps, his backpack slung over his shoulder. He was heading straight for the stairs.

"Hey," Hailey said, "you gonna say good-bye to your dad?"

Josh mumbled a "bye" without turning around.

"That was a bit lame," his mother said.

"Dad says I'm a liar," he said, holding his position at the top of the stairs to the first floor.

"What?" Hailey asked. "And what happened to your finger?"

"It's nothing," Paul said. "Josh, I never said you were a liar." Josh glared at him without comment. "I just—look, come here."

The boy moved his way as though his running shoes had lead soles. Paul said, "Maybe I was wrong."

"Maybe?" Josh said, then spinning on his heels and disappearing down the stairs.

Hailey gave her ex-husband a reproachful look but voiced no criticism. "Good-bye, Paul," she said, then, almost as an afterthought, glanced at his wife. "Charlotte."

Charlotte nodded.

Once they'd heard the front door close, Paul shook his head and said, "Shit."

Twelve

While Charlotte hosted her open house, Paul spent much of the afternoon cloistered in his office. He read more articles online about Kenneth Hoffman, and when he thought he'd found pretty much everything on the subject, including several video segments from local news stations, and an item on that NBC show *Dateline*, he broadened his search to include think pieces on why people do bad things.

That covered a lot of territory. Why do people lie? Why do they steal? Why do they have affairs? And, most important, why do they kill?

He scanned articles until he felt he would go blind, and by the end of it, he had no clearer sense of why Hoffman murdered those two women. Paul found Hoffman's motivation to kill *him* the simplest to explain. Paul was a witness. He had seen those two women in the back of the Volvo. Hoffman had to kill Paul if he was to have any chance of getting away with his crime.

Paul thought he would like to talk to him about it.

Face-to-face.

He thought he was up to it. His reaction to unexpectedly seeing Kenneth's son, Leonard, was not, Paul believed, an indicator of how he'd react to sitting down with the killer of two women, if that could be arranged. For one thing, he'd be prepared.

He was about to do a search on how one arranged a visit with an inmate when his thoughts turned to Josh.

He'd really botched things with his son that morning. There

really was no reason for Josh to lie about tapping away at the typewriter in the middle of the night. And it didn't make much sense for him to have done it in the first place. He hadn't gone near the thing since catching his finger in it.

He had to accept that there was only one logical explanation: he'd dreamed it.

Yes, he'd told Charlotte he'd continued to hear the *chit chit chit* as he went down the hallway, but maybe he hadn't shaken the dream by that point. Maybe he was half sleepwalking.

What pained him was that he and Josh had had such a nice—albeit short—time together, aside from the troubling aspects of the Batman movie. And Paul had sabotaged it at the end.

Damn it.

But Paul was pretty sure he could fix things with Josh. He'd make this right. The next time Josh came out from the city, they'd do something really special. Maybe go for a drive to Mystic, check out the aquarium.

Maybe Charlotte would even want to come.

Things definitely seemed better with her. They'd hit a few bumps in the road, but if there was any upside to his nearly getting killed, it was that it had made Charlotte reassess not just their marriage, but also the expectations she had for herself. As she'd told him more than once since the incident, she'd been questioning where she was in her life. Was she where she'd hoped she'd be ten years ago?

While she was doing respectably as a real estate agent, it had never been her goal. She'd entertained, at one time, the idea of a career in, well, entertainment. Living in New York, she'd done off-*off*-Broadway, even had three lines one time as a day care operator in a *Law & Order* episode. (Paul suspected Charlotte had actually gone on a date or two with one of the stars, on the *Law* side, but she would never confirm nor deny.) Sadly, she never got the big break she'd strived for and reached the point where she had to make an actual living. She'd held sales jobs, worked hotel reception. When

Paul met her, she was the early-morning manager of a Days Inn. So, where her career was concerned, she had settled.

If there was little glamour in being a real estate agent, there was even less in being married to a West Haven College professor. Yes, it was a decent place to teach, but it wasn't Harvard, and it lived in the shadows of nearby Yale and University of New Haven. If Charlotte had ever viewed what he did as a noble calling—molding young minds into leaders of tomorrow, ha!—Paul doubted she did anymore. Before the attempt on his life, she'd rarely asked him about his work, and why would she? It was boring. What was there for him to aspire to now? Where did one go next? The dizzying heights of department head?

So this was what Charlotte's life had become. Selling houses in a drab Connecticut town, married to a man of limited ambition.

And then there was the baby thing.

Paul had not brought up the subject in a long time, but he'd hoped he and Charlotte would one day have a child. Had he stayed with Hailey, he was sure Josh would have ended up with a baby brother or sister. Hailey had as much as said she and Walter were trying. But Charlotte had not warmed to the idea of becoming a mother herself.

Well, fuck all that.

This was a new day, Paul told himself. This was the day when he took control. This was the day when he stood up to the demons. This was the day when he would start rebuilding himself and his marriage.

He was going to tackle this Hoffman thing. He was going to write something. He was going to write something beyond the notes he'd already made. He was going to write something *good*. He didn't yet know what shape it would take. Maybe it would be a memoir. Maybe a novel. Maybe he'd turn his experience into a magazine piece.

It had everything.

Sex. Murder. Mystery.

Coming back from the brink of death.

The fucking thing would write itself, once he decided which direction to take it in. This was the key to putting his life and marriage back together. He wasn't doing this just for himself. He was doing it for Charlotte. He wanted her to see that he could be strong, that he could get his life back.

Enough of this sad-sack bullshit.

Maybe he could even be the man she'd want to have a child with.

But hey, let's take things one step at a time.

Paul reflected on how he'd come across these last few months. Christ, even Bill seemed worried he might kill himself. Yes, he'd been depressed. He'd been traumatized not just by the event itself—the nightmares, the anxiety—but also by physical manifestations. Headaches, memory lapses, insomnia. Who wouldn't be depressed?

But suicidal?

Had he come across as that desperate? Maybe.

"See how you are when you've got Kenneth Hoffman visiting your sleep every night," he said to himself.

Shit.

Of course.

The typing he'd thought he'd heard was clearly part of a Hoffman nightmare. Paul must have been dreaming about those two women typing out their apologies. Charlotte's gift of that antique Underwood had triggered a Hoffman dream that zeroed in on that aspect of his crime.

That was the *chit chit chit* he'd heard in the night. Jill Foster and Catherine Lamb tapping away.

Paul got out his phone. Josh was very likely at the game now, so Paul wasn't going to call him. But Josh might see a text.

Paul quickly wrote one.

Hey pal. Luv you. Sorry about this morning. Ur Dad was a jerk. Hope u r having fun at the game.

He sent it. Paul stared at the phone for a long time, waiting for the dancing dots to indicate his son was writing him a reply.

When none came after three minutes, Paul put his phone back into his pocket.

Thirteen

"So, Gavin, how did you spend your weekend?" Dr. Anna White asked as the two of them settled into their respective chairs in her office.

Gavin appeared thoughtful. "Reflecting."

Anna's eyebrows raised a fraction of an inch. "Reflecting?"

He nodded. "About the hurt I've caused, and if there's any way I can make amends."

"Amends."

"Yes. Do you think it would be possible to arrange a meeting with the people I've wronged so that I might apologize?"

Anna eyed him warily. "I don't know that a face-to-face would be the way to go. I think it could end up badly for all concerned."

Gavin, innocently, asked, "How so?"

"I think the woman whose cat you hid would be too fearful, and that father you called . . ." At this point she shook her head. "I hate to think what he might try to do to you if you were in the same room."

"You might be right," he said. "Maybe I should write something instead."

"We'll get to that. But besides reflecting, what else did you do with your weekend?"

"Not much," he said. "Well, I worked Saturday. I usually work evenings at Computer World, but they're not open Saturday night, so I did a day shift."

"Did you work Friday night?"

Gavin nodded. "I did."

"What time did your shift end?"

"Nine," he said slowly. "Why are you asking me?"

Anna hesitated. "A troubling thing happened to someone on Friday night."

"Someone? You mean, someone you know?"

Anna slowly nodded.

"Another one of your patients?" he asked.

Anna studied him for several seconds, weighing how to proceed. She ignored his last question and continued. "Someone did a very sick, very cruel thing to her."

"This person you know who might be a patient," Gavin said.

"Her dog was recently run over by a car. Someone snuck into her house and hung a dead Yorkshire terrier in her bedroom. According to the tag, the dog had belonged to a family in Devon. They were making up the missing posters when the police notified them."

Gavin sat back in his chair and put a hand over his mouth. "Wow. That's pretty sick."

"Yes," Anna said. "It is."

"So, you're telling me this why?" he asked.

Anna hesitated. "The other day, when I came in here, you were standing over there. Behind my desk."

Gavin looked at her blankly, then shrugged. "Uh, I guess."

"What were you doing over there?"

Gavin glanced over to that part of the room. "Just looking at the books."

"You're interested in psychology texts?"

Another shrug. "You don't know what a book actually is until you look at it." He grinned. "You could use a few more graphic novels."

"When you were over there, Gavin, did you look at my computer?"

"Huh?"

"My laptop. Were you looking at my laptop?"

Gavin's eyes narrowed. "Holy shit. Let me guess. This lady with the dead dog hanging on her door, she *is* a patient, and you think I was fucking with her head?"

"I didn't say the dog was hanging from her door."

Gavin blinked. "Yes, you *did*. That's exactly what you said. Jesus Christ, you're actually accusing me of this."

Anna hesitated. "I haven't accused you of anything, Gavin."

"Of course you are. What did I do this weekend? Where was I Friday night? This is unbelievable. I come here for *help*. I come here, *trusting* you to help me deal with a personal crisis, and what happens?" He shook his head. "This is fucking unbelievable. So I guess every time something bad happens to anyone in Milford, I'm immediately the number one suspect. Was there a hit-and-run this weekend? A bank robbery? Did someone steal a candy bar from the 7-Eleven? Do you think I had anything to do with those things, too?"

Anna had begun to look slightly less sure of herself. "You have to admit, Gavin, that what happened to that woman is not unlike the stunt you pulled, the one that landed you here."

"I swear, I don't even know who that woman is. What's her name?"

"I can't tell you that."

"Yeah, well, if you think it's me, you might as well, since I'd already know it, right? But I don't. If I'm the prime suspect, why haven't the police been to see me?"

Anna said nothing.

"So wait, not only are you accusing me of doing this horrible thing, but you think I'm snooping around in your computer? Checking out who comes to see you and what their problems are?" He shook his head and adopted a wounded expression. "Wow. So this is the kind of help and understanding I'm getting. I'm sure going to get better coming to see you a couple of times a week."

"Gavin—"

He stood. "I can't do this."

"Gavin, killing an animal is a sign of a more serious issue than any we've dealt with so far. You need to understand that—"

"Understand what?" he shouted. He jabbed a finger in her direction. "I should report you or something. There must be some kind of ethics commission or something for you people. They need to know!" He stood.

"Gavin, sit down!"

"No, I think I've had just about—"

The door suddenly swung open. Paul Davis stood there, looked quickly at Gavin, then at Anna.

"I'm sorry," he said. "I heard—are you okay, Dr. White?"

She got out of her chair. "We're fine here, Paul."

"I heard shouting and—"

"Whatever your fucking problem is," Gavin said to Paul, "don't expect *her* to help you."

Paul gave Gavin a long look. "You need to calm down, buddy."

"Buddy?" Gavin said. "Are we buddies?" He regarded Paul curiously, as if wondering whether they had met before. "You're Paul? Did I hear that right?"

Slowly, Paul said, "Yeah."

"Well, Paul, good luck."

He started for the door so quickly that Paul didn't have time to step out of his way. Gavin put his hands on the front of his jacket to toss him to one side, knocking Paul's head into the jamb.

"Shit!" Paul said, touching his head for half a second, but just as quickly pushing back. Gavin stumbled from the office to the small waiting room.

"Asshole," Gavin said.

Now they were both pawing at each other, each trying to grab the other by a lapel so as to make it easier to land a punch with a free hand.

"Gavin, stop it!" Anna screamed.

They stopped, looked in unison at her. As each released his grip on the other, Gavin turned and ran for the door.

"Paul, I'm so sorry," Anna said.

He brushed himself off, as though some of Gavin had somehow stayed with him. "I'm okay."

"Your head," she said. "Did you hit your head in the same spot?"

He touched it again. "No, it's okay. I'm fine. What about you?"

"I'm okay," she said, then frowned.

"What the fuck is *his* problem?" Paul asked, glancing at the door through which Gavin had departed. "What was his name? Gavin?"

"I think I just handled something very badly."

"What?"

She shook her head. "Nothing. Mr. Hitchens is my problem, not yours. Do you still want to talk? I'll understand if all this—"

"I'm okay, if you're okay."

"I just need a minute," she said, taking her seat.

"You're shaking," Paul said. "We don't have to do this."

"No, no, we do. What just happened here, it's still nothing compared to what you've been through." She sat up straight, raised her chin, and said, "I'm ready."

"You're sure?"

A confident nod to assure him she was back on track. "So, tell me what's happened since we last spoke."

He filled her in on his online research and how it was having an empowering effect, although it hadn't stopped the nightmares. He told her that Charlotte's gift of an antique typewriter had triggered a bizarre dream that seemed so real, he ended up blaming his son for something he clearly had not done.

"I texted him an apology. It took him the better part of a day to reply." He paused, reflecting. "Do I seem borderline suicidal to you?"

"Why would you ask that?"

"It was something a friend said. He seemed worried I might do something stupid."

"I would say no," Anna said. "But you'd tell me if your thoughts were trending in that direction?"

"Of course." He also told her about not remembering his drive home one day, forgetting about texts he'd sent, other memory lapses.

"When do you see the neurologist again?"

"Couple of weeks." Another pause. Then, "Do you know anything about visiting someone in prison?"

"Not much."

Paul nodded. "From what I read on the state website, the inmate needs to put you on a list. Unless you're, you know, a police detective or a lawyer or something."

"You still want to see Kenneth Hoffman."

Paul bit his lip. "I think so. I know closure is a huge cliché, but a sit-down with him might provide some. You always hear it on the news. How the family of a murder victim gets closure on the day the accused is convicted."

"I'd say that's something of a myth," Anna said. "But I won't stop you from looking into a visit. In the meantime, you can think about what you'd want to say to him. What you'd want to ask him."

"I'd like to know if he's sorry."

Anna smiled wryly. "Would it make a difference?"

Paul shrugged. "If I can get in to see him, I don't want to go alone."

Anna nodded. "You'd want to take Charlotte."

"No. I'd want you to come."

Anna's eyebrows went up. "Oh."

"I don't know if I could come back here and give you an accurate account of what happened. Having you there to observe could be helpful."

Anna appeared to be considering it. "I don't normally do house calls."

Paul grinned. "You mean, *Big* House calls."

WHEN PAUL WENT OUT TO HIS CAR, HE COULD NOT FIND HIS KEYS. Anna said if she found them, she'd let him know. He called Charlotte, who picked him up at Anna's, drove him home, and unlocked the door. Once he had his spare keys, Charlotte drove him back to Anna's so he could retrieve his Subaru.

That night, over dinner, he told Charlotte about what had happened at Anna's before his session had started.

"Some people," he observed, "are even more fucked-up than I am."

They killed off a bottle of chardonnay while watching a movie. At least, part of one. Halfway through, Charlotte ran her hand up the inside of Paul's thigh and said, "Is this movie boring or what?"

"It is now," he said.

When they turned the lights out shortly after eleven, Paul thought, *Things are getting better.*

AND THEN, AT SIX MINUTES PAST THREE, IT HAPPENED AGAIN.

Chit chit. Chit chit chit. Chit. Chit chit.

Fourteen

B efore the sounds of the Underwood reached him, Paul had been dreaming.

In the dream, he has a stomachache. He's on the bed, writhing, clutching his belly. It feels as though something is moving around in there. Something *alive*. It's like that *Alien* movie, where the creature bursts out of John Hurt's chest as the crew of the *Nostromo* eat lunch.

Paul pulls up his shirt, looks down. There's something in there, all right. There's something poking up from under the skin. And then, as if a zipper ran from his ribs down past his navel, he opens up. But there's no blood, no guts spilling all over the place. His belly opens up like a doctor's bag.

Paul looks at the gaping hole in his body and waits.

What come up first are fingers. Dirty fingers with chipped nails. Two hands grasp the edges of his stomach. Something—someone—is pulling itself out.

Holy shit, I'm having a baby, Paul thinks.

Now there's the top of a person's head. It's Kenneth Hoffman. Once his head clears Paul's stomach, he looks at Paul and grins. He's saying something, but Paul can't make out what it is.

It turns out he's not saying actual words. He's making a sound. The same sound, over and over again.

Chit chit chit. Chit chit.

Paul reaches down, puts his hands over Kenneth's face. He doesn't know whether to push Kenneth back inside himself, or try to drag out the rest of him. He feels Kenneth nibbling at his fingers.

Chit chit chit. Chit chit.

Paul opened his eyes. He was breathing in short, rapid gasps. He touched his hand to his chest and found it wet. He'd broken out in a cold sweat. He craned his neck around to look at the clock radio glaring dimly at him from the bedside table.

3:06 A.M.

He didn't want to close his eyes and return to that nightmare. Slowly, so as not to disturb Charlotte next to him, he swung his legs out of the bed and onto the floor.

He decided to take a leak.

As his eyes adjusted to the darkness, he looked at Charlotte. She was sleeping with her back to him, head on the pillow, hand slipped beneath it. He could just barely make out her body slowly rising and falling with each breath.

Dressed only in a pair of boxers, he padded silently across the floor to the bathroom and closed the door. The plug-in night-light glowed dimly.

He lifted the toilet seat, drained his bladder, cringed as he flushed, hoping the noise wouldn't be too disruptive. He rinsed his hands at the sink and dried them, waiting for the toilet tank to refill before opening the door.

The tank refilled, and silence again descended.

As his fingers touched the doorknob, he heard it.

Chit chit. Chit chit chit.

He held his breath.

I am not dreaming. I am awake. I am absolutely, positively, awake.

It was the same sound from the other night. A typing sound.

He waited for it to recur, but there was nothing. Slowly, he turned the knob, opened the door, and took a step out into the hallway. He froze, held his breath once again.

Still nothing.

All he could hear was the distant sound of the waves of Long Island Sound lolling into the beach, and Charlotte's soft breathing.

Could something else have made a noise that sounded like keys striking the cylinder? Something electrical? Water dripping somewhere in the house? Maybe—

Chit chit.

A small chill ran the length of Paul's spine. He wanted to wake Charlotte. He wanted her to hear this, too. But waking her would also create a commotion. Whoever was fooling around with that typewriter—and clearly it was not Josh, who was miles away in Manhattan, but it had to be *somebody*—was going to stop once they heard talking on the floor above.

Paul wanted to catch whoever it was in the act.

No, wait. He should call the police.

Right. Great plan. *Hello, officer? Could you send someone right over? Someone's typing in my house.*

Paul reached the top of the stairs, then tiptoed down, one soft step at a time. When the house was rebuilt after Sandy, a new staircase had gone in, and there wasn't a single squeak in the entire flight.

As he reached the second step from the bottom, he heard it again.

Chit chit. Chit chit chit.

He looked across the kitchen to the closed door of his study. There was no light bleeding out from below it. Just like the other night. How was someone supposed to mess around with that Underwood in total darkness?

A miniflashlight. Sure. Whoever was in there wasn't going to want to attract attention by turning on the lights.

Yeah, like that made sense. They were already attracting attention with the typing.

Paul moved barefoot across the floor. As he closed the distance between himself and the door, he wondered whether he needed some kind of weapon. As he sidled past the kitchen island, he carefully extracted a long wooden spoon from a piece of pottery filled with kitchen utensils.

He had a pretty good idea how ridiculous he looked, but the spoon would have to do. You went into battle with what was at hand.

Paul reached the door, gripped the handle. With one swift motion, he turned and pushed.

"Surprise!" he shouted, reaching with his other hand to flick the light switch up.

And just as it was when he thought Josh had been fooling around in here, the room was empty.

The typewriter sat where it had been since Charlotte bought it for him, seemingly untouched. No paper rolled into it.

Paul stood there, blinked several times. "What the fuck," he said to himself. He scanned the room, as if someone could hide in a place that wasn't any bigger than a closet.

Suddenly, struck by an idea, he ran to the steps that led down to the front door. Someone could be making a run for it. Quietly, for sure, but did anything else make sense?

Paul ran his hand along the wall, hunting for the switch. He flipped it up, illuminating the stairs and the door at the bottom.

There was no one there. From where he stood, he could see the dead bolt on the door turned to the locked position.

In his rush, his left foot slipped over the top step and dropped to the next, throwing him off balance. He canted to the right, reaching frantically for the railing to break his fall, but missing it altogether. His butt hit the top step, then bumped down two more, hard, before he came to a shuddering stop.

"Fuck!" he shouted. He suddenly hurt in more places than he could count. Butt, thigh, foot, arm.

Pride.

Upstairs, Charlotte shouted. "Paul! Paul!"

Wincing, he yelled back, "Down here!" He grabbed his right elbow, ran his hand over it delicately. *"Jesus!"*

He heard running on the upper floor, then thumping down the stairs. "Where are you?"

Charlotte sounded panicked.

"Down here," he said, struggling to his feet. His boxers had slid halfway down his ass, and he gave them a tug up, hoping to preserve what little dignity he had left. She arrived in the kitchen, her white nightgown swirling around her like a heroine in a romance novel.

"What's happened? Did you fall? Are you okay? What's going on?"

Instead of telling her, Paul wondered whether there was something worse than nightmares and memory loss.

Going batshit crazy.

Fifteen

The sun wasn't even up, and her dad was at it already.

Anna White, dressed in an oversize T-shirt that hung to her knees, was awakened not by her alarm but by the sound of the rowing machine. She tossed back the covers and padded down the hall to her father's room. She gently pushed open the door. Frank, in his pajamas, was stroking away on the machine, watching the cartoon channel.

"Dad," she said softly, "it's five-thirty."

Anna believed the cartoons put her father into a kind of trance, keeping him from any awareness of how long he had been on the machine. She was convinced he was going to have a heart attack at this rate.

He either didn't hear her, or had chosen to ignore her. He laughed as Daffy Duck took a shotgun blast to the face, spinning his bill to the other side of his head.

"Dad," Anna said, stepping forward, putting a hand on his upper arm. She was amazed at how hard it felt. Her father's head jerked in her direction.

"What?"

"You should go back to bed. It's too early to be up. It's sure too early to be up doing this."

"This one's not over."

The remote was on the floor. She knelt down to reach it, hit the POWER button. The screen went black.

"Why'd you do that?"

"Dad, please. Go back to bed."

"Not tired. Gotta take a whiz," he said, getting off the machine and walking down the hall. Anna sat on the edge of his bed, waiting for him to return. He wandered back in after a couple of minutes, a dark coaster-size stain on the crotch of his pajama pants.

Always hard to get that last drop, Anna thought.

She stood, allowing her father to get into the bed. Then she plopped herself back down on the edge once he had his head on the pillow.

"You going to read me a story?" he asked.

She felt a twinge of fear. Was he joking, or did he think he was five years old?

"Something raunchy'd be nice," he said, grinning.

Okay, a joke.

"No, I am not going to read you a story," she said. He hadn't called her Joanie, so maybe this was one of his moments of clarity. She hoped so.

"I'm not going to get back to sleep, you know," he said. "I'm usually up by six, anyways."

"Yeah. Who am I kidding."

Frank rubbed Anna's arm affectionately. "Sorry if I woke you up."

"Don't worry about it, Dad." It struck her that he seemed very much with it at this moment. "Since we're both wide awake, let me ask you something."

"Okay."

"You were always my go-to guy when I was wondering what to do with my life."

Frank waited.

"I wonder if I'm in a rut," Anna said. She then added quickly, "And not because of you. This has nothing to do with you. I'm talking about my work. It's interesting, and I like it, but there are times when I need to get out of my comfort zone."

Frank nodded.

"I've got this one patient, doesn't matter who, but he wants to set up a meeting, in prison, with the man who tried to kill him. And he wants me to go with him."

Frank looked intrigued. "Wow."

"Yeah. I'm not sure he's in the right frame of mind for an encounter like that, but he seems pretty determined, so it might be better if I were with him."

"I think you should go," her father said. "Sounds damn interesting."

"Yeah," she said, nodding. "I shouldn't always just play it safe, staying in the office."

Her father blinked at her several times. She wondered whether she was losing him.

"Isn't that why you asked me to move in? To feel safer?"

She gave his hand a squeeze. "It was one of the reasons. A good one, too."

"It made me feel safer, too." He smiled in a way that seemed almost childlike. "I like that feeling. It's a warm feeling."

Anna patted his hand. "I'm gonna have a shower, and then I'll start the coffee."

Her father's brow wrinkled slightly, as though he was considering something.

"What is it?" Anna asked.

"Just wondering if I need to pee again."

She grinned. "I think only you know for sure."

He thought one more second, then said, "No, I'm good."

She looked back at him as she was stepping into the hall, and his eyes had shut. In two seconds he appeared to have fallen back asleep.

The shower could wait, Anna thought.

She returned to her bedroom and crawled back under the covers. It didn't take her much longer to nod off than it had taken her father.

So she was out cold when the police stormed the house five minutes later.

Sixteen

─────────

S o what'd you tell her?" Bill asked, sitting on the locker-room bench, lacing up his shoes. "What'd you tell Charlotte?"

Paul shrugged, twirling the squash racket in his hand, waiting for Bill to get ready. "I told her I thought I'd heard someone knocking."

Bill chortled. "What, like Girl Scouts going door-to-door selling cookies in the middle of the night?"

"Like someone trying to get in."

Bill shook his head. "Are you sure you're up to this?"

"I want to get back to doing the things I used to do."

"Yeah, but *this*?" Bill held up his own racket. "Doctor gave you the okay?"

"Didn't ask," Paul said. "I want to hit the ball, move around. I'm not going to do anything heroic. The ball lands in the corner, I'm not going in after it."

"So I'll take it easy on you," Bill said. "Like always."

"Fuck you."

They walked out of the locker room and into the West Haven College athletic facility. They strolled past exercise machines and an indoor track before they got to the squash courts. There were five, all backed with glass walls for the benefit of spectators.

"Does Charlotte know you're doing this?" Bill asked.

"No."

"This is a bad idea."

"I'm telling you, I'm fine."

Two women were playing in the court they had booked. Bill

glanced up at a wall clock. "They've still got two minutes. Okay, so Charlotte finds you on your ass on the stairs and you say you heard someone at the door, but there *was* no one at the door."

"Isn't that what I said?"

"Why didn't you tell her the truth?" Bill asked, his eyes on the two women in the court.

"I had already accused Josh of messing with the typewriter in the middle of the night. What's Charlotte going to think if I tell her I heard the same thing again?"

"That you're losing it?"

"Yes, thank you."

"But you're telling *me* what you really heard. Suppose *I* think you're losing it?"

"Do you?"

Bill sighed. "I haven't got any other explanation." He tapped the edge of his racket on the glass. When the women turned around, he pointed to an imaginary wristwatch. The women ended their game and exited. One of them gave a long smile to Bill as she blotted her neck with a small towel.

"You're as bad as Hoffman," Paul said as the woman headed for the locker rooms.

"Hey," Bill said, "that's low. He was married. I'm not."

They ducked through the low door and entered the court.

"So you *do* think I'm losing it," Paul said.

"I'm not saying that," Bill said. He was holding the ball. He tossed it a couple of feet into the air and whacked it against the far wall.

Paul returned the serve. "What are you saying?"

Bill, swinging, said, "You've been totally stressed-out and this is how it's manifesting itself." The *pings* of the ball bouncing off the walls echoed within the court. "There's no evidence anyone was in the house, right?"

Paul swung, hit the ball. "Right."

"The door was locked, you didn't see anyone, you didn't hear anyone running down the stairs."

Paul ran to the right side to hit the ball. "Yeah."

"So no one was there, and you couldn't have heard what you thought you heard. Which means one of two things. You heard something else that *sounds* like that typewriter, or you heard it in your head."

Bill went into the corner for the ball as Paul said, "What else sounds like a manual typewriter?"

"So you dreamed it."

"I didn't. I was awake." He let the ball sail past him.

Bill shrugged. "I don't know what to tell you. Are we stopping?"

"I'm feeling a little light-headed," Paul said, looking ashamed to admit it.

"Then let's stop before I end up killing you."

"Thanks."

The court was still theirs, so they stood there as they continued talking. Bill shook his head, struggling on Paul's behalf for an explanation.

Bill snapped his fingers. "I got it."

"What?"

"Mice." Paul rolled his eyes. "No, hear me out. You've got mice, and they ran over the keys in the middle of the night."

"Even for you, that's pretty dumb. Even if we did have mice, which we don't, a mouse weighs so little, the key wouldn't go down. And you'd need an entire troupe of dancing mice to make as much noise as I heard."

Bill held up his palms in defeat. "Call the Ghostbusters."

Paul ran his hand over the back of his neck. "I didn't even work up a sweat." As they turned for the door, Paul said, "I think I'll move it."

"What?"

"The typewriter. I'll put it in the laundry room or something."

Bill nodded thoughtfully. "That'll make Charlotte happy. Her special gift relegated to the laundry."

"Shit."

"And what, exactly, would that prove? Where's the logic? If you believe someone, somehow, is breaking in, hiding the typewriter isn't the answer. A fucking dead bolt is the answer."

"We've got a dead bolt on the door."

"Windows all secure?"

"Yes."

"You got an alarm system?"

"No."

"Maybe *that* should be your first step. If you still hear keys tapping in the night after that, well, then maybe you really do need the Ghostbusters." He grinned.

"Who ya gonna call?"

Bill's face lit up. "Here's what you do. Roll in a sheet of paper and see if there's a message in the morning."

"*That's* the strategy of a crazy person," Paul said.

———————

THAT NIGHT, AT DINNER, PAUL SAID, "WHAT WOULD YOU THINK ABOUT our getting a security system?"

"Seriously?" Charlotte said, digging her fork into her salad. "What, you're getting me a priceless jewel collection?"

"Just asking."

Charlotte shrugged. "Sure. I can get some recommendations at the agency. But what's prompted this?"

Paul pressed his lips together hard, debating with himself whether to get into it. His mouth was dry, so he picked up his glass of water and took a long drink. "So you know, that thing with Josh? When I said I heard typing noises in the night?"

"Yeah?"

"I heard it again."

"The typewriter?"

Paul nodded slowly. "That's why I was up. I didn't hear someone at the door. I heard someone on the typewriter."

Charlotte shrugged. "So you were dreaming. Or, more specifically, having another nightmare. Was it about Hoffman?"

"It was."

"What happened in it?"

He touched his stomach without thinking about it. "I don't even want to say."

"Okay."

"But . . . but at the end, he was trying to talk to me, but the sounds coming out of his mouth were like typewriter sounds."

"So it *was* a dream."

"But then I got up. I went to the bathroom. I started hearing it again."

Charlotte studied him for several seconds. He could see the skepticism in her eyes. She didn't have to say anything.

But finally, she spoke. "So, if you hear it again, wake me up."

Paul nodded. "Deal."

AND THAT NIGHT, THERE WAS NOTHING.

Paul lay awake for hours, staring into the darkness, waiting for the *chit chit chit* to begin.

It did not.

When he rose the following morning—he thought he'd finally fallen asleep around five—he was exhausted and bleary-eyed, but also slightly relieved.

But the more he thought about his situation, the less relieved he was. If the typing sounds were imagined, even when he was certain he was fully awake, was his head injury to blame? Were there symptoms the doctor had not discussed with him?

Had he been sleepwalking? Had he been in some kind of trance?

At breakfast, Charlotte said, "So, no *tippity-tap* last night?"

"No," he said groggily. "I listened for it all night."

"Oh, babe, you gotta be kidding. No wonder you look like shit."

"Yeah, well, I feel like shit, too."

She went back to the counter and filled a mug from the coffee machine. "I've just renewed your prescription."

He stared into the black liquid and said, "Can you inject this directly into my veins?"

"Look, I gotta go," she said, leaning in to give him a light kiss on the cheek. "Maybe the mystery typist will return tonight and we can all have a drink together."

Paul didn't see the humor in the comment.

"What have you got on today?" she asked.

He shrugged. "Just my project."

After Charlotte had left for work, he continued sitting at the kitchen table, sipping his coffee, hoping the caffeine would kick in. He noticed his hand was slightly trembling.

"God," he said to himself. "You're a mess."

The door to his small study was open, and from where he sat, he could see the black Underwood typewriter sitting atop his makeshift desk, dwarfing the laptop next to it, facing in his direction.

The semicircular opening to the cathedral of keys struck Paul as a kind of garish smile.

"What the fuck are you looking at?" Paul said, and went back to his coffee.

Seventeen

The following morning, more than twenty-four hours after it had all happened, Frank White still found himself trembling at the memory of it.

Anna, who had canceled all her appointments for the previous day but expected to return to work today, was sitting with her father at the kitchen table, stroking his hand. He'd hardly touched the scrambled eggs she had made for him.

"It's okay, Dad."

He nodded, slipped his hand away from hers and picked up his fork. "This looks good," he said.

"There's ketchup there if you want it."

The doorbell rang. Frank's entire body stiffened.

"It's okay. It's someone from the police." She did half an eye roll. "Someone I'm *expecting* from the police. Who can maybe answer a few questions for us. Would you be okay here on your own for a few minutes?"

"Of course," he said, a tiny bit of egg stuck to his lower lip. "I'm not a child."

Anna smiled and, considering what he had just said, resisted the temptation to pick up his napkin and wipe his mouth.

Frank said, "I thought they were going to shoot me. I thought they were going to shoot you."

"I know. But it didn't happen. You're okay and I'm okay."

The doorbell rang again.

"Neither of us has a scratch on us." She gave him another smile, hoping she could coax one out of him. "Never a dull moment around here, right?"

He nodded.

"And there's more coffee if you want it."

Finally, a smile from her father. "I could probably use something a bit stronger."

She got up and left the kitchen. She opened the front door and found a short, heavyset black man in his forties standing there. His bushy black mustache made up for the few strands of hair he had on his head. He wore a sport jacket, dark blue shirt and tie, and jeans. He was ready with a badge to display for Anna.

"Hi," he said. "Detective Joe Arnwright. Milford Police."

"Come in," she said.

"How are you today?" he asked, taking a seat in the living room. It wasn't a polite greeting. He was clearly asking how she was compared to the day before.

"My father's still very upset. *I'm* still very upset."

Arnwright nodded sympathetically. "Of course."

"They *stormed* in here," she said. "We were *asleep*."

"To be fair, they managed to open a window and came into the house very quietly in an effort—"

"Don't you people do something to confirm that what someone's telling you is true?"

"Dr. White, we've—"

"My father gets up to take a pee and finds men with guns in the hallway. It's a wonder you didn't give him a heart attack, let alone shoot him."

Arnwright nodded patiently. "Their information, as you know, was that a man had already shot his wife and was going to shoot his daughter next. That's what our officers believed they were coming into. They needed to assess the situation as quickly as possible to eliminate any threat. And that threat, they would have presumed, was against you. The daughter."

"You were conned," Anna said.

"I'm not disputing that."

"They made my father lie on the floor and pointed guns at his head!" Anna said through gritted teeth. She managed to convey her anger without raising her voice. She did not want her father to hear all this. "An old man! With dementia!"

"I understand that you're—"

"You *understand*? That's encouraging. My father and I came this close to getting killed."

"I don't believe that's the case. The members of that team are very professional."

Anna took a second to compose herself, to go in another direction. "Have you arrested him?"

"Mr. Hitchens, you mean."

"Who else would I mean?"

"We have interviewed him, yes."

Anna eyed him warily. "And?"

"We've interviewed him and we are investigating," he said. "We believe the 9-1-1 call was placed from a cell phone, a kind of throwaway one they call a burner that—"

"I know what a burner is. I watch TV."

"We're going to try and find out where that burner was purchased, then see if we can determine who the buyer was."

"He didn't have the phone on him? Did you search him?"

"As I said, we are investigating," Arnwright said.

"What did the caller sound like? The one who called 9-1-1?"

"It sounded like an elderly man. But there are all sorts of voice changer apps out there. Did Mr. Hitchens ever threaten to do something like this to you? A crank call of this nature."

"No. But it's his style. My father's suffering from dementia. Hitchens would just love to scare a confused, old man."

"We need a little more than that," Arnwright said.

Anna sighed. "I think he might have killed a dog, too."

Arnwright, pen in hand, looked ready to take down details. "Go on."

She bit her lip. "I can't . . . I don't have any proof of anything."

Arnwright put the pen away and stood. "Again, I'm sorry about what happened here. I'll let you know if there are any developments."

Anna showed him to the door. She went into the kitchen to see how her father was, but he was not there.

"Dad?" she called out.

She went upstairs to his room, expecting to find him on his rowing machine. But he wasn't there either.

She thought she heard a muted *whack*.

Anna went to her father's bedroom window, which looked out onto the backyard. There he was, golf club in hand—it looked like a driver—swinging at half a dozen balls he had dropped onto the well-manicured lawn, except for those spots where he had done some serious divots.

It was him, she told herself. *I know it was him.*

Eighteen

Paul was ready to begin.

He'd typed up plenty of notes, copied and pasted paragraphs from online news accounts of the double murder, but now he was ready to take that leap. To write the first sentence of whatever it was he was going to write. Memoir? Novel? A true-crime story? Who knew?

What Paul did know was that however the story came together, one thing was certain: it was *his* story.

And so he typed his first sentence:

Kenneth Hoffman was my friend.

Paul looked at the five words on his laptop screen. He hit the ENTER key to bring the cursor down a line. And he wrote:

Kenneth Hoffman tried to murder me.

That seemed as good a place to start as any. From that springboard, he jumped straight into the story of that night. How, while returning from a student theatrical presentation at West Haven, he'd spotted Hoffman's Volvo station wagon driving erratically down the Post Road.

About a thousand words in, Paul started finding the process therapeutic. The words flowed from his fingertips as quickly as he could type them. At one point he glanced at the bulky Underwood beside the laptop and said, "Like to see *you* crank out this shit this fast."

When he got to the part where he saw the two dead women in the back of Kenneth's car, Paul paused only briefly, took a deep mental breath, and kept on writing. He took himself to the point where the shovel crashed into his skull.

And then he stopped.

He felt simultaneously drained and elated. He had done it. He had jumped into the deep end of the cold pool, gotten used to it, and kept on swimming.

When Charlotte got home that evening, he could not wait to tell her about his progress.

"That's fantastic," she said. "I'm proud of you. I really am." She paused. "Can I read it?"

"Not yet. I don't know exactly what it's going to be. When I feel it's coming together, I'll show it to you."

She almost looked relieved. She'd had a long day that had finished with an evening showing, and all she wanted to do was go to bed. As she did most nights, she fell asleep moments after her head hit the pillow. She rarely snored—Paul knew he could not make the same claim—but he could tell when she was asleep by the deepness of her breathing.

He turned off the light at half past ten but lay awake, he was sure, for at least an hour, maybe two.

Paul felt wired.

For the first time since the attack, Paul felt . . . *excited*. If he'd ever doubted the wisdom of tackling this whole Hoffman thing head-on, he didn't anymore. But would this change in attitude manifest itself in different ways? Would writing about Hoffman have an exorcising effect? Would the nightmares stop? Maybe not all at once, but at least gradually?

If the writing continued to go well—*Let's not get ahead of our-selves, it's only Day One*—then maybe it would be fun to do it in another location. After all, he could take his laptop anywhere. And he was *not* thinking about the closest Starbucks. More like Cape Cod.

If Charlotte could get a few days off, they could drive up to Provincetown, or take the ferry to Martha's Vineyard. He could even toss a few recent bestsellers into his suitcase, maybe find something worth adding to his popular fiction course.

He'd talk to Charlotte about it in the morning, although he feared her answer. Too much going on, she'd say. You can't sell a house when you're not here. *You* can't work twenty-four/seven, he'd tell her. If he could talk her into taking the time, he could see if Josh wanted to come, too. He could call Hailey, see if she'd be okay with that.

No, maybe not. If he was to have a chance of talking Charlotte into the idea, it had to be just the two of them. It wasn't that Charlotte didn't like Josh. Paul was sure she liked him. But did she *love* him? Was it even fair to fault her for that if she didn't? Josh was not her son, and had been in her life for only a few years.

It was about then, thinking about a Cape Cod getaway, whatever time it happened to be, that he fell asleep.

But it was 3:14 A.M. when he woke up. He didn't wake up on his own.

He was awakened.

Chit chit. Chit chit chit.

HIS EYES OPENED ABRUPTLY. WAS IT A DREAM AGAIN? HAD HE EVEN *been* dreaming? Even if it was hard to recall the details of a dream upon waking, Paul could usually tell whether he'd actually been having one.

He did not think so.

And he was sure that he was, at this moment, awake.

He pinched his arm to be sure.

Yup.

He held his breath and listened for the typing sound to recur. There was nothing. For several seconds, all he heard was the pounding of his own heart.

Then, there it was.

Chit chit. Chit chit chit.

This was not a dream. This was the real deal.

What had Charlotte suggested he do the next time this happened? Wake her up. Get yourself a corroborating witness.

He sat up in bed, touched Charlotte gently on the shoulder.

"Charlotte," he whispered. "Charlotte. Wake up. Charlotte."

She stirred. Without opening her eyes, she said, "What?"

"It's happening," he said. "The sound."

"What sound?"

"The typewriter."

Her eyes opened wide. She withdrew her hand from under the pillow, sat up, blinked several times.

"Just listen," he whispered.

"Okay, okay, I'm up."

"Shh."

"Okay!" she said.

"Be quiet and listen."

Charlotte said nothing further. The two of them sat there in the bed, waiting. After about ten seconds, Charlotte said, "I don't hear anything."

Paul held up a silencing hand. "Wait."

Another half a minute went past before Charlotte said, "You must have dreamed it."

"No," he whispered sharply. "Absolutely not. I'm going downstairs."

"I'll come with you."

"Be real quiet. It could start up again at any second."

Together, they padded down the hall to the stairs and descended them slowly. Twice, Paul raised a hand and the two of them froze.

Nothing.

When they reached the kitchen, Paul reached over to a panel of four light switches and flipped them all up at once. Lights came on over the island and dining table, under the cupboards, and in the adjoining living area.

"We know you're here!" Paul shouted.

Except no one was.

Paul bolted down the stairs that led to the front door, careful to grab the railing this time so he didn't land on his butt.

"Paul!" Charlotte screamed.

The door was locked, the dead bolt thrown. He opened a second, inside door that led to the garage, disappeared into there for fifteen seconds, then reentered the house, shaking his head. He trudged back up the stairs to the kitchen.

"Paul?"

"I thought . . . I thought I could catch whoever it was."

"No one was here," Charlotte said softly.

He headed for his think tank, flicked on the light, and stared at the Underwood. Charlotte slowly came up behind him, rested a hand on his shoulder. Neither of them spoke for several seconds, but finally, Paul broke the silence.

"You think I'm crazy."

"I never said that."

"I know what I heard." Paul bit his lower lip. His voice barely above a whisper, he said, "This is the third time. Three nights I've heard it."

Charlotte, her eyes misting, said, "Believe me, it's the dreams. Go back to bed. In the morning, things may seem a lot clearer."

"I'm not losing my mind," Paul insisted.

"You're tired and you're stressed and you worked all day writing about—"

"Enough!" he shouted, throwing down his arms and taking a step back from his wife. "I swear to God, if I hear the word *stressed* one more time, I don't know what the hell I'm going to do."

"Fine," Charlotte said evenly. "I'm sorry."

"Bill said the same thing, that I must be dreaming it. But"—Paul was slow to say the words—"he did have an idea."

"You talked to Bill?"

"We met up for a game and—"

"*Squash?*"

"It was a very *gentle* game. I didn't want—"

Charlotte was enraged. "Are you out of your mind? You've had a serious blow to the head and you set foot in a squash court? Have you any idea how stupid that is? You could bash your head—"

"Would you just stop!" he shouted. "Fuck! Just shut up!"

Charlotte took a step back. "I'm trying to help you."

Paul lowered his head and held it with both hands. "I feel like my fucking brain is going to explode."

Charlotte, softly, said, "It's going to be okay." She waited a beat. "You said Bill had an idea."

Paul sighed. "Yeah. I don't know if he was joking, or humoring me, or what."

Charlotte waited.

"He said I should roll some paper in."

Charlotte blinked. "He said what?"

Paul pointed at the typewriter. "He said, if this thing's making noises in the night, put some paper in and see what it's saying."

Charlotte said nothing.

"You think I should do that?" Paul asked.

"That's ridiculous," she said.

Paul shrugged. "He mentioned the word *ghost*. Well, actually, he mentioned the Ghostbusters."

"Jesus. He can be such an asshole." Charlotte rolled her eyes, threw up her hands, and said, "Go ahead."

"What?"

"Do it. Roll in a sheet of paper. If you think you hear something again in the middle of the night, and there's nothing on it, then you'll know."

"Know what?"

She touched her index finger to her temple. "That it really is a dream."

Paul's jaw hardened. He met his wife's eyes for several seconds before breaking away, stepping over to the printer, and taking out one sheet of paper from the tray. He set it into the typewriter carriage and rolled it in, bringing an inch of paper above where the keys would strike.

"Great," she said. "I'm going to bed."

She turned and walked out.

Paul stayed another moment and stared at the typewriter. He ran his fingers along the middle row of letters, depressing the occasional key just enough to see the metal arms bend toward the paper, as if with anticipation.

Nineteen

Later that week, Anna White was at her desk, adding a few notes to a patient's file in her computer before Paul Davis arrived for his weekly session, when she thought she heard a noise from upstairs. The only one up there was her father.

She worried he might have fallen.

She bolted from her chair, ran from the office wing on her house to the living area, and up the stairs as quickly as she could. She rapped on her father's closed bedroom door.

"Dad?"

There was no answer.

She tried the door and was surprised to find she could open it only an inch. Through the crack she could see that a piece of furniture was blocking the door. It was her father's dresser. That was what she had heard. Her father dragging his dresser across the room.

"Dad!"

Frank's face appeared in the sliver. "Yes, honey?"

"What are you doing?"

"Can't be too careful."

"Dad, the police are not coming back. That's not going to happen again."

"They're not getting in here, that's for damn sure."

Anna, her voice calm, said, "You can't stay in there forever, Dad. What are you going to do when you have to go to the bathroom?"

He disappeared, only to reappear five seconds later with a waste-paper basket in one hand, and a roll of toilet paper in the other. "Thought of everything," he said.

"Okay," Anna said. "And when you get hungry?"

"You can bring something up for me."

"And who do you think's going to empty that pail for you? Because I can tell you, it's not going to be me."

"Window," he said.

Jesus, she thought, picturing it. She had one last card to play, and knew she'd hate herself for it. "And what about when it's time to go to the home to visit Joanie?"

Frank stopped and puzzled over that. He clearly hadn't thought through every eventuality.

"Oh," he said. "You've got me there."

"Why don't you put the dresser back where it was, Dad? And put on the TV. Maybe they're running some Bugs Bunny cartoons now."

She heard the dresser squeak as he pushed it back. Anna opened the door wide and watched him move it across the room. She didn't offer to help him. All those hours he spent on the rowing machine, he could probably get a job with the Mayflower furniture movers.

Dresser back in place, he grabbed the remote and turned on the television. He propped himself on the corner of the bed, as if nothing had happened.

Anna, wearily, went back downstairs.

The moment she entered her office, she let out a short scream.

Gavin Hitchens was sitting in his usual chair, waiting for her.

"Jesus Christ," she said.

He made an innocent face. "I never canceled. This is when I come."

"Leave."

He raised his palms in a gesture of surrender but did not get out of the chair. "I came here to tell you I forgive you."

Anna blinked. "You what?"

"Forgive you. For thinking I had something to do with that woman and that dead dog, and with whatever happened here a couple of days ago that made you send the police to see me. I know you probably violated some kind of doctor-patient privilege when you did that, but I'm willing to overlook it."

"I mean it, Gavin. You need to leave."

"Because, you see, I think maybe I deserved that. When you've done the kinds of things I've done, you've got no one to blame but yourself when you find yourself facing false accusations. You've set yourself up. I appreciate that now."

"I'm calling the police."

Gavin's look of innocence morphed into one of hurt. "Does this mean you're not going to be counseling me anymore?"

"You could have gotten my father killed."

"I don't know what you're talking about. Well, yes, I do, because the police told me. It must have been awful, a SWAT team coming into the house like that."

"You're sick, Gavin. I hope someone can help you, but it's not going to be me. Honestly, I don't know that anyone can."

He stood. "If you want to know what I think, I think it's some kind of a copycat. Someone who knows I'm seeing you and wants to frame me. You might want to look at your other patients and see who might be capable of something like that."

Anna strode into the room, past Gavin, and went behind her desk. She reached for the phone. Before she could lift the receiver, Gavin put his hand atop hers, pinning it there.

She looked into his smiling face.

He said, "Did you know, when you sleep, you don't snore, but when you exhale, your lips do this adorable little dance?"

Anna felt a chill run the length of her body. She wanted to scream but couldn't find her voice.

Gavin released her hand and grinned. "Just kidding." He walked to the door but turned one last time before leaving. "Good thing you don't have any pets," he said.

Anna slowly dropped into her chair and gripped the arms to stop her hands from shaking.

Twenty

The first thing Paul did when he got up was head straight to his office. Charlotte was still under the covers when he slipped out of bed and trotted barefoot down to the kitchen in his boxers.

He hadn't heard any more typing noises in the night, but it was possible, he told himself, that he'd slept through them. If the keys of the typewriter had—somehow—been touched in the remaining hours of the night, the evidence would be on that sheet of paper he had rolled into it.

This is crazy, Paul told himself. *Why am I even doing this?*

He swallowed and felt his heart flutter as he slowly pushed open his office door.

The Underwood sat there.

The page was blank.

Paul put a hand on the jamb for support and took a breath. He didn't know whether to feel relieved, or disappointed.

"I really am losing it," he whispered.

In the light of day, the events of the night seemed clearer. As much as he had fought Charlotte's conclusion that he'd been dreaming, what other possible explanation was there?

Think about it. Does it make any sense at all that someone would sneak into your house in the dead of night to tap on the keys of an old typewriter?

Paul knew the answer.

He'd mention it today at his session with Dr. White. He'd ask some questions. Could someone be half-awake and half-asleep at the same time? When he thought he was awake and hearing *chit chit chit* was it possible he was not fully conscious? Could it be a kind of sleepwalking?

That, he had to admit, made more sense than anything else.

He went back up to the bedroom and slid under the covers as Charlotte was waking.

"Hey," she said groggily. She blinked a couple of times, pulled herself up into a sitting position and said, "How are you doing?"

"Good," he said, putting a hand on her arm. "I just wanted to say I'm sorry."

"About what?"

"How I acted last night. I was short with you, and you were only trying to help."

"It's okay," she said. "Don't worry about it."

When he told her what he was going to ask Dr. White, Charlotte nodded with enthusiasm. "That could explain everything," she said.

Paul looked down as his face flushed with embarrassment. "I went down and checked."

"Checked?"

"To see if anything had been typed onto that page."

"And?"

He looked up. "I think you know the answer."

PAUL FELT OPTIMISTIC ON THE WAY TO HIS SESSION. HE COULDN'T wait to tell Anna White that he not only had made a good start on his writing project, but also had come up with a theory about the noises in the night.

He'd decided to pop into Staples for some printer cartridges and the Barnes & Noble for a quick look at new fiction releases first. He was heading south on River Street when he saw the Volvo.

It pulled out in front of him from Darina Place, just ahead of the underpass below the railroad tracks. The driver either didn't see

Paul, or didn't care. Paul had to hit the brakes to avoid broadsiding the vehicle.

Paul didn't get to see who was behind the wheel, but that might have been because he was consumed with looking at the entire vehicle.

The Volvo was a station wagon. It was dark blue. It was the same vintage as Kenneth Hoffman's.

Paul felt his heart starting to race. His hands almost instantly began to sweat. His breathing became rapid and shallow.

As the car settled into the lane ahead of him, Paul looked to see if one of the taillights was broken. But as he tried to focus, he found his vision blurring.

I'm having a panic attack.

I'm going to pass out.

Paul hit the brakes and steered toward the edge of the road. Behind him a horn blared. He got the car stopped under the bridge and huddled over the wheel, his head resting atop it. He closed his eyes, fighting the dizziness.

Suddenly, overhead, the roar of a passing commuter train.

Paul's heart was ready to explode from his chest.

"Breathe," he told himself. "Breathe."

It took him the better part of five minutes to pull himself together. Slowly, he raised his head from the wheel, propped it against the headrest. He released his fingers from the wheel and wiped his sweaty palms on the tops of his legs. When he was confident his heart rate and breathing were back to normal, he continued on his way.

ANNA WHITE WASN'T IN HER OFFICE.

Paul peeked in from the waiting area and did not see her behind her desk or seated in the leather chair she used when they had their chats.

He allowed a couple of minutes to go by before he poked his head into the main part of the house and said, "Dr. White? Anna?"

He thought he heard the sound of clinking cutlery, as though someone was doing dishes in a sink. He followed the noises to the kitchen, where Anna, her back to him, was standing at the sink.

"Anna?" he said.

She whirled around, her eyes wide and fearful. In the process, a wet glass slid from her hand and hit the floor, shattering into hundreds of pieces.

"Oh God, I'm sorry," Paul said, moving forward. He scanned the floor to assess the level of risk. "Don't move your feet."

Anna surveyed the bits of glass around her feet. "Shit." She looked apologetically at Paul. "You startled me."

As he knelt down to gather up the larger pieces of glass he said, "When you weren't in your office I . . . I should have just waited."

When she started to kneel down to help pick up glass, he said, "No, I've got this. As long as you don't move you won't step in any of it."

But she ignored him, crouching and gathering pieces around her feet.

"Oh for fuck's sake," she said, holding up her index finger. Blood trickled down the side.

"Hang on," Paul said. "Hold it over the sink. I've got almost all of it."

With a dish towel, he swabbed the floor of any shards that were too small to pick up with his fingers.

Standing, he said, "Where do you keep your first-aid stuff?"

She pointed to a drawer. Paul found a package of Band-Aids and peeled one from its wrapping. Standing shoulder to shoulder with Anna, he gently took her wrist in his hand and ran some water over her bloody finger.

"You're trembling," Paul said.

"I'm . . . a little on edge today is all." She shook her head. "I don't even know why I was doing this. I have a dishwasher. I just . . . needed to clear my head."

Paul turned off the tap and gently dried her finger with a paper towel. He studied the cut closely.

"I don't see any glass."

Paul wrapped the tiny bandage tightly around her finger. "If it's none of my business, you don't have to answer, but what's got you on edge? Is it your father?"

"No," she said. "Well, some."

"What happened?"

"A fake 9-1-1 call. The police came, guns drawn. My father was pretty shook up."

Paul held on to her hand a few more seconds before letting go. "There. You should be okay now."

IN THE OFFICE, IN THEIR RESPECTIVE CHAIRS, ANNA SAID, "I REALLY *am* sorry. I should have been in here when you arrived." She took a breath.

"We don't have to do this today," he offered.

She raised a hand, waving away any further debate. "I'm good. Go ahead."

"I actually thought I was going to be late," Paul said. He told her about what had happened when he saw the car that looked like Hoffman's. "I don't know all the symptoms of a panic attack, but I think I might have had one. I know it wasn't Hoffman, and I don't even think it was his car, but seeing it triggered something. I've really felt like I've been moving forward these last couple of days, but that was a real reminder that I've got a way to go."

Anna wanted to be sure that he was okay now, and that he would be okay to drive home. Paul said he was confident that he was.

"But I should tell you . . . it happened again."

"What happened?"

"Those typing noises in the middle of the night. And I was as sure as I could be that I was awake. I got Charlotte up, but she never heard a thing." He tossed out his theory about being awake and asleep at the same time.

"Possibly," Anna said, "but that's not really my area of expertise. But yes, I think it's possible. You were still under the influences of a dream while you presented as awake."

Paul stared at her for several seconds. "I think that has to be it. Unless," and at this point he forced a chuckle, "it's a ghost. That's what Bill—a friend of mine—suggested, although he was joking."

Anna managed a wry smile. "If that's the problem, you're absolutely in an area I don't know much about."

As the session came to its conclusion, Paul again asked Anna how she was.

"Better," she said, holding up her bandaged finger and offering a crooked smile. "You're my new hero."

Twenty-One

"I gave Bill shit today," Charlotte said over dinner.

"What for?"

"Seriously? Letting you get into a squash court with him?"

"Oh, that."

"I don't know who's the bigger idiot, you or him."

Paul smiled. "Tough call."

She gave him a sharp look. "It's not funny."

They moved on to other things. She asked if he had the ticket for the dry cleaning. She'd be going by there tomorrow and could pick it up.

"What dry cleaning?" he asked.

"The dry cleaning I asked you to drop off."

"You didn't ask me to drop off any dry cleaning."

"This morning, I said to you, please drop off the dry cleaning. I pointed to the bag on the chair in our room. And you said, no problem, you'd do it on the way to your session."

Paul stared at her. "No, you didn't."

Charlotte said, "Maybe this will help you remember. I said, tell them to be careful with that black dress. And you said, the one that looks like it's painted on? And I said, why, you got some paint remover? Does *that* help?"

Paul's face fell. "I don't remember any of that."

Charlotte tried to look upbeat. "It's no big deal. I'll drop it off tomorrow."

TO HIS SURPRISE, PAUL SLEPT WELL. MAYBE TACKLING THE HOFFMAN business was having an impact, Volvo incident aside.

When he woke up at five minutes after seven, he heard water running. He threw back the covers and traipsed into the bathroom. Charlotte stood naked behind the frosted shower door, her head arched back to allow the water to splash across her face.

"Hey," he said loudly to be heard over the water.

She turned the taps off and opened the door far enough to retrieve a towel hanging on a hook.

"When did you come to bed?" she asked. "I waited for you for about twenty minutes before I finally went to sleep."

"I stayed up for a while, that's all," he said. "I was doing some writing."

Paul studied his face in the mirror, examined his eyes. Charlotte dried off behind the glass, then opened the door and stepped out, the towel wrapped around her.

"But you slept through the rest of the night?" she asked.

"I did," he said. "I feel kind of logy, but I slept pretty good."

Paul knew what she was really asking. Had he heard anything in the night? He ran his hand over his bristly chin and neck. He opened a drawer, brought out a razor and shaving cream.

"You want to start the coffee while I get dressed?" she asked when he was done shaving.

He nodded wearily and, after another look at himself in the mirror, said, "It's gonna take more than coffee to fix this."

He slipped out of the bathroom and headed to the floor below. Charlotte took off her towel, dried her hair as best she could, and retrieved a handheld dryer from the cabinet below the sink. She plugged it in, flipped the switch, the small room suddenly sounding like the inside of a jet engine. She aimed the device at her head and let her hair fly.

Less than a minute later, Paul stood at the bathroom door, his face drained of color. She turned the machine off.

Twenty-Three

_____

' Charlotte said, staring at the page in the typewriter,
ng around to look back into the kitchen. "Someone

aid, gripping her shoulders. "No one's here now, and
evidence that anyone's been here at all. I've checked
ows. I've been through the whole place. I'm certain
ere after we went back upstairs."
now that," she said.
me," he said. He walked her over to the stairs that
front door. "Look."
looking at?"

single dark blue running shoe on the floor by the

oing that the last few nights. One shoe, up against
eone opened it, the shoe would have moved."
ared, dumbfounded, at the shoe, then at Paul. "So
? I don't understand."
you get that typewriter?" Paul asked.
At a yard sale. Some people were moving, clearing

linked several times, trying to recall. "It was on Lau-
A two-story, three baths, double-car garage. I didn't
, but I drove by, you know, because I like to be aware

"For Christ's sake, didn't you hear me?" he said.

She waved the dryer in front of him. "With this on?"

"Come downstairs."

"What is it?"

"Just come."

She ducked into the bedroom to grab her robe, threw it on, and
quickly knotted the sash. She ran after her husband, who was already halfway down the stairs.

"What's going on?" Charlotte asked.

He led her straight to the small office, stood just outside the door,
and pointed to the typewriter.

"Look," he said.

"Look at what?"

"The paper," he said. "Look at the paper."

From where she stood, she could make out the letters. A partial
line of them on the sheet of paper Paul had rolled into the machine
a few days earlier.

"What the hell?" she whispered.

She slowly stepped into the room, bent over in front of the black
metal typewriter, close enough to read the words that had somehow
appeared between the time they'd gone to bed and now:

**We typed our apologies like we were asked but it
didn't make any difference.**

Twenty-Two

I don't want to alarm you, but it's possible someone got into the house without our knowing it, so we need to be on our guard. I debated whether to even tell you, because I didn't want to upset you."

Frank White looked at his daughter with weary eyes. "Someone broke in?"

Anna reached across the kitchen table and put both hands over his. "I don't know. He might have been just trying to rattle me."

"Who is this?"

"One of my patients. Well, a former one," she said. "It was something he said yesterday."

"Is he the one you think sent the police here?"

"I don't have any proof, but yes, that's what I think. The police have already talked to him about the other incident. But they don't have any real proof for that one, either. But some things you just know. I've been through the whole house. I've checked the windows, the sliding glass doors, everything, and they all look secure."

Frank nodded slowly, then said, "We need to tell Joanie all this."

"Of course," Anna said.

"But don't make too big a deal of it. I don't want to worry her needlessly."

"I'll look after it."

Her father smiled. "Or I could tell her when we go see her."

She smiled. "Sure."

"What did you do to your finger?" he asked, looking down at the Band-Aid and lightly touching it.

"It's nothing," she said. "
"There's something else on

Frank waited.

"It's a bit of a profession
that this one patient might
whether I need to warn ther

Frank's eyes seemed to g
to solve her problem, but a
just the same. "I've already
some of what he's done is a
ethical concerns are minima

Frank nodded, then pu
stood. "I'm gonna hit a few b
She gave him a sad smile.

Oh, my Goc
then whir
really *is* here."

"No," Paul
I don't see any
doors and win
no one got in

"You don't

"Come wit
led down to t

"What am

"That shoe

There was
door.

"I've been
the door. If so

Charlotte
what's going

"Where di

"I told yo
out their stuf

"Where?"

Charlotte
relton Court.
have the listin

of the houses in Milford that are on the market, and they were having this sale. I saw that typewriter and knew instantly that you'd like it." She paused. "I sure called that wrong."

"Could you find the house again?"

Charlotte gave him a *"seriously?"* look.

"We need to talk to those people," Paul said.

"Why? Why does it *matter* where it came from? It's just a fucking typewriter! Paul, honestly, you're scaring me."

"I need to know who else has used it. I need to know who has used this machine."

"Hundreds of people could have used it," Charlotte said. "Please, tell me what you're thinking?"

"Read it again."

"What?"

"Go on. Read it again."

He led her back to the small room, grabbed the sheet of paper by the top, and ripped it out of the typewriter. "Just read it."

"I've read it."

Paul read it aloud: "'We typed our apologies like we were asked but it didn't make any difference.' That doesn't mean anything to you?"

"Paul, I swear."

"That's what Kenneth made them do. Before he killed them. Before he killed those two women."

Charlotte stared at him blankly for several seconds, then back to the page in his hand. "This is insane."

"No kidding. You think I don't feel nuts even suggesting it?"

"And what the hell *are* you suggesting?"

He shot her *"seriously?"* look right back at her.

Charlotte said, "Hang on, let me try to get my head around what I think you're saying. You believe those women are sending you a message? Through this typewriter? Paul, listen to yourself."

Paul hesitated. "Look, I know it sounds ridiculous. But what if this . . . what if this is the very same typewriter those apologies were written on?"

"But how could that typewriter end up in a yard sale? Wouldn't the police have it? Wouldn't it be in evidence?"

Paul thought about that. "That's a good question. You'd think it would be. I honestly don't know. It was days later that I remembered Kenneth putting something in that Dumpster. The police might never have found it. Maybe someone else did."

"Okay, so maybe it is, and maybe it isn't the actual typewriter. Regardless, how do you explain this?" She took the sheet of paper from his hand and waved it in front of his face.

"I don't know." He thought a moment. "I'm going to call that woman."

"What woman?"

Paul edged around her, sat in his cheap office chair, and fired up his laptop. "The reporter who wrote the story. I can't remember her name. She wrote a feature with lots of details about the case. It was the first thing I read when I decided to throw myself back into this."

He tapped away on the keyboard, scrolled down through the results of a search. "Here it is. Here's the story. Gwen Stainton. She's the one. At the *New Haven Star*. She seemed to know more about this case than anyone else."

Paul executed a few more keystrokes. "Okay, here's the *Star* staff list . . . hang on. Yeah, Stainton. I'll send her an email." As he typed, he read his message aloud. "Dear Ms. Stainton, I have read with interest all your stories about the Kenneth Hoffman case, and I have one question. What happened to the typewriter on which the apologies were written? Do the police have it? If you know the answer, I'd be most grateful if you could tell me. If not, please pass along the name of someone who might know."

He turned and looked at Charlotte. "How does that sound?"

Hesitantly, she said, "Fine, I guess."

"What? You don't sound like you mean it."

"I'm worried about you."

He pointed to the typewriter. "I have to know more. You get that, right?"

Charlotte glanced down at the typewritten sheet she was still holding, dropped it on the desk, and looked back at her husband. "Go ahead and send it, I don't care. I've got to get ready for work."

She slipped out of the room as Paul turned his attention back to the laptop. He moved the cursor over the SEND button and clicked.

The email to Gwen Stainton vanished from the screen with a *whoosh.*

"Okay," he said to himself.

His eyes moved to the antique Underwood. He stared at it for several seconds, then took a fresh, blank sheet from the nearby printer and rolled it into the typewriter, positioning it just as he had the other piece.

"Just in case you have anything else you want to say," he whispered.

Twenty-Four

I'll drive you to work," Paul said when Charlotte had returned to the kitchen to make herself some breakfast. He had already run upstairs and quickly dressed so that he'd be ready to leave when she was.

"I need a car in case—"

"No, listen, I want to see if we can find the house where you got the typewriter."

Charlotte appeared to wilt. "Paul, listen to yourself."

"I just want to talk to them. The people who had the yard sale. Ask them where it came from, how they got it. Look, if they've had it for fifty years, fine. But if they got in the last eight months, then there's a chance—"

"I need my car," she repeated.

"Okay, fine. We'll take your car, and I'll grab a cab home from your office."

"You think we could get a coffee along the way?"

Paul sighed. "Fine."

Before she descended the stairs, she looked into his study. "You rolled in another sheet of paper."

"Yes."

She began to move in that direction. "You really think—"

He took her arm. "Come on, let's go."

As Charlotte got behind the wheel, she dug her phone from her purse. "I don't know how this is going to go, so let me call the office and tell them I might be a bit late."

"Good idea," Paul said, getting in on the passenger side.

She tapped a number, put the phone to her ear. "Yeah, hi, it's Charlotte. Look, uh, Paul and I are running a couple of errands this morning so it's probably going to be around nine-thirty before I get in." She nodded to whomever was on the other end, then said, "Yeah, sure, the file's on my desk. See you in a bit." She returned the phone to her purse. "Okay, let's do this. And don't forget, you promised me coffee."

Charlotte headed out of the neighborhood, and when she reached New Haven Avenue, she hung a right. Up ahead was a Dunkin' Donuts. She wheeled into the parking lot and said, "You're buying."

Paul went into the store and returned with two paper cups of coffee. She took a sip of hers, then put it into the cup holder between the seats. She keyed the ignition, backed out of the parking spot, and they were off.

She drove confidently back through the downtown Common, then a series of rights and lefts until they had reached Laurelton Court.

"It's a dead-end street," she said. "An attractive feature if you're selling or buying. Minimum traffic. No one uses your street as a shortcut."

She brought the car to a stop out front of a house with a SOLD real estate sign out front.

"This is it," she said.

Paul had the door open before she had the car in park.

"God, slow down—"

He was already out of the car, heading for the front door. He rapped on it hard before he'd even looked for a doorbell button. When he spotted that, he jammed it with his index finger.

Charlotte wore a worried expression as she watched from the car. She reached for the coffee and took another sip.

Paul knocked on the door again. And for a second time, he rang the bell. No one came to the door. Charlotte watched as he peered through the window in the door, using his hands as a visor to get a better look. His shoulders slumped. He turned and walked slowly back to the car.

"What?" Charlotte asked as he settled into the passenger seat.

"I looked inside. The house is empty. Cleared out. Not a stick of furniture. They're gone."

Charlotte gave him a sympathetic look. "Sorry."

"You could find out, right?" he said.

"What?"

"Who owned the house? And where they went? Do you know the agent who had the listing?"

She nodded. "I do."

"If you can get a name, wherever they've moved to, I could call them."

"Sure," Charlotte said. "I could do that."

Paul frowned. "You don't sound crazy about the idea."

"No, it's fine."

"What? What is it?"

"I *said* I would do it."

"I can tell by your voice you don't want to."

Charlotte said nothing for several seconds, then shifted in her seat so she could look at her husband more directly. "The thing is," she said, her voice softening, "maybe where the typewriter came from doesn't matter."

"Of course it does."

"The only way it would matter is if we were to accept that—I don't even know what to call it—there was some kind of supernatural or psychic or whatever connection between the typewriter and anyone who might have used it. And Paul, I'm sorry, but that just doesn't make any sense."

"You saw the message," he said, bristling. "You saw those words.

We weren't dreaming when we saw them. They were there, on that piece of paper."

"I know."

"And I can't find anything to suggest someone got into the house," Paul continued. "I mean, yeah, Josh has a key, and maybe Hailey has a key, for all we know, but that shoe, Charlotte. That shoe, I'm pretty sure it hadn't moved."

"I know," she said again.

"So what's your solution, then?" he asked her. "If nothing else makes any sense, how the hell do you think those words got on that page?"

She looked away, turned the key, and started doing a three-point turn on Laurelton.

"Answer me," Paul said.

"I wonder, and I don't want you to take this the wrong way, but I wonder if it's possible there's one other explanation," she said.

"What?"

"Did you ask Dr. White if it was possible to be partly asleep and awake at the same time?"

"Yeah," he said slowly. "She said maybe."

"So think about that." She guided the car out of the neighborhood and headed toward her office.

"Just spit it out," he said.

"If you could hear something that really wasn't there, maybe you could *do* something you have no memory of."

"Oh, fuck," he said, turning and looking out his window.

"You stayed downstairs a long time last night before you came up to bed. Maybe you nodded off before you joined me. Or maybe you got up in the night and I didn't hear you."

"You think I typed that note."

"All I'm saying is that you need to consider the possibility."

He didn't speak to her the rest of the way. A block away from her office, she said, "Look, I'll run you home. You don't have to get a taxi."

"Just fuckin' drop me off anywhere."

"Please, I never meant to—"

"Save it," he said.

She pulled into the parking lot of the real estate agency. Paul got out without saying another word and slammed the door.

Twenty-Five

"I'm sorry, I don't have an appointment," Paul said later that morning to Dr. Anna White. "I know I was here only yesterday."

Anna had a surprised look on her face when she found him at her door—everyone had to ring in now, no walking straight into the waiting room—looking distressed. "Paul," she said, "I've got someone coming in five minutes, but what's wrong?"

She invited him in and guided him into her office.

"Sorry to just show up," he said again.

"What's happened?"

He hesitated. "Let me ask you something, and I need you to give me a straight answer."

"Of course."

"Do I strike you as someone who could be totally delusional?"

"What's brought this on?"

"I'm pretty sure Charlotte thinks I'm losing my mind."

"I don't believe that. Why would she?"

"Something really strange has happened and I don't know how to explain it."

"Just tell me."

So he told her about finding the sheet of paper in the typewriter with the message written on it.

"I see," Anna said slowly.

"I don't like the sound of that 'I see' very much," Paul said. "My theory is, well, it's pretty out there, but I think Charlotte has one that's a little more down to earth."

Anna nodded slowly. "That it's you? That you typed it yourself?"

Paul nodded slowly.

"Do you think that's possible?" she asked.

"No," he said quickly. But then he bowed his head, and added, "God, could it be?"

"Talk to me about that."

"Charlotte has never heard the typing in the night. I'm the only one. I mean, yeah, I suppose it's possible I dreamed it, even though it seemed very real."

"Okay."

"But a message in the typewriter, that's totally different. That's something you can hold on to. It's concrete. Charlotte saw it just as clearly as I did."

"Let's try to look at this logically," Anna said. "If we accept the fact, as I do, that there are no spirits or supernatural forces actually at work in our world, except in the movies and in the pages of Stephen King novels, then we have to consider that the stresses you've been under are manifesting themselves in creative ways you may not even be aware of. And you have, in the last week or so, made a conscious decision to revisit the circumstances of Kenneth Hoffman's attempt to kill you."

"So I typed that note and don't even know I did it."

"I think we have to look at that as a possibility."

Paul ran a hand over his mouth and chin. "Charlotte and I had this entire conversation yesterday about the dry cleaning that I have no memory of. There are texts I don't remember sending. And, of course, those typing noises in the night, before an actual note showed up. But composing a crazy note and not remembering it, that's something totally . . ."

"I could do some research on it," Anna offered. "People have done some amazing things while sleepwalking. A lot more than walking. People have been known to get in their cars and drive around with no memory of having done it. I think if someone could do that, typing out a few words is not such a stretch."

Paul let out a long breath. "Well, whatever I'm doing while I'm asleep is making me crazy while I'm awake."

Anna looked ready to ask something but was holding back.

"What is it?" Paul asked.

"Is your house secure?" she asked.

He nodded.

"So you don't think it's likely that someone could have entered the house and put that note into the typewriter."

Paul shook his head. "I don't think so. And I can't think of any reason why anyone would."

Anna did not say anything for several seconds. Then, "There's something I need to tell you. I don't honestly think it has any bearing on this, but you know that patient the other day? The one who got angry and stormed out?"

Paul nodded. "Yeah. Gavin, was it? Hitchcock or something?"

"The name's not important," Anna said. "But this patient may, and I stress *may*, be harassing some of the people I see. I can't prove it, but if he were, it would be consistent with the behavior that sent him to me in the first place."

"What's he done?"

Anna hesitated. "Do you know anything about computers?"

Paul shrugged. "About as much as most people."

"How long would someone need to download files from a computer with one of those little sticks? You know the kind I mean?"

Paul let out a long breath. "I don't know. Not long, probably. Why?"

She shook her head. "You understand this is an awkward situation for me, but I can tell you what's already part of the public record. There was a news item. He called a grieving father, pretending to be his deceased son."

"Jesus. Who would do something like that?"

"He seems to get off on exploiting people's weaknesses."

"Do you think—"

"No," she said quickly. "But I only mention it so that you'll be on your guard. A kind of heightened alert. If you should see him around your house or anything like that, call me, or call the police, even."

———

PAUL DIDN'T WANT TO GO STRAIGHT HOME FROM ANNA'S OFFICE. HE thought he'd drive around for a while and think.

Just what kind of tricks could your mind play on you? he wondered. Sure, he'd been under plenty of stress, but he'd not had any actual delusions. Okay, once in a while, he heard Hoffman's voice in his head, and for a second, maybe he thought the Volvo that had pulled out in front of him was his former colleague's car.

But those were fleeting illusions, nothing more.

Was it wrong to wonder, even briefly, if the message in his typewriter was actually from the people it purported to be? Were Catherine Lamb and Jill Foster trying to communicate with him?

Don't go there.

That led him to speculate whether he was dealing with something worse than the fallout from a blow to the head. Was he suffering some form of mental illness? Paul had known, over the years, two individuals diagnosed with schizophrenia. They had believed, with absolute certainty, they were the victims of elaborate conspiracies. One was convinced the U.S. government was after him, that the president himself was overseeing a scheme to remove his brain. The second, a mature student at West Haven College who'd attended for only a single semester, was convinced her entire body was being devoured by lesions, yet she had skin as beautiful as a newborn baby's.

I'm not like that, he told himself. *I am aware of my reality.*

And yet, didn't those two people believe they were, too?

After driving around Milford for the better part of an hour, he decided to head for home.

He pulled into the driveway, got out of the car, and stood there for a moment. He took out his cell phone, brought up the number of Charlotte's cell, tapped on it, and put the phone to his ear.

"Pick up, pick up, pick—"

"Hello?"

"Hey," he said.

"Hey," Charlotte said.

"I'm sorry. I really lost my shit this morning."

"It's okay."

"I went by Dr. White's," Paul said. "Kind of barged in. The thing is, I'm willing to consider all the options, even the one you were getting at."

"I never really said—"

Dee dee, diddly-dee, dee dee, dee-da, dee-da, dee da dee.

"It's okay," he said.

"What's that noise?"

Paul glanced down the street at the approaching vehicle. It was the same ice cream truck he and Josh had run out to on Saturday night. The one that had been driven by Kenneth Hoffman's son.

"I have to go," he said.

"I've got a call in to find out who sold that house. When I—"

"Later," he said, tucking his phone away.

Stick with the program. Don't be distracted. You set out to confront this shit, and confront this shit you shall. So there've been some strange bumps in the road. Keep on going.

The truck slowed as two kids from a house half a block away ran out, waving their arms. The truck slowed to a stop.

Dee dee, diddly-dee, dee dee, dee-da, dee-da, dee da dee.

Paul strode down the street. He waited for the two kids to get their orders, then stood up to the window. The heavyset young man with the LEN name tag pinned to his chest said, "What do you want?"

Paul said, "Medium cone, just plain."

No more fear. No more turning away.

As Len began to prepare it, Paul said, "You're Leonard Hoffman, right?"

Leonard turned and looked at Paul. "Yeah."

"Do you know who I am? Do you recognize me?"

Leonard stopped swirling the cone under the soft ice cream dispenser, set it on the counter. "I don't think so," he said.

"I'm Paul Davis."

Realization slowly dawned behind Leonard's dim eyes. "You . . . I know that name."

"Your dad . . . I was the witness. Your father was charged with attacking me, that night. I wondered—I know this may sound odd—but I wonder if I might be able to talk to you about your father."

Leonard's eyes narrowed. "Why?"

"I just . . . it's hard to explain. These last few months have been difficult for me, and I've been trying to—how do I put this—confront the things—"

"You're a bad man," Leonard said.

"What?"

"It's all your fault."

"*My* fault?"

"That my dad went to prison."

"Uh, no, I don't think so, Leonard. It was your dad's fault, because he killed those two—"

"You stopped. If you hadn't stopped, he wouldn't have been arrested."

So maybe this wasn't such a great idea after all.

"Because you stopped, it made my dad stay there too long. And then the police came."

Paul blinked. "If the police hadn't come, I'd be dead. Your father would have finished me off."

"He should've," Leonard said, flicking the ice-cream cone off the counter with the back of his hand. It bounced off Paul's chest, leaving a dripping, white mess on his shirt.

"No charge, asshole," Leonard said. He went back to the front of the truck, put it in gear, and drove off.

HE WENT BACK INTO THE HOUSE FOR A CLEAN SHIRT AND STUFFED the other one into that bag of clothes that he was supposed to have taken to the dry cleaners. It was still up in the bedroom. He'd grab a fresh shirt from the closet.

Mockingly, he said to himself, "Hey there, Leonard. Wanna talk about your killer dad? Sit down, really get into it about your homicidal father?"

He passed through the kitchen on the way upstairs.

Glanced in the direction of his office.

Saw the typewriter on the desk.

Something caught his eye.

"No," he said under his breath.

From where he stood, there appeared to be a black line on the new sheet of paper he had rolled into the machine that morning.

A line of type.

Slowly, he approached the door to the small office and stepped in, as though a tiger might be hiding behind the door. His pulse quickened and his mouth went dry. Paul blinked several times to make sure that what he was seeing was real.

The latest message read:

Blood was everywhere. What makes someone do something so horrible?

He stumbled back out of the room.

I did not do this, he told himself. *I did not do this. I have no memory of doing this. I wasn't even here. There's no way I—*

A loud *ping* rang out from inside his jacket, startling him. He took out his phone, brought the screen to life.

He'd received an email. He opened it, saw that it was from Gwen Stainton of the *New Haven Star*.

It read:

Dear Mr. Davis:
I thought I recognized your name as soon as I saw your email address. I covered the Hoffman double homicide from the very beginning and can tell you that the typewriter used in the case was never recovered. What makes you ask?
Sincerely,
Gwen Stainton

Twenty-Six

Paul's mind raced.

If he had not written this note and left it for himself—as Charlotte would probably theorize if she were here—and if those two dead women really were *not* trying to connect with him, then there remained only one possible explanation.

Someone really was getting into the house.

But the house had been locked when he got back here. He clearly remembered sliding the key in, turning back the dead bolt.

Could someone have come in through the garage, then entered the house through the interior door that connected the two?

Paul ran downstairs, went out the front door, and tried the handle on the garage door. He couldn't turn it. It was locked as well.

He went back into the house, checked the balcony doors off the living room and the bedroom, in case somehow someone had scaled the wall. But those doors were not only locked, they were also prevented from being slid open by wood sticks in the tracks.

No one could have gotten into this house.

He was sure of it.

He returned to the kitchen, then went back into his study long enough to grab the laptop that was sitting next to the typewriter, which he brought out to the kitchen island. He pulled up a chair. He could not bring himself to remain in his tiny office. He was, at this moment, too freaked-out to be in there with that relic. The very thought of going back into that closet-size space made him feel short of breath.

He thought of that movie, the one with *paranormal* in the title, where they set up the camera in the bedroom. In the morning, the couple living in the house saw all these freaky things happening while they'd been asleep. Covers being pulled off them, doors opening and closing.

Except, Paul reminded himself, *that* had been a movie.

This was for real.

He thought back to the moments before he and Charlotte had left to find the house where she had bought the Underwood. Was it possible he'd written this line on the typewriter seconds before they left? But he wasn't even remotely asleep at that point. He'd been up for hours.

"I didn't do it," he said under his breath. "I'm sure I didn't do it."

He opened the mail program on his laptop to take another read of the message he'd first seen on his phone, the one from Gwen Stainton, saying that the Hoffman typewriter had never been recovered.

"What makes you ask?" she'd written before signing her name.

He found the *New Haven Star* page he'd looked at earlier and called the main phone number.

"*New Haven Star*," a recording said. "If you know the extension you're calling, please enter it now. If you had a problem this morning with the delivery of your paper, please press one. If you would like to register a vacation, suspend delivery, or cancel your paper, press two. If you would like to place an ad, please press three."

"For fuck's sake," Paul said.

"If you would like to be connected to the newsroom, press four. If—"

Paul pressed four, thinking that anyone calling in with a hot tip would probably have given up by now.

"Newsroom," a man said.

"Gwen Stainton."

"Hang on."

The line went dead for nearly ten seconds, then, "Stainton."

"Ms. Stainton, it's Paul Davis. I emailed you this morning about Kenneth—"

"Yeah, the typewriter question. We talked, right? Back when I wrote a feature on the case, after Hoffman pleaded guilty."

"That's right."

"How are you doing?"

"I'm okay."

"I know you got hurt pretty bad, but in a lot of ways, you were pretty lucky."

"I guess you're right about that. So, about the typewriter. I don't think this ever even came up—it wasn't in your story—but the night I saw Kenneth, he tossed something into a Dumpster. I think it had to be the typewriter he made the women write those notes on. But because of my head injury, I didn't even recall that for a few days. I suppose, by then, that the Dumpster could have been emptied."

"Possibly," Gwen said. "Like I said in my email, Mr. Davis, what makes you ask?"

He paused. "Is this off the record?"

A pause at the other end. "Yeah, sure."

"I've been seeing a therapist since the incident. To, you know, deal with the trauma. As a way of confronting it, I've decided to write about what happened to me. A kind of therapy, I guess you'd call it. But reviewing everything about what occurred that night, there's this one, well, kind of a loose end. About the typewriter."

"You sound like a modern-day Columbo," Gwen said.

"Maybe so," Paul conceded.

"You probably know as much or more than I do. After he killed those two women, Hoffman wanted to get rid of the evidence. That being their bodies, and the typewriter, which would have had a lot of blood on it. I imagine it would have been impossible to get the blood out of all the little nooks and crannies in an old machine like that."

From where he was sitting, Paul looked at the Underwood. If

this was that typewriter, someone had cleaned it up. Or maybe it had rained after Hoffman dumped it. Nature gave it a good rinsing.

"Sure," he said.

"So, yeah, he tossed it. And it wasn't found. But the police didn't need it to make their case, since Hoffman confessed. I'm sure the police did try to find it, but like you said, it probably was in a dump somewhere, buried under tons of trash, by that time."

Paul couldn't take his eyes off the typewriter. He was unable to shake the feeling that it was looking at him. Except, typewriters didn't have eyes. The old ones, like this Underwood, were nothing more than hunks of metal. They were machines, plain and simple. They could neither see, nor hear, nor talk, or—

Maybe *talk*.

"Mr. Davis?" Gwen said.

"I'm here," he said. "In your story, you said the typewriter was an Underwood. How would you know that, if it was never found?"

Gwen hesitated. "I'm pretty sure one of the detectives told me. He said Hoffman had called it an Underwood."

Paul continued to stare at the machine.

"Mr. Davis? Is there anything else I can help you with?"

"No," he said. "I mean, maybe."

"What?"

"Have you ever spoken with him? With Kenneth Hoffman?"

"Briefly," she said. "It wasn't an interview. But there was an opportunity to have a few words with him one day when he was being brought from the jail to the courthouse."

"What was your impression?"

"He was charming," Gwen said. "Positively charming."

PAUL HAD PUT THE PHONE DOWN FOR ONLY A SECOND WHEN HE thought to call back Charlotte.

"Why'd you cut me off before?" she asked.

"It was the ice cream truck."

"You cut me off to get an ice cream?"

"You said you were going to ask around about some home security companies?"

"Yeah, it's on my list," she said with a hint of weariness. "That, and finding the former owners of that house. Why? Has something else happened?"

Did he want to tell her that he'd found another note? While he considered how to respond, Charlotte said, "Paul?"

"No, nothing's happened," he said. "I just wanted to remind you, that's all."

"I'll ask around. Listen, there's a call I have to take."

"Go."

He put the phone down on the counter and sat there, thinking.

And then it hit him.

"Fuck," he said.

He got back onto the laptop, opened a browser, and went to Google. He entered several key words. *Gavin* and *dead* and *pretend* and *son* and *father* and *Hitchcock*.

Paul found the news story, even though he had the last name wrong. It was Hitchens, not Hitchcock. It was as Anna had described. The sick bastard tormented a man by pretending to be his son who had been killed in Iraq.

Paul remembered Gavin Hitchens bumping into him as he stormed out of Anna's office. The brief tussle they'd had.

And then Paul couldn't find his keys.

Twenty-Seven

I t all made sense.

If this psycho had gotten into Anna White's files, as she feared, then he knew all about Paul's history. If Hitchens had googled Paul just as Paul had googled Hitchens, he'd know all about what had happened with Hoffman. He'd know Paul had nearly died. He'd know about the notes Hoffman had made the women write.

He'd know about the typewriter.

Hitchens would know more than enough to fuck with him.

Paul called up the online phone directory and entered Hitchens's name. A phone number and a Milford address popped up. The guy lived on Constance Drive.

"You son of a bitch," Paul said.

He felt rage growing within him like a high-grade fever. He wanted to do something about this bastard.

Right fucking now.

He got out his cell and phoned Anna White's office. The first, logical course of action was to get in touch with her.

Voice mail.

"Shit," he said, and ended the call.

He looked at the screen again, focusing on Gavin Hitchens's address. He closed the computer, grabbed the extra set of keys he'd been using the last few days, and headed for the stairs to the front door.

But wait.

What about the shoe Paul had sometimes been leaving just inside the door? If Hitchens had been in the house, how had he left the shoe there on his way out?

Paul ran down to the front door. He picked up a shoe, opened the door, and stepped outside. He got down on his knees, and with the door open no more than four inches, he snaked his arm in, up to the elbow, then crooked it around and set it up against the back of the door.

It could be done, he thought. He had to admit he'd not checked exactly how close the shoe had been to the door. If it had been sitting out an inch or two, would he have noticed?

But wait.

How would Hitchens even know he needed to set that shoe back in that position? If he'd snuck into the house in the middle of the night, he might have heard the shoe move. The sole might have squeaked as it was pushed across the tile.

Minor details, Paul thought. Somehow, this Gavin asshole had figured it out.

While his rage continued to grow, Paul felt something else. There was *relief*. He'd come up with an answer to what had been going on, and it wasn't that he was crazy.

That was good news.

But he was going to deliver some *bad* news to Gavin Hitchens.

Paul grinned. "I'm comin' for ya, you motherfucker."

THE HOUSE WAS EASY ENOUGH TO FIND. IT WAS A WHITE, TWO-STORY house with a double garage. A blue Toyota Corolla sat in the driveway. Paul parked two houses down and started walking back.

He had no plan.

Well, he wanted his goddamn keys back. He had *that* much of a plan.

Paul was still one lot away when he saw him. Gavin Hitchens came out the front door, heading for the Corolla.

Paul picked up his pace. He cut across the lawn, the grass underfoot silencing his approach.

Hitchens reached the driver's door and was about to open it when Paul came up behind him, grabbed the back of his head with his outstretched palm, quickly gripped Hitchens's hair, and drove his skull forward into the roof of the car.

Hitchens let out a cry.

Paul pulled his head back, barely noticing that he'd put a small dent into the roof of the Corolla.

"You bastard!" Paul said, driving Hitchens's head into the car a second time. But he wasn't able to do it with as much force this time. Hitchens was resisting. He managed to do half a turn, wanting to see who his attacker was.

"Fucker!" Paul said, spittle flying off his lip. "You sick fuck!"

Hitchens twisted, freed himself from Paul's grasp. He made a halfhearted attempt to take a swing at Paul, but the blow to the head had disoriented him, and he slid halfway down the side of the car.

Paul brought one leg back and kicked Hitchens in the knee. Hitchens screamed and slid the rest of the way to the driveway.

Paul stood over Hitchens, who was now bleeding profusely from the forehead. "I know it was you," Paul said. "I know what you did, and I know how you did it."

Hitchens moaned. He looked up blearily and said, "Police . . ."

"Good idea," Paul said. "You can tell them about breaking into my house, trying to drive me out of my fucking mind. Where are my keys? I want my goddamn keys."

Hitchens managed to sit upright, his back against the front tire. "You're in such deep shit," he said.

"Nothing compared to what you're in," Paul said.

His phone started to ring inside his jacket.

"Breaking and entering, that's what they'll get you for," Paul said. "And if there's a charge for trying to drive someone out of his fucking mind, they'll add that to the list."

He felt a pounding in his chest. He wondered if he might give himself a heart attack. The thing was, though, it felt *good*. Paul hadn't felt this good, this empowered, in a very long time.

When he looked down at Hitchens, he saw Hoffman, too.

The phone in his jacket continued to ring.

Paul finally dug it out of his pocket and saw that it was Anna. He put the phone to his ear.

"Yeah?"

"Paul?"

"Yes?"

"It's Anna. You called. But listen, I found them."

Paul blinked. "What?"

"Your keys. They'd fallen behind a chair. I just found them. Drop by anytime to pick them up."

Twenty-Eight

A neighbor saw the whole thing and called the police.

Paul didn't see the point in running. He was hardly going to lead the cops on a high-speed chase throughout Fairfield County. He sat on the curb in front of Hitchens's home and waited for them to arrive. They got there about a minute after the ambulance.

The neighbor, a woman in her seventies, knelt next to Gavin, trying to comfort him.

"What kind of monster are you?" she shrieked at Paul. She stayed with Hitchens until the paramedics assessed him. When the police arrived, she pointed to Paul.

"He did it!"

Paul sat, arms resting on his knees, doing his best impression of someone who did not present a threat.

The officers approached. "Sir, would you stand up please?"

Not long after that, he was cuffed, thrown into the back of the cruiser, and on his way to the station.

———

HE WAS ALLOWED TO CALL CHARLOTTE WHEN HE GOT THERE.

"Do you know any lawyers?" he asked.

"Tons," she said. "I'm in real estate."

"It's not a real estate lawyer I need."

When Charlotte recovered from his news, she said she would find someone and meet him at the station.

Paul was placed in a cell to wait, which gave him plenty of time to think about a great many things.

Anyone else in his predicament might have been thinking about what charge awaited him. Would it be assault? Would it be something more serious, like attempted murder? Would his afternoon behind bars turn into six months or a year? Or more?

But Paul wasn't thinking about any of that.

He was thinking about the typewriter.

Gavin Hitchens had not taken his keys. Gavin Hitchens had not broken into his house. And Gavin Hitchens had definitely not typed that message.

Which presented what one might call a bit of a mind fuck.

Hoffman's typewriter had not been found. It was within the realm of possibility that the machine Charlotte had picked up at that yard sale was that typewriter.

And if it was . . .

Paul examined the tiny cell. A bench to sit on, a toilet bolted to the wall. It seemed so . . . restful in here. Charlotte and whatever lawyer she could find could take their time as far as he was concerned.

It was nice to have a place to contemplate things, uninterrupted.

So, if it was the same typewriter, Paul had to decide whether to think the unthinkable.

Were Catherine Lamb and Jill Foster trying to communicate with him through that typewriter? If so, what were they trying to say? What was the message?

What did they want from him?

This is crazy. They'll lock me up, but it won't be in a place like this. It'll be a psych ward.

Why contact him? Maybe they'd have reached out to anyone who possessed this typewriter. (Paul made a mental note: when Charlotte found the previous owners, he'd ask if they'd noticed anything spooky about the Underwood. Maybe that was why they'd sold it.) But making a connection with Paul, who was directly linked to the women through Kenneth Hoffman, had to mean something.

Sitting in the cell, Paul had something of an epiphany. He needed to talk to more people. He needed to talk to everyone connected to this case, or at least try.

The dead women's spouses. Other women Hoffman had affairs with. His wife, Gabriella. The more he learned, the more he might understand why messages were appearing in that typewriter.

CHARLOTTE SHOWED UP WITH A LAWYER NAMED ANDREW KILGORE, who didn't look as though he'd seen his twenty-fifth birthday yet.

"Mr. Davis, I've arranged for your release but you're going to have to appear for a hearing—"

"Sure, whatever, that's fine," Paul said as the cell door was opened and he was led, along with the lawyer, toward the exit.

"Mr. Davis, I'm going to need to sit down with you to discuss our options. Your wife tells me you've been under considerable strain and that you suffered a head injury eight months ago, which could be very useful to us—"

"I want to get out of here," he said.

He found Charlotte waiting out front of the station. She threw her arms around him. Her smeared eye makeup suggested she'd been crying.

"Are you okay?" she asked.

"Fine," he said, breaking free of her and reaching for the car door. "Let's go."

Kilgore had more to say to him, but Paul wasn't even listening. He had a plan now, and he just wanted to get to it.

Twenty-Nine

When Paul and Charlotte got home—they first had to go over to Constance Drive to fetch Paul's car—she found the latest note sitting in the Underwood:

> **Blood was everywhere. What makes someone do something so horrible?**

"Paul?" she said. "What's this? You didn't tell me about this. What's going on? Why did you attack that man?"

"I have to go out," he said.

"Paul, we just got home. For Christ's sake, tell me what's going on?"

"I have things to do."

"IS HAROLD FOSTER IN?" PAUL ASKED AT THE MILFORD SAVINGS & LOAN customer service desk.

"Do you have an appointment?" the woman behind the desk asked, flashing him a Polident smile.

"No," he said.

"Um, would you like to make one?"

"If he's here now, I would like to see him."

The woman's smile faded. "Let me check. What's the name?"

"Paul Davis."

"And what's it concerning?"

"It's a personal matter," he said.

"Oh." She picked up the phone and turned away so that Paul could not hear her discussion. After fifteen seconds, she replaced the receiver and said, "Have a seat and Mr. Foster will be with you shortly."

Shortly turned out to be five minutes. Finally, a short, balding man in a dark blue suit appeared.

"Mr. Davis?" He wore a quizzical look.

Paul stood. "Yes."

"Come on in."

He led Paul down a carpeted hallway to an office about ten feet square. The wall that faced the hall was a sheet of glass. Foster went behind his desk and sat while Paul took a chair opposite him.

The man's desk was stacked with file folders. "Excuse all the mess. So much paperwork." He grinned. "Everything has to be in writing, I always say."

"Of course."

"How may I help you? You weren't very forthcoming with our receptionist, but I understand financial matters are very personal. Whether you've got a million to invest, or you owe the same to the credit card companies"—he grinned—"these are all things that aren't anyone else's business."

"It's not that kind of thing," Paul said.

"What could it be, then?"

"I teach at West Haven College. Well, not at the moment. But I'll be going back in the fall."

The three words prompted an almost instantly darker look from Foster. "Oh?" He studied Paul a moment longer. "What did you say your name was again?"

"Paul Davis."

Foster leaned back in his chair. "My God, you were . . . you were there."

Paul nodded. "I was."

"He tried to kill you."

"Yes."

"If you hadn't stopped . . . the police wouldn't have found him." He let out a long breath. "And then we might never have found out what happened to them. To Jill, and Catherine."

"I'm very sorry about your wife. I knew Jill, of course. Not well, but I ran into her occasionally at West Haven. The one I knew much better, or at least thought that I knew, was Ken—"

Foster held up a hand. "Stop right there."

"I'm sorry?"

"Don't even say his name," he said, his voice bordering on threatening. "Do not say that man's name in my presence. Never."

Paul nodded. "I understand."

Foster calmed himself. "Well, what is it you want?"

"I . . . I hardly know how to begin this, but I want to ask you some questions, about Jill, and what happened."

"Why?"

He couldn't bring up the typewriter, but he could tell this man about how he was attempting to deal with his post-traumatic stress.

"I'm . . . writing something. I'm writing about what I went through, about my recovery."

"A book?"

"I don't even know yet. The immediate goal is to get it all out, to face what happened to me. Maybe, at some later date, it'll be a book, or a magazine piece. I don't know what shape it's going to take."

"Oh."

"Yeah, well, anyway, that's why I'm here. To ask you—"

The hand went up again. "Enough," he said.

"I just wanted to—"

"Stop. I'm sorry for what happened to you, Mr. Davis. And I suppose I owe you some thanks. You probably, inadvertently of course, helped bring . . . that man to justice by coming upon him when you did. But I don't want to talk about this. Not with you, not with anyone else. I've no doubt these last eight months have been hell for you. Well, they've been hell for me, too. And your way to deal with it may be to turn it into some creative writing exercise, but I have no interest in baring my soul to you or answering your prurient questions about my wife."

"Prurient? Who said anything—"

Foster pointed to the door.

"Get out or I'll call security."

Paul nodded, stood, and left. Foster trailed him, a good five paces behind, until Paul had left the building.

Thirty

Anna White heard the doorbell ring.

It was the front door this time, not her office door. It was after five, and her last appointment had just left. She met weekly with an obsessive-compulsive man who associated leftward movements with evil. When driving, he would go around a block, making three right turns, so as not to make a left. He tried to use his left hand so little that muscle tone in that arm had degenerated. If he meant to walk left, he would rotate his body three-quarters of a turn, then head off in the direction he had to go. It was all rooted in the Latin word *sinister*, which means "to the left" or "left-handed." Not surprisingly, his politics were right-wing.

Anna was making very little progress with him. She hoped that if Gavin Hitchens had actually managed to download many of her files, that he didn't get hold of that one. A psychopath like Hitchens would have far too much fun with him.

She was about to make some postsession notes when she heard the doorbell. She hurried through the house, wanting to get to the door before her father, should he choose to come downstairs to answer it. But a glance through a window revealed that he was outside, chipping away at the lawn with a nine-iron.

Anna opened the door to a woman she did not recognize.

"Hello?"

"Paul's gone over the edge," she said.

"I'm sorry?"

"I'm Charlotte. Charlotte Davis? Paul's wife?"

"Yes, okay. What's happened?"

"May I come in?"

Anna opened the door wide to admit her.

"They arrested him," Charlotte said.

"They *what*? Who? The police?"

"He attacked some man."

"What man?"

"Someone named Hitchens."

Anna's face fell. "Oh my God no."

"What?"

"I shouldn't have—I wanted to warn him but I never thought—"

"Warn Paul about what?"

"Please, tell me what happened."

Charlotte told Anna what she'd been able to learn from Paul and the police. "He has this crazy idea this total stranger got into our house. Or at least, he did, until he got some call from you."

"I'd found Paul's keys, in my office. He must have thought Hitchens had them."

Charlotte wiped a tear from her cheek. "I don't know how much more of this I can take. Lately, Paul's been so . . . I was going to try and make an appointment with you anyway, to talk about him. But then, when this happened . . ."

"I can't discuss my patients," Anna explained. "Not even with their spouses."

Charlotte nodded quickly. "Of course, I understand that. But I have to tell you what's been going on."

"I really don't know that—"

"Please. I thought Paul was getting better, but these last few days, he's getting worse. He's losing it."

Anna hesitated, then said, "Go on."

"He's hearing things in the middle of the night. Things that *I'm* not hearing. Like someone tapping away on an old typewriter I bought him. And now he's *finding*"—she put air quotes around the word—"messages in the typewriter he thinks are coming from these two women Kenneth Hoffman murdered. And he's already told you about the nightmares, right?"

She replied with a cautious, "He has."

"I don't know what to think. Messages from the dead?" She shook her head, reached into her purse for a tissue, and blotted up more tears from her cheeks, then her eyes. "Unless you believe in ghosts, which I don't, the only possible explanation is that he's writing these messages himself."

Charlotte's chin quivered. "What should I do? I'm so worried about him. He's had such a tough year. The nightmares, the physical recovery. I thought maybe his idea of diving right into what happened to him, writing about it, might help, but it's having the opposite effect. I think writing about it is . . . it's like he's being dragged into some black hole."

"I'll talk to him. I'll bring him in for some extra sessions."

"I'm so worried that he—you don't think there's any chance he'd do anything, you know, to harm himself, do you?"

Anna's brow furrowed. "What have you observed?"

Charlotte hesitated. "I don't know. Nothing I can put my finger on exactly. But he's been down so long, and now, he's having . . . are they delusions? I don't know what else to call them. What's next? That message in the typewriter, it's like a text version of hearing voices. What if the next message tells him to kill himself?"

"If I see anything that leads me to think your husband would harm himself I'll take the appropriate steps."

"I mean," Charlotte continued, "they *are* delusions, right? I mean, are they delusions if he's doing it deliberately?"

"What are you getting at?"

"The noises he claims to be hearing, the typed message, at first I was thinking it was all in his head, that even if he's writing the messages, he's doing it unconsciously, he doesn't know he's doing it. But what if he *does* know? What am I dealing with then? Why would he put on an act like that? Is he trying to make *me* crazy?"

"I can't think of any reason why he would do that," Anna said.

"So then is it a hallucination?"

"I don't know."

"Has he been prescribed something that would be messing with his head? Some kind of weird side effect?"

"No."

Charlotte was shredding the tissue in her hand. "I don't know what to do. I don't know how to help him."

Anna asked her to wait a moment. She went to her office, grabbed the keys she had been holding for Paul, and gave them to Charlotte when she returned to the front of the house.

"You don't have to take all this on yourself," Anna told her. "That's what I'm here for. To help Paul through this period. We need to give him some time."

"Please don't tell him I was here."

"Why don't *you* tell him? It might actually mean a lot to him, to know that you're this concerned."

"I don't know," she said, more to herself than Anna. "I just don't know."

Charlotte turned for the door, then stopped. "When I said I didn't believe in ghosts, you didn't respond to that. I'm guessing, I mean, I'm sure you've seen everything in your line of work. Have you ever encountered anything that would suggest there's anything to, you know, messages from the . . ." Her cheeks went red, as though she were too embarrassed to complete the sentence. "What I'm trying to say is, you've never seen anyone actually get a message from the *beyond*."

Anna offered a smile. "Not in my experience."

"I don't even know if that's a comfort. If those two dead women really *were* trying to communicate with my husband, well, at least that would prove Paul wasn't crazy, right?"

Thirty-One

O nce he'd recovered from his encounter with Harold Foster, Paul found himself at the Connecticut Post Mall.

He needed to walk around, gather his thoughts before he did anything else. So he wandered the shopping concourse from one end to the other, not going into a single store, but finally ending up in the food court, where he bought himself a cup of coffee and sat down to drink it.

He'd had, when he'd left the house, the roughest idea of a plan. Talk to Jill Foster's husband, then Gilford Lamb, spouse of Hoffman's other victim, Catherine. He was also thinking of getting in touch with Angelique Rogers, the West Haven political science professor who'd also had a fling with Hoffman, and had been interviewed in that story by Gwen Stainton.

The meeting with Foster's husband hadn't gone well, but that didn't mean he wasn't going to press on. He knew there was no reason to think that any of these discussions would go well. He might be the *only* one seeking a greater insight into Hoffman's soul. Maybe everyone else just wanted to put the whole nasty business behind them. Foster wouldn't even allow Hoffman's name to be spoken in his presence. Kenneth's wife, Gabriella, Paul feared, might be the hardest to talk to of all of them. If there was anyone who might want to be moving on with her life, it could be Gabriella. And yet, she might, more than anyone else, be the one who held the key to the secrets of Hoffman's personality.

But for now, Paul needed to clear his head. The mall's food court wasn't quite as isolating as a jail cell, but it would do.

As he sat there, watching mothers pushing strollers, teenagers hanging out and laughing, an elderly couple sitting across from each other saying nothing, he wondered whether this quest for understanding was a worthy pursuit.

What guarantee was there that no matter how many people he talked to, no matter how many questions he asked, he'd ever get his answers?

Sometimes people did bad things. End of story.

But now there was more to it.

Something was not right.

That fucking typewriter.

Paul had exhausted all rational explanations for those messages. As unsettling as it would have been to learn Gavin Hitchens had been sneaking into his house to plant them, it would have been a relief to find out he was responsible.

The only other "real world" explanation? Paul was doing it himself. But he wasn't ready to accept that yet. Sleepwalking was one thing. But inventing messages from the dead and having no memory of it? That was a bridge too far.

That was crazy.

The problem was, the only explanation left to him wasn't any less insane.

Was it possible the typewriter was some sort of conduit for Jill Foster and Catherine Lamb? Were those two women actually trying to talk to him?

No.

Possibly.

Did Paul believe things happened for a reason? If the answer was yes, then some unseen hand had guided Charlotte to that yard sale. Some force he could not possibly understand told her to get out of the car and check out the junk these people were trying to sell.

And that force knew that when she saw that old Underwood, she'd immediately think it would be the perfect gift for her husband.

The mystical heavy lifting was done.

Once the typewriter was in the house, Jill and Catherine could begin their communication with him.

"God, it's fucking nuts," Paul said.

"You talking to me?"

Paul turned. Sitting at the table next to him was a woman he guessed to be in her eighties, blowing on a paper cup of tea, bag still in, the string hanging over the side.

"I'm sorry," Paul said. "Excuse my language. I . . . I was just thinking out loud."

The woman's weathered, wrinkled face broke into a smile. "That's one of the first signs."

That brought a smile to his face for the first time that day. "In my case, you might be right."

"Are you okay?" she asked, grabbing the string and bobbing the tea bag up and down.

"I'm fine," he said. "Thank you."

"You look like a troubled young man."

He forced another smile. "I've had better days."

The woman nodded. After what seemed a moment of reflection, she said, "I come here every day and have a cup of tea. I look forward to it. It's the high point."

"That's nice," he said, although he wasn't sure whether that was nice, or sad.

"And I watch the people, and I think about their lives, and what they're going through. I used to read books, but I find it harder to concentrate on them now. So I make up stories about the people I see."

Paul thought it was time to move on.

"A lot of times, when I see a man sitting here having a coffee, it's because he's waiting for his wife to finish shopping. But I don't think that's the case with you."

"And why's that?"

"You don't keep looking at your watch, or your phone. So you're not waiting on someone. You're here on your own."

"You're good," Paul said.

The woman nodded with satisfaction. "Thank you." She cocked her head at an angle and asked, "What's fucking nuts?"

It jarred him, his words coming back to him, from this sweet old lady.

What the hell, he thought. It might be easier to ask a stranger this question than someone he knew well.

"Do you think," he asked hesitantly, "that the dead can speak to us?"

The woman reacted as though this were the easiest question she'd ever been asked. "Of course," she said, taking out the tea bag and setting it on a napkin. "I hear from my husband all the time. Do you know what he did?"

Paul waited.

"He died in October. This'd be in 1997. He'd been sick a long time and knew what was coming. So, four months later, a dozen roses arrive at the door. He figured he wouldn't make it to February, so he had ordered my Valentine's Day flowers back in September." She smiled. "How about that?"

"Well," Paul said. "He must have been something."

She took a sip of her tea. "He had his moments."

Paul stood. He tucked his napkin into the empty coffee cup. "You have a nice day," he said.

He dropped the cup into the trash and headed for the escalator that would take him from the food court down to the main part of the mall. He glanced back for one last look at that woman, thinking he would give her a friendly farewell wave.

She was gone.

Thirty-Two

He decided his next stop would be Gilford Lamb.

The one-time director of human resources at West Haven had not returned to work after his wife's murder. His initial time off for bereavement leave had turned into an extended sick leave. From what Paul had heard, he had never recovered emotionally from the loss.

Paul looked up his address online and found that he lived in the Derby area of Milford in a simple two-story house. He pulled into the driveway next to a twenty-year-old rusting Chrysler minivan. As he got out of his own car he took note of the uncut lawn choked with crabgrass, the crooked railing alongside the steps to the front door, the paint flecking off the house.

God, Paul thought. *It's only been eight months.*

When Paul pushed the button for the doorbell, he didn't hear anything. Must be broken.

So he knocked.

Not too hard, the first time. But when no one answered, he tried again, this time putting his knuckles into it.

From inside the house, a muffled, "Hold on."

After ten seconds, the door opened. An unshaven Gilford Lamb looked through a pair of taped glasses at Paul, blinked twice, and said, "Paul?"

"Hi, Gil."

"Well, son of a bitch. What brings you here?"

Paul guessed Gilford was in his midforties, but he looked more like a man in his sixties. His hair had thinned and turned gray, and Paul bet the man was thirty pounds lighter than the last time he'd seen him, which would have been about nine months ago. His plaid shirt was only half tucked into a pair of jeans that looked like they'd last seen a wash when the first Bush was president.

"I was going by, thought I'd drop in. It's been a while."

"Goddamn, yes, it has. Come on in."

He opened the door, and the second Paul stepped into the house he wanted to leave. The place smelled of sweat and piss and booze and old meat. The living room, or what was once a living room, was a clutter of newspapers, magazines, bottles, and, of all things, an oval model train track on the dirty carpet. But the Lionel steam train would have had a hard time making the loop, given that portions of the track were littered with dropped items including a coat and a busted computer monitor.

"You want anything?" Gilford asked.

"No, that's okay."

"Well, I think I will," he said and disappeared briefly into the kitchen. Paul heard the familiar *pfish!* of a pull tab. Gilford returned with a can of Bud Light in his hand. "Gosh, it's great to see you!" His smile seemed genuine. "I was thinking about you the other day, wondering how you were doing."

"Good to see you, too," Paul said, working to hide his shock at how Gil's life appeared to have spiraled downward so severely.

"Grab a seat."

That was definitely something Paul did not want to do, but he could see no way to refuse. He moved aside some old magazines—science journals, train enthusiasts' magazines, even a few comic books—from the stained cushion of a lounge chair while Gilford dropped his butt right onto a layer of newspapers that acted as a couch cover. He crinkled as he got comfortable.

"Not many folks from the college come by," he said. "Well, I guess the truth is, none of them come by. Hear from human resources occasionally, but that's about it. You probably know I'm still on a leave."

"Me, too," Paul said. "But I expect to be going back in September."

"Head's all healed?"

"Getting there. How about you?"

"Oh." He smiled. "I'm never going back. I'll ride out the medical leave long as I can and then quit. I'll never set foot on that campus again."

"How are you . . . managing?" He tried not to look about the room as he asked.

"Oh, it's day by day." He chortled. "I don't much give a fuck."

Paul didn't see the point in avoiding the obvious. "It hit you hard," he said.

"Hmm?"

"Catherine."

Gilford studied him for a moment, stone-faced, then looked away. "Yeah, well." His gaze drifted, as though he could see through the wall to the outdoors. "I guess the guilt kind of ate away at me."

Paul felt a chill. "The guilt?"

"I loved that woman more than anything in the world. I truly did."

Softly, Paul said, "I'm sure. But I don't understand the guilt part. It wasn't your fault, Gil."

He focused on Paul and said, "Wasn't it? I sure as hell think it was."

"It was Kenneth's fault."

"Kenneth," Gil said softly.

"You can't blame yourself."

"Maybe he's the one who slit her throat, but I'm the one who put her there with him," Gil said. "I drove her away. I was . . . I don't know. I'd become distant. I took her for granted. I hadn't remembered her birthday in six years. I know that sounds like I didn't love her, but I did. I just . . . I'd just stopped being attentive in any way whatsoever. I was living in my own world. I see that now, how I sent her into the arms of another man. And not just any man, but a homicidal maniac."

"No one saw it coming," Paul offered. "No one knew Kenneth was capable of something like that."

Gilford shrugged. "Doesn't matter anymore, anyway. So tell me this. What brought you to my door this afternoon? I saw you looking around when you walked in here. I know I look like some kind of deranged hermit, but I'm not so far gone that I don't know when someone is lying to me. You weren't just driving by and decided to say hello."

"That's true."

"So what's up?"

"I've been thinking a lot about Kenneth lately."

"I've never stopped."

"I'm sure. I can't really explain this, but some things that have happened lately have prompted me to look for answers."

"Answers to what?"

"To what made him do it."

"What sort of things?"

Paul hesitated. How did you tell a man his dead wife was sending you messages? He decided to take a chance with Gilford, to at least touch on the more recent developments involving Hoffman.

"Do you think it's possible," Paul asked slowly, "for the things that we use in our everyday lives, for them to—how do I put this—hold some kind of energy, to retain something of us in them?"

Gilford said, "What?"

"I'm not putting this well. But let's say you had something of your grandmother's. Like a mirror. Do you think that mirror possesses some of her soul?"

Gilford drank from his can of Bud Light. "Where might you be going with this, Paul?"

"What if I told you that I've come into possession of something, something that has a particularly dark history, and that individuals who used this item, somehow, in a way that I can't begin to imagine, are trying to communicate with me?"

"I guess I'd say, what the hell are you talking about?"

"It's a long story how it all came to be, but I think I have the typewriter."

Gilford squinted. "The what?"

"The typewriter. The one Kenneth . . . the one he made Catherine and Jill write their apologies on."

Gilford studied him. "You don't say."

Paul nodded.

"That'd be quite something."

"Yeah," Paul said.

"And what makes you think this typewriter you've got is that very typewriter?"

Paul licked his lips, which had gone very dry. "Well, to begin with, it's the same kind. And Kenneth's typewriter was never found by the police. So it's at least possible that this is the same one." He paused. "I've been finding messages in it. Words on sheets of paper that I've left rolled in. Asking why Kenneth did it."

Gilford leaned forward. "And who's doing the asking?"

"Catherine and Jill."

"Well," Gilford said. "That's nothing short of amazing."

Paul waited to see whether he had more to add. When it appeared he did not, Paul asked, "You have any thoughts or questions?"

He nodded very slowly. "I do."

Paul edged forward in his seat. "Okay."

"All you have to do is look around here and you can tell I'm not doing so well. I'm not like one of those nutcases you see on an episode of *Hoarders* who seems oblivious to their surroundings. I know this is a pigsty. I am aware that I'm living in a hellhole. The thing is, I don't give a flying fuck. I haven't given a shit about anything since that son of a bitch took Catherine away from me. I know the clock is running out on me before I drink myself to death one night or leave something on the stove and burn this place down or maybe one night I just take out that gun I've got in the bedroom dresser and blow my brains out, which is something I give some thought to every single fucking day. It would certainly spare me the humiliation of being that crazy person you see wandering the street pushing a shopping cart full of everything they own."

Gilford Lamb paused to take a breath, then continued. "But never, not once in these last eight months, have I had a notion as ridiculous as the one you just came up with. As bad as things have been for me, I've never lost touch with reality. But that, my friend, sounds like what's happened with you, and you have my sympathy. I know you've been through a lot, too. What I'd suggest, before it's too late, is that you get help, that you find someone to talk to about this, because I'm guessing you got hit harder in the head than you realize."

"I am talking to someone about this," Paul said.

"A neurologist, I hope."

"Him, too."

Gilford nodded slowly. "Well, that's a good thing, no doubt about it. It's been a pure delight having you drop by, Paul, even though I still don't understand quite why you did. If, the next time you're driving by, you get the urge to visit me again, I hope you won't be offended if I ask you now to just keep on going."

Thirty-Three

Paul was lucky to catch Angelique Rogers when he did.

Paul hadn't needed to look up an address for the West Haven political science professor. A launch for a book she had written about women in the Civil War had been held at her place a couple of years ago, and Paul and Charlotte had attended. A local bookseller was hawking copies, and Paul had bought one. Paul had embraced the idea of a book that examined the role of women during that period in the country's history, but the academic writing style had made it a tough slog. He hadn't been able to make it through the first chapter. The book had sat, ever since, on his study shelf, unread, and while he'd told Angelique he'd thoroughly enjoyed it, he lived in fear she would ask him which chapter was his favorite.

She lived on Park Boulevard in Stratford in a sprawling ranch house with flagstone-style siding. On the other side of Park was a narrow strip of land, and then Long Island Sound. It was a stunning view, Long Island itself nothing more than a sliver of land on the horizon.

There was a green SUV in the driveway, tailgate open. The cargo area was half-filled with luggage and bags. As Paul turned into the drive, Angelique came out of the house dragging a small, wheeled suitcase. Her eyes widened with surprise as she spotted him getting out of his Subaru.

"Paul," she said. "Oh, my."

There was still a trace of her French accent. She had told Paul her history once, about moving to America from Paris when she was only ten. Her parents had both been offered teaching positions at Cornell University. When she spoke, it was evident she was not from around here, but several decades removed from France had made it difficult to pinpoint her origins. She was a petite woman with gray-blond hair that hung in wisps over her eyes.

He waited for her around the back of the car and reached for the case when she got there.

"Let me," he said.

He grabbed the case and tucked it into the back.

"Thank you," she said, "although don't be offended if Charles rearranges it. He packs the trunk like it's a game of Tetris."

Charles, Paul recalled, was not the name of her former husband. Angelique caught his blank expression and smiled. "My new boy-friend. We've rented a place in Maine for the next three weeks."

"Sounds fantastic," Paul said.

"You look well," she said.

He wasn't so sure about that, but he accepted the compliment with a shrug. "Forgive me for showing up unannounced."

She smiled. "No one comes along here by accident. I'm a bit off the beaten path."

He nodded. "No, it's not an accident."

Paul told her, as briefly as he could, about his project but this time leaving out anything to do with the typewriter.

"So you're trying to figure out what makes Kenneth tick," she said.

"In a nutshell. You told the newspaper you were surprised."

"Who wasn't surprised? He is an enigma, our Kenneth. He cast his spell over me for a while. I never thought I'd be the kind to—"

A tanned, trim, silver-haired man in shorts came striding out of the house. "What happened to you?" he called out to Angelique. "There's still the food to—"

He stopped when he saw that she was talking to someone. "Oh, sorry."

Angelique introduced Charles and Paul to each other. While she mentioned Paul was a colleague, she did not get into what had happened to him.

"I bought this car from Charles," Angelique said.

He smiled. "She came into the dealership, and I thought, I don't care if I sell this woman a car, but I definitely want her phone number."

"Love, just start filling the cooler with the stuff on the right side of the fridge," she said.

If Charles understood he was being dismissed, he offered no clue. "Sure. Nice to meet you, Paul."

Paul nodded. As Charles went back into the house, Angelique said, "If there's something you want to ask, now's your chance."

"Tell me about him."

She cast an eye out over the sound. "Like I said, an enigma. He was a charmer. Did you know he wrote poetry?"

"I'd heard," he said.

"I'd sometimes find, in my interoffice mail, or under my door, a short poem he'd typed up. Little love poems." She grinned. "Quite terrible, actually." She gave Paul a knowing smile. "I would imagine an English professor would be better at that sort of thing, but Kenneth, well, there's not a lot of romance attached to math and physics. But he tried."

"Do you remember any of them?"

She shook her head. "They were forgettable, and at some point I threw them all away. I remember one, about how beautifully shaped women are, one of nature's most glorious achievements." She laughed. "It was embarrassing. I look back and wonder what possible clues there were that I did not pick up, that would have offered a hint to what he was capable of."

The same poem he'd tried out on Charlotte, Paul recalled. Maybe Kenneth had only had one poem in him.

"Let me tell you a story. After our . . . is *dalliance* too precious a word? Although, at the time I may have taken it more seriously than that. Anyway, it was over, and had been for some time, and he and I happened to be in the faculty lounge. Not talking, not interacting at all, and I was aware he was there. It was awkward; I tried to avoid him. I was about to leave when I got a call on my cell that my son, Armand, had been injured. He was eight at the time, and a car had clipped him at a crosswalk by the school. He'd been taken to the hospital. It turned out, thank God, not to be life threatening, but it was serious. I nearly collapsed. My husband was out of the country on business. Kenneth asked what had happened. He took me to the hospital—I was in no condition to drive—and he stayed with me there the entire night. I told him to go home, but he wouldn't leave. God knows what he told Gabriella about where he was, but he kept me company, went and found a doctor when I hadn't had an update in hours. He looked after me. And there was never a hint that he wanted anything in return. He saw I needed help, and he helped me."

She paused. "And that's the man who slit those women's throats."

PAUL DECIDED TO TAKE ANOTHER SHOT AT HAROLD FOSTER.

He recalled a book he'd once read by a legendary Miami police reporter. Often, when she'd call the family of a murder victim, hoping to add some personal details to her story, she'd get a slammed phone in her ear. So she'd wait a few minutes and try again, saying she'd somehow been cut off. Often, in the interim, another family member would argue in favor of talking to the press, that the world needed to know that, no matter what the cops might say, their dead relative was a decent human being, not some lowlife who had it coming.

Harold's situation was not quite the same, but he might have had a similar change of heart.

After his visit with Angelique, he took a route that went past Milford Savings & Loan. As he neared the bank, there was Foster, coming out the front door, heading for the adjacent parking lot.

Paul quickly pulled over to the curb, turned off the car, and got out. The banker was nearly to his car when he saw Paul approaching. He stopped.

"Harold," Paul said, trying to sound agreeable.

Foster was speechless.

"I'm hoping, since we last spoke, you might be willing to reconsider answering a few more questions."

"What the hell is wrong with you? Leave me alone."

"Listen, I'm sorry about this, I really am, but if you don't want to help me now, then I'll be back tomorrow. And if you won't help me then, I'll be back the day after that."

"Mr. Davis, I understand that what happened to you was traumatic. Guess what? What happened to *me* was traumatic. Why can't you get that through your thick, damaged skull?"

"So, I'll see you tomorrow then."

Foster sighed with exasperation. "Fine. What the hell do you want?"

Now that Foster appeared to have surrendered, Paul had to work up his courage to ask his question.

Paul nodded sheepishly. He felt his face flush.

"The truth is, I really have just one question for you, and you're going to think it's a strange one. Or, I don't know, maybe you won't."

Foster stiffened.

"Have you ever, since your wife passed away . . . have you ever felt—this is the strange part but bear with me—that she was trying to connect with you in some way?"

"Excuse me?"

"What I'm wondering is, have you ever felt as though she was talking to you? You know how, when you lose a loved one, in some way they're still with you?"

"A loved one," Harold Foster said flatly.

"Yes."

"You're quite serious."

"I am."

"And you're asking this why?"

Paul hesitated. "I'd be grateful if you indulged me without my having to explain."

"Fine," he said. "I'll answer your goddamn question." A sly grin crossed his face. "Sometimes I *can* imagine Jill speaking to me. I hear her voice in the back of my head."

"You do?" Paul felt his heart do a small flip of encouragement.

"I do."

"What do you hear her saying?"

"She's saying, 'You lucky bastard. Kenneth Hoffman did you a real favor, didn't he?'"

Paul's mouth opened. He was struck not just by the comment, but also by Harold Foster now being willing to utter his wife's killer's name.

"And you know what I say back to her?" Foster continued. "I say, 'You're damn right.' That's what I say. Hoffman rid me of a two-timing, conniving bitch." He shook his head. "Since she died, if you want to know the absolute fucking truth, I've never felt better. It's like I've been cured of cancer. I feel that I can start my life over."

Paul wondered if he looked as stunned by Harold's words as he felt.

"It was so much easier, honestly, than a divorce. So many times I considered asking her for one, but the thought of the process stopped me. The fights, the recriminations, the lawyers, the sleepless nights, the division of property. It's endless. How easy it would be, to avoid all that, to just kill your spouse. But, of course, I'd never have done such a thing. I'd never even have contemplated it. But what Hoffman did, it makes me realize now, what a magnificent time saver murder is. There are times I wonder if I should write him a check."

Paul couldn't think of a follow-up question.

"Does that about take care of it?" Foster asked. When Paul said nothing, the man unlocked his car, got in, and started the engine.

Paul was still standing there as Foster drove out.

———

PAUL REALIZED, AS HE TURNED ONTO HIS STREET, THAT CHARLOTTE'S car was directly in front. She hit her blinker, turned into their driveway, and he drove in right behind her. They each got out of their cars at the same moment.

"Hey," Charlotte said, walking toward him.

"Hey," he said.

She approached him tentatively, eyes down, the way a girl might act if she were asking a boy to dance. But it wasn't shyness. She appeared almost fearful.

"There's something I want to tell you I did, because I don't want you finding out on your own and getting angry, wondering why I didn't tell you."

"What are you talking about?" he said worriedly.

She looked him in the eye. "I went to see Dr. White."

Paul said nothing.

"I'm just so worried about you, Paul," she said. "You're scaring me half to death. I'm not sorry I went to see her. I don't care how mad you get. I had to talk to her."

Paul wasn't angry. He put his hands on her shoulders. "It's okay." He paused. "What did she say?"

Charlotte, eyes brimming with tears, said, "What *could* she say? She's not allowed to say anything. You're her patient. I'm not."

"What did you tell her?"

"I don't know what's happening with you. You assaulted a man! You come home, then you take off. I don't know where you're going, who you're going to see. You think you feel like you're losing your mind? Well guess what? Me, too."

He tried to pull her into his arms, but she resisted. When he pulled a little harder, she allowed him to hold her.

"I'm sorry," he said.

"I need you to listen to me," she said. "I want you to get help. You have to promise me that if Dr. White can't help you, you'll see someone else. You'll get to the bottom of all this. You'll find out why you're . . . why you're doing the things you're doing."

"That's what I've been trying to do. I've been out all day, talking to people."

"What people?"

Paul told her, prompting a concerned sigh.

"Do you really think that's the best thing to do? Getting all those people involved. I mean, the more people you talk to, the more people who are going to think you're—"

She stopped herself.

"The more people who are going to think I'm what?"

"Nothing."

"Crazy? The more people are going to think I'm crazy? Is that what you wanted to say?"

"That's not what—I can't take any more. I just can't."

She turned. Her keys were still in her hand, and she used them to unlock the front door. She went in, closed the door behind her, leaving Paul standing there in the driveway.

I'm losing her, he thought. *If she doesn't believe me, where am I?*

Without Charlotte's support, he wasn't sure he had the strength to get through this. Whatever *this* was.

The front door reopened. Charlotte stood there, crying.

"What's wrong?" he asked. "What is it?"

"It's not funny anymore, Paul," she said.

"What are you talking about?"

"Why are you doing this? Why are you doing this to *me*?"

"Charlotte, what are you talking about?"

She pointed a finger over her shoulder. Paul ran past her and into the house, taking the steps up to the kitchen two at a time. When he reached the top, he froze.

The kitchen floor was littered with paper.

Single sheets. The same kind of paper that was loaded into his printer. At a glance, twenty, maybe thirty sheets. Scattered all over the room.

A line typed on each one.

Paul bent over, started grabbing the sheets, one by one. Reading them. He tried to keep his hands from shaking, but each page in his hands was like a leaf in a windstorm.

Blood everywhere

Laughter as we screamed

What did we do to deserve this?

We were unfaithful but that shouldn't be a death

sentence

Paul lifted his gaze from the clutch of pages in his hand and looked toward the study door.

The Underwood, without a sheet of paper in it, stared back at him.

Paul felt himself being watched and turned to see Charlotte standing at the top of the stairs.

"Just tell me the truth," she said. "Is it you?"

He looked her in the eye. "No. I swear."

She nodded very slowly, turned to look at the typewriter, and said, "Then we have to get that fucking thing out of here."

Thirty-Four

P aul didn't need any time to come up with a plan.

"We take this thing, we put it in the trunk, we drive to the middle of the bridge, and drop it in the goddamn Housatonic."

Charlotte nodded. "We could. We could do that. I *like* that idea."

Paul eyed her skeptically. "I'm hearing a *but*."

"Okay, if that's what you want to do, fine, but you better do it at night. You toss something into the river and you'll be up on some environmental charge. Littering, something. And how are you going to explain yourself if the police come by? Why does a person drop a typewriter off a bridge? What's your story going to be? And even at night, there are probably traffic cameras."

Paul shook his head slowly. "Is there another bridge, another place where—"

Charlotte raised a hand. "Look, for now, let's get it out of *here*. We can talk about where to get rid of it permanently later." She thought for a moment as they stood, shoulder to shoulder, looking at the Underwood. "The garage."

Paul bit his lip. "How does that solve the problem? If there's really something going on with this thing, moving it out of here won't make it stop."

"Neither would dropping it into the river, but whether it's there, or in the garage, you'll stop hearing it in the night," Charlotte said. "This . . . *thing* can type out as many notes at it wants in the garage. If we don't know about it, we don't have to care."

"Okay," he said, a hint of defeat in his voice. "I'm in."

He got his hands under the typewriter. It was, he realized, the first time he had ever moved it.

"This thing *is* heavy," he remarked.

"I told you," she said. "It's a fridge with keys."

Careful not to slip on any of the sheets of paper still on the floor, Paul walked the typewriter across the kitchen and down to the first floor. At the foot of the stairs, at right angles to the front door, was the second door—also fitted with a dead bolt lock—that led into the garage. Charlotte got ahead of Paul, turned back the bolt, opened the door, and held it for her husband. Being an interior door that led to a garage, it had a spring-loaded hinge to guard against possible carbon monoxide mishaps.

She flicked on the light switch. The garage was littered with cardboard boxes, several old bicycles, unneeded furniture.

"That," Paul said, nodding at something in the corner.

Charlotte pointed to a wooden antique blanket box tucked up against the wall. "This?"

Paul nodded, shifting the weight of the typewriter from one arm to the other. "Yeah. Open that up. See if there's anything in it."

The box was about three feet wide, a foot and a half high and deep. Charlotte lifted the lid.

"There's a bunch of old *Life* magazines and *National Geographic*s and stuff in there."

"God, why do we have those? They were my *parents'*. Can you shove them over, make enough space for this thing?"

Charlotte got down on her knees and started piling magazines over to one side, creating a cavity on the left.

He leaned over and set the typewriter into the bottom of the box. When he let go, he flexed his fingers to get the blood circulating in them again. "That is one heavy son of a bitch. Okay, close it."

Charlotte closed the lid of the blanket box as Paul scanned the room.

"What?" she asked.

"Looking for something heavy to put on top."

"Jesus, Paul, it's not the clown from *It*. It's not going to break out and attack us."

Paul had nothing to say to that. He found three liquor store boxes with the word BOOKS scribbled on the side in black marker. He set them on top of the blanket box.

"That should do it," he said. "Those things weigh a ton." He clapped his hands together, as if dusting them of dirt.

Charlotte linked an arm in his. "Do you think maybe you can relax a bit now?" When he said nothing for several seconds, she said, "Paul?"

"There's one more person I want to talk to."

"Who?"

"Gabriella Hoffman," he said, and saw the doubt in his wife's eyes.

"What can that possibly accomplish?"

"Locking that typewriter in a box doesn't mean I don't still have questions."

"I don't know, Paul. Maybe this has been a mistake. Maybe you need to put all this behind you, stop dredging up everything." She glanced at the blanket box weighed down with the boxes of books. "I never should have bought that thing."

"What if you were *meant* to buy it?" Paul asked.

"What are you saying?"

"What if this is all part of some plan?"

Charlotte looked away, not wanting to listen.

"Hear me out. Whatever the reason for those messages, it's possible that typewriter belonged to Kenneth Hoffman, that this is the machine he forced those women to write their apologies on. What are the odds you'd be drawn to that very yard sale, find that very machine, by chance? To buy something linked to someone I know, to an issue I'd already been thinking I might write about? What are the odds of that?"

Quietly, Charlotte said, "Long."

"Exactly. Incalculably long. But it's a lot more believable if it was somehow preordained. What if there were some sort of force leading you to it?"

"Jesus, Paul. What force? Whose plan?"

"I don't know. Did you find out whose house it was?"

"I told you, I've made calls but haven't heard back yet."

"Maybe it doesn't even matter. Maybe we're not meant to know. The typewriter just *is*. It has no history other than what Hoffman made them write on it. It lives in that *moment*."

"It's like a *Twilight Zone* episode."

Paul couldn't help but laugh at that. "No shit. But I think I'm meant, for whatever reason, to pursue this. And that means talking to Gabriella, and ultimately, Kenneth, who can—"

"Wait, hold it. Kenneth?"

"In prison. I want to talk to him in prison. Maybe Gabriella could expedite that process, if she's willing."

"Why would she?"

"Maybe she won't. But it's worth a try." He took hold of Charlotte's shoulders. "Who knows. Maybe she's as desperate for answers as we are."

"I'll come with you."

He shook his head. "No, it's okay. I think this is something I have to do alone."

Charlotte looked less sure. "I'm worried about you. Out there, asking questions that seem . . ."

"Insane."

She sighed with resignation. They crossed the garage to the door that would take them back into the house. As Paul closed it, he took one final look at the blanket box, then turned off the light.

Thirty-Five

"I was afraid maybe you wouldn't want to see me," Paul said to Gabriella Hoffman.

"Not at all," she said, opening the door for him. "It would seem the least I can do."

Instead of dropping in as he had done with the others he'd wanted to talk to about Kenneth, Paul phoned Gabriella first. She had not asked what it was about, which led Paul to wonder whether she'd always expected he would call, someday.

While Paul and Kenneth had been colleagues, Paul had never been in the Hoffman home. It was a stately two-story in north Milford, set back from the road. Paul was expecting some level of inattention, not necessarily along the lines of Gilford Lamb's place, but when tragedy strikes a household, sometimes other things slide.

But the yard was beautifully maintained. Blooming flower gardens, perfectly trimmed shrubs. He parked alongside a black Toyota RAV4, rang the bell, and was admitted.

Gabriella, tall, thin, with silvery hair that came down to her shoulders, was described as forty-nine years old in the Gwen Stainton article, but she looked older. Despite that, she looked fit, and held her chin high, as though she had nothing in the world to be ashamed about.

She said they'd be more comfortable talking in the kitchen, and led him there. She offered coffee from a half-full carafe and set two mugs on the table. They sat across from each other.

"Many times, I've thought about getting in touch with you," she said.

"You have?"

She nodded. "When you discover you've been married to a monster, you can't help but feel responsible for some of the monstrous things he's done."

"I'm not blaming you. It's never occurred to me to do that."

Gabriella smiled and touched his hand. "That's kind of you. The truth is, I never found the courage to approach you. And as much as I've wanted to offer condolences, something, anything, to Harold or Gilford, I have to admit that I haven't the courage there, either. What would I say? Can I make it all up to them by bringing over a dozen home-baked muffins? I think not. Several times I've tried to write letters to them, and to you, but every time I end up tossing them into the garbage."

Paul did not know what to say.

Gabriella continued, "I was reading one time about a case in Canada. A respected military man who turned out to be a serial killer, and his wife had absolutely no idea. I think about her, and wonder, how does she get up every day, knowing she lived with someone like that, that she didn't see it, and that if she had, maybe she could have done something about it?"

"I can't imagine."

"What Kenneth did wasn't quite as horrific as that, but my God, it came pretty close. If there is anything to be grateful for, it's that you survived."

"Well," Paul said, "I guess there's that."

She put a hand on his arm. "I think we met a few times at faculty events."

"We did."

"Did you know?"

Paul felt a jolt. "Did I know what?"

"That Kenneth was sleeping with anyone who'd let him into her pants?"

The bluntness threw him for a second. He was ashamed by the answer he was to give. "Yes." He paused.

"I suppose everyone did."

"I can't speak for everyone, but I think it's likely," he said. "Now, sitting here, I feel somehow complicit, too. It's not in my nature to be judgmental, but maybe if I'd called Kenneth out on what he was doing, it might have made a difference."

"Oh, I didn't mean to make you feel guilty. I just wondered. Don't feel badly. I certainly knew."

"You did?"

"Oh please," she said. "I knew there was the odd one here and there. I knew what kind of man he was. Although, carrying on with two at the same time, that came as something of a surprise."

"Yes, I suppose it did."

She placed her palms on the table and straightened her spine, as though signaling a change in the conversation's direction. "Kenneth spoke of you often. In fact, he still does."

Paul's eyebrows rose. "Really?"

She nodded. "I visit him every couple of weeks. The man does feel, whether we choose to believe it or not, remorseful. I think he feels especially bad about you. You were a good friend."

"I don't know which I'm more surprised by. That he would mention me, or that you visit him in prison."

"He's still my husband."

"You've never—forgive me, this is probably none of my business—but you've never taken any steps to end the marriage? The affairs alone would be cause for divorce, but since Kenneth did what he did . . ."

As Paul asked the question, it struck him where, exactly, he was sitting.

He was in the kitchen of the Hoffman home. This was where it had happened. His eyes wandered down to the table. Could this be the same one? Was this where the typewriter had sat? Was the chair he was sitting in the one Jill Foster had been bound to? Or Catherine Lamb?

What must it have taken to clean this place up after he'd slit their throats? Was there still blood buried in the grains of this wooden table's surface? Was this where two women pleaded for their lives, where they hoped that a couple of typewritten apologies might save them?

"Paul?" Gabriella asked.

"I'm sorry, what?"

"It looked as though I'd lost you there."

"My mind, it drifted there for a second. What did you say?"

"You were the one talking. You were wondering why I haven't divorced Kenneth."

"I'm sorry. It's none of my business."

She smiled. "As difficult as it may be to imagine, he's a victim, too. A victim of his own impulses. Since he's been in prison . . . he's tried to take his own life. At least once that I know of. Kenneth is my husband. For better or for worse. That was the vow I took. Vows mean something, you know."

"Kenneth took those same vows. About being faithful and forsaking all others."

Gabriella smiled sadly. "He wasn't very good at sticking to those, was he?"

Paul felt a shiver.

"What about the house," he said. "Have you thought of selling it, moving away from Milford?"

"Good luck with that," she said. "Your wife, she works in real estate, doesn't she?"

"Yes."

"She'd probably know all about how hard it is to sell a house where something horrific has happened. In time, maybe, but what Kenneth did, it's far too fresh in people's minds." She paused. "For me, it always will be."

She took a sip of her coffee, set down the mug. "So what was so important that you needed to see me?"

Best to come right out with it.

"I'd like to see Kenneth."

"Oh?"

"I thought it might help if you spoke to him, paved the way, had him put me on a list of accepted visitors."

She considered the request for a moment, then said, "I don't suppose that would be a problem, but I have to ask. Why?"

"At first, I wanted to see him just"—he shrugged—"to talk to him. These past eight months—and I know they've been very difficult for you—but they have been pretty hard on me. I guess what I have is PTSD, post-traumatic stress disorder. I've had recurring nightmares, bouts of memory loss. Even . . . moments where I may be perceiving things I believe are real, but they're not."

Gabriella eyed him with sympathetic wonder. "Oh my, that's awful, but do you think seeing him will help you with any of that?"

"I do. I might be totally wrong, but I do. I think coming face-to-face with him, of turning him back into an actual person, instead of some kind of demon that comes to me in the night, may help."

If she was offended by having her husband referred to as a demon, she didn't show it.

"I'm writing about what happened to me. I don't know what it'll turn into. A memoir, a novel, or maybe just something I write for myself that'll never be read by another living soul. But I think the process is helping me come to terms with what happened. I've been talking to the others touched by Kenneth's actions."

Gabriella put a hand to her mouth. "Oh, dear. You mean, like Harold and—"

"Yes."

She appeared to be deflating. "What have they said to you? How—no, don't tell me. I don't think I'm ready to hear it."

"I understand."

Gabriella took a second to collect herself. "You're seeing a therapist, I presume."

"I am."

"Does he think it's a good idea?"

"She. She's not convinced it's a good idea, but she's not stopping me. In fact, I want to take her with me, if I am able to get in to see Kenneth."

"Well," she said. "You said, *at first*. Is there another reason you want to see him?"

"Before I answer that, I want to ask you something else, something that may seem strange."

"Go ahead."

"Do you ever feel . . . haunted by the women Kenneth killed?"

Her head cocked slightly, as though no one had ever asked her this before. "I suppose I do."

"In what way?"

"I don't know . . . I guess sometimes, I can see them, at this table. Asking me why."

Paul nodded. "Yes. When you see them, how real are they?"

"Far too real. I mean, even though I never saw what happened, I can imagine it, sadly." Gabriella sharpened her focus on him. "Why do you ask?"

Here we go.

"I think it's possible," Paul said, "that I have the typewriter."

Gabriella's face froze.

"I'm sorry, what?"

"I think I have it. The typewriter Kenneth made them write their apologies on."

"That's not possible. The typewriter was never found. How could you have it? Kenneth got rid of it the night of the murders. The police never found it. No, that's simply not possible."

Before he could tell her more, she asked: "What kind of typewriter is it? Describe it."

"It's an Underwood. Very old. Black metal. You know. An antique manual typewriter. My wife acquired it recently at a yard sale."

She appeared to be trying to remember. "It's funny, you see it sitting around the house every day, and now I'm trying to think, was it a Royal? A Remington? An Olympia? All names I remember from my childhood. But I think, yes, I think it's possible our old typewriter was an Underwood. But there are millions of them. You can find one in almost any secondhand shop. What would make you think it was ours?"

Paul had thought about how he would answer. "That's something I would be prepared to discuss with Kenneth."

"You should tell me." Her face darkened. "After all I've endured with that man, surely I'm entitled to know whatever you're holding back."

"I'd like to tell Kenneth first. If he wants to tell you what I've told him, I have no problem with that."

She didn't look pleased with that, but she didn't fight him. She did appear ready to ask him something else, but they were interrupted by what sounded like a truck pulling up to the house.

"My son's home," she said.

"Can you get in touch with Kenneth and ask him if he'll see me?"

Gabriella stood up, evidently eager to greet her son. "I'll see what I can do. Sometimes these things can be arranged more easily than you think. And what's the name of the person you want to take with you?"

Paul told her. She nodded and started walking toward the front door.

It opened before she got to it. Leonard Hoffman, still in his ice cream–stained apron, came into the house.

He looked at Paul and said, "You."

Thirty-Six

"Hello, Leonard," Paul said.

Gabriella was startled. "You know each other?"

"This is the bad man I told you about," Leonard said.

"Wait, what?" she said.

"Leonard sells ice cream on our street quite often," Paul said defensively. "Earlier today, I admit, I mentioned to him that there was, well, a connection."

Gabriella looked as disappointed as she was angry. "Why would you do that? Why would you drag my son into this? Don't you think he's suffered enough from what his father has done?"

"I'm sorry, I—"

"He called me saying some man asked about his father, but I had no idea it was you."

Paul looked apologetically at Leonard. "I'm sorry. I didn't mean to upset you."

"Leonard, why don't you go in and have a snack while I see this man out."

Leonard hesitated, not sure that he was ready to be dismissed. But finally he said, "Okay." He glanced over his shoulder, adding, "Don't come back here again." He disappeared into the kitchen.

"Really, I'm sorry," Paul said to Gabriella.

"Something we never got to," she said, keeping her voice low, "was how hard this has been on Len."

"I can well imagine that—"

"No, you can't. Len's not been the easiest boy in the world to raise. He's got his share of difficulties, but say what you will about Kenneth, he loves his son and was always there for him."

"What's Leonard's—"

"If you were going to say 'problem,' Leonard doesn't have a problem. He was always just a little slower than the other kids, but there's nothing wrong with him. He might not have been college material, but he's got this job now driving that ice cream truck and that's done the world for how he feels about himself. Can you imagine what it's been like for him having a father go to jail for what he did? I just thank God he's years out of school. The other kids would have tormented him to death."

"I should go," Paul said.

"Maybe you should."

But Paul hadn't moved toward the door, and Gabriella guessed why. "I'll still do it for you. I'll get in touch with Kenneth, and the prison."

"Thank you. Can I give you my cell number?"

She went for a pen and a piece of paper. When she returned he gave it to her and she wrote it down.

"Okay," she said.

"When I talked to Leonard," Paul said hesitantly, "he said it was my fault."

"What?"

"Because I came upon Kenneth. Because maybe if I hadn't, Kenneth would have been gone by the time the police came."

"Does that surprise you?" she asked. "I think, at some level, Leonard can't believe it's true. That there must be some sort of extenuating circumstances. His father couldn't have done what they said he's done."

Paul nodded. "Thank you for your time, Gabriella."

IT WAS NEARLY TEN WHEN PAUL GOT HOME.

He locked the front door once he was inside. As he was about to climb the steps upward, his gaze was drawn to the door to the garage.

Paul reached out for the doorknob, but then pulled his hand back.

There's no need to check, he told himself.

But the longer he stood in that spot, the more he knew he was going to have to prove it to himself. It was like going back into the house to make sure you'd turned off the stove. You knew you'd done it, you knew it was off, but you had to *know*.

He turned back the bolt on the door, opened it, and reached his hand around to flick on the light. He stepped around the various boxes and pieces of furniture until he was in the far corner of the garage, where the cartons of books were piled atop the wooden blanket box.

This is crazy, he told himself. *Of course it's in there.*

He held his breath, listening. If the keys were tapping away in that box, he'd surely hear them.

And he was hearing nothing.

Which was a good sign, right?

And even if there had been anything going on in that box since Paul put the typewriter in there, he had not left any paper in it. So the machine wouldn't be able to do any communicating.

No, wait.

Not true.

What about those sheets of paper scattered all over the kitchen? How in the fuck had *that* happened?

How did countless sheets get rolled into the typewriter? And how the hell did they get pulled out?

Paul began moving the cartons of books off the blanket box. Once he had it cleared off, he knelt down, slipped his hand into the groove under the lid to allow him to lift it up easily.

Just do it.

Lift it up and look inside.

Paul took a deep breath, and brought the lid up.

"Paul!"

"Jesus!" he shouted, dropping the lid and whirling around. His heart jackhammered in his chest.

The interior door to the garage was open about a foot, Charlotte's head poking in.

"What are you doing?" she said. "I thought I heard you come in, but then you didn't come upstairs."

"You scared me half to death," he said, still kneeling.

"What's going on?"

"Nothing," he said. "I was . . . checking. That's all."

He turned back to the blanket box and lifted the lid, casting light down into it.

The typewriter was there. There was no paper rolled into it, no other paper to be found, not counting the stacks of old magazines.

Paul swallowed, lowered the lid, and stood.

"Well?" Charlotte asked.

"It's here," he said.

"Well, of course it is. For God's sake, come to bed."

He nodded sheepishly and walked across the garage, hit the light, and closed the door as he went back into the house.

Thirty-Seven

Paul was in front of his laptop when his cell phone rang shortly after noon the following day. It was Gabriella Hoffman.

"It's set up for tomorrow," she told him. "For both of you."

"I can't thank you enough," he said. "He's willing to see me?"

"He is."

Then he called Anna White and told her they were set for a prison visit with Kenneth Hoffman, if she was still interested in coming.

"Yes," she said without hesitation. She would have to clear her schedule for the day, and make sure that she could get Rosie, a retired nurse who lived next door who often checked in on her father whenever Anna had to be away for any length of time.

"Why don't I drive," she said.

Paul was going to ask why, then figured, if he were dealing with someone who'd suffered a head injury and from all indications was borderline delusional, he'd want to be the one behind the wheel, too.

"Okay," he said. "I'll come to your place, then we'll head up in your car."

"WAS THERE EVER ANY TALK OF CHARLOTTE COMING WITH US?" ANNA asked as they backed out of her driveway. The prison facility where Kenneth Hoffman was serving his time was near Waterbury. Anna figured it would take the better part of an hour to get there. She entered its address into the in-dash GPS system on her Lincoln SUV.

They'd start out by taking Derby-Milford Road up to Highway 34, jogging west, then heading north on 8.

"She knew I was trying to arrange a visit with Kenneth, but when she knew you'd agreed to go with me, she thought that was best. She told me she came to see you."

Anna glanced over. "I told her she should. There was no reason to keep it a secret. She's worried about you."

Paul nodded. "More now than ever."

"Well, you are going through more now than you were before."

"It's not just that," he said. "She just seems . . . more caring. In between moments where she thinks I'm totally nuts. Anyway, she decided to take a day herself and get out of town. Her mother's in Tribeca, and she hasn't been into the city to visit her in weeks. They're not that close, actually, so I was a little surprised, but anyway, I dropped her off at the station this morning. Knowing Charlotte, she'll also make time to hit Bloomingdale's before catching the train home. I don't know when we'll be back so I told her to take a cab home from the station."

Anna swerved too late to miss a pothole. A loud, metallic rattle came from the rear cargo area. It sounded like it was inside the vehicle. Before Paul could ask, Anna said, "Golf clubs."

"Oh. You play?"

"Some. Every time I play there's at least one club missing. My dad keeps taking them so he can hit some balls in the backyard and never puts them back." She changed topics. "What are you really hoping to get out of this? Seeing Kenneth?"

"I'm not going in with any expectations. I guess I'll see how it goes."

She noticed a manila envelope on his lap. "What's in there?"

"Something I want to show him, if they'll let me."

"You want to show me?"

He slid several pages out of the envelope. They were the messages he had found in the typewriter and scattered across the floor.

Anna glanced over several times as Paul leafed through them for her. "I simply don't know what to make of them, Paul."

"They're proof," he said.

"Of what, exactly?"

He glanced at her. "Maybe you think they're proof that I've gone mad. I think they're proof that Jill and Catherine Lamb are trying to reach me."

Anna decided not to respond.

They drove a few more miles in silence until Paul said, "Tell me about Frank, about your father."

"Well, he's a wonderful man. A retired animator. Worked for Warner Bros., actually knew Walt Disney. Still watches cartoons every single day. He's been living with me since my mother passed away. The last year or so, things have . . . started to happen. Confusion. Sometimes he thinks I'm my mom, his wife. Other times he wants me to take him to visit her. I fear we're on a slippery slope."

"It happens," Paul said.

Her lips compressed before she spoke. "He's been a great help to me for so long. He's been telling me I need to find a place for him. Like he's worried about being a burden to me." The lips pressed tightly together again, as if somehow that would ward off tears. "Says there's no reason for me to be keeping him around."

"Is he laying a guilt trip on you?"

"It's not like that at all. He's genuinely worried about me." She let out a short laugh. "Wants me to get *out there*. You know what he called this trip of ours, to a prison? A fun outing."

Paul laughed.

Anna was silent for a moment. Then, "I don't know what I'm going to do. I mean, eventually. We're managing okay now, but in six months? Hard to say. That visit from the SWAT team shook him up badly." She looked his way and smiled. "You would be amazed at how many therapists' lives are a complete mess. We offer advice to others on how to get their shit together when our own is a total disaster." She laughed self-deprecatingly. "We're the evangelists who get caught with a prostitute while preaching morality to the masses."

Paul smiled.

Anna continued, "We're just people. We're just people like anyone else, with a fancy piece of paper on the wall. At the end of the day, we have the same doubts as anyone else. Are we making any progress? Are we making a difference? Are we really any help to anyone at all?"

"You've helped me," he said.

Her mouth formed a jagged smile. "I hope so. And yet here we are, driving off to meet with a murderer. For the life of me, I don't know that this is going to do you an ounce of good."

"It's a journey into the unknown for us both."

"Yeah, well, I wish this GPS could tell us if we're doing the right thing."

Paul looked at her hands gripping the steering wheel. He didn't see any bandage.

"How's the finger?" he asked.

She flashed him a smile. "It healed up nicely, thank you."

A warm feeling washed over Paul. He wanted to touch Anna, rest his hand on her arm ever so slightly. Make a physical connection, no matter how small. He recalled holding her hand under the running water, their shoulders touching.

THEY BARELY SAID A WORD THE NEXT HALF AN HOUR. NOT UNTIL THE GPS voice advised Anna to take the next exit off the highway. A few more miles, and a few more turns later, they spotted a facility in the distance surrounded by an unusually tall metal fence with thick coils of barbed wire strung along the top.

"Doesn't look much like a day care center," Anna said.

"No," Paul said. He turned and looked at her as the car approached the gate. "All of a sudden, I'm not sure this is a good idea."

"You don't have to do this," Anna said. "I can turn around and take us back."

Paul pressed his lips tightly together. "We're here," he said. "Might as well check the place out. If they send me here for what I did to Hitchens, maybe Kenneth and I will end up as roommates."

Thirty-Eight

Charlotte had not lied to Paul about going into Manhattan. She hadn't even lied about going to visit her mother. She intended to do that, if she had time. And Paul was right when he had joked as he'd dropped her off at the Milford station that she would try to find time to visit Bloomingdale's.

But she was not going into New York for either of those reasons.

When she got off the train and entered Grand Central Terminal, she exited through the market and flagged down a cab almost immediately on Lexington.

"Sixty-Third and Park," she said as she closed the door.

The taxi moved south, the unshaven, overweight man behind the wheel steering over to the left lane to make a turn onto Forty-First Street. One long block later, he went north on Third while Charlotte struggled with muting the annoying mini–TV screen bolted to the partition in front of her.

"Nice day," the driver said.

Charlotte was not interested in small talk.

Traffic, as always, was heavy, but fifteen minutes later the taxi was slowing on Sixty-Third with Park only half a block away. "Where 'bouts?" the driver asked.

"Anywhere here," she said. "Just pull over."

The cab aimed for the left side of the street. Charlotte slid a ten and two ones into the tray below the Plexiglas divider and got out. As she hit the sidewalk she glanced up to check the numbers. She had never actually been to this address before, but she knew, from checking Google Maps early that morning, that her destination had to be practically right in front of her.

Then she saw the sign.

BENJAMIN MARKETING

It was a subtle bronze marker, not much bigger than a license plate, affixed to the side of a building at eye level, next to a set of revolving doors. Charlotte pushed through and found herself in a small, marble foyer. A security guard at the front desk looked up.

"Help you?"

"Here to see Hailey Benjamin," she said, knowing there was probably no need to add the name of the firm.

"A moment," he said, picking up a phone.

Charlotte had figured this would happen. She was waiting for the question.

"Name?" the guard asked, looking at her.

"Charlotte Davis."

The guard repeated the name into the phone, hung up, and said, "Go on up. Sixteenth floor."

Charlotte got onto the elevator, imagining what Hailey's reaction must have been when she was told who was here to see her. She'd be so dumbfounded the wife of her ex-husband was in the building that she'd hardly refuse to see her just because she didn't have an appointment.

As the elevator passed the fourth floor, Charlotte wondered whether Hailey would notify her husband, Walter, that she was here. Walter Benjamin was the president of Benjamin Marketing, and while his wife technically worked for him, it was, from everything Charlotte had heard, more of a partnership.

When the elevator doors parted on the sixteenth floor, Hailey was standing there in front of the wall with the firm's name stretched out over twenty feet in big blue letters.

"Charlotte," she said, saying the word as a half welcome, half question.

"Hailey," she said.

"Taking a day off to see the city?" Hailey said, forcing a smile.

"Something like that. Is there someplace we could talk?"

"Uh, sure. What's this about? Has something happened? Is everything okay?"

"Let's get settled first."

Hailey said something quietly to the man on the reception desk before leading Charlotte down a glass hallway to a door labeled CONFERENCE ROOM B.

Inside was a rectangular glass table big enough to sit a dozen people. Hailey pulled out a chrome-and-black-leather chair for Charlotte before sitting herself in the one next to her.

"Can I get you something? Sparkling water? A cappuccino?"

"No," Charlotte said. "Hailey, I know you and I have not exactly been best friends over the years."

Hailey said nothing, waited.

"But this isn't about me. This is about Paul. I know there's got to be some part of you that still cares about him, and—"

"Of course I care about Paul," Hailey said. "Just because things didn't work out between us doesn't mean I have no feelings for him. We had a child together, for God's sake. What's going on? Is he okay? Is he sick? Is this about what happened?"

"Yes . . . and no. He's not himself. He's—he's believing in things that don't make any sense."

"Like?"

"First of all, he's hearing things."

"What do you mean? Do you mean *voices*? Paul's hearing voices?"

"Not exactly," Charlotte said. "But—"

The door opened. A tall, gray-haired man in a dark blue suit, open-collared white shirt, and no tie stepped in.

"Charlotte?"

"Walter," Charlotte said.

She started to stand, but he raised two palms, as though he could keep her in her seat through some invisible force. "Please, don't get up. How nice to see you. Is something wrong with Paul?"

"Why would you ask that?" Charlotte asked, her voice tinged with suspicion.

"I just—" He cut himself off, looked at Hailey.

"I told Walter you were heading up in the elevator," Hailey said, "and all we could think was that Paul was in some sort of trouble. Has he been back to see the neurologist? Is that what this is about?"

"He hasn't," Charlotte said. "It's a different issue than that. I came here because, I think you need to know that Paul is going through a very difficult time, and I don't know that I can handle it all alone."

Hailey shrugged hopelessly. "Tell me about these voices he's hearing."

"Jesus, hearing voices?" Walter said.

"I never said voices," Charlotte said. "More like sounds, in the night, sounds I don't hear."

"It's a good thing you're telling us this," Walter said. "Thank you."

Charlotte shot him a look. "Thank you?"

"Well, it's good to know," he said. "Because of Josh." Walter glanced at his wife. "Right? If there's something wrong with Paul, we need to know."

"What's that supposed to mean?" Charlotte asked.

Hailey looked apologetically at Charlotte. "It's just, well, if Paul is unstable, I mean, that's something we'd have to take into account when it's your turn to have Josh."

"There's nothing wrong with me," Charlotte said. "And I'm not suggesting Paul's *dangerous*."

"Of course not," Hailey said earnestly. "But I can't help but be concerned about the environment Josh is in. It could be very troubling to him, to be there if his father is having . . . episodes. He was very upset after his last visit to your house."

Charlotte slowly shook her head.

Walter was nodding, as though he'd seen this coming all along. "We know that what's happened with Paul isn't his fault. He didn't ask that man to attack him. It's a terrible tragedy, all the way around. But we have to deal with the fallout from that, whether it's fair or not."

"I don't believe this," Charlotte said.

"Well, if he's delusional," Walter said, "it's simply out of the question that Josh can be spending any unsupervised time with him."

"I have to agree with Walter," Hailey said.

Charlotte pushed her chair back and stood.

"Nice to know you're all so very concerned," she said.

"No, Charlotte, please," Hailey protested, placing a hand on Charlotte's arm. Charlotte shook it off.

"I came here looking for some help, or failing that, some sympathy, maybe even a shred of insight," she said. "But look what you're doing. Seizing on Paul's misfortune as an opportunity to keep sole custody of Josh."

"That's ridiculous," Hailey said.

"How dare you," Walter chimed in.

"That's what you'd like, isn't it? Full custody. Force Paul right out of his son's life. In his current state, he needs the love of his son more than ever. He needs to know people love him."

"That's absurd," Hailey said. "I would never do that to Josh, or to his father."

"Seems to be exactly what you're proposing. Maybe it'd make your whole life easier if Paul just did go ahead and kill himself."

Hailey gasped and recoiled. "Where did that come from? How could you say such a thing? Is Paul *suicidal*?"

Charlotte burst into tears. "I don't know! I hardly know anything anymore." She quickly pulled herself together. "All I'm saying is, it *would* make it simpler for you." She fixed her eyes on Walter. "Then you could stop bitching and moaning about getting stuck on the FDR while coming out to Milford."

"I think it's time for you to leave, Charlotte," Walter said.

"I couldn't agree more."

As Charlotte moved for the door to the conference room, she stopped, as if she'd forgotten something.

She looked at Hailey.

"How did you let yourself in the other day?" she said.

"What?"

"Into our house. You had the door open before anyone could get down there to open it for you. Do you have a key? Did you make a copy of Josh's?"

"What on earth are you implying?" Hailey asked.

Charlotte left without saying another word to either of them.

Thirty-Nine

P aul and Anna were not allowed to take much of anything into the main prison area. Car keys, purse, wallet, even spare change, all had to be checked. The guard asked what was in Paul's envelope and he said "papers." The guard flipped open the end of the envelope and peered inside long enough to see it did, in fact, contain papers and nothing else—Paul wondered if he was expecting to find a couple of joints in there—but did not pull them out far enough to see what was typed on them. Paul was allowed to keep them.

"You got lucky," Anna whispered to him as they were led through two sets of gates.

It had been arranged for them to meet with Kenneth Hoffman in a room separate from the common visiting area. Paul had never set foot in a prison before—Anna said she'd been on a couple of "field trips" to correctional institutions during her training—and he found himself trying to take in everything along the way to their appointment. The cinder block walls painted pale green, the clang of gates closing, the smell of desperate men. It felt, in some strange way, like a high school, except instead of windows, there were bars, and instead of young kids bouncing off the walls, there were people without hope.

Plus, there was the feeling that at any moment, someone would stick a shiv in your side.

Paul had a dozen questions for the guard—the man was built like an armoire—leading them through the prison. Had there ever been a riot? Had anyone escaped? Did people really try to hide metal files inside cakes? But not wanting to look like an idiot, he kept all the questions to himself.

"Here we go," the guard said as they reached a metal door with a small, foot-square window at eye level. He unlocked it and showed them into a drab, gray space about ten by ten feet. The only things in there, aside from a camera mounted up by the ceiling in one corner, were a table and three chairs—two on one side, one on the other. Paul noted the metal ring bolted to the top of the table, and brackets that attached the table legs to the floor with bolts.

"Have a seat," the guard said, motioning to the two chairs that were side by side. "I'll be back." He left, closing the door behind him.

They sat.

After three minutes, Paul looked at Anna and said, "I hope they don't forget we're here."

Eight minutes after that, the door reopened. The guard stepped in, followed by Kenneth Hoffman.

Paul stood and took in his one-time friend, stunned by what he saw. Dressed in a short-sleeved, one-piece orange coverall, Hoffman would probably have been six feet tall, but he had become round-shouldered, as though an invisible boulder were perched at the back of his neck. And a man who had once come in at around 180 pounds didn't look much more than 150. His arms were thin and ropy, and beneath his scrawny gray beard—Paul had always known Hoffman to be clean-shaven—his cheeks were hollow. He'd lost much of his hair, his pink scalp visible through wisps of gray.

All this in eight months.

But what struck Paul most were Hoffman's eyes. There was no sparkle, no depth to them. It was as though they were layered with wax paper.

Dead eyes.

"Paul," Hoffman said, his voice low and leaden.

"Kenneth," Paul said. He was going to extend a hand, but they'd been cautioned about no physical contact.

"And you are?" Hoffman said, looking at a still-seated Anna.

"Dr. Anna White," she said.

"A head doctor, I understand," he said. He smiled, showing off teeth tinged with brown. "You're not here to give me a rectal exam."

"Sit down," the guard said. As he slipped out the door, he said to Paul and Anna, "Need anything, just shout."

Hoffman sat. He hadn't taken his eyes off Anna since she'd introduced herself.

"It seems like the dumbest thing in the world to ask," Paul said, "but all I can think of is, how are things?"

Kenneth smiled weakly. "Just lovely."

"Thanks for seeing us," Paul said.

"I don't get a lot of visitors," he said, and shrugged. "Nice to break the monotony. And you're the first one from West Haven to see me." Kenneth shook his head. "I would have thought you'd have been the absolute last. How are things there?"

"I haven't gone back yet," Paul said. "I've been on a leave." He said it without a hint of irony.

"Oh, yes," Kenneth said. "That." He looked Paul straight in the eyes. "If you've come here looking for an apology, you can have one."

Paul glanced at Anna. Her eyebrows went up a tenth of an inch. She knew Paul was not necessarily expecting one, and even if he had been, she figured he wouldn't have been expecting it this quickly.

"I'm sorry you got dragged into my mess," Kenneth said. "I mean, I did what I felt I had to do at the time, but I wish it hadn't happened that way." He paused. "If I was going to be caught anyway, I'm glad you lived." He smiled wryly. "Getting rid of two bodies was going to be hard enough, but three? I'd have probably died from a heart attack digging a third grave." He smiled, turned over his hands to show his palms. "If not that, the calluses would have been brutal."

Paul sat with his hands clasped in front of him and smiled. "It's nice to catch up."

Anna had spotted something on the inside of Kenneth's left wrist, what looked like a fresh scar.

"I was surprised to hear that Gabriella visits you," Paul said.

"She's a saint, she is."

"I might have thought she'd want nothing to do with you."

Kenneth shrugged. "Go figure." He smiled sardonically. "It must be the hypnotic hold I have over women, even those I've wronged." He looked at Anna. "What do you think?"

"Even Charles Manson had his admirers," she said evenly.

"Ooh, that stings," he said. He looked down at the envelope on the table, and then to Paul. "So why are you here?"

"Three reasons, I guess," he said slowly, building up to it. "It's been a rough eight months. There's the physical recovery of course. That's been hard enough. But there's the mental one, too. You haunt me, Kenneth. You come to me more nights than not. I've been looking for ways to deal with that, and believed one way would be to meet with you. To sit down with you. To remind myself that you're not some, I don't know, all-powerful evil force, but just a man. Nothing more. And seeing you here has helped me already. You're a shell of what you used to be. You don't look like you'd be much of a threat to anyone." Paul leaned forward. "You're broken, Kenneth. You're a sad, broken man who's tried to take his own life. So tonight, when I go to sleep, that's the image of you I'll take with me. Not the man who tried to kill me, but a pitiful, beaten man."

Kenneth held Paul's gaze. "Glad to be able to help in that regard. Number two?"

"I wanted to ask why. Why did a man I thought I knew do something so utterly horrible? What happened?" Paul tapped his own temple. "What snapped in here to make you do what you did? Or do you even know?"

Kenneth appeared to take the question seriously. "You don't think I've asked myself that question a thousand times since it happened? You know what I think? I think that inside of all of us—

you, me, even you, Dr. White—is a devil just dying to break out. Most of us, we know how to keep him penned up. We lock him away in a personal jail with bars of morality. But sometimes, he's able to pry those bars apart, just enough to slip out. And if he's been in there a long time, when he does get out, he wants to make up for lost time." He smiled. "Does that answer your question?"

"No," Paul said. "But it's probably as close as we're going to get."

Kenneth smiled. "And number three?"

Anna glanced over at Paul and the envelope under his palm.

Paul said, "Remember yard sales? Driving around the neighborhood, people putting out all their junk to sell."

"Of course. I haven't been in here forever."

"Charlotte picked up something interesting the other day at a sale in Milford."

"Okay."

"An old typewriter. An Underwood."

Kenneth blinked. "So?"

"It was an Underwood that you made Catherine and Jill type their apologies on, wasn't it?"

"Yeah," Hoffman said. "It was."

"I'm going to tell you a story you're not going to believe, but I don't care. You may laugh, but I don't give a shit. The typewriter that's sitting in my house is, I'm certain, the typewriter you made Catherine and Jill use before you killed them."

Hoffman leaned back in his chair and crossed his arms. He looked dumbstruck for several seconds, then chuckled.

"That's not possible," he said. "It was never found."

"Well, someone found it. Not the police, I grant you that. But someone found it."

"Bullshit. I tossed it into a Dumpster. It would have been picked up the next day. It's long gone. It's buried in a landfill."

"No," Paul said.

He turned back the flap on the envelope and pulled out the pages.

He set them out for display, one at a time, for Hoffman to read. He studied each sheet as it was placed before him.

"What the hell are these?"

"Messages. From the women you killed."

Kenneth looked up from the pages into Paul's eyes. "What?"

"They've been showing up in that typewriter. All by themselves."

Kenneth tilted his head to the right, then the left, almost in the manner of a dog that can't make sense of what it's seeing.

"This is some kind of joke."

"Not a joke."

Kenneth laughed, but it sounded forced. "No, really. This"—he tapped his index finger on one of the pages—"is complete and total bullshit."

Paul slowly shook his head. He noticed Anna had leaned back some from the table. This was his show.

"I wish it were a joke. I was skeptical at first, too. I heard the typing in the night, when the only ones in the house were Charlotte and me. I'll admit, I had to consider alternative explanations for a while. One, that someone was breaking in and doing it. Two, that I was losing my mind and writing these myself without even realizing it. But I've discounted both those theories. And I believe Dr. White here is with me on that one, am I right?"

Paul looked at Anna, waiting for a reassuring nod that did not come.

"Anyway," he continued, "I was left with only one possible explanation. That there are powers out there beyond our understanding, and that Catherine and Jill are reaching out. Looking for answers."

"You haven't forgotten what I taught, have you, Paul? Math, physics? I dealt in the world of the rational. And what you're saying is nuts."

"It would be nuts for messages like these to show up in a typewriter that was *not* the one you used."

Kenneth took another look at the pages. He ran his index finger over the typing. "The *h*," he said, little more than a whisper.

"It's slightly off center," Paul said. "And the *o* is a bit faint. Do you remember that from your Underwood?"

Kenneth seemed to be struggling to recall.

"I think I know what's going on," he said.

Paul and Anna waited.

"You and your shrink here are running some kind of game on me. I don't know what it is, exactly, and I have no idea why, but that'd be the theory I'd go with, because I am telling you, one hundred percent, that this is a crock of shit."

"Why?" Paul asked. "Why isn't it just possible something's going on here that's beyond our understanding?"

Kenneth flattened his palms on the table and weighed his response. "I told you. The typewriter. I threw it away."

"Someone must have spotted it in the garbage," Paul said. "Before the trash was picked up. Had no idea how it got there, didn't care. And then it wound up in someone's house, and they put it out one day to sell before they moved away from Milford. Tell me it couldn't have happened that way."

For the first time, Kenneth's face registered doubt. "Maybe, just maybe, that's possible. But these notes? That's nuts." He looked down at them one last time.

"What are you looking at?" Paul asked.

"The *e*'s," he said. "They're a bit filled in . . ." Hoffman seemed to be drifting for a moment, then looked up. "The police don't have the typewriter, but they have the notes . . ."

"The notes you made Catherine and Jill write," Paul said, getting ahead of Kenneth's thinking. "Of course. They could compare these pages to the ones they have in evidence. Back in the day, samples of typing were like fingerprints. They could match them to specific machines."

Paul brightened and looked at Anna. "Why did I never think of that? Do you think the police would let us see that evidence?"

"I don't know," Anna said. "They might."

Kenneth did not share Paul's excitement. He asked, "Is there blood on it? Is there blood on the typewriter?"

Paul thought a moment and said, "Not that I've noticed." There was Josh's blood, of course, from when he caught his finger in the machine, but Paul knew that was not worth mentioning. "But there could be traces, I suppose, down between the keys. I guess whoever was selling it did their best to clean it up. I mean, who'd buy a used typewriter that was covered in dried blood?"

Hoffman's forehead wrinkled. His eyes went slowly around the room, then settled back on Paul.

"What are you going to do with it?" he asked. "The Underwood."

"Why?"

Hoffman shook his head angrily. "I just want to know."

Paul shrugged. "I haven't really thought about that. For the time being, it's going to stay in my house."

"Are you going to give it to the police?"

Paul turned to Anna again. "Should I, if it's evidence?"

She shrugged. Before she could answer, Kenneth said, "What's the point? You want to get my fingerprints off it?" Kenneth laughed. "They've got me. You think they want to convict me again? Instead of getting out in a hundred years, it'll be two hundred."

Forty

Neither Paul nor Anna said a word until they were out of the prison and back in the car. Once the doors were closed they let out a collective breath, as though they hadn't taken one for the last couple of hours.

Anna turned to Paul and asked, "How are you? Are you okay?"

"I'm a little shaky," he said, "but yeah, I'm okay. How about you?"

"I'm fine." She found herself smiling, almost against her will. "It was actually kind of exhilarating. Creepy, but exhilarating."

"Is *creepy* a psychological term?"

She laughed. "Pretty much."

"I don't feel . . . scared of him anymore."

"You made that pretty clear."

Paul was quiet for a moment as Anna started the engine and steered the car out of the prison parking lot. "I almost, for a second there, I almost felt sorry for him. When he was talking about how we all have this devil hiding inside us. I thought that almost made sense, in a way."

"Or else it was just an excuse," Anna said. "Listen, I want to apologize for something in there. When you said I'd come to the same conclusion as you had about the source of those notes, I wasn't exactly supportive."

"I noticed."

"I should have said something."

"Maybe I'm the one who should apologize. I presumed when I shouldn't have."

She hesitated. "I don't think Hoffman was convinced those letters were actually written by Catherine and Jill, that two dead women are speaking to you through that typewriter." Another pause. "I'm having a hard time with that, too."

"You aren't willing to consider that there might—just might—be forces at work in the world that are beyond our understanding? You think it's impossible that something like this could happen? Because, for me, I've pretty much exhausted all other options."

Anna kept staring ahead through the windshield. "It'll be almost dark by the time we get home."

"Isn't that what you call avoidance?"

She glanced his way for a second. "I'm going to tell you something I probably shouldn't."

"Okay."

"Twelve years ago, well, going back even further, my mother was not well. It was a long decline. Life's so unfair that way, you know? Sometimes I think it would be so much better if we went just like that." She took a hand off the wheel and snapped her fingers. "None of this lingering. It can be so hard on everyone."

"Sure," Paul said.

"This is something I've never told anyone. Not my father, not any of my friends, not my ex-husband, although we'd split by this time."

Paul nodded. "Okay."

They were back on the main road, picking up speed.

"It was a Tuesday night, just after three in the morning." She stopped, breathed in through her nose, steeling herself. "I was sound asleep. And I heard my mother speak to me. As clearly as you talking to me now. She said, and I'll never forget this, she said, 'It's time to come and say good-bye.' I woke up, and I could still hear her in my head, saying that. I looked at the clock, and it was eleven minutes after three. I don't want to make too much of this, but my mother was born on the eleventh of March."

Paul nodded slowly.

"She was in a hospital chronic care wing at the time. I knew it was irrational, I knew she couldn't actually speak to me like that, but I felt I had to go to the hospital. I threw on some clothes and drove there as quickly as I could and I went to her room."

The car went over a bump and the golf clubs in the back rattled like old bones.

Paul realized he was barely breathing. "What happened?"

"She was awake. She was looking at the door. It was like she was waiting for me to arrive. She smiled and reached out a hand."

Anna put her own hand to her mouth. Paul could see a tear running down her cheek. She needed a moment before she could continue.

"It was so small. Her hand. Just skin and bone. I took it, and she said to me, I swear, she said, 'I'm glad you got my message.' I know it sounds crazy, but that's what happened." She glanced with moist eyes at her passenger. "Pretty nuts, right?"

Paul slowly shook his head. "No. It's not nuts at all."

"And I sat with her, and twenty minutes later, she was gone."

Paul didn't know what to say.

"I called my father, woke him up, told him a lie, that the hospital had called me. That Mom had passed away. I told him I was on my way." She sniffed. "I couldn't tell him the truth."

"No," Paul said, understanding.

"How could I explain that I was there? How could I tell him that she'd gotten in touch with me, and not him? Why didn't she somehow contact my father, too?"

"Maybe she tried," Paul said. "He just didn't hear her."

Anna hit the blinker and steered the car over to the shoulder. Once it had stopped, she put it in park.

"I need a second," she said. "I'm sorry." She allowed the tears to come. She pointed to the glove compartment. Paul opened it, spotted a shallow box of tissues. He pulled out half a dozen and handed them to Anna.

"God, this is so embarrassing," she said as she dabbed her eyes, then blew her nose. She dropped her hands into her lap. "Not to mention unprofessional. I'm the one who's supposed to be keeping it together."

"It's okay."

I can touch her. It's okay.

Paul reached over and placed a hand on hers. Gently, he said, "By not telling your father, that tells me you believe what happened was real."

She looked at him. "Even if I didn't believe it, even if it really was only a dream, and a complete coincidence that I got to the hospital just in time, I couldn't tell my father because *he* might believe it. And think how hurt he would feel. So I could never tell him."

She took her hand out from under Paul's, placed it on top of his, and squeezed. "It's haunted me all these years. It truly has. It was good to finally tell someone."

Paul fought the urge to put an arm around her. He wanted to do it more than anything.

"So," she said, freeing his hand, putting the car back in drive, and checking her mirror to see whether it was safe to pull back onto the road, "I guess the bottom line is, yes, the jury is still out, but I can't tell you that what's been happening to you isn't really happening. I just don't know."

"I understand," he said.

God, I just want to hold her.

But they were back on the road now, Anna pushing down hard on the accelerator. A few miles later, she said, "I think this trip did you some good. If your only takeaway is that Kenneth Hoffman is no longer the boogeyman you'd built him up in your dreams to be, then it was worth it."

"I suppose. And I got to show him those notes. Maybe . . . maybe I was hoping he'd think they were real. If he had, I'd be able to think, okay, I'm not the only one who's starting to believe in the unbelievable."

"I think they rattled him," Anna said. "Although I'm not sure which troubled him more. The notes, or the fact you'd come into possession of what might be his typewriter."

Paul's phone rang. He dug it out of his jacket, saw the caller's name, and frowned.

"What does she want?" he said, more to himself than Anna.

"Who is it?" Anna asked.

Paul put the phone to his ear. "Hailey, is everything okay? Is Josh—what . . . Charlotte came to your office and what . . . yes, I *have* had a hard time, but . . . I know Josh has a key. Why would she . . . okay, okay . . . okay. Thanks for telling me . . . okay . . . good-bye."

He held the phone, made no effort to put it back into his jacket.

"That was weird," he said, staring straight ahead.

"What's happened?"

"Charlotte said she was going to see her mother but she went to see Hailey, supposedly because she was worried about me, and wanted to get Hailey's take. But then there was something about Josh's key, and . . ."

"What is it, Paul?"

He shook his head, as if that might make things come clear. "Something I'll have to talk to Charlotte about when I get home."

Anna decided not to push it. "Okay."

———

ANNA PULLED INTO HER DRIVEWAY NEXT TO PAUL'S CAR AND TURNED off the engine. She glanced up at her father's bedroom window, noticed that the light was on.

"Thanks again for everything," Paul said, pulling on the handle of the passenger door.

"You're welcome. Thank *you*. It was quite a day."

Paul held his position. He looked at Anna and knew, at that moment, what he wanted to do. Something he couldn't. Something he wouldn't.

"Time to go, Paul." She smiled. "See you at our next session."

"Right, of course," he said.

He got out, closed the door, found his keys, and unlocked his car. Anna waited until he was out of the driveway and heading up the street before she got out and went into her house.

———————

DRIVING HOME, PAUL FELT AWASH IN GUILT.

He'd done nothing wrong, he hadn't acted on his feelings, but the fact he'd had them made him remorseful. Just when Charlotte was being so supportive, sticking by him, helping him through the worst crisis of his life, he finds himself attracted to another woman.

He'd spent so much time lately with Anna. He could tell her things he could tell no one else. She listened.

Of course, you idiot. It's her job.

At an intellectual level, Paul knew that. Her concern for him was rooted in professionalism. He'd be a fool to think she felt anything for him that went beyond that.

Except it didn't change how he felt.

He had to push her out of his mind. Any other kind of relationship with Anna White was a nonstarter.

If there was anything Paul needed to work on, to *reward* and *nourish,* it was his life with Charlotte.

Don't make a complicated life even more complicated.

So he struggled to replace thoughts of Anna with a review of his meeting with Kenneth Hoffman.

Had the encounter been helpful? Was Anna right, that if nothing else, seeing Kenneth face-to-face had diminished his stature? He was, indeed, a broken man. Paul thought the days and weeks ahead would be the test of whether seeing Kenneth was a good thing. Would the nightmares fade? Would he stop hearing Kenneth in his head?

He hit the turn signal indicator, turned down his street, then pulled into the driveway behind Charlotte's car.

Well, there was some good news. He actually remembered driving here.

As he wearily got out of his car, it occurred to him he'd had nothing to eat in hours. On the way up, he and Anna had joked about dining on prison food, but once they were inside, they pretty much lost their appetites. He figured Charlotte was home from New York by now. Maybe she'd made dinner and set aside a plate for—

Oh God.

The front door was wide open.

Forty-One

Paul charged into the house, shouting, "Charlotte!"

He threw the door closed behind him and took the stairs up to the kitchen two steps at a time. As he reached the top, Charlotte came around the kitchen island, her face full of alarm.

"What?" she asked.

He put on the brakes. "The door was open. I was worried. I didn't know—"

"I left it open," she said, cutting him off. "You know how you were asking about a surveillance system, getting the locks changed? Well, I found a guy and took the first step today. I'd set up an appointment for late in the day, after I was back from the city. We've got new locks. I'd left the door open a crack so you'd be able to get in. I guess the wind blew it all the way open. God, you're a nervous wreck."

"I'm sorry," he said, glancing back down to the front door to be sure it was closed. "I'll close it now." He scurried down the flight, turned the dead bolt, and returned. Charlotte was standing by the island.

"Give me your keys," she said.

He handed her his set. On the granite countertop was a single key that looked, at a glance, identical to Paul's house key. Charlotte picked up his set and worked the house key off the ring, then replaced it with the new one. She took his old key and tucked it into the front pocket of her jeans.

"You did this because of Hailey?" Paul asked.

"What about Hailey?" Charlotte asked, looking nervous.

"She called me."

"I was gonna tell you," Charlotte said, looking like she'd been caught in a lie. "I knew there was a chance Hailey'd rat me out. But you remember the other day, how she strolled right in here?"

"You don't really think Hailey snuck in here and—"

"I don't know, okay?" she said defensively.

"What did you tell them?"

"I told them I was worried about you. So shoot me. I've been worried sick about you, and honestly, I can't predict what you're going to do next. Not these last few days. Not since I bought that goddamn thing and put it in your think tank."

Paul glanced at the open door to his study, as if to confirm that the typewriter was no longer there. He mentally breathed a sigh of relief to see that it was not. He knew where it was, but he was not going to go into the garage to check this time.

You could take paranoia a little too far.

"Whatever's going on, whatever the cause," Charlotte said cautiously, "I see it driving you to the brink of . . ."

Paul gave her a look.

"Just hear me out here. What if Hailey *is* behind this? She had a key. She could sneak in. What if it's a custody thing? What if she and that smug asshole Walter are somehow setting you up, trying to make you seem mentally unfit, so they could go after sole custody of Josh?"

"No!" he said firmly. "She wouldn't do that! She wouldn't do it to Josh. She wouldn't keep him from me."

"Sometimes," Charlotte said, "you don't know what people are capable of."

Paul sighed, moved his head from side to side sorrowfully. "I just spent the afternoon learning that lesson."

He recounted his prison visit for her.

"Are you glad you did it?" Charlotte asked.

He told her he thought he was, and why.

"Good," she said. "You know what I'd like?"

"What would you like?"

"One night where we don't talk about any of this. Nothing about Hoffman. Nothing about typewriters. Nothing about your legal problems with that asshole Hitchens."

"God, him. There's been so much going on, I nearly forgot I might be going to jail myself." He tried to laugh.

"Stop."

"Okay."

"I want one night that we devote just to ourselves."

"Sold."

"Have you eaten?"

"I'm so hungry, I'd eat airline food."

He perched himself on one of the island stools while Charlotte pulled out an already prepared plate from the refrigerator. She said, "Spinach-and-ricotta-stuffed cannelloni with tomato sauce. Sorry, I had mine about an hour ago. I was starving."

She put it into the microwave, then went back to the fridge and brought out a bottle of red wine. "Got this, too." She found a corkscrew in a drawer, opened the bottle, and filled two wineglasses.

Charlotte handed one to him, raised her glass to make a toast. "To a new beginning. To putting the bad behind us, and looking forward to the good."

Paul, struggling to be enthusiastic, clinked his glass to hers and drank. "I like that."

Charlotte, wineglass in hand, turned back to the microwave to check on the progress of her husband's dinner. "Three minutes."

"I'm gonna wash up," he said, leaving his glass and heading for the stairs to the top floor.

"Be quick," she said.

By the time he returned, his dinner was waiting for him and

Charlotte was refilling her glass. "It is my intention," she said with mock seriousness, "to get drunk and make some bad decisions."

Paul smiled as he retook his spot on the stool. "Sounds like a plan," he said, picking up his glass and downing the rest of his wine in a single gulp.

"Hit me," he said, setting the glass back down. Charlotte filled it to the brim, then looked at the trickle left in the bottle.

"Good thing I have more than just this one," she said.

Paul cut into the cannelloni with the side of his fork and blew on it before putting it into his mouth. "This is not bad."

Charlotte smiled as she went to the fridge again. "All I want is for you to be happy," she said. She scowled at the second bottle she had pulled out. "A screw top. Is that too down market?"

"Seriously?" he said. "For me, who doesn't know a Chablis from a chardonnay?"

"Yeah, and really, the more you drink, what does it matter?"

She opened the bottle, set it on the island at the ready. Paul went through his second glass in half a dozen gulps. The moment his glass was empty, Charlotte refilled it.

"Do you forgive me?" she asked.

"For?"

"Talking to Hailey and Dr. White."

He nodded. "I do."

"If the roles were reversed, wouldn't you have done the same thing?"

Paul thought about that. "I guess I would have." He had polished off the dinner and pushed the plate away from him.

"Are you wondering what's for dessert?" Charlotte asked.

"It's okay," he said. "I'm good."

"You should reconsider," she said, setting down her glass, coming around the island, turning his head to face her, and putting her mouth on his.

Paul felt himself instantly responding. He slid off the stool, put his arms around Charlotte, and pulled her in to him, their lips parting. She slid her tongue into his mouth as he cupped his hands on her buttocks.

Charlotte wedged a hand down between them, felt his hardness beneath his jeans. She pulled back slightly, creating enough space between them that she could undo his belt and the button at the top of his zipper. As his jeans began to fall, allowing her to slip her hand into his shorts, Paul freed her blouse from her pants and ran his hands over her bare skin, heading toward her back and the clasp of her bra.

"Are you going to take me here on the island?" she whispered.

"If it were a desert island, maybe," Paul said. "But I think a bed might be more comfortable than granite."

"Well, Romeo, if we're moving this party to the bedroom, you better pull up your pants so you don't trip on the stairs."

"Wise advice."

"Turn off the lights on the way up. And bring that bottle."

———

WHEN THEY WERE DONE, PAUL SLIPPED NAKED OUT OF THE BED, STAG-gered into the bathroom long enough to take a piss, guided by the moonlight filtering through the window blinds. He flopped back down on the mattress, staring up at the ceiling. Charlotte, naked and exposed with the covers down around her ankles, had barely moved since they finished making love. The second wine bottle and two glasses all sat empty on her bedside table.

"Whoa," she said quietly.

"No kidding," Paul said, reaching his hand out across the sheet and touching his fingers lightly on her arm. "You know, I'm not as young as I used to be."

"Welcome to the club."

"What I mean is, four glasses of wine—"

"It was five."

"Whatever. I'm feelin' it."

"Like I said, welcome to the club."

Paul turned onto his side and shifted closer to Charlotte. She found the energy to roll onto her side, too, so that he could tuck in behind her, spoon-style.

"Covers," she said.

Paul reached down for the comforter and dragged it up over them. He put his arm around Charlotte, caressing her breasts, and put his head deep into his pillow.

Within seconds, he was snoring.

———————————

HE WAS DREAMING, PERHAPS NOT SURPRISINGLY, ABOUT NEEDING TO go to the bathroom. As he slowly started to come awake, opening his eyes briefly, he thought that killing off a couple of bottles of wine at bedtime will do that to you.

Paul tried to ignore the urgent message from his bladder and closed his eyes again. The two of them had barely moved. Paul was still tucked up against Charlotte, his arm resting over her hip.

He could hear her breathing softly.

He almost drifted back into sleep, but he was being forced to face the inevitability of his situation. He was going to have to get up. The question was whether he could disentangle himself from Charlotte without waking her.

First, he gently raised his arm from her hip and let the comforter settle back onto her. Then he slowly edged his body toward his side of the bed, trying to keep the comforter from dragging across Charlotte.

At the same time, he turned himself over so that his back was to hers, and he was facing the wall beyond his side of the bed.

The room was dark, and the moon had shifted in the intervening hours, so there was almost no light slipping through the blinds.

He wondered what time it was. He was worried it might be four or five in the morning. He did not want it to be that close to daybreak. He was weary, and hoping for several more hours of sleep once he was back under the covers. One or two o'clock, even three, would suit him just fine.

The clock radio on his bedside table was showing no display.

That led Paul to wonder if the power was off. If it had gone out, and come back on, the clock would be flashing "12:00." But right now, there was nothing. It struck him as an odd time for the electrical grid to collapse. There were no high winds, no storm of any kind.

But hang on.

There was a discernible glow coming from the direction of the clock radio. As if the display were on, but at a tenth of its usual illumination.

Lying on his stomach, he extended his left arm, reaching for the clock.

His hand hit something.

It was as though he'd bumped into an invisible wall.

He felt around. Something cold and metallic sat on the bedside table between him and the clock radio. He gave it a slight push, but it did not budge. His fingers scrabbled across the object. One side was smooth, but when his fingers worked around it, he felt countless round pads that recessed slightly at his touch.

Paul felt a chill run from his scalp to his toes.

No longer worrying about disturbing Charlotte, he swung his legs out of the bed and fumbled in the dark under the shade of the bedside lamp, his fingers struggling to find the switch.

He found it, turned the lamp on.

Paul screamed.

Still screaming, he slid off the side of the bed and hit the floor on his back. His scream had morphed into actual words.

"No no no no!"

Charlotte sat bolt upright in bed, throwing back the covers.

"Paul?" She spun around, expecting to see him next to her but seeing only his head above the edge of the bed.

She saw the look of horror on his face, then followed his gaze.

And then she screamed, too.

The typewriter sat there on the bedside table, positioned so that it was facing the bed. Charlotte found three words:

"Oh my God!"

And then the room went silent as the two of them stared at the hunk of black metal.

"Paul," Charlotte whispered.

He did not respond. He did not look at her.

"Paul," she said again.

Slowly, he focused on her. His eyes were wide with shock.

"Paul, there's paper in it."

It was true. A piece of paper was rolled into the machine. There were two words of type on it.

Slowly, Paul got to his knees, then stood and approached the typewriter, as though it were a coiled snake ready to strike.

Without touching it, he peered over the machine to read the message that had been left on the single sheet.

It read:

We're back.

Forty-Two

Paul, naked and trembling, took a step back from the typewriter and said, "This is not happening. This is not fucking happening!"

Charlotte was in the middle of the bed, crouched on her knees, staring disbelievingly at the antique writing machine. "Paul, how did . . . how is this possible?"

He turned at her and shouted, "I don't know! This can't be happening. This has to be a nightmare. I have to wake up. I have to wake up. This can't be real!" He put his palms to his temples, as though posing for Edvard Munch's *The Scream*.

"I was asleep," he said. "I was right here. Not two feet away. How could this happen? How did it get in here? It can't be here. It *isn't* here."

"Paul, Paul, listen to me. Paul?"

He looked at her, his eyes wide. "What?"

"This isn't a dream, Paul. That fucking thing is *here*."

"How did it get here? How?" He whirled around.

"Someone's in the house!" Charlotte said. "Has to be!"

Paul was not about to argue for a supernatural explanation at this point. He ran from the room, barefoot. Charlotte could hear him tearing down the stairs, shouting.

"Where are you?"

Charlotte got off the bed and grabbed a long T-shirt from her dresser.

"Come out, you son of a bitch!"

She pulled it on over her head, then picked up Paul's boxers from the floor and ran for the stairs.

"You bastard if you're here I'll find you!"

All the kitchen lights were on by the time she reached it, as well as the light in Paul's small study. But he was not there. She went down the next set of steps. The front door remained locked, but the inside one to the garage was not. She opened it, found the lights already on.

Paul was on the far side of the garage, staring into the open blanket box.

"It was here," he said. "It was *here*." He shook his head angrily. "Shit! Shit shit shit! I forgot to put the books back on top."

He pointed to the boxes he had lifted off the blanket box during his last visit in here, when he had checked to make sure the typewriter was where it was supposed to be.

"It got out," he said softly with a tone of wonder. "It escaped."

"Paul, listen to what you're saying."

"What?"

"You're talking about it like it was some . . . some animal or something."

"It moved. It *moved*."

"It *can't* have moved! That's not possible! Not by itself!"

"Well then what the hell happened?"

Charlotte took a second to calm herself, then said, "Call Dr. White."

"What?" It was as though there were some invisible barrier between them keeping him from comprehending her words.

She crossed the garage, handed him his shorts. "For God's sake, put these on. It's cold in here."

"It was open," he said. "The box was open when I came in here." He looked imploringly at Charlotte. "How did it do that? How?"

"Paul, I'm begging you."

"The front door was locked," he said. "With a new set of locks!"

"Yes," she said quietly.

He nodded, putting it together. "That pretty much settles it.

There was no one in here." He smiled, as though this were good news. "Don't you see? No one got in. It did it. It did it on its own."

"Paul."

His face went red with rage. "What the hell else can it be?"

She took a step back. "Will you call her, please?"

"What are you talking about? This is not a fucking *psychological* problem. I need a goddamn exorcist or something. That thing is *possessed*. There are people that do that. I'm sure of it. They come in, they get rid of evil spirits. It should be easy in this case. It's not a house. It's just that *thing*."

"If you won't call her, I will."

"You're not getting this at all."

"I think I am."

She turned for the door, went back into the house. As she was mounting the stairs, the door behind her opened and Paul started coming up after her.

"You're not calling her," Paul said.

"You can't stop me."

"It's the middle of the night, for Christ's sake!"

"I don't care."

Paul gained on her, grabbed the hem of her shirt to stop her progress.

"Let go!" Charlotte said, stumbling to her knees. Her left one hit the edge of a stair. "Jesus! You're hurting me!"

"Please, please, don't."

He was holding her down, keeping her from moving farther up the stairs. She flung back blindly with her arm, catching Paul in the side of the head. It stunned him enough that he fell over to one side and let go of her. He rubbed at his temple.

"Oh, God," she said, realizing where she had struck him. "Is that the same spot where—"

"It's okay," he said, taking his hand away from his head.

"I'm sorry. But, Paul, you need help."

She got back on her feet and managed to reach the kitchen without him attempting to grab hold of her again.

"I don't need help," he mumbled as he followed her.

"Yes, you do. Help from me, help from Dr. White. We all want to help you."

"Christ, don't be so fucking patronizing. How the hell do you think that typewriter got up two flights and parked itself right next to my fucking head? How do you think *that* happened?"

"What did it do, Paul? Did it walk up? Did it fly? Did it use its tiny fucking keys to turn the knob on the garage door? Did it go through walls?"

"It did *something*!" he said. "If it didn't get itself up here how the hell did it happen?"

Tears were forming in the corners of her eyes. "Please don't make me."

"Don't make you what?"

"Please don't make me say it. I'm here to help you, to support you."

"Did you feel me get out of bed?"

"I was drunk," Charlotte said. "We could have had an earthquake and I wouldn't have noticed."

"Don't give me that. I was right up next to you. I had my arm around you."

"I didn't feel you get up before you found that thing next to your bed. Maybe you got up one other time. I'm just saying, Paul, we have to consider the possibility . . ."

"That I'm losing my mind?"

"I did not say that." She threw her hands into the air. "I don't know what to do! What should I do? You tell me."

"For starters, you can get that fucking thing out of the house."

"Fine. Fine. If that's what you want, I'll do it right now."

She stormed up the second flight, Paul in pursuit. "What are you going to do?" he demanded.

"Just watch me."

She returned to their bedroom, went straight past the bed to the sliding glass doors that opened onto the small balcony. She first drew back the blinds, then unlocked the door and slid it open. Cool air blew into the room, and the sounds of waves lapping at the beach became a soft soundtrack.

"Charlotte?" Paul said, standing at the foot of the bed.

"Get out of my way," she said, pushing past him.

She got her fingers under the typewriter and, with a grunt, lifted it off the bedside table.

"It's heavy," Paul said. "Let me help—"

"I told you, get out of my way."

She had to put her back into it. She arched her spine and tilted her head back as she struggled to carry the machine across the room and out the door. Once she reached the balcony, she took a deep breath and heaved the Underwood up and onto the railing, balancing it there.

Charlotte glanced back at Paul, who stood in the doorway, seemingly mesmerized by her actions.

"If you think this thing is alive, well, I'm about to kill it," she said.

"Wait," Paul said.

She looked stunned. "Seriously?"

"Just . . . wait."

The typewriter teetered precariously on the railing. All she had to do was take her hand away and it would plummet to the cement walkway below.

"I . . . appreciate what you're doing," Paul said. "I do. But what if . . ."

"What if what?"

"What if they have more to say?"

Charlotte closed her eyes briefly, signaling she had reached her limit.

Forty-Three

By the time Anna White arrived nearly an hour later, Paul had calmed down some. He'd never been a fan of hard liquor, but he'd knocked back a couple of shots of vodka to calm his nerves.

"I hope that wasn't a bad thing," Charlotte said once Anna was sitting at the kitchen table, talking to Paul. For someone who'd been in bed less than an hour earlier, Anna was alert and attentive. She'd come over in a jogging suit, her hair pulled back into a ponytail, her face devoid of lipstick or other makeup.

"That's okay," she said. "How are you now, Paul?"

"Better," he said.

"Tell me everything that happened."

He told her, even the parts about he and Charlotte killing off a couple of bottles of wine and having sex. But the story really started with the discovery of the typewriter next to his bed.

"Is it still up there?" Anna asked.

Paul shook his head. "We got it out of the house. It's in Charlotte's car." He gave his head a slow, deliberate shake. "It's not coming back in here unless it knows how to get out of a locked trunk."

Anna didn't say anything to that.

Paul leaned in closer to Anna and whispered, "Either that thing got up here on its own tonight, guided through the house by the spirits of those two women, or I brought it up here and have no memory of it." He sighed. "Which would be worse? And if I did bring it up here, if I wrote all those notes, if I did all that, does it

"I know, I know. I'm all for getting it out of here. I am. I'm just not sure it should be smashed into a million pieces."

"What, then?" she asked. Before Paul could come up with a suggestion she had one of her own. "I'll put it in the trunk of my car. And then I'm going to put it someplace where it won't be found. How about that?"

Paul considered the offer. "Okay, yes. Okay."

"But I'm doing it on one condition. You have to call Dr. White."

Paul hesitated. "I don't know. I don't see what she can do."

"I'll let this go," she said, nodding toward the typewriter. "Believe me, I don't care what happens to this thing. I'm happy to see it busted into a billion bits. You should be, too, but I'm willing to do it your way. Pick up your phone and call her."

Paul looked back into the room. With the typewriter off the bedside table, he could see the time. He thought it had to be around three or four but was surprised to see that it was only 1:23 A.M.

"It's late," he protested. "I'll be waking her."

"So what?"

"I'll do it. But let's put that into your trunk first."

"Fine," she said. "But do you think you could carry it? I just about broke my arms getting it this far."

Paul came out to the balcony and carefully took the typewriter from Charlotte. He felt a chill as he took the Underwood into his arms, cradling it as though it were some demonic infant.

"Let's do this quickly," he said.

Charlotte got ahead of him on the stairs, grabbing her car keys from a bowl in the kitchen along the way. She held the front door for him, then hit the button on her remote to pop the trunk on her car. The lid swung open a few inches, and she lifted it the rest of the way.

Paul leaned over the opening and set the machine onto the trunk floor. There was a small tarp rolled up in there, which he took and draped over the typewriter, as though smothering it. Then he slammed the lid.

He dusted his hands together and rubbed them on his boxers, as if somehow touching the machine had contaminated him. He turned and looked at Charlotte.

And fell apart.

"Oh, God," he said, and started to cry. He put his hands over his face. "Oh God what is happening, what is happening, what is happening." The cries turned into racking sobs.

Charlotte took him into her arms and squeezed. "Let it out," she said. "Let it out."

His arms limply went around her. "I can't take it anymore, I just can't."

"It's going to be okay. We're getting rid of it. It's in the car." Charlotte suddenly found herself crying, too. "I'm so sorry." She buried her face in his shoulder. "I'm so, so sorry."

Paul, between sobs, managed to say, "It's not your fault. There was no way you could know."

"I shouldn't have . . . I never should have . . . it was a bad idea," she said, weeping. "At the time . . . it seemed . . ."

"Stop," Paul said. His breaths had turned rapid and shallow. "I feel, I feel like I'm going to pass out."

"Come in. Get in the house."

She got him to the door. Once inside, she locked it, checked that the door to the garage was also secure, and the two of them trudged upstairs. She managed to keep him on his feet until they reached the kitchen table, at which point he dropped into a chair.

He was still crying. He put his elbows on the table, rested his head in his hands.

"Maybe it's some kind of nervous breakdown," he said. "I'm willing to admit that. I don't know what else it could be. I must be . . . I must be doing these things. I have to be."

Charlotte had grabbed his phone, which had been recharging from an outlet by the kitchen sink.

"Dr. White," she said, handing it to him.

He nodded, surrendering. He looked at his hand, which was shaking. "You call her. I can't do it. I don't even know if I could hold the phone."

Charlotte found the number in his contacts, and tapped. "It's gone to message after three rings," she said.

"That'll be her office phone. Keep calling it. She'll hear it eventually from the other part of the house."

She ended the call, entered the number again. The fourth time, it worked.

A frantic Anna White answered, "Yes, who is this? Paul, is this you?"

"I'm so sorry," Charlotte said after identifying herself. "Paul's in a bad way. A *really* bad way."

Calmly, Anna asked, "Tell me what's happening."

"He's shaking, he can't stop crying. You need to come over. He needs to talk to you, he—"

"Charlotte, if he's in a psychotic state, then—"

"What the hell is that? How am I supposed—"

"Let me speak to him."

Charlotte said to Paul, "She wants to talk to you."

He nodded weakly, steadied his hand as he took the phone, and pressed it to his ear.

"Yes?"

"Paul?"

"Yes."

"Talk to me."

Paul didn't say anything. He seemed to be struggling to find th words.

"Paul?"

Finally, with great effort, he said two words before handing phone back to Charlotte.

"Help me."

mean I'm crazy, or that I'm somehow possessed by the ghosts of Jill and Catherine? Anna, Jesus, there's no good answer here."

"Sitting here, talking to you, you do not strike me as someone who's detached from reality, Paul."

"Something's crazy. It's either me, or the situation."

Anna took out her phone. "I have to make a quick call to my father. I had to wake him before I left. I didn't want him waking up and not finding me at home."

"Of course."

"Dad?" she said into the phone. "I'm just checking in. Okay. I'll call you again in half an hour, unless you really think you can get back to sleep." She nodded. "Okay. Love you, Dad."

As she put her phone away, Charlotte was getting out hers. "Who are you calling?" Paul asked.

She glanced his way. "Bill."

"Bill? Why are you—"

"He's your friend. Maybe it would help if he came—Bill?"

She turned away, walked toward the stairs where she wouldn't be disturbed by Paul and Anna.

"It might be good to talk to him," Anna said.

"I hate her waking him up in the middle of the night."

Anna managed a smile. "But it was okay for me."

"I'm sorry."

"Kidding. What would you like to do, Paul? If you want, I could have you admitted."

"Admitted?"

She put a hand on his arm. "For observation. For a day or two. And I know you've resisted in the past, but once we have you seen by a psychiatrist, and there are a couple of very good ones I can recommend, there might be a pharmacological approach to treatment that we—"

"Drugs," he said.

Anna nodded. "Yes."

"I don't want to be on drugs."

"You want to just stick with vodka?"

He frowned. "Your point?"

"I'm saying that if you drink, you're self-medicating. There may be other, more productive approaches. But as a psychologist, I can't prescribe for you. That's where an assessment by a psychiatrist could be very helpful."

"That's your answer? Go into the loony bin and get doped up."

"We don't have to do that," she said, her voice steady and measured. "As long as you're not a danger to yourself or anyone else, no one's going to force you to do that."

"I wonder what Charlotte thinks," he said.

"Why don't we ask her?"

Although still within earshot of the others, Charlotte had moved over to the stairs and taken a seat on the top step. She said into her phone, "I hate to call you in the middle of the night, but I thought you'd want to know about Paul."

"What's going—hang on, I'm just turning on the light here—what's happening over there?" Bill asked.

"His therapist just came over. He had a full-blown meltdown." Charlotte sniffed, then said, "He's really messed up."

"Are you crying?"

"Of course I'm crying."

"Okay, okay," Bill said. "What do you want me—"

"Hang on, Paul wants to ask me something."

Paul said, "Do you think I should go into the hospital?"

"The hospital?" she said. "Like, what do you mean?"

"The psych ward," Paul said. "It's an option. They could keep an eye on me and they might give me something. You know, to mellow me out, I guess."

"Shit, no," said Bill, who could hear them both talking.

"Hang on," Charlotte said to Paul. Into the phone, she said, "I'm trying to talk to Paul here."

"Put him on," Bill said.

Charlotte held out the phone to Paul. "Bill wants to talk to you."

Paul held the phone to his ear. "Sorry. Charlotte shouldn't have gotten you up."

"Don't worry about it," Bill said. "What's this about the hospital?"

"I'm talking about it with Anna."

"You do *not* want to go into the hospital. There's no *way* you want to do that."

"But they might be—"

"No, you listen to Bill here. Going into a place like that, it'll only mess you up further. Those places are filled with crazy people, and you are *not crazy*. You hear me? Once you let them lock you up, they'll never let you out."

"I don't know," he said.

"Look," Bill said, "how do you feel right now? Right this second?"

"Shaky."

"But shaky enough to go into a hospital?"

"I don't know. Maybe you're right."

"You bet I'm right. Whaddya say you give it a couple of days. I have to go out of town tomorrow—shit, it's already tomorrow—but when I get back, you and me, we'll get together, do something to take your mind off all these things. But not squash. We're not putting that head of yours at risk. How does that sound?"

Paul nodded slowly.

"Are you there?" Bill asked.

"Yeah," Paul said. "Okay, I'll do that. I'll give it a couple of days and see how it goes. Charlotte's taken the typewriter away."

"There ya go," Bill said. "You hang in there, pal."

Paul handed the phone back to Charlotte and turned to face Anna, who was now standing by the kitchen table.

"You can go home," he told her. "I'll be okay."

Forty-Four

Charlotte stayed up most of the night with Paul, waiting until he finally fell asleep. Rattled as he was, he eventually lost the fight to exhaustion. Once he'd succumbed, Charlotte slipped into bed next to him.

Every time he moved or made a sound, she woke up.

Just after seven, she sensed he was fully awake, and asked, "How are you?"

He said, "Did all that really happen?"

"I'm afraid so."

He quickly turned over and looked at the bedside table. Seeing nothing on it but a lamp and his clock, he said, "I thought it might have come back."

Charlotte had nothing to say to that. It wasn't clear whether Paul was attempting to make a joke. He rolled onto his back and stared at the ceiling. "I'm sorry I put you through all that."

"It's okay," she said, raising up on her elbow and turning to face him. "What does it mean, exactly, that you're saying you're sorry?"

He turned his head slightly to look at her. "I don't know. I guess . . ."

"You guess what?"

"I know I may have looked like I was sleeping all night, but I was awake a lot, too. Thinking."

"Okay." Gently, she asked, "And what are you thinking?"

"That maybe Anna—Dr. White—was right."

"Right about what?"

"That maybe I should be admitted."

"You want to go into the hospital?"

"I don't *want* to, but I'm wondering if it's the only thing that makes sense. But I keep thinking about what Bill said, that once they have you in there, they'll never let you out. If I could go in for, I don't know, a couple of days, maybe that would be long enough to figure things out."

"I guess that's something you could revisit with Dr. White."

He managed a nod with the back of his head still buried in the pillow.

"You seem . . . almost calm," Charlotte said. "Certainly a lot calmer than in the middle of the night."

"There's only one way to explain this," he said. "And now that I've settled on that, I guess I do feel a little more at peace."

"And that way is?"

"Think of all the small memory lapses I've had. Forgetting where I'd driven. Forgotten texts and messages. The dry cleaning. Not remembering seeing that car across the street, nearly blacking out when I saw a car like Kenneth's. I must have gotten up in the night and brought the typewriter up and put it next to the bed. I *had* to. And I don't recall doing it."

"So you've moved past thinking it . . . did it itself."

He gave her a sad smile. "I have." He chuckled. "I mean, try to picture it. A typewriter opening the door. Coming up the stairs. It's comical if you think about it."

"I guess I haven't been able to see the humor in all this," Charlotte said.

He grimaced. "Yeah, well, I don't blame you there."

Charlotte threw back the covers and got out of bed. "I'm going to call in sick today."

"No."

"Yes. Any big house deals come along, someone else can take them."

"No, you don't have to do that. I'll be okay. I'll get in touch with Dr. White and talk to her about whether to go in for, you know, observation or something."

Charlotte shook her head. "I think you need to listen to Bill on this one. Why don't you give it a couple of days. Then, if you still feel that's what you want to do, then do it."

Paul sat up. "Okay."

"And you need to call that lawyer back."

"Call him back?"

"I told you. He called yesterday. He thinks he can get you off with a suspended sentence or something, that there are extenuating circumstances up the wazoo that the court will be sympathetic to. But you have to get it sorted out."

"When did he call?"

"I told you all about this last night," Charlotte said.

"You see?" he said. He tapped his head with his index finger. "This needs a tune-up."

"And I think you need a break from your project. No more talking to grieving husbands and jilted wives. No more holing up in your study, writing about what happened to you. You need to get out. You need to *do* things."

Paul considered her advice. "I don't even know if I care about it anymore. I've met with Kenneth. Maybe my demons have been exorcised. Maybe it's time to move on. I don't have to turn my experience into a brilliant work of literature." He grinned. "Let someone else win the Pulitzer."

PAUL MANAGED TO TALK CHARLOTTE INTO GOING TO WORK. "HONestly," he told her, "I'll be fine."

And up until the time she left for the real estate office, he thought he would be.

But once the house was empty, anxiety rushed in to fill the void. He could not stop certain thoughts running through his head:

1. *It's me. I did it.*
2. *No. I didn't do it. I couldn't have done it.*
3. *Someone broke in and did it.*
4. *No, the locks were changed. No one could get in.*
5. *So maybe I did do it.*
6. *Or maybe . . . the ghosts of Catherine and Jill are REAL.*

He avoided his study. Even if he'd not been considering abandoning his project, he knew he wouldn't have been able to write this morning. He couldn't focus. It would be impossible.

If he couldn't accomplish anything on that score, maybe he could do something practical. He could focus on items 3 and 4. He could satisfy himself, once and for all, that the house was secure.

He checked all the windows, even those up on the third floor that only a human fly could access, for weakness. He found them all properly latched. The main garage door was locked and did not appear to have been tampered with in any way.

Paul grabbed a ladder from the garage and hauled it up two flights of stairs, chipping paint on the wall with the legs as he made some turns, to allow him to reach the one access panel to the attic. Flashlight in hand, he climbed to the top of the ladder and gave the square panel door enough of a nudge to slide it to one side. Then he went up one more step and poked his head into the space.

He turned on the flashlight and did a slow 360-degree sweep of the attic. There was nothing up there but rafters and insulation. They'd never used the space for storage. It was too difficult to get anything up there and then, later, bring it back down.

He returned the ladder to the garage.

Well. So that was that.

Now he almost wished the typewriter was not tucked away in the trunk of Charlotte's car. If it were here, he would place it next to the laptop, look at it, and say, "I'm here. What would you like to talk about?"

At one point, the phone rang. It was Anna.

"I wanted to see how you were doing," she said.

"Okay. Thanks again for coming out in the middle of the night."

"I've an opening at two if you'd like to come in."

Paul thought for a moment. "No, I'm good."

"Are you sure? You weren't so good a few hours ago."

"Don't worry. I think I've come to some sort of . . . realization. An acceptance."

"And what's that, Paul?"

Paul said nothing.

"You there?" Anna asked.

"I'm here," he said.

"Look, I'm going to leave that two o'clock open. If you change your mind, just come in. You don't have to call."

"Okay. Good to know."

Anna said good-bye and Paul put away his phone.

———————

CHARLOTTE WAS RIGHT. HE NEEDED TO GET OUT OF THE HOUSE.

That didn't mean he had to jump in the car and drive to Mystic. But some fresh air wouldn't be a bad idea. Maybe a walk to downtown. Lunch someplace.

As he came out the front door, he was almost knocked back, as if by a fierce wind, but there was not so much as a breeze.

It was music that nearly knocked him off his feet.

Dee dee, diddly-dee, dee dee, dee-da, dee-da, dee da dee.

It was the Tastee Truck driven by Leonard Hoffman. It was stopped almost directly across the street. Leonard was not behind the wheel. He was more likely at the serving window, but it was on the side of the truck that Paul could not see. Leonard had clearly been stopped by one or more of the neighborhood kids. Paul then noticed one pair of legs, from the knees down, visible through the underside of the truck.

Paul huddled by his front door. He did not want to engage with Leonard. He did not want to see him. He considered going back in the house but concluded he could wait here until the truck moved on down the street.

The truck rocked on its springs ever so slightly as someone moved inside it. And then there was Leonard, settling back in behind the wheel, putting the truck into gear, and pulling forward.

As the truck exited Paul's field of vision, he saw who Leonard's customer had been.

It was a man, holding an ice-cream cone. Late twenties, early thirties. His face was severely bruised and a bandage was wrapped about his forehead. One arm was in a sling.

Jesus, Paul thought. *That guy's had the shit beat out of him.*

And then he realized who he was looking at.

Gavin Hitchens gazed across the street, locked eyes with Paul, smiled, and took a lick of his ice-cream cone.

Paul felt his insides turn to liquid.

He stared back for several seconds before summoning the strength to approach. Crossing the street, he shouted, "What the hell do you want?"

Hitchens held his spot, had another lick. "I wanted an ice cream," he said.

"I'm betting that guy goes through your neighborhood, too," Paul said, stopping within ten feet of the man. "Get the hell out of here."

Hitchens nodded slowly. "Soon as I finish. Can't drive and eat an ice cream with one hand."

Hitchens took one more lick, tossed the unfinished cone at Paul's feet, then turned and walked slowly up the sidewalk to his car, limping severely. He opened the driver's door and gingerly got behind the wheel.

Paul watched until Hitchens had reached the end of the street, turned, and disappeared.

_____

ANNA WHITE SAT AT HER OFFICE DESK AND GLANCED AT THE WALL clock. It was nearly three in the afternoon.

Two o'clock had come and gone.

Paul Davis had not shown up.

Forty-Five

I t was almost the time when Charlotte, on a slow day, might have
gone home. But then a couple from Boston came into the office without an appointment. They had been driving around Milford when they spotted a house for sale on Elmwood Street, half a
block from the sound. It was a beautiful three-story with a strong
Cape Cod influence. Cedar-shingle siding, a balcony on the third
floor. Two-car garage. And out front, a FOR SALE sign with the name
CHARLOTTE DAVIS on it.

Charlotte sent Paul a text to tell him she would be home late.
He'd gotten plenty of texts like that before.

Charlotte showed the couple the Elmwood house and drove
them around town to check out a few more properties.

It was nearly nine-thirty by the time they were done.

Charlotte had a small briefcase with her that was stuffed with
various documents and real estate flyers. She decided to toss it in the
trunk of her car, where it would be out of sight.

She got the remote out of her purse and hit the trunk release
button. Lights flashed, and the trunk yawned open a few inches.
She lifted it up and set the briefcase next to the tarp-shrouded typewriter.

She pulled the tarp back and stared, briefly, at the exposed Underwood. She then pulled the tarp back over it and slammed the
trunk shut. She got into the car, turned on the engine and headlights, and pointed the car toward home.

She saw the emergency lights as she turned onto her street.

There were so many, they were almost blinding. It was difficult to tell just how many vehicles there were up ahead. She could see at least two police cars, an ambulance, and what even looked like a fire truck.

They appeared to be clustered either right in front of her house, or just beyond it. Either way, the street at that point was impassable.

A male officer standing in the middle of the road held up a hand to stop her. She powered down her window.

"Road's closed, ma'am," he told her.

"My house is right there." She pointed. "Can I get that far?"

Her words made an impression on him. "*That* house?"

She nodded.

"Okay, go on ahead."

"What's going on?" she asked.

"Just go on ahead."

She put the window back up and crept the rest of the way, edging past a Milford Police cruiser and turning into the driveway behind Paul's car. As she opened her door she found a uniformed female officer waiting for her.

"You live here?" she asked.

"Yes," Charlotte said.

"What's your name?"

"What's going on?" she asked.

"What's your name, ma'am?"

"Charlotte Davis. Could someone please tell me what's happening?"

"Please wait here."

"Can I go inside?"

"Please wait here."

The cop walked off, threading her way between the emergency vehicles blocking the street. Charlotte saw her conferring with someone. A fortyish black man in plainclothes with what appeared, at least from where Charlotte was standing, a badge of some kind clipped to his belt.

The man looked in Charlotte's direction and approached.

"You're Mrs. Davis?" he asked.

"Yes. What's going on?"

"My name is Detective Arnwright. Milford Police."

"No one will tell me what this is all about. Give me a second. I want to let my husband know I'm home."

"What's your husband's name, ma'am?"

"What? It's Paul. Paul Davis."

Charlotte had reached her front door, tried opening it first without a key, and when that did not work, started fiddling with the set of keys still in her hand.

But before she could insert it into the lock, Arnwright said, "Mrs. Davis, I have some difficult news for you. There's been an incident."

Charlotte turned to look at the detective. "What are you talking about? What kind of an incident?"

"There was . . . a drowning," Arnwright said.

"What?"

The detective nodded solemnly. "A man was found on the beach. His body had been washed up."

"Why are you—what are you saying?"

"The man was fully clothed, and his wallet was still tucked down in the pocket of his jeans. We found a driver's license and some other ID in there."

"Oh please, no, no. He couldn't have. He told me he was going to be okay. He *promised* me."

"He told you he'd be okay?" the detective asked.

"It's a mistake," Charlotte said defiantly. "It can't be him."

"Well, I'll want to address that shortly, Mrs. Davis. But you seem to be suggesting that maybe your husband was going through a difficult time."

"He . . . he has been. He's been under a great deal of stress. And . . . other things."

"What kind of other things?"

Charlotte began to ramble. "Dr. White, she talked about admitting him, but he didn't want to go to the hospital, he wanted to see if he'd feel better, and now that the typewriter was out of the house and wouldn't be sending him any more messages he probably thought things really would get better but now if—"

"Mrs. Davis, slow down. What's this about a typewriter? And you said Dr. White? Anna White?"

Charlotte became angry. "Why are you asking me these questions? Whose ID did you find?"

"We found several items of identification for a Paul Davis in the wallet," Arnwright said gently. "Some with photos. The reason I ask about your husband's state of mind is, as I said, he was fully dressed. He wasn't in a swimsuit or anything like that. It's the early stages of the investigation, but it appears he may have simply walked out into the water."

"Oh, God," Charlotte said again. "No, please, no." She started shaking her head back and forth.

Arnwright put a hand on her shoulder. "Mrs. Davis, I am so very sorry . . ."

"Is that him?" she said, pointing toward the street.

Arnwright spun around. Two male attendants were rolling a gurney to the back of an ambulance. A body was atop it, draped in a sheet.

"Paul!" she screamed, and started running.

"Mrs. Davis, please, wait!" Arnwright said, jogging after her. But Charlotte had a good head start.

"Stop!" she shouted at the attendants. One of the two men looked her way and mouthed *shit*.

They stopped wheeling the gurney as they opened the back doors of the ambulance, allowing Charlotte a chance to come up alongside it and grip it by the side rails.

"Is it him?" she asked, clearly unable to bring herself to pull down the sheet and reveal the face. "Is it?"

The attendants looked to Arnwright for guidance. Everyone went silent as the detective decided what should be done.

He nodded.

The attendant slowly pulled the sheet far enough back to reveal the dead person's head.

It was a man, hair wet and matted, the face dirtied with beach sand. But his facial features were undamaged, and even in this condition, he was easy enough to identify as Paul Davis.

"No!" Charlotte said.

As her knees buckled, she collapsed onto the street.

Forty-Six

When Anna White found Detective Joe Arnwright at her front door the next day she thought he must have more news about Gavin Hitchens. He'd made a brief stop at her office a day earlier to confirm that Paul Davis, who'd been arrested for assaulting Hitchens, was also one of her clients.

Anna was between appointments and making some notes when she heard the doorbell to the main house.

"Detective," she said. "Come in."

He smiled grimly. She did not like that look.

"What's going on?" she asked.

"You recall we talked the other day about Paul Davis," he said. "In connection with Mr. Hitchens."

"Yes," she said regretfully. "A terrible situation all around. Has something happened?"

"I'm afraid he died last night."

"Gavin Hitchens?"

"No, Mr. Davis."

Anna stood stock-still for five seconds. Slowly, she raised both hands and placed them over her mouth.

"Oh, God," she said, lowering her hands and looking for something for support. She moved to a nearby chair and put one hand on the back of it to steady herself. "This is terrible. This is awful. What happened?"

"A drowning. That's what everything points to."

Anna looked dumbstruck. "A drowning? How could he have drowned? I don't even think he owned a boat."

Joe Arnwright said, "It appears Mr. Davis took his own life."

Anna's body wavered. "I need to sit down," she said. "Come to my office." Once they were there, she took the chair she occupied when working with her clients. Joe Arnwright sat across from her.

"This is just . . . I can't believe it," Anna said. She bit on the end of her thumb. "This can't be." She looked imploringly at the detective. "Are you sure it wasn't some sort of accident? Did he fall off the pier? Something like that?"

"His wife told us he'd been seeing you for a period of time, that he'd been deeply troubled about a number of things. And, of course, I know now that he was nearly killed by Kenneth Hoffman eight months ago. That there was a lot of fallout from that."

"Yes," she said. "We even went up to visit him, this week, in prison."

Arnwright looked stunned. "You did? Why?"

Anna explained it as best she could. Arnwright had a small notebook in his hand and was scribbling things down.

"Would that explain why he might be inclined to take his own life?"

"If anything," she said, "I would have thought that the visit helped. I can't . . . this is horrible. How is his wife? How's Charlotte?"

"Extremely distraught, as you can imagine. She was telling me that Mr. Davis was suffering from a delusion of some sort."

Anna reached for a tissue from a nearby box. She dabbed her eyes and wadded the tissue in her fingers.

"I don't quite know how to respond to that," she said. "I suppose the short answer is yes."

"Something about a possessed typewriter," Arnwright said, without a hint of derision or skepticism.

"Yes."

"He believed it was the typewriter Kenneth Hoffman made his victims write notes of apologies on."

"That's correct," Anna said.

"I'm not a mental health expert, but that makes me wonder, had he been diagnosed with schizophrenia?"

"No."

"Was he depressed?"

"He was certainly down, but I did not believe he was clinically depressed."

"But doesn't getting messages from dead people count as hearing voices? Isn't that a symptom of schizophrenia? His wife said he was writing the notes himself, but unaware that he was doing it."

Anna sighed. "I know how that sounds. And now, in retrospect . . ." She could not finish the sentence.

"Were you concerned he might harm himself? That he might take his own life? Could he have received one of these so-called messages telling him to kill himself, to walk out into the sound?"

"I just . . ."

"And I understand you were recently out there? Two nights ago? He'd had an episode?"

"Oh, God, what have I done," Anna said and began to curl in on herself. "What did I fail to do?"

As the tears came, she grabbed for more tissues. "I suggested to him that he go to the hospital, that he be admitted for a short period so that he could be observed. But he wouldn't do it."

"Why not?"

Anna shook her head. "His friend talked him out of it."

"What friend?"

"Bill. I don't know his last name, but I think he works with Charlotte. She's a real estate agent."

Arnwright flipped to an earlier page in his notebook. "Bill Myers?"

"Possibly. Charlotte phoned him when I was there. Bill asked to talk to Paul, and after that Paul said he didn't want to go to the hospital. He might have come to that decision on his own, though. Paul did not believe there was anything wrong with him mentally, although toward the end, he seemed more open to considering the idea that maybe he was responsible."

"Responsible?"

"For the strange things that were going on."

"Do you agree with the wife? He *was* writing them?"

Anna looked at the detective with red eyes. "Yes."

Arnwright nodded and closed his notebook. "So it appears what happened is, Mr. Davis was in a very distressed state of mind, walked out into Long Island Sound with the intention of killing himself, and was successful. Is there anything you can tell me, as a professional who was treating Mr. Davis, that would run contrary to that finding?"

Anna struggled. To say no was an admission that she had not done her job, that she had failed him. To say no was to admit responsibility.

To say yes would be to lie.

"No," she whispered. "No, I can't think of anything that would contradict that finding."

Arnwright offered a slow, sympathetic nod. "For what it's worth, Dr. White, we have all been there. We're all just trying to do the best we can."

"I didn't," Anna White said. "Not even close."

Forty-Seven

"I killed him," Bill Myers said. "I killed Paul."

"I'm sorry?" Detective Arnwright said. "What do you mean?"

They were meeting at The Corner Restaurant on River Street, a cup of coffee in front of each of them. Arnwright had suggested Paul's friend order something to eat, but he'd declined, saying he didn't have much of an appetite. That was when he made what had sounded to the detective like a confession.

"Mr. Myers, I should tell you, that if you're about to admit something here, I'm obliged to inform you that—"

"It's nothing like that," Bill said, waving his hand in the air. "I didn't drag him out into the sound and hold his head underwater, for God's sake, but I might as well have."

He made two fists, opened his hands, then made them again.

"I just . . . I can't believe he did that. I can't. He wasn't crazy." He leaned in closer to Arnwright. "He was going through some shit, he really was, but I never, *never* thought he would do anything like that. Otherwise, I would have told him to take his therapist's advice, to check into the hospital. But no, I had to talk him out of that." He grimaced. "I have to live with that for the rest of my life. That's what I mean when I say I killed him. I talked him out of getting the help he so clearly needed."

"It's hard to know what's going through people's heads," Arnwright said. "When did you last see Mr. Davis?"

"We met up for a squash game the other day but didn't really play that hard. You know he had a head injury, and I didn't even think he should be playing, but he was sick of treating himself with kid gloves. But after a few minutes, he came to his senses, and we cut our session short."

"How did he seem to you?"

"Upset. You know about the nightmares? The typewriter thing?"

"Yes."

"Well, there you go."

"Were you close friends, you and Paul?"

Bill hesitated. "Friends, for sure. Maybe not super close. We knew each other in university, UConn, and we sort of kept in touch. We both ended up in Milford, and he knew what I did for a living, and when Charlotte was getting into real estate, he asked if there was any way I could help her out. We found a spot for her at the agency."

"So all three of you were friends."

"I guess. Sure."

"Are you married, Mr. Myers?"

"I have been, but not now." He appeared to be considering whether to tell Arnwright something. "Let me tell you a story."

"Okay."

"I had a cousin, she lived in Cleveland. And around the time she was turning twenty, she started believing that she was being pursued by Margaret Thatcher."

"The British prime minister?"

Bill nodded. "She said she was getting messages from her, telepathically. And here's the thing. Her parents, they wanted to *believe* that it was really happening. That somehow, for reasons they could not explain, the prime minister of England was out to get their daughter. You know why?"

"I think so."

"Because the alternative was even more horrible to imagine. That their daughter was seriously mentally ill. They were in denial about that. But eventually, of course, they had to accept the fact that my cousin Michele was delusional. A delusion became the only rational explanation."

"And that's how you feel about Paul and his obsession about that typewriter."

Bill shrugged.

"What happened to Michele?" Arnwright asked.

"She jumped off the Hope Memorial Bridge into the Cuyahoga River at the age of twenty-four."

———

DETECTIVE ARNWRIGHT HAD TO WAIT NEARLY A MINUTE FOR HIS knock to be answered at Gavin Hitchens's house.

When the door finally opened, Arnwright's eyebrows went up a notch. He knew Hitchens had been seriously injured by Paul Davis, that he'd suffered a blow to the head, that his elbow had been sprained, that one of his knees had been hurt. So the sling, the bandage on his head, and the wrapped knee were to be expected. Arnwright was just expecting Hitchens to be wearing more than a pair of boxers.

"Yeah?" he said.

Arnwright introduced himself. Hitchens nodded knowingly and smiled.

"Let me guess," he said. "That son of a bitch wants to charge me with harassment or something." Hitchens grinned maliciously. "Fucker puts me in the hospital, and *I'm* supposed to be the dangerous one."

"You're talking about Mr. Davis," Arnwright said cautiously.

"Is that what he did? File a complaint about me? Because if he's saying I did something, I didn't do anything."

"What do you think he might have said?"

"Look, okay, I was on his street. I was looking at his house. But that's all. I was getting an ice cream."

"And when was this?"

Hitchens blinked. "Hang on. Is that why you're here or not?"

"If you think I'm here about Paul Davis, yeah, you're right about that. So when was this?"

"Yesterday, kind of midday."

"You had words?"

Hitchens shrugged. "He told me to move on, and I did. End of story."

"But there's a lot of bad blood between you."

"Wow," said Hitchens. "I can see why you're a detective."

"What's the source of this trouble?"

The young man shrugged. "I've been through this. I gave a statement. This Davis guy is some kind of mental case. Thinks I was trying to drive him insane or something, but believe me, his crazy train had already reached the station."

"Did you speak again with Mr. Davis later yesterday?"

"No, that was it."

"What was your purpose in standing out in front of his house?"

Gavin Hitchens looked away. "I don't know. It was a place to be."

"Were you trying to scare him? Intimidate him? Make him think you were going to get even?"

Slowly, he shook his head. "I mean, he might never even have seen me if he hadn't come out when he did, so you can't really scare a guy if he doesn't know you're there."

Arnwright studied the man for several more seconds.

"Okay," the detective said finally. "Thanks for your trouble."

He turned to leave but Gavin said, "Hey, hold on. That's it?"

Arnwright turned. "That's it."

"Is that bastard going to go to jail for what he did to me?"

"Doubtful," Arnwright said.

Forty-Eight

The following day, Charlotte Davis sat on the bed she had shared with her husband and looked out through the sliding glass doors at the sun reflecting off the waters of Long Island Sound.

There were things she had to do, but she was having a hard time getting started.

Finally, she stood and opened the closet so that she could select a suit for Paul. The funeral home had been asking. Paul had only one good one. As a professor, he could get through almost any function with a sport jacket, jeans, and a tie. Even during graduation ceremonies, when he might be called upon to wear a gown, he could get away with smart casual undercover. The last time Paul had worn a suit, Charlotte thought, was to attend the funeral of a cousin in Providence.

And so he would wear one to a funeral again.

Charlotte pulled a dark blue suit from the hanger, laid it out on the bed. It had not seen any outings since its last trip to the dry cleaners. The tag was still attached. She took the jacket off the hanger, held it up to the light from the window, turned it around.

There was a small smudge on the back that the cleaners had missed, but really, did it matter? Even with an open casket, no one was going to see that. The matching pants, she noticed, had been on the hanger so long they had a crease at the knee, but again, was anyone going to see anything below the waist? Wouldn't only the upper half of her husband's body be viewable, not all of him?

Charlotte hadn't even discussed with the funeral home director the possibility of a closed casket. Was that the way to go? It wasn't as though Paul had been in a bad car accident. Death by drowning had left his face relatively unscathed. He was, in a word, presentable.

She decided she would press the pants, regardless. And at least try to get the spot off the back of Paul's suit jacket. The man deserved that much.

Her cell phone rang.

She'd left it on the dresser. She took a step toward it, looked at the screen to see who it was.

BILL

She held the phone for several seconds, letting it ring six times in her hand before declining the call.

She did not want to talk to Bill. Not now. She'd not spoken to him since the call in the middle of the night, when Bill had told Paul not to go to the hospital. Bill was not the only one from whom Charlotte was not taking calls. She was ignoring calls from Hailey, too.

Except for one.

Paul's ex-wife, her husband, Walter, and her son were coming to the service the next day. Josh, Hailey had told Charlotte, was utterly destroyed by the death of his father. He only stopped crying to sleep, which had only come because he was exhausted from weeping.

"Well," Charlotte said, "the good news is, you and Walter got what you wanted. Full fucking custody."

Hailey had gasped. Before she could respond, Charlotte ended the call. When Hailey tried to call her back, Charlotte did not pick up.

Charlotte set up the ironing board in the small downstairs laundry room and placed the suit pants on it. While she waited for the iron to heat, she went up to the kitchen for a cup of coffee. She had started a pot earlier but had yet to have the first cup. Nor had she bothered yet with any breakfast.

The kitchen island was covered with nearly a dozen empty cardboard liquor boxes. She pushed a couple of them aside to make a working space for herself. She grabbed a small plate from the cupboard and some butter from the fridge. She put a slice of whole wheat bread into the toaster, but before she could push it down, the doorbell rang.

She glanced down at herself. She was only a step up from pajamas—a pair of jeans and a T-shirt, hair pinned back, no makeup. She was not ready for unexpected visitors coming to pay their respects.

She sighed, scurried barefoot down the steps to the front door and peered through the narrow window that ran down the side.

It was Anna White.

Charlotte unlocked the door, swung it open.

"Dr. White," she said.

Anna nodded. "Mrs. Davis. I'm sorry to bother you at a time like this, but would you have a moment?"

Charlotte raised her arms in a gesture of futility. It was far from welcoming, but she said, "Sure, come on in."

"Thanks," Anna said, following her up the stairs.

Once they'd reached the kitchen, Charlotte said, "I've left the iron plugged in, be right back."

Charlotte disappeared downstairs.

Anna looked at the empty boxes on the island. As she turned slowly to take in the rest of the room, her gaze landed on the open door to what had been Paul's minioffice.

Anna felt a chill that ran the entire length of her spine.

There, on the desk, next to the laptop, was the Underwood.

Anna assumed it was *the* typewriter. The machine Paul had believed was sending him messages from beyond the grave. The machine that, one might argue, drove him to the brink of madness. The machine that played a major part in the man's suicide.

It had not been here the other night. Paul had said it was in Charlotte's car, that it wasn't coming back into the house unless it was smart enough to unlock the trunk.

She walked slowly to the office and entered. Cautiously, as

though it were electrified, Anna touched the typewriter with the tips of her fingers.

She actually felt something akin to an electric shock but knew it was nothing of the kind. It was an emotional reaction. The metal casing of the typewriter was cool and smooth to the touch.

Anna was reminded of that movie, the one by Stanley Kubrick, where the ape reaches out to touch the black obelisk. Fearfully at first, then, when he realizes the black slab isn't going to bite him, he runs his hands all over it.

Anna ran her fingers across the keys, gave the space bar a tap.

There didn't appear to be anything ominous about it, but how the hell did it get back up here if—

"Dr. White?"

Anna turned to see Charlotte standing there. "You startled me," Anna said. She nodded in the direction of the typewriter. "I just had . . . to look at it. How did it get back up here? Paul had said it was locked in your car."

Charlotte gave her a quizzical look. "I put it there," she said.

"Oh, well, of course," Anna said.

Paul's wife frowned. "Tell me you didn't think it got up here on its own."

"No, no, I didn't think that," Anna said, her face flushing. "I'm just surprised to see it."

"When I went out to get boxes, I needed the trunk space, so I put it back in here. When I get around to Paul's stuff"—her voice began to break—"I'll have to decide what to do with it."

"I guess, if it were me, I'd have . . ."

"You'd have what?"

"It's none of my business," the therapist said. "I'm in no position to judge."

"No, tell me."

Anna hesitated. "I think I'd have headed for Stratford, stopped on the bridge, and dropped that thing into the Housatonic."

Charlotte's chin quivered. She took several seconds before answering. "That's exactly what Paul wanted to do. I should have let him."

"You still could," Anna said.

Charlotte nodded slowly, and said, "Maybe I just have to know."

Anna let that sink in but said nothing.

Anna emerged from the office and wandered back to the island, where she stood beside a stool, not wanting to perch herself on it unless invited.

"I was getting his suit ready," Charlotte said. "The pants are wrinkled, and there's some kind of spot on the back of the jacket. Silly, right? Like anyone's going to notice."

"It's not silly," Anna said. "You need to get everything the way you want it. You want to do right for Paul." Anna looked at the empty boxes.

Charlotte didn't wait for the question. "I'm going to have to sort through Paul's things sooner or later."

"This is definitely sooner."

"I was wandering through the house yesterday and everywhere I looked I saw him. His books, his clothes, his CDs. I know the mourning is just beginning, but these reminders, everywhere I turn, are going to make it go on and on. Better to rip the bandage right off."

"I guess that's one way of handling it, but you might be moving a bit fast."

"You don't approve."

"I didn't say that. I know people who've dealt with loss this way. I knew a woman who lost her teenage son in a car accident, and she stripped the house of everything that reminded her of him. A week after he died, you'd have never known he lived there."

"Did it help?" Charlotte asked.

"If you're asking did it make her forget, the answer is no," Anna said.

Charlotte was quiet for a moment. Then, "That detective came by late yesterday. Arnwright."

"He came to see me, too."

"He was here two, three times, asking me about Paul, but I guess yesterday's visit was his last. He had the official coroner's report, which also meant that they were able to release his body to the funeral home. That Paul did die from drowning."

"I'm so sorry."

"He said they couldn't officially rule it a suicide. I mean, we can't know what was in his head, and it's not like he left a note. But based on his behavior the last few weeks, it's the most likely explanation. So they've called it something like 'death by misadventure.'" Her eyes reddened. "Like it was some sort of fun outing that went wrong."

Charlotte sighed. She raised her head and looked squarely at Anna. "Why are you here?"

The question struck Anna with the force of a slap. She sought some reservoir of inner strength and said, "I'm here to say I'm sorry."

"You said that five seconds ago."

"This sorry . . . is different. I'm sorry I failed Paul. I failed him badly. You came to me. You told me. You were worried he might do something to himself. I should have done more."

Charlotte looked at her, steely-eyed. "I guess you should have."

Anna stood there several more seconds before she realized there was not much else to say. "I shouldn't have come." She stopped on her way to the stairs. "But I'd like to come to the service and pay my respects. It's tomorrow?"

Charlotte nodded. "Two o'clock."

"I'll be there."

"Wonderful," she said with more than a hint of sarcasm. "Now, if you'll forgive me, I have a suit to press."

Forty-Nine

A nna had thought there would be more people.

About forty showed up for the funeral, which was held in a small church on Naugatuck Avenue. While Charlotte and Paul were not affiliated with any Milford church, the funeral home had found a minister who was not only amenable to hosting the service, but also willing to say a few words about Paul.

Paul's mother, who lived in a nursing home in Hartford, had been driven down by one of the facility's care workers. In her nineties with twiglike arms and legs, she was wheeled in and given a spot near the front, in the center aisle. She gave every indication of being oblivious to what was going on.

At one point, Anna was pretty sure she caught a glimpse of Arnwright at the back of the church, but then she lost sight of him.

Several of those attending were evidently from West Haven College. Anna walked in with a woman who, she learned after some brief small talk, was the college president. She introduced Anna to a few of Paul's colleagues. Anna forgot the names as soon as she heard them. When anyone asked how she knew Paul, she said simply, "He was a friend."

She felt ashamed to admit her connection. Everyone, she believed, would know how she had failed him. She felt doubly ashamed that she did not want to admit it.

Not that there weren't people there who knew. Charlotte, of course, and there was Bill Myers, who had been huddled over to one side of the church, reviewing some notes. Anna recognized him from real estate signs she'd seen around town over the years.

Anna also figured out who Hailey and Walter must be. They were the couple with the crying boy. That he was Josh there was no doubt. Anna could see the resemblance. He was a miniature Paul in a brown suit, red tie, and shined-up shoes. He sat with his mother and stepfather in the front pew to the left of the aisle, while Charlotte sat on the right. They did not exchange greetings nor look at one another.

It struck Anna that Charlotte was very alone. She was on the aisle, so she could only have someone on her right. Anna figured that would be a spot reserved for family, but once he had finished reviewing his notes, Bill took that seat space on the pew. He seemed to know the two women and one man to his right, which led Anna to think they were others from the real estate agency. Bill gave Charlotte a comforting hug, followed by the others.

A work family seemed to be all Charlotte had in attendance. Maybe the trip out from New York was too much for Charlotte's mother.

Anna came up the right side of the church and slipped into a pew at the halfway point. She ended up sitting next to a man in a gray suit who turned and nodded.

"Hello," he said.

Anna nodded.

He extended a hand. "Harold Foster," he said.

"Anna White," she said.

Foster?

There were probably plenty of Fosters in Milford, but Anna was pretty sure that Jill Foster's husband's name had been Harold.

He must have sensed the question she wanted to ask but would not. "Yes," he said. "*That* Foster. My wife worked at West Haven."

"Were you and Paul friends?"

"Not . . . really. But there is, I suppose, a connection." He took a moment to form his thoughts. "My wife, and Catherine Lamb, and now Paul. All victims, one way or another."

Anna could see the reasoning.

"Taking his own life," Foster said, shaking his head. "One can only imagine the torment he was going through."

Anna could only nod. She was relieved to see the minister heading for the pulpit. "It looks like things are about to begin," she said.

The minister took his place. He read several passages from the Bible that Anna did not recognize but assumed were relevant. She'd never been particularly religious, and her parents had rarely attended church. The minister called on Bill Myers to say a few words. Bill stood, gave Charlotte's hand a squeeze, and mounted the steps to the pulpit.

"Boy, this is tough," he said, reaching into his pocket for a folded sheaf of papers that contained his remarks. "If there were two words to describe Paul, they would have to be *good guy*. That's what he was. He was a good guy. But he was more than that. He was a good husband, and he was a wonderful father to his son, Josh."

Bill looked at Josh, sitting on the front row bench, dwarfed between his mother and stepfather, staring down into his lap. The mention of his name brought his head up briefly.

"And the fact that Josh is such a fine young man is a testament to what a good man Paul was. He was also a devoted educator. He cared about his students. I know that all the people here today from the college would say that about him, too."

Bill cleared his throat, shuffled his papers. He seemed to have lost his place. He flipped the pages over, his handwritten scribbles briefly visible for the congregation to see.

"Here we are. Sorry," he said. "I'm a little nervous. I first knew Paul back in our own college days, and we kind of drifted apart after that. Then we both turned out to be living in the same town, and we reconnected. I'm glad I got to know him again, even if it was only for a few years. These last few months were not easy for Paul. He suffered a trauma he clearly could not move past. I think for those of us close to Paul, the signs were right in front of us, but we blinded ourselves to them. We thought things would be okay. There's a lesson here for us all. When we see friends in trouble, we have to be there for them. We have to do everything we can to make them get help. We can't assume they'll pull through." Bill paused. "I failed Paul in that regard, and have to live with that the rest of my life."

There were some murmurs in the church. Someone whispered, "He's being too hard on himself."

Bill shuffled his papers again, and sniffed. He appeared on the verge of tears.

"I got a lot more stuff written down here, but to be honest, I'd be saying the same thing over and over again. We'll miss him." He gazed toward the casket, which had been closed for the service. "We'll miss you, man, we really will."

He stepped down and returned to his spot next to Charlotte, head bowed. She patted his back twice.

When the service was over, Harold Foster got up abruptly and cut in front of other mourners to be among the first out of the church. Maybe he was one of those people, Anna mused, who left the baseball game at the top of the ninth. Wanted to beat the rush getting out of the parking lot.

Anna wanted to get out of there as quickly as she could, too, and scanned the church looking for a less crowded exit path. But before she could settle on one, she heard a voice behind her.

"Sad, huh?"

A chill ran the length of her spine. Anna knew the voice. She turned to find Gavin Hitchens standing there in jeans, a sport jacket that was frayed along the lapels, and a loosened plaid tie.

She'd not seen what Paul had done to him. His arm was in a sling, his forehead bandaged. Anna guessed he was favoring one leg, as he had one hand firmly gripped on the back of a church pew for support.

"Gavin," she said.

"Some cop came by, asking weird questions about Paul, but he never said he was dead. But then I heard about the drowning." He shook his head. "A real tragedy."

"Stay away from me."

She started to turn away when he said, "I've got some good news, though."

Anna held her spot.

"The charges got dropped." Gavin grinned. "They gave that dead soldier's dad three voice recordings to listen to, and he couldn't pick mine out. Plus, the coffee shop surveillance video's time code is all fucked-up. They can't tell for sure when I was actually there. So, there you have it." A broad smile. "I'm an innocent man."

"There's a big difference between not guilty and innocent," Anna said.

"But I was thinking, we could still have our sessions. I liked our little talks."

Anna was about to turn away, unable to endure his smug expression another moment, when she saw Arnwright sidling up behind him. Gavin saw her looking beyond his shoulder and turned to see the detective.

Arnwright exchanged a nod with Anna, leading her to think he wanted to speak with her, but that wasn't the case.

"Mr. Hitchens," he said.

"What's up?" Gavin said breezily.

Arnwright smiled. "Guess whose surveillance system's time code is working just fine? And crystal clear, too?"

"I don't know what you're talking about."

"A house in Devon," Arnwright said.

Gavin started to pale. "Uh, what?"

Arnwright appeared to be struggling to keep the smile from growing into a grin. "Yeah. Seems some folks lost their dog. Got the whole thing on video." Arnwright looked Anna's way. "Nice to see you, Dr. White. You have a nice day."

She felt herself being dismissed, but she walked away with a sense of relief. Maybe Hitchens was finally going to get what was coming to him. Her encounter with him had delayed her enough that she was now among the last to file out of the church.

Anna found herself trailing behind Charlotte and Bill. They walked with heads lowered, shoulders touching. Soon, they'd be outside, where many were waiting to say a few words, if not to Charlotte, then to Hailey and her son.

She worked to push Gavin Hitchens out of her mind. If she had to, she thought, she'd get a restraining order. She'd talked to Arnwright about that.

Anna had already decided against offering any more words of comfort or regret to Charlotte. Her visit the day before had not gone well. Once Anna had cleared the church doors, she headed for her car. She had left her father in the care, once again, of her retired neighbor, but she didn't like to take advantage.

As she trailed Paul's friend and widow, Anna had her chin down, close to her chest. If she'd been holding her head high, she might have failed to notice Bill reaching out a hand to hunt for Charlotte's.

He found it, and when he did, he did more than simply hold it. He laced his fingers in with hers in a gesture that struck Anna as more than comforting.

There was something almost intimate about it.

Well, it's a difficult time, Anna thought.

Almost as quickly as he had found Charlotte's hand, he let it go and thrust his own hand into his pants pocket.

But then he turned to Charlotte, leaned in closely to whisper something in her ear.

Two words.

Anna was close enough that she was able to make them out, although even as the words were whispered, she questioned whether she had heard correctly.

Yet they had been as clear as if Bill had whispered them into her own ear and not Charlotte's.

"It worked," Bill said.

Fifty

Yes, Charlotte thought. *It did.*

But just because they'd pulled it off didn't mean they could start getting careless. What the fuck was Bill thinking, reaching for her hand like that, whispering in her ear, with people all around them. Sure, he'd be expected to console her, but he needed to dial it back a bit.

This was when they had to be the most on their guard.

Charlotte was already worried that she'd made a mistake, going out and getting all those empty boxes at the liquor store. The way Dr. White looked at them had made Charlotte nervous. She hoped she'd explained herself well. The truth was, she'd been itching to start packing up Paul's stuff from the moment she and Bill had decided what they were going to do.

But they had to be careful.

Which was exactly why she had been declining Bill's calls since Paul's death. It didn't look good for them to be talking. Sure, the occasional phone conversation could be explained, should they ever be asked. But the smarter course was to not talk on the phone at all. That was also how Charlotte had wanted it in the months leading up to Paul's so-called death by misadventure. Even though Bill and Charlotte worked together, only so many calls could be attributed to real estate.

There were plenty of opportunities for them to talk at work. In person. Those kinds of interactions didn't leave a trail.

And, of course, there were all those empty houses.

Not every home that went on the market was occupied. Many people who'd put their places up for sale had already moved. Some were homes that developers had built on spec, awaiting a first buyer.

When you slipped into a house like that for a fuck, you didn't have to worry about the homeowner coming back early.

Most of these empty houses had been "staged." Furniture was moved in to make the place look lived-in. Books were put on shelves. Magazines fanned out on coffee tables. Pictures hung on the walls. A bowl of fruit—preferably plastic—on the kitchen table. Maybe one bedroom was done up as a nursery, another as a teenager's room, with sports posters on the wall. And they'd dress up a master bedroom, too, with a king-size bed and fancy linens and assorted throw pillows.

Charlotte and Bill had access to many such places.

Not only was it a hell of a lot cheaper than going to a hotel—and to play it safe they'd have had to go to one well outside Milford—you didn't have to use a credit card. Nor did you have to worry about why your car was parked out front of your coworker's house.

They often joked about how much more convenient it was to have an affair when you worked in real estate.

The other thing they joked about, at least up until Kenneth Hoffman had nearly killed him, was how nice it had been of Paul to bring them together. Putting in a call to his old college friend, now working in real estate, to see if he had any advice for his wife, new to the whole business of buying and selling houses.

"Send her around," Bill said. "I'll see what I can do."

Charlotte went to the agency for a visit. Bill took an instant liking to her and was very interested to learn that she had been, at one time, an aspiring actress.

"That'll serve you well here," he told her. "You'll find yourself working for a seller and a buyer, working both sides, and they both have to believe all you care about is getting the very best deal you can for them. Some performance skills will come in very handy."

She saw something she liked in Bill, too.

She liked all the things he was that Paul was not. More self-assured, more handsome, in better shape. And even though he had one failed marriage behind him, there were no kids, and his former wife was remarried and living in France. Paul, Charlotte soon came to understand, had enough baggage to fill a 747's cargo hold. There was always something with Paul's ex. Working out the visits with Josh, the plans that were always changing. Having to listen to Paul complain about Walter's superficiality and name-dropping. Paul's real complaint, Charlotte knew, was that Hailey had traded up. She'd found a go-getter, a man with ambitions, a man who did not spend his evenings grading essays and writing next week's lecture on Ralph Waldo Emerson but was out meeting with company bigwigs and sports team owners about how to raise their profiles.

It was Charlotte who now had the guy who spent his evening grading essays and writing next week's lecture on Ralph Waldo Emerson.

And was there anything wrong with that? she sometimes asked herself. Maybe not. Unless you'd suddenly woken up to the fact that you wanted more.

It was Bill who'd reawakened her, who had shaken her out of her complacency.

There was an energy about him. When he wasn't working deals, he was taking a long weekend to London with some woman he'd just met. Or driving up to Quebec to ski and returning with a bad back, and it hadn't been on the slopes where he'd damaged it. Another weekend, with another woman, it was hot air ballooning.

He seemed . . . electric.

God, and the man even owned more than one suit.

Bill was always looking to try something new.

I could be something new, Charlotte thought.

One time, she said to Paul, "Have you ever thought about packing a bag full of Agent Provocateur lingerie and just heading into New York and booking into The Plaza and fucking our brains out?"

And Paul had said, "Agent Who?"

So one day, hosting an open house with Bill where no one had shown up for the better part of an hour, she tried the same question.

He looked at her and said, "Tonight works."

They didn't make it to The Plaza. At least, not that night.

There was the ritual of self-recrimination the first few times. Maybe they thought it was expected of them.

"This did not happen," Charlotte said, splayed across the covers in the oversize master bedroom of a three-thousand-square-foot ranch that was close to schools, had a finished basement, and had dropped ten thousand in price in the last week.

"I know," Bill said. "It just . . . Paul's my friend. I mean, he was my friend. Maybe not so much now. This was just one of those things, right? It won't happen again."

But it did.

One night when Charlotte had told Paul she was showing a condo to a woman from Stamford, but instead was in a darkened empty house with her head in Bill's lap, Bill said to her, "I'd like it to be just you."

She looked up and said, "What? What does that mean?"

"Is there a way? Is there a way that we could do this without having to be in a different fucking house every time? A way where we didn't have to pretend anymore? A way where we could just go wherever we want and do whatever we want? Because if there is, I'd want that. Just with you."

Which would mean, of course, that she would have to leave Paul. That she would have to *divorce* Paul.

It could be done. It would be messy. It would be hateful. It would take time. But it could be done.

Paul had already been through one divorce, and from the tales he'd told her, it had nearly destroyed him. He had not made it easy, he had to admit, for Hailey when she wanted to separate. Lots of pleading. Plenty of late-night calls. Failing to see things as they really were.

Refusing to accept that it was *over*.

"I made a fool of myself," he conceded. "I kept thinking I could win her back when it was clear she'd made up her mind."

He'd been afraid to commit to another marriage, so great was his fear of failing again. "But there's something about you," he told Charlotte. "I'm willing to take a leap of faith."

Leap he did.

And now, Charlotte was going to give him news she knew would destroy him. She'd met someone else. Hey, and guess what? It's your old college pal, Bill!

But she was prepared to do it. It would be horrible, but she told herself, if you didn't seek out your own happiness in life, no one else was going to do it for you.

She wanted to be happy with Bill.

And then Paul nearly died.

He stumbled upon Kenneth Hoffman getting rid of those two women he'd murdered. Kenneth clubbed him on the head. Paul went down. Kenneth knelt down beside him, ready to finish him off.

Enter the police.

Charlotte was willing to admit, to herself, that her feelings had been mixed. If only Kenneth had gotten away with it. If only that single blow to Paul's head had been fatal. It wouldn't have been her fault. She'd have been blameless. An innocent beneficiary.

So close.

Charlotte wondered, should she feel guilty, thinking that way? Because she didn't. What she felt, overwhelmingly, was *frustrated*. It was a bit like checking your lottery ticket, thinking you have every number, then double-checking and finding that you're off by one.

Paul had lived. Therapy had followed. He had to take a leave from West Haven while he recovered, and that recovery was slow with numerous setbacks. There were the nightmares. Waking up at three in the morning in a cold sweat, screaming.

Paul Davis was a broken man.

"You can't do it now," Bill said. "You can't tell a man who's coming back from a fucking attempted murder that you're divorcing him. Think what it would be like for us. At the agency? In this town? You, the woman who left a guy at his lowest point, when he needed your support more than ever before, and me, the guy you left him for." He shook his head. "I can tell you one thing for sure. We'd never sell another house in this market."

Charlotte considered all of his points. She went very quiet.

"What?" Bill asked her. "What are you thinking?"

"Maybe," she said, "there's another way."

Fifty-One

Anna White kept wondering whether she could have heard it wrong.

Maybe Bill Myers had not whispered the words "It worked" into Charlotte's ear as they were walking out of the church together. But what else could it have been? What sounded similar to "It worked" but was not "It worked"?

Surely not "It sucked." Bill wouldn't have said that about the service, unless he was being self-deprecating about his own words honoring Paul's memory. Yes, perhaps that was it, Anna thought. He believed his eulogy was inadequate. He should have said more. And he'd whispered those two words to Charlotte as an apology. He could have done better. Maybe he was looking for some reassurance, hoping that she would then tell him he was wrong, that his words about Paul were from the heart and that they definitely did not suck.

Yes, Anna thought. That could have been what she heard.

But even if he had said what she initially believed she'd heard, so what. "It worked" could have referred to any number of things. The service *worked*. What the minister had said *worked*.

And yet Anna couldn't shake the feeling the words meant something very different.

If all she'd heard were those two words, she might have been able to let it go. But it was what she saw in the seconds before Bill leaned in and whispered in Charlotte's ear.

The way he took her hand.

292 // Linwood Barclay

He did not simply hold it. He entwined his fingers with hers. Gave them a squeeze.

Anna told herself she was reading too much into the gesture. At times like these, people did strange things. Charlotte had lost her husband. She was grieving. It made sense that she would accept comfort from a friend.

But then Bill Myers did something Anna could not explain. He withdrew his hand quickly and thrust it into his pocket.

It was as if he feared someone might have seen what he did.

Anna continued to walk along behind them as they exited the church. As Charlotte and Bill emerged into the daylight, they encountered people who had been waiting for Charlotte so they could offer their condolences. Charlotte found herself in the arms of one person after another. Bill stepped back, gave her some space.

As Anna came out of the church, she moved slowly past those paying their respects to Charlotte, down the steps, and toward the sidewalk. But instead of heading for her car, she stood close to the street and watched.

She thought more about what "It worked" might have meant.

It means nothing.

Yet Anna could not shake the feeling there was something conspiratorial in the way Bill had said it. That it was their secret.

That they had pulled off something.

No, Anna thought. *I'm just looking for a way to ease my own conscience.*

She'd barely slept since Paul's death. She had not been able to shake the guilt she felt. Paul's suicide was proof she'd failed him. She should have pressured him to go into the hospital that night. She should have told him his friend Bill was wrong to talk him out of—

Bill talked him out of going to the hospital.

"It worked."

The words suggested the successful execution of a plan. What plan? Some kind of plan that would result in Paul's death?

Could you really make a man take his own life?

No, impossible.

Unless you could somehow drive him to it. Push him to the brink of madness. Make him believe something that was unbelievable.

"It worked."

Anna had accepted that there was only one explanation for the notes in that old Underwood. Paul was writing them. He might not have known it, but he was. His memory lapses were evidence that it was possible.

There was, however, something about Paul's typewriter delusion that left her troubled. Simply put, it was insufficiently elaborate. It was not wide-ranging. It was too specific. It did not live up to the standard set by other patients she'd seen over the years who'd endured hallucinations. She'd had clients who'd spun out conspiracies of great intricacy. One man she had seen three years ago was convinced Russian president Vladimir Putin was trying to brainwash him into turning over U.S. government secrets. Putin was communicating with him through various household appliances, including his toaster oven. That part was strange enough, but why would this man be tapped to hand over top secret information, when he worked at Dairy Queen?

That job was just a cover, he explained to Dr. White. He was, in fact, in touch with people from the CIA and the NSA. That's why it all made sense.

No matter how much she challenged his fantasy with logical questions, there was always an answer. She finally had him see a psychiatrist, who wrote out a scrip to keep his delusions in check.

But Paul, well, Paul was not like that.

His delusion was not immersed in multiple hallucinations and conspiracy theories. It was far from elaborate. It was specific. In every other respect, Paul Davis presented as a completely sane individual.

He didn't fit the pattern.

He didn't behave like a delusional man. Believing that Paul wrote those notes required some forcing of the proverbial square peg into a round hole.

What if, Anna wondered, there was no delusion at all?

The notes were real. But they were not coming from those two dead women.

"It worked."

How would you do it? Anna wondered. How could you make someone believe something so fantastical?

The crowd was breaking up. Word had quietly spread that Paul was to be cremated, so there would be no trip to a cemetery for burial. Everyone who had wanted to pass on a few comforting words to Charlotte was now heading to the church parking lot. Doors opened and closed, car engines came to life.

The minister came out to say a few words to Charlotte. Bill had rejoined her, standing alongside, nodding earnestly as the minister spoke.

And then it was over.

Charlotte thanked the minister and shook his hand, then turned and headed for the parking lot. Bill walked with her. Maybe he was going to drive her home.

No. Charlotte took a key from her purse, unlocked her car. Bill opened the driver's door for her.

A true gentleman.

They were talking. Bill said something that prompted Charlotte to shake her head. Then she seemed to cast her eye beyond them, as if checking to see whether anyone was looking their way.

Anna feigned disinterest. She glanced at her watch. But from the corner of her eye, she observed.

Before getting behind the wheel, Charlotte rested her hand on the top of the door. Bill Myers placed his over it and held it there for a good ten seconds. Then Charlotte pulled her hand away, sat in the driver's seat, and closed the door. Bill stepped back as she keyed the engine, and he turned in Anna's direction.

Quickly, he drew his suit jacket together in front and buttoned it. He then slipped a hand into the front pocket of his pants and started walking across the parking lot toward another car.

Anna was almost certain she knew what he had just done. She couldn't have sworn to it in a court of law. She'd have been laughed at. She'd have been mocked for professing to have astonishing observational skills.

But she was sure he was struggling to conceal an erection.

Not the usual response at a funeral, Anna mused.

Bill got into a car, fired it up, turned left onto Naugatuck. Charlotte had pulled out seconds earlier, heading right.

Anna rushed to her own car and got behind the wheel. She pondered what, if anything, to do now. To head home, she would have turned left out of the lot but found herself heading right.

After Charlotte.

Did she want to talk to Charlotte one more time? Start by telling her again how sorry she was, how she'd failed Paul? And then ask what Bill Myers had meant when he whispered those two words in her ear?

And if Anna were to do that, what, seriously, did she expect to achieve?

It was a stupid idea.

And then it hit her.

She was following the wrong car. Bill Myers was the one she wanted to talk to.

Anna checked her mirrors, did a quick U-turn, and went after the other car.

Fifty-Two

It would be so much better if he just got hit by a bus," Bill had said to Charlotte one night a few weeks earlier when Paul believed she was helping a retired couple decide how much their East Broadway beach house was worth. In fact, Bill and Charlotte were sitting naked in the hot tub out back of a nice three-bedroom on Grassy Hill Road that was listed at $376,000.

"What did you say?" Charlotte asked, trying to hear him over the bubbling of the jets.

"Nothing," he said. "It was stupid."

"No, tell me."

So he repeated it.

Charlotte said, "It's stupid because you can't wait around for something like that to happen. You can't wait for the bus driver to take his eyes off the road. You can't wait for a pedestrian to make the mistake of not looking both ways." She thought a moment. "The only way it would work would be if you could make someone *decide* to step in front of the bus."

Bill rubbed his feet up against hers under the water. "Well, that's not exactly possible."

She moved closer to him, reached below the water, and took him firmly in her hand. As she stroked, she said, "It doesn't have to be a bus."

She told him her idea. How Paul's current mental state played right into it. She had just about every detail worked out.

"That's . . . pretty *out* there," Bill said, managing to concentrate despite the distraction.

"I don't think so," she said. "But I'm going to need help. A lot of help. Some of it technical."

"Like what?"

"Can you set up a phone's ring to be anything you want? Like, if I recorded something, could I turn it into a ringtone?"

Bill, closing his eyes briefly, said he was pretty sure that could be done.

"And I have to find an old typewriter. In all the stories I read, there was one reference to an Underwood. We need to find one of those. It doesn't have to be an exact replica, but close. The good thing is, it's within the realm of possibility it could still be out there. The real one was never found."

"You're sure?"

Still moving her hand up and down, she smiled. "I called the police. Made up a story about being from some crime museum starting up in New York. Said that typewriter would make an excellent exhibit. Never recovered, they said."

Bill said he would start checking antique shops. He even knew a couple of business supply stores that might have something like that, almost as a novelty item. And there was always eBay and Craigslist.

"Nothing online," Charlotte cautioned. "No trace."

"Hang on," Bill said. He closed his eyes, shuddered, gasped. Charlotte took her hand away.

"This is where the creative part comes in," she said. "Paul has to believe this is *the* machine used in the murders."

They would type up all the messages ahead of time, she said. Bill could feed him the idea of leaving paper in the machine if he didn't think of it himself. Charlotte could hide them in the house and roll them into the typewriter or scatter them about the house as opportunities presented themselves. She'd make Bill a key, so he could sneak into the house and plant them. Or, she could do it herself.

Like the morning Paul wanted to find the yard sale where Charlotte had said she'd bought the Underwood. She didn't call the real estate agency to say she'd be late. She called Bill, signaling that the house would be empty for the next hour or so. He went over and rolled a message into the typewriter. The morning that Paul arose late and found Charlotte in the shower, she'd already been down in his study, putting a message in place.

Over the next week, they worked out the details. With a new phone, she recorded the sounds of typing by banging away at the keys. She turned that into a ringtone. The muted phone would be left atop one of the kitchen cupboards, programmed to ring only when called from Charlotte's personal phone. She'd keep that one under her pillow and make the calls once Paul was asleep.

They did some test runs. Bill held the new phone while Charlotte called it, using her own.

Chit chit. Chit chit chit. Chit. Chit chit.

"Oh my God," he said. "It's perfect."

She'd even be able to do it if Josh were staying with them. He slept with iPhone buds in his ears.

Bill had some ideas of his own. "Remind him of conversations that never actually happened. Ask him if he picked up things you say you asked him to get, but never did. Reinforce the notion that his memory's faulty."

Charlotte liked that. She said she could tell Paul she'd seen a car parked outside the house, the same one he'd seen days earlier. Except, of course, he'd never mentioned seeing a car. She could send texts from his phone, leaving him baffled when he received the replies.

"And I can visit his therapist, and Hailey. Tell them all the disturbing things I've witnessed. Plant the seed that he's losing it." She smiled. "It's nice to get back to acting. I don't see winning an Emmy, but I'll have you."

Bill came up with what he called *the clincher.*

"One night, we go for broke. You get him drunk, slip something into his drink, show him the best night in bed ever. I sneak in, put that fucking typewriter right next to him. If that doesn't drive him round the bend, he's made of stronger stuff than any of us."

Charlotte said she'd tell Paul she'd had the locks changed, even when she hadn't. He'd be even more convinced there were supernatural forces at work.

They found a suitable typewriter in an antique shop in New Haven. The notes were written.

Bill identified one huge flaw in the scheme.

"This is all designed to drive him crazy, push him over the edge, make him step in front of that metaphorical bus."

"Right," Charlotte said.

"But what if he doesn't?"

Charlotte smiled. "Oh, I have that figured out, too."

Fifty-Three

Anna was not an expert at the whole "following cars" thing.

She'd grown up watching *The Rockford Files* and *Miami Vice* and *Cagney & Lacey*, and it always looked so easy on those shows when the detectives had to tail someone. They didn't have to worry about traffic or red lights or pedestrians texting at crosswalks. The road was always clear for them.

The only way she could keep Bill Myers's car in sight was to practically ride on his bumper.

She tried to back off when she could but was so afraid of losing him that she stuck too close to him. She was sure he'd notice he was being followed.

But maybe that wasn't so bad. Didn't she want to talk to him? She wasn't tailing him so much to find out what he was up to as to find a moment to have a few words with him.

Right.

Except what was she going to say? What was she going to ask him? Anna was starting to think maybe she hadn't thought this through.

Myers led her into a nice area of south Milford. He put on his blinker and turned into a development on Viscount Drive, a few hundred feet from the beach. He lived in a collection of attached townhouses, and turned into the driveway of one of them.

She kept on driving.

She had planned to stop, flag down Mr. Myers for a conversation, but then lost her nerve. She carried on to the next stop sign and turned.

Anna circled the block, came back, and parked out front of Bill's house. She killed the engine, sat there, frozen by fear and indecision.

Knock on the door or leave?

While she considered what to do, she dug her phone out of her purse. She needed a distraction. She decided to check and see whether she had any messages. She'd muted the phone during the funeral. If anyone had texted, emailed, or phoned her, she wouldn't have known.

Well, what do you know, there were two emails and one voice mail. She checked the latter first.

It was Rosie, her neighbor keeping an eye on her father while she was out, asking when she thought Anna would be back. The woman had an eye appointment at four. Anna called her immediately and said she would be home soon, long before the woman had to be at the doctor's.

Then she turned her attention to the emails. One was junk, and the other was from someone asking if she was taking on new clients. Anna tapped on the reply arrow and was about to write back when she nearly had a heart attack.

Someone was rapping hard on her window.

Anna was so startled she dropped the phone into her lap and put her hand to her chest. Bending over, his nose pressed up to the glass, was Bill Myers.

"Can I help you?" he asked.

COMING HOME, BILL MYERS WAS PISSED.

He wanted to see Charlotte, *needed* to see Charlotte. Not at the funeral, but privately. She'd been putting him off, and sure, he understood the need for caution. But they hadn't gone through all this to *not* spend time with each other. He needed her. He needed her in every way.

It was this need that made him take her hand as they were leaving the church. To link his fingers with hers. What he wanted to do, right there in the church, was put his mouth on hers, take her in front of everyone.

See the look on their faces.

But he wasn't *that* stupid. And he'd already let her know a few minutes earlier what was on his mind. Sitting in the front pew, next to her, he had taken her hand and subtly shifted it to his lap so that she could feel how hard he was.

Charlotte had given him the tiniest squeeze before withdrawing her hand back to her own lap.

He saw that as a good sign. He'd been hoping for one, given Charlotte's avoidance since Paul's death. Not taking his calls, ignoring texts. Yes, she'd told him, weeks earlier, that whenever it was done, they had to be discreet. They did not want to attract any undue attention.

Fine. He got that. But the thing was, he had questions. Like, how long would they put up with the charade? They did work together, after all. How long before he could stay at her place, or she could sleep over at his? It was nobody else's business what they did now. Paul was dead. Wasn't Charlotte entitled to move on with her life?

But son of a bitch, just like he'd whispered to her, it had worked. Better than he had ever imagined.

He paced the house. Antsy. Anxious.

He happened to glance out the window, saw a Lincoln SUV parked across the street. He'd noticed the car in his rearview driving home. He squinted, tried to see who was behind the wheel.

It was a woman, and she looked familiar. Bill thought he had seen her at the funeral. What the hell did she want?

There was only one way to find out.

He went out the front door, crossed the street, and while the woman was engrossed in her phone, went up to the window and knocked on it with his knuckle. Asked if he could help her. Gave her quite a start.

The woman put down the window.

Bill, thinking maybe she hadn't heard him through the glass the first time, asked again, "Can I help you?"

"Mr. Myers?"

"Yes?"

"I'm Anna White. I was Paul's—"

"I know who you are," he said, nodding. "You were there, the other night, when Paul, you know, when things got really bad."

"I'm sorry to bother you. I'd hoped to talk to you at the service but missed you. And now I've been sitting out here, like an idiot, trying to work up the courage to speak to you. I wasn't sure whether to bother you at a time like this, what with Paul being your friend and all."

Bill studied her for a second. "Uh, well—"

"It wouldn't take long. I just want to have a few words."

Bill shrugged. "Come on in."

She got out of the car, locked it, and walked to his front door with him. "I thought your eulogy was very heartfelt."

He shrugged. "Thanks." He opened the door for her and invited her to sit in the living room.

Anna settled into a soft chair. "How is Charlotte doing?"

"Well, she's devastated, of course," he said.

"I can imagine. I dropped by to see her, after it happened. But I think it was a mistake. Did she tell you I visited her?"

"No," he said. "So, what did you want to talk about?"

"I suppose I wanted to tell you what I told Charlotte. That I feel terribly sorry. That I feel I failed your friend. It's all been weighing heavily on me."

"Yeah, well, you're not the only one. I mean, I guess we all played a role there."

"Did you see the signs?" she asked earnestly.

He nodded slowly. "Like I said in the church, I guess we all did. Charlotte for sure. And anytime I saw Paul, I could tell he was pretty troubled."

"Troubled, yes. But anything that suggested to you he'd take his own life?"

"Well, come on. Look at everything that was going on. The attempt on his life, the nightmares, thinking his typewriter was somehow possessed or something? That must have been some scene the other night."

"It was."

"I don't know how he did it. Without waking up Charlotte."

"You mean . . ."

"Going down to the garage, bringing up the typewriter, putting it right there by the bed. Shit, I still can't get my head around it. You're the expert. Do you think he knew what he was doing? Was it like a split personality or something? One part of him was doing all the typewriter stuff, and another part was scared shitless by it?"

"I don't know," Anna said.

"Well, if *you* don't, given your expertise, I guess we'll never know," he said.

"So, looking back, you're not surprised Paul took his own life?"

"What's the phrase?" Bill asked. "Shocked, but not surprised."

"I get that. So that's why I'm a little puzzled."

"Puzzled?"

"The other night."

"Yes?"

"What puzzles me is what you said to Paul when he got on the phone with you."

"What are you talking about?"

"When the subject came up about him going to the hospital, you advised against it."

Bill was, briefly, at a loss for words. "I don't know that I'd go that far."

"I'm sorry?"

"I mean, I may have pointed out the drawbacks to being admitted to the hospital, but it's not like I told him *not* to do it."

"I got the sense you were quite adamant. You persuaded him not to go."

"I don't see why you're laying this on me," he said defensively. "You're his therapist, for Christ's sake. If you thought he should have been put into a psych ward, you should have overruled me."

"I couldn't force Paul into the hospital against his wishes, not if he didn't present an immediate danger to himself, and I was not sure at that moment he did. But you've just told me that you saw indications that Paul might harm himself. That he *might* take his own life. And you've just told me you believed he was writing the messages himself, moving the typewriter around, *himself.* That one part of his mind was doing all this, while another part was unaware."

"I don't think I said that *exactly.*"

Anna smiled. "You're right, I may have paraphrased slightly."

"I don't get where you're going with all this, Dr. White."

"Let me be clear, I'm not absolving myself of any blame," she stated. "But I don't understand why you talked your best friend out of getting more intensive psychiatric care when, from everything you've told me, you believed he was suicidal and carrying out actions his conscious mind was unaware of."

"It's not like the way you're making it sound," Bill said. "He was my friend. And a lot of it's Monday morning quarterbacking, you know? You didn't realize you were seeing the signs until it was too late."

"Right," she said. "I totally understand."

There was a silence between them.

Bill broke it by saying, "I don't know what else to say." He stood, signaling it was time for Anna to go.

"What worked?" Anna asked, still seated, looking up.

"Huh?" he said.

"In the church, as we were walking out, you said to Charlotte, 'It worked.' I wondered what you were referring to. What was it that worked?"

He stared at her for two seconds and said, "I don't remember saying that. You must have misheard me." Bill smiled weakly as he moved toward the door. Then the lightbulb went off. "Oh, I remember. I *did* say that. I was referring to my little speech. I had it all written up at the office, did it on the computer there, and I couldn't get it to print out. There wasn't a soul there, because everyone else was on the way to the funeral, so I actually called Charlotte about it—like she had nothing more serious to worry about at a time like this—and she said the office printer had been acting up, that it was probably jammed, so I opened the printer up and sure enough she was right. So I cleared it, and then I was able to print out the eulogy. So that was the reference. To the printer. That I got it to work."

Anna nodded. "That makes sense."

He smiled as he opened the door. "You have a nice day."

"You, too," Anna said. She stood, left the house, and headed for her car.

Bill needed to know—right fucking now—what Anna White had said when she'd visited Charlotte. If Charlotte declined his call, he'd show up on her doorstep.

I hope we don't have a problem.

Fifty-Four

Once Anna White was back behind the wheel of her car, and before she turned on the engine, she lightly drove the heel of her hand into her forehead.

"Idiot," she said.

It was as simple as that. A printer that would not print.

And then, with advice from Charlotte, it became a printer that *did* print.

"It worked."

There you had it.

How she'd let her imagination run away with her. She'd gone from zero to sixty in under three seconds. Two simple words and suddenly she had Bill Myers and Charlotte Davis plotting to drive Paul crazy.

Next thing, Anna thought, she'd be believing 9/11 was an inside job, that doctors had a cure for cancer but were keeping it hidden, that there really were aliens at Roswell.

Didn't that kind of prejudging go against everything she'd learned in her professional life? You don't size up your patients in three seconds. You listen to all the facts. You talk to them. You dig below the surface and look for clues that are not immediately evident. What she had done was reach her conclusion first, then look only for evidence that would support it.

"Stupid stupid stupid," she said, and started the engine.

Realizing how seriously she had misjudged the situation made her feel more than just foolish. Ashamed, for sure. But not in any way relieved. If Bill and Charlotte had been in cahoots—boy, there was a word she hadn't thought of in years—then some of the responsibility would have been lifted from her shoulders. Her failure to accurately predict Paul's self-destructive behavior would be mitigated.

As she continued driving back toward her house, she thought that if she'd tipped her hand with Bill Myers, if she'd really let it slip that she suspected something monstrous of him, she'd have felt obliged to write him a letter of apology.

It would be the only decent thing to—

Anna slammed on the brakes.

Behind her, a horn blared.

She swerved the car over to the side of the road. Her heart was racing as she threw the SUV into park.

Write him a letter of apology.

She thought back to the service when Bill Myers was making his remarks about his good friend Paul.

How when he got lost and had to search through his notes, how he'd turned the pages over.

From where she sat, Anna could clearly see pages covered with scribbling.

Handwriting.

He had not printed out his speech.

Bill Myers had lied to her.

Fifty-Five

B ack during the planning stages, Charlotte had agreed Bill was right. There was no guarantee, no matter how much they nudged him in that direction, that Paul would kill himself.

"You may have to help him with that," Charlotte said.

Bill and Charlotte weren't in the hot tub for this conversation. They were simply sitting in his car, parked behind a furniture store. He was in the driver's seat, hands gripped tightly on the wheel, even though they were not moving.

"Charlotte," he said.

"You've had to know this was a possibility."

Of course he did. But he'd been trying to fool himself, thinking they could actually accomplish this without getting their hands dirty. Well, *really* dirty.

"Look, maybe he'll actually do it," Charlotte said, looking for a silver lining. "But at some point, we have to—what did my father always like to say?—shit or get off the pot."

Once they'd planted the notes, and Charlotte had spoken with Dr. White and visited Hailey in Manhattan, and Bill had managed to get that typewriter placed on the bedside table right next to Paul, well, fuck, if that didn't send him over the edge, what then?

When Dr. White came over in the night and suggested to Paul that he go to the hospital, Charlotte had panicked. She'd called Bill and told him to talk Paul out of it. They were hardly going to be able to move forward if Paul was in a locked ward.

So Bill had talked him out of it.

The question had always been how to do it. If Paul's suicide was going to need a little help, what was the most convincing way for it to happen? Once Bill got over his initial squeamishness, he actually came up with a few good ideas. His best was to have Paul "jump" from the second-floor balcony, or the one off the master bedroom, one floor higher. But was it enough of a drop? Charlotte wondered. What if Paul survived, and told the police what Bill had done? (It would have to be Bill; Charlotte didn't have the physical strength to heave him over.)

Bill was confident it would work. If Paul survived the fall, Bill would twist his neck.

So when Charlotte learned that Paul had drowned, she didn't have to feign shock when Detective Arnwright gave her the news. Why hadn't Bill told her he'd had a change of plan?

Maybe because then she really *would* look shocked.

She couldn't bring herself to talk to Bill those first few days. Their first conversation had been at the funeral. Play it safe, she kept thinking. Give it time.

Soon, they'd reconnect.

Soon, he could tell her why he'd decided to drown Paul. She wondered how he'd done it. Dropped by after dark, invited him for a walk on the beach? Then suddenly grabbed him, pushed him down into the water, held his head under?

Anyway, it was done.

She and Bill could get on with a life together. She was aching for him as much as he was for her. She hoped she would always want him the way she wanted him right now.

God, I hope I don't get bored with him, too.

No, no, that would not happen. They had a bond that was unlike any other.

It had been an interesting experience, all this. Charlotte had learned a lot about herself, what she was capable of. And she'd learned a lot about Bill, too.

She knew he had more of a troubled conscience than she did. She hoped that would not be a problem down the road.

What had he said to her one night?

"What we're doing, you know it's wrong."

Right. And she'd taken only a second to fire back with:

"If you were going to worry about that you should have said something a long time ago."

Fifty-Six

Detective Joe Arnwright's desk phone rang.

"Arnwright," he said.

It was the front desk. "Got a Dr. White wants to see you."

"Sure, send her in."

It struck Arnwright as oddly fortuitous that Dr. White would choose to drop by at this particular moment. He had, on his desk, and his screen, the report on the death of Paul Davis. Everything about the investigation appeared in order. It was still impossible to say, definitively, that Davis had committed suicide. He had gone into the water, and he had drowned. Had he intended that to happen? In the absence of a suicide note, there was no way to know his state of mind.

One thing seemed certain. He had not gone for a swim. People did not generally go swimming in jeans, shirt, and shoes.

It was possible he'd fallen off a nearby pier and washed up onshore. There was a dock over by the bottom of Elaine Road. And there was that outcropping of rock at Pond Point to the west. Maybe he'd gone for a walk out there and lost his footing.

But the interviews Arnwright had conducted with the man's current and former wives, friends, and therapist painted a picture of a deeply troubled man.

And yet, there was one small detail that bothered Arnwright. In all likelihood, it didn't mean anything. But it nagged at him just the same. Maybe one more visit with Charlotte Davis was in order. Arnwright would have to think about that. He didn't want to bother a woman who'd recently lost her husband with what might be a totally trivial question.

Anna White appeared at the door to the detectives' room. Arnwright stood and gave her a wave. Anna threaded her way between some desks until she was at Arnwright's.

"I know I should have called, but—"

"That's okay. Sit. Can I get you something?"

Anna declined. They both sat. Arnwright closed the folder that was on his desk and minimized the program on his screen.

"Hitchens giving you more trouble?" Joe Arnwright asked. "Because we've got him good on this dognapping thing."

"I'm pleased to hear that," Anna said. "But that's not why I'm here." She sighed. "I'm not even sure that I should be here."

Joe waited.

"You know, when you came to see me the other day, I told you how responsible I felt about what happened to Paul."

Joe nodded.

"I told you I felt I failed him, and I still do feel that way, so this thing that's been on my mind, I have to question my own motives. I may be looking subconsciously for a way to lessen the guilt I feel."

"Can't be all that subconscious if you're aware of it," the detective said.

"Yes, well, you make a good point there."

"So what's on your mind?"

Anna took a second to compose herself, and said, "I don't think Paul was having delusions."

"What do you mean?"

"I mean, I don't think there was anything wrong with him. Yes, he'd been depressed. But I don't think he was imagining the things he claimed to be hearing in the night. I think he heard *something*, but I don't know what. And I don't think he wrote the messages he was finding in the typewriter. Not consciously, or subconsciously. I don't think he was having hallucinations. I don't think he was mentally ill in any way whatsoever."

Arnwright leaned back in his chair and took in what Anna White had said. "Okay."

"I do concede that Paul was, during these last few days, extremely agitated because of what was going on at home. And that last night I saw him, he was incredibly distressed."

"So, I'm not sure what you're trying to say here. Are you saying you don't think he committed suicide?"

"I'm not saying that."

"So you think he did."

"I don't know."

Joe Arnwright smiled. "Dr. White, I—"

"I think he *might* have done it. But, then again, I think he might *not*."

"So you're leaning toward this being an accident? Because that's still within the realm of possibility."

Anna White bit her lower lip. "I shouldn't have come in. I'm making a fool of myself."

"No, you're not. What I do, Dr. White, is often based on a hunch, a feeling. Do you have a feeling about what happened?"

"I do."

"And what is that feeling?"

"That if Paul did kill himself, he was driven to it."

"Driven to it?"

Anna nodded. It took everything she had to force out the next few words. "And if he didn't take his own life, someone took it for him." She put her hands in her lap decisively, as though she had just gotten the toughest word at the spelling bee.

"You're saying you think someone might have murdered Mr. Davis?"

Anna White swallowed. "I think it's a possibility."

"What makes you say that?" Arnwright asked.

"Because of what he said," she blurted.

"Something Paul said?"

"No, not Paul. His friend. Bill Myers. I heard him whisper 'It worked' to Charlotte."

"That's it," Arnwright said. "Just those two words."

Anna nodded sheepishly. "When I asked him what he meant by that, he came up with a story about how he got a *printer* to work so he could have a copy of the eulogy he gave. But he didn't read a printed speech. It was handwritten. I saw it. He lied to me."

"Okay," Arnwright said, doing his best to tamp down the skepticism in his voice.

"I also asked Mr. Myers about talking Paul out of going to the hospital." She paused. "It's like he wanted to make sure Paul was where he could get to him. Almost like he didn't want Paul to get away, to get help."

Arnwright frowned. "Okay, so all these things that happened with the typewriter, you're suggesting it was a setup?"

Anna nodded.

"Why?"

Again, Anna struggled to get the words out. "I think Bill Myers and Charlotte Davis might be having an affair."

"You have any evidence of that?"

Anna hesitated. "Not really."

"So that's just a feeling, too, then."

"It was the way . . . they held hands. And . . . I guess that's all. Body language, I suppose." Another anxious swallow. "I've learned to read that kind of thing over the years."

"Body language," Arnwright said.

"I know. I must sound ridiculous."

"You said you think Mr. Davis was set up. How on earth would they do that?" the detective asked.

"I . . . have no idea." She shook her head. "There's something else."

"Yes?"

"The boxes."

"Boxes?"

"When I visited his wife, after his death, she had all these empty boxes."

Arnwright looked at her, waiting.

"She'd gone out and gotten all these empty boxes to start packing his things. Who does that so fast after someone dies? It's like, it's like she couldn't wait to get at it."

Joe Arnwright took a long breath, put both palms on the desk and said, "Anything else?"

Anna sat there, feeling increasingly ridiculous. "No," she said.

"Well, I want to thank you for coming in. It's all very helpful." He stood, implying the therapist should do the same.

Anna got up. "I know what you're thinking."

"And what's that?"

"That I'm trying to get myself off the hook. That I've come up with this elaborate fantasy so that I won't feel Paul's death was my fault."

"That's not what I'm thinking."

"I didn't know what else to do but come and see you."

"And I'm glad you did. If I need to talk to you again about this, I know how to get in touch."

Dr. White knew she'd been dismissed. She stood and said, "Just about every meeting I've had lately I've regretted immediately afterward. I guess I'll add this one to the list." She nodded her good-bye and walked out of the detectives' room.

Arnwright sat back down and reopened the folder on his desk, as well as the report that had been on his screen.

He read, for maybe the fifth time, what had been found on Paul Davis's body.

There had been the wallet, of course. Despite his body having been tossed about by the waves after he had—presumably—walked out into the waters of Long Island Sound, and then subsequently washed back onto the beach, the wallet had not been dislodged from the back pocket of his jeans. It was solidly in there, and it had taken some effort for the police first on the scene to extricate it from the tight, wet clothing.

His watch, an inexpensive Timex, remained attached to his left wrist. It was still working. His tightly laced Rockport walking shoes remained on his feet. Retrieved from the front pocket of his jeans were a gas station receipt, wadded tissues, three nickels, four quarters, one dime, and a dollar bill.

That was it. None of those things had been washed out of Paul Davis's pockets during his time in the water.

Arnwright had been troubled not by what was in his pockets, but by what was not.

He thought back to that night, when Paul Davis's wife got out of her car and went to the front door of her house.

It was locked. She had her keys in her hand, and used one to open the front door.

How had the door been locked in the first place? Presumably, Paul Davis had locked it as he exited the house, on his way to the beach or to a pier or wherever.

So where was the key?

Why was there no key in his pocket?

Fifty-Seven

Charlotte wasn't surprised to see her phone light up with Bill's name on the screen. Not two hours since the funeral and already he was calling her. So much for discretion. But then again, a guy who puts your hand on his dick in the middle of a funeral service clearly has a problem with delayed gratification, not to mention subtlety.

She figured if she ignored the call, he'd just keep trying. So she accepted it.

"Hello?"

"We need to talk," he said.

"Why, Bill," she said, feigning a casual tone. "It's good of you to call. I know I already told you, but I thought what you said about Paul was lovely. Straight from the heart. He'd have been touched to know how you felt."

Bill paused. It took him a second to catch on. There was either someone in the room with her, or Charlotte thought someone was listening to her calls. She had no reason to believe that was happening, but why risk it? She'd actually gone online, looked up bugging devices and where they were most commonly hidden, and then had searched the house to make sure it was clean.

No fool, she. You didn't hear *her* whispering "It worked" in the middle of a crowded church.

"Yeah, well, thanks for that," Bill said. "Like you said, it was from the heart."

"The house feels so empty with him gone."

"Yeah, right. Uh, like I said, there was something I needed to talk to you about. In person."

Charlotte sighed. Maybe it was time. Besides, there were some things she wanted to discuss with *him*.

"Fine, then," she said. "I'm here."

"See you in a few minutes," he said, and ended the call.

Did he want to tell her how he did it? Was he overwhelmed with guilt and needed to talk about it? Did she even *want* to know every detail? As long as it was done, that was all that mattered.

Charlotte figured it would take Bill the better part of twenty minutes to come over, but the doorbell was ringing in fifteen. She glanced out a second-floor window before running down the stairs, and while she could not see him at the door, she spotted his car parked half a block up the street.

At least that was smart. She wasn't ready for people to see his car parked at her house yet.

She went down the stairs and opened the door. Bill charged into the house and blew straight past her. As he mounted the steps to the kitchen, he said without glancing back, "We've got a problem."

She hurried up the stairs after him. "What are you talking about?"

He went straight to the fridge, took out a bottle of beer, twisted off the cap, and took a long drink.

"Is there anybody else here?" he asked warily.

"No."

"The way you were talking on the phone, I thought maybe—"

"I was being careful. But the house is safe. Say what you have to say."

He leaned up against the island. "Okay, you're gonna be pissed, because this is my fault, but you're going to have to move past that so we can deal with the situation."

"Just tell me, for Christ's sake!"

His eyes looked upward. He couldn't face her. "Someone heard me. What I whispered."

"Whispered when?"

"In the church. What I said when we were walking out. That what we did, that it *worked*."

"For fuck's sake, Bill! Jesus! Who? Who heard you?"

"The therapist. Anna White."

"How do you know?"

"She came and saw me. She came to my fucking *house*. Started talking about this and that, worked her way around to the fact I talked Paul out of going to the hospital. Asked if that was what I was referring to when I told you it worked."

Charlotte shook her head disbelievingly. "You're an idiot."

"All right, all right, I'm an idiot."

"And putting my hand on your cock in the middle of—"

"Okay!" he bellowed. "I get it! I'm a fucking moron. Can we get past that and deal with what's happening right now?" As he shook his head in frustration, his eyes landed on the typewriter. "Jesus, you brought that back into the house?"

"I needed trunk space," she said, waving her hand at the boxes that still covered up much of the island. "Look, let's think about this." Her voice was calmer. "What does Dr. White really have? She heard you say two words, and she's suspicious that you didn't want Paul to go to the hospital. It's nothing. It's absolutely nothing. What did you tell her when she asked what you meant?"

"I said it was about getting the office printer to work."

"What?"

"If she asks, I called you about that. That I was trying to print out the eulogy."

Charlotte looked exasperated. "She's supposed to believe that the first thing you told me after the funeral for my dead husband is that you got a printer to work."

"I didn't have a lot of time to come up with something. Important thing is, I think she bought it. I'm more worried about the other thing, about talking Paul out of going to the hospital."

Charlotte was thinking. "No, that's okay. What you said made perfect sense at the time. Why would you want your friend to be locked up in a psych ward? Those places are horrible. You had a natural reaction. You're worrying about nothing. Let it go."

"She said she came to see you, too."

"Yeah. But she came by to say she was sorry, that she misread the signals. She was feeling all guilty. That's probably why she came to see you. She wants to lay this off on you so she doesn't feel responsible."

He took another long pull on the bottle. "I guess. But I didn't like the way she was asking questions. I had a bad feeling about it."

"Well, get over it. Even if she went to the police, what does she have, really? You think Detective Arnwright is going to give a shit about something like that? The medical examiner's report, all the statements from us and the doctor and Hailey? It all points to suicide."

"Yeah," he said. "It does. Okay." He grinned. "And wonder of wonders, that's what actually happened."

Charlotte took a step closer. "What?"

"Well, unless you dragged Paul into the water yourself and drowned him, he really did it. What'd you think I meant when I said it worked? He actually fucking offed himself."

Charlotte stared at him, open-mouthed.

"All this time," she said, "I wondered why you didn't give me any warning that you were going to do it that night. We'd talked about that. So I'd be ready."

"Why do you think I was calling you so often before the funeral?" Bill asked. "I was as stunned as you."

"Oh my God," Charlotte said softly. "You didn't kill Paul. *We* didn't kill Paul."

Bill grinned. "Sometimes things just have a way of working out."

Fifty-Eight

Anna White walked out of the Milford Police headquarters feeling like a fool.

"Idiot," she said under her breath as she got into her SUV.

She headed home. She'd canceled so many appointments over the last week that there were still clients she'd been unable to reschedule. It was already late afternoon—God, she had to get home so Rosie could make her eye appointment—so she wasn't going to be able to see any of them today. But she could start sorting out the next few days.

Despite being dismissed by Detective Arnwright, Anna still believed something was very wrong. She'd spent her professional lifetime reading people, and the story she believed she'd seen developing between Charlotte and Bill was one of deception.

Paul was not, Anna believed, the only one who'd been deceived.

The number one dupe was herself. Anna now could not help but wonder if Charlotte had been putting on an act when she showed up unexpectedly at the office to tell her how worried she was about Paul.

I was played, Anna thought. *I'm their corroborating evidence.*

If Charlotte and Bill were having an affair, as Anna suspected, and were plotting against Paul, who better to back up their story that Paul was unstable than the dead man's therapist?

But if what Anna suspected was true, what could she do about it? She'd gone to Arnwright with nothing more than a hunch, and it was just as well she didn't mention what Bill was trying to conceal after he saw Charlotte to her car.

Hey, Detective, he had a hard-on. That's proof, right?

It would have been the last thing Arnwright needed to be convinced that she was a nutcase. And sex-obsessed.

So what was there to do? If she couldn't get the police interested in taking another look at Paul's death, was she going to conduct an investigation herself?

I am not Nancy Drew.

She was not going to snoop about like some amateur sleuth in a hackneyed mystery novel. That wasn't the real world. She had no idea how to go about such a thing. She was not going to try tailing someone again. She was not about to hide microphones in Charlotte's house or Bill's townhouse.

All she knew how to do was talk to people. And more than that, to *listen*. And to watch. That was how you got below the surface, to where the truth was buried.

She wanted to talk to Charlotte again. When she'd last spoken to her, Anna had not held the suspicions she did now. Anna wanted to look her in the eye when she asked her some of the same things she'd asked Bill Myers.

And for sure, she'd ask about his call to her about the printer. What a crock of shit that was.

Anna believed she would come away from a meeting like that knowing, in her heart, whether her suspicions were warranted. If she found they were, she might not have enough for the police to open an investigation, but at least she'd have a good idea what really had happened.

I have to know.

Paul's death would always weigh on her. She would always feel responsible. But there were degrees of responsibility.

When she returned home and gave the neighbor her freedom, she checked on Frank, whom she found in the backyard knocking some more chip shots with a nine-iron. The woods behind the house, Anna imagined, were littered with hundreds of golf balls.

Then she went about rescheduling. Once she was done with that, it was nearly seven, and time to pull something together for her father and herself for dinner.

"Dad," she said, finding him back in his bedroom on the rowing machine, "are you okay with a frozen pizza? I know it's pretty sad, but it's been that kind of day."

"Okay by me, Joanie," he said, sliding back on the machine.

Knowing he'd be okay with it, but still feeling she needed to apologize for it, she had already preset the oven. By the time she got back to the kitchen, it was time to slide the pizza into it.

Half an hour later, sitting at the table with her father, he studied her and said, "What's on your mind, pumpkin?"

His pet name for her since she was a child. So at least for the moment, he knew she was his daughter.

"I have to confront somebody about something," she said. "I'm not looking forward to it."

Frank smiled sadly. "It's okay. I can handle it."

"Oh, God, Dad, it's not *you*," she said, laying a hand on his.

"If there's something you gotta tell me, I can take it."

"It's something else entirely. Really."

"Okay, then."

"I might have to go out tonight."

He nodded. "Sure thing."

"And I need to know you'll be okay if I do. I can't impose on Rosie again."

"Not a problem."

She was relieved that her father no longer seemed traumatized by their visit from the SWAT team. He seemed to have forgotten all about it.

"What is it you have to do?" he asked.

"I kind of have to work myself up to it."

Another nod. "If you decide not to, I was thinking we could go visit your mother tonight."

It never ceased to amaze her how he could drift in and out this way. Be perceptive enough to tell there was something on her mind, and then propose an outing based on a fantasy.

"We'll see," Anna said.

He offered to do the dishes—there was little more than a baking sheet, two plates, and two glasses—so Anna told him that would be great. She wanted him to feel useful whenever possible.

When he was finished and had retreated upstairs to his bedroom to watch the cartoon channel, Anna made some tea. When it was ready, she poured herself a cup and sat at the kitchen table to drink it.

She spent the better part of an hour on it.

"Sooner or later," she said under her breath, "you're gonna have to do this thing."

But that didn't have to mean she couldn't have another cup of tea first while she thought about it.

Fifty-Nine

They felt a celebration was in order.

And why not? Bill and Charlotte never had to be worried about being arrested for murder because—Breaking News, folks!—they had not murdered anyone.

Sure, they might have *driven* Paul to take his own life, but how was anyone ever going to prove that? There was no so-called smoking gun. No fingerprints, no DNA, no incriminating hairs or fibers. None of that stuff you saw on TV.

The pages of faked messages from Catherine and Jill weren't evidence. They'd been written on that typewriter, and so far as anyone knew, Paul had written them. About the only thing Bill thought they needed to address was that extra smartphone with the typewriter ringtone.

He grabbed a chair from the kitchen table and brought it over to the cupboards, stood on it, and retrieved the device that had been sitting up there since they'd put their plan into action. It had been plugged into an outlet near the ceiling that had originally been installed to power accent lighting.

He stepped down off the chair, phone in hand.

"No need to throw this out," he said. "All I have to do is change this ringtone."

He fiddled with the phone's settings for several seconds, then placed it screen down on the island.

"Done," he said. "Consider our tracks covered."

Charlotte had apologized for being so angry about the overheard whisper. "Who cares what Anna White heard? I could have gone down on you in the middle of the church and there wouldn't be a damn thing they could do about it."

"We got what we wanted, but son of a bitch, our hands are clean," Bill said. "I have to admit, I didn't see that coming."

"You," Charlotte said, "are a lot smarter than you look."

"Maybe," he said. "But you were the one who really had to pull it off. You had to be here. You had to play along. You deserve an Oscar."

She'd brought out a bottle of wine from the fridge and was already on her third glass. Bill was into his fourth beer. No more meeting in empty houses. If anyone came by, his presence here was totally legitimate. He was consoling the widow.

He had some very serious consoling in mind for later.

"It's really—shit, you know—it really was the so-called perfect crime," she said. "You know why? Because there *was* no crime."

"Are there even laws for what we did?" Bill asked. "Even if someone could prove we used that thing"—he pointed to the typewriter—"to mess with someone's head, was it even illegal? We could say it was like a practical joke that got out of hand. Or even better, we were *helping* Paul."

"Helping?"

"No, not helping. *Inspiring.* The same thing you told him when you gave it to him. He wanted to write about what Kenneth had done to him, and what we did was designed to inspire him with that effort. Really get him into it. That's all. We couldn't have known he'd take it the way he did."

"*That's* a bit of a stretch," Charlotte said.

"Anyway, it's a moot point. It's never going to get to that." He became reflective. "I still can't believe he did it. Walked right out into the water. I mean, how would you do that? If you fall out of a boat or something like that, and you can't make it to shore, sure, you drown. There's nothing you can do. But walking in? You'd think, once your lungs started filling up, your natural instincts would take over, you'd try to save yourself, turn around and run back for shore."

Charlotte shook her head. "No, it could happen. I've seen stuff like that on the news." Her face went dark. "God, it must have been awful." She looked at Bill and her eyes misted. "The water is so cold." She mimed shivering, but the chill was real.

It was a rare moment for her. She almost felt sorry for what they'd set into motion.

"Listen," he said. "It's done. We don't look back. We look forward." He pulled her into his arms. "It's all over now. We made our decisions and now we live with them." He tightened his squeeze on her. "We got what we wanted."

"I was worried about you for a while," she said. "I thought you were getting cold feet at one point. That you were having some crisis of conscience."

"Not anymore."

He bent his head down and put his mouth on hers. She placed her hand at the back of his neck and latched onto him.

"That's the spirit," Bill said, breaking free long enough to take a breath. He grasped her around the waist and lifted her onto the island so that her face was level with his. She wrapped her legs around his torso, locked her ankles, trapping him. They explored each other that way for another minute before Charlotte put her hands on his chest and gently pushed back.

"Upstairs," she said.

Seconds later, they were in the same bed where Charlotte and Paul had spent their last night together. If she had any qualms about that, she did not show it. The sex with Bill was fast and animalistic. The second time was slower but no less passionate.

By that time, night had fallen. They lay together in the bed, weary and lethargic. Moonlight coming through the blinds cast prison-stripe shadows across their nakedness.

"This is probably the wrong thing to say," Bill said, glancing at the bedside clock, which read 9:57 P.M., "but I could use something to eat."

"Don't give me straight lines," Charlotte said. "Is this where I say you've been doing that for the last two hours?" She turned onto her side, threw a leg over his, pinning him to the mattress. "Just stay where you are. Close your eyes."

"I might be hungrier than I am sleepy," he said.

"Oh shut up," she said. "I'm exhausted and you should be, too."

"My dick could sure use a nap," he said.

"Close your eyes," she said again.

He did. In less than a minute, he could hear soft breathing from her pillow. And shortly after that, he succumbed.

But it seemed to him that he had been asleep only a few minutes when his eyes reopened. He glanced at the clock. It was only 10:14. He'd been asleep barely fifteen minutes.

Something had woken him up.

A sound.

It had sounded like—

No, no way.

He propped himself up on an elbow and listened. The only thing to be heard was Charlotte's breathing in and out.

It was nothing, he thought. Whatever he thought he'd heard, it had to have been part of a dream.

He put his head back down on the pillow, closed his eyes.

And then immediately opened them when he heard the sound again.

Chit chit. Chit. Chit chit chit.

From downstairs.

Sixty

"Wake up!" Bill whispered to Charlotte.

She grunted, opened her eyes. "What?"

"Shh!" He had a finger to his lips. "Listen."

Chit. Chit chit chit.

She blinked a couple of times. "It's nothing," she said groggily.

"You don't hear that?"

She nodded. "It's the phone. You must not have changed the ringtone."

Bill considered that. "Okay, maybe, yeah. I should have tested it."

"Fix it in the morning," she said, putting her head back down onto the pillow.

"But wait," he said. "Someone has to call it for it to ring."

Charlotte raised her head again, turned to look at her bedside table. "Where the hell—"

She shifted over to the edge of the bed, looked down to the floor, felt around with her hand. "There it is," she said.

"What?"

"My phone. I must have knocked it off the table. I guess it called you."

That placated Bill for only a second. "Your phone's not going to make a call just by hitting the floor."

"What about pocket calls? Isn't that kind of how those happen?"

In the few seconds they'd been whispering, there had been no more sounds of typing.

"Maybe," Bill said.

"Or," she said, "someone else called the phone. It didn't have to be me. You never got a wrong number? Or a telemarketer's call? Even on your cell? They don't have to know your actual number. They just keep dialing and sooner or later they hit yours."

"We planned for that," he reminded her. "We programmed the phone to only ring when you called it. Otherwise, it was on mute."

"Oh, yeah," she said. "So maybe there was a glitch. It's accepting other calls now."

"I'm gonna go down and power it off completely," he said.

She grabbed onto his arm. "Stay here."

He allowed her to hold on to him. He dropped his head onto the pillow and stared at the ceiling.

Chit chit. Chit chit chit. Chit.

"Oh, fuck it," he said, and threw back the covers.

Charlotte sighed. "I really was asleep, you know."

"Since I'm going down, you want anything?" he asked, pulling on his boxers.

"You're still hungry?"

"We didn't exactly have dinner."

"I guess not. Bring me up some crackers and cream cheese or something."

"That's it?"

"Jesus, just go."

She flopped back down on the bed and pulled the covers up over her head. Within seconds, she felt herself falling back to sleep.

And then it was her turn to be awakened by a now familiar sound.

Chit chit. Chit. Chit chit chit.

And then:

Ding!

She opened her eyes and sat up in bed. Charlotte reached over for

Bill, but her hand hit mattress. She patted around, confirmed that he was not there.

Ding? she thought.

That was the sound a typewriter made when you reached the end of the line. It was the signal to hit the carriage return. That had never been part of the ringtone programmed into the phone.

That sounded like a real typewriter.

Like the typewriter downstairs.

So what the hell was Bill doing playing with that damn thing at—she looked at the clock—10:34 P.M.

Boy, she'd fallen back asleep quickly. But even though Bill had not been gone long, all he had to do was mute a phone and grab something to eat. Why stay downstairs and goof around with the typewriter?

"God," she said, slipping out from under the covers. As she pulled on an oversize T-shirt, she couldn't help but wonder if she had traded a man for whom she'd lost all love for a man who was an enormous pain in the ass.

"Hey!" she called out as she headed for the bedroom door. "What the hell are you doing?"

As she approached the top of the stairs she noticed there were no lights on in the kitchen.

"Bill?" she called. "What's going on?"

No reply.

"You're freaking me out. Talk to me, for Christ's sake."

She slowly descended the stairs, step by step. Listening.

There wasn't any sound coming from the kitchen. Even the typewriter had gone silent.

"Bill?"

As she went to step onto the kitchen floor, her hand reached for the light switch.

Standing there, directly in front of her, was a very tall, heavyset man. Definitely not Bill. The first clue was that he was fully clothed.

The second was that he was wearing a name tag.

It read: LEN.

"Hi," he said, and then closed his meaty hands around her neck.

Charlotte barely had a moment to scream.

Sixty-One

It took three cups of tea—followed by two glasses of wine—before Anna was ready to do what she knew she had to do.

But now that she'd worked up her courage for a show-down with Charlotte Davis, Anna worried that she had left too late.

It was dark out. It was after ten.

Chances were Charlotte was already in bed. With, or without, Bill Myers.

Whoa, Anna thought.

Why hadn't she considered that possibility? That when and if she went to see Charlotte, Myers would be there.

She had to stop thinking that way. She was looking for excuses not to go.

I am going to do this.

And catching Charlotte off guard, possibly waking her up, well, so what? That might work to Anna's advantage. The thing was, Anna knew *she* wasn't going to be able to get to sleep tonight. So what if she kept someone else up, too?

As for Myers, she'd look for his car. If she drove over there and saw it in Charlotte's driveway, she'd reassess at that point.

Charlotte might not even be home. She could be at Myers's house. Would she go back there? She'd make that decision if and when she had to.

Anna went upstairs and rapped lightly on her father's door.

"Hello?"

She pushed the door open. Frank was under the covers, in his pajamas.

"Sorry," she said. "I'm going to go do this thing I was telling you about. I'll be back soon."

"What time is it?"

"It's late. Go back to sleep."

"Where are you going?"

"I'll tell you all about it in the morning. Rosie won't be here. It's too late for her to come over. You'll be fine for a while, okay?"

Her father said sure.

Back downstairs, she pulled on a light jacket, turned off a few lights, and decided she would exit the house from the office wing. As she was passing through, she heard the familiar ding of an incoming email. She slipped in behind her desk and discovered not one new email, but five, from patients about rescheduled appointments.

Anna opened the datebook beside her computer, made a note of the new times for her clients, then wrote quick replies to confirm the changes. Then she slipped out the side door, locked it, jumped into her SUV, and headed out.

She rehearsed in her head the questions she was going to ask Charlotte. Were there ways she could trip the woman up? Get her to say things she didn't want to say? While she'd been having her tea—not so much when she was drinking the wine—she'd scribbled some thoughts down on a paper napkin.

Not so much questions, but things to watch for, like the things people do when they lie.

Stalling by repeating a question. Excessive blinking. Long pauses. Coming up with overly complicated responses. Impersonal language—fewer references to *I* or other people by their actual names, so more use of *him* and *her*.

Of course, one of the other possible reactions from a liar would be to attack.

Anna was hoping it wouldn't come to that.

Sixty-Two

Charlotte took a moment to place the large man who had her pinned to the wall with his hands around her neck.

She didn't recognize him at first. She wasn't used to seeing him outside his ice cream truck. But it took only a few seconds to remember him from the times she'd bought a cone from him. She also remembered this was Kenneth Hoffman's son.

Leonard.

What was he doing here? Why was he in her house? Why was he trying to kill her? And where was Bill? What had happened to—

Oh God.

Out of the corner of her eye she saw him. He lay on the floor to the right of the kitchen island. He was not moving, and his head seemed positioned at an odd angle to his shoulders, as though his neck had been twisted.

If he was breathing, Charlotte could see no sign.

She struggled to do any breathing of her own. She wanted to scream, but nothing would come out, so she tried to mouth some words.

"Stop," she croaked. "Please stop . . . can't breathe . . ."

She flailed pitifully against the man, trying to slap him with her hands, but it was like trying to repel a bear with a flyswatter. When Leonard pushed her up against the wall, he lifted her slightly, so her feet were only barely touching the floor. She couldn't get any leverage to kick him.

Charlotte felt herself starting to pass out. Her brain was being starved of oxygen. Her eyes darted about the room, catching movement in the doorway to Paul's small office.

There was someone standing there.

A woman.

"Not her, too, Leonard," said Gabriella Hoffman. "We need to talk to her."

Leonard relaxed his grip on Charlotte's neck. She slid an inch back down to the floor, and as Leonard took his hands away she dropped to her hands and knees, hacking and coughing. As she struggled to get air back in her lungs, Gabriella walked in her direction, stopping in front of her.

Charlotte looked up, her neck already purplish with bruising from Leonard's grasp.

"What have you done to Bill?" she asked hoarsely.

"Don't worry about him," Gabriella said. "Worry about you."

"I . . . I know you."

"I think we met at faculty events once or twice," Kenneth Hoffman's wife said. "I'm Gabriella. And you are Charlotte." Her eyes shifted in the direction of Bill's body. "I don't know him. Who is he?"

"Bill," Charlotte said, her voice shaking. "Bill Myers."

"A West Haven professor? I don't recognize him."

"No. We sell real estate together."

"It looks like you do more than that together," Gabriella said. "This is my son, Leonard."

Leonard nodded.

"Most people call me Len," he said.

Charlotte, fully able to breathe again, asked, "Is . . . is Bill dead?"

"Yes," Gabriella said. "Leonard snapped his neck."

Charlotte slowly got to her feet, then took one step back from Gabriella. Leonard hovered to one side like a pet gorilla awaiting instructions.

"What do you want?" Charlotte asked. "Why are you here?"

Gabriella waved her hand toward the Underwood. "That."

"The typewriter?"

"Yes."

"What . . . what about it?"

"Your husband went to visit Kenneth in prison with some ridiculous story about those women, the ones my husband was convicted of killing, trying to talk to him through this machine."

"Yes," Charlotte said, her voice little more than a whisper.

"Paul gave Kenneth quite a scare. Not because of those messages. Those were laughable."

"I don't understand."

"What I needed to see—to get—was that." Again, she indicated the Underwood. "But when we came before, it wasn't here."

Charlotte's eyes went wide. "You were here before?"

Gabriella smiled. "Your husband said the typewriter was in your car's trunk, but I didn't believe him. But I guess he wasn't lying, because it wasn't here. So we've come back. We were going to ask you for your car keys, but then we saw the typewriter sitting right here."

"You saw . . . Paul?"

"Leonard and I just wanted to talk to him. About the typewriter, and the letters. We met him outside. He'd been out for an evening stroll." Gabriella smiled. "Things didn't quite go right. When he understood my concern, well, he became very agitated. And when Leonard here tried to calm him down, he ran off toward the beach."

"Oh, my God," Charlotte said. She looked at Gabriella's lumbering son. "He didn't kill himself. *You* killed him."

Leonard's look bordered on sorrowful. "I didn't really mean to. I guess I held his head under the water a little too long."

Gabriella sighed. "We took Paul's keys and searched your house, but he wasn't lying. The typewriter wasn't here."

"I still don't . . . I don't understand why . . ."

"As I said, those messages that the typewriter was supposedly spewing out were ridiculous. They gave Kenneth pause, for a moment, he was willing to admit that, but he figured it had to be some kind of joke. A trick. But," Gabriella said slowly, "it is still possible—however remotely—that this is the real typewriter."

"I don't understand," Charlotte whispered.

"Kenneth got in touch after Paul's visit. Said I needed to act before Paul did something like ask the police to compare his notes to the ones Catherine and Jill wrote."

She held some sheets of paper of her own. "So I just was doing a little comparing of my own."

She waved one of them in front of Charlotte. "These are from some notes I made when I audited a West Haven philosophy class some years ago." She smiled. "One of the perks of being married to a faculty member." She looked off almost dreamily at a point in the distance. "I've always liked the feel of a real typewriter. So much more *satisfying* than a computer. Don't you?"

Gabriella ended her reminiscing with a small shake of the head. She pointed to the Underwood. There was a piece of paper rolled into it, and a line of type.

"Remember 'Now is the time for all good men to come to the aid of the party'?" Gabriella asked.

Charlotte shook her head.

"You're too young," Gabriella said. "That's what they'd always have you write to test a typewriter. A nice, crisp sentence. That's what I was doing. That's the noise you heard. I was about to compare my class notes to what I just typed here, but that was when your Mr. Myers came down."

Charlotte struggled to piece together what was happening, how whatever she had set in motion was now blowing up in her face. Her eyes kept being drawn to Bill's lifeless body.

Her mind was able to cut through the panic and confusion to ask, "So what if it's the actual typewriter? What difference does it make?"

"Oh, a great deal," Gabriella said.

Gabriella leaned over and peered into the inner workings of the

Underwood. "And it looks as though Kenneth was right to be concerned."

"What the hell are you talking about?" Charlotte asked.

Gabriella raised her head. "Blood. There's dried blood in the keys." She looked at Charlotte. "It's nothing short of amazing that you found it. At a yard sale, yes? What are the odds? Someone must have found it in the garbage before the Dumpster was emptied, or maybe it was found at the dump. Then it ended up for sale in someone's driveway, and of all the people in the world who could buy it, it was you."

"I didn't buy it at a yard sale! And that blood is Josh's!"

"Josh?"

"Paul's son. He got his fingers caught in it. You're right, it would be amazing if this were that typewriter. But it isn't."

Gabriella frowned. "I don't understand."

"I didn't buy it at a yard sale. I bought it at an antique store. We—me and Bill—were trying to find a typewriter like the one Kenneth made those women write their apologies on."

Gabriella's expression was one of genuine puzzlement. "Why?"

A tear escaped Charlotte's right eye and ran down her cheek. "We did a terrible thing. A terrible, terrible thing."

Gabriella, intrigued, smiled and said, "They say confession is good for the soul." The smile twisted into something jagged. "Although Kenneth might not entirely agree with that."

Charlotte gave her the broad strokes of what she and Bill had done.

"Why ever would you do that?" Gabriella asked, her face full of wonder.

Charlotte swallowed hard. "We wanted to make it look like he was losing his mind. And, then, when we . . . when we killed him . . . everyone would think it was suicide. Except we thought he'd actually done it. Killed himself. But it was you."

Gabriella's wonder morphed into one of irritation. "So all our worries have been for nothing?" She ran her fingers along the Underwood's space bar. "This was all something you and your *lover* cooked up?"

"Yes!" Charlotte said with sudden enthusiasm. "You don't have to worry! And I don't even understand why you *are* worried. What is it about the blood? Why were you concerned about that?"

Gabriella glanced at Bill's body, then gazed pityingly at Charlotte. "Every time you think you're done, there's always one more thing left to do."

Sixty-Three

Anna White drove slowly down Point Beach Drive. She had her window open slightly, and she could smell the brisk salt air wafting in from the sound. The last time she'd had to find the Davis house it had been dark, and so it was that again she had to rely on artificial light to check house numbers.

She did recall that the house was near the end of the street, although she couldn't remember any particular characteristics.

But then she spotted Charlotte Davis's car in a driveway and, to Anna's relief, the only other car in the driveway was Paul's. She did not see Bill Myers's car there. If she had passed it coming down the street, she had not noticed it.

Luckily, there was a space on the street directly out front of the Davis house that she was able to pull straight into. She killed the engine, got out of the car, and closed the door softly. She wasn't sure she wanted anyone to know she was here until she rang the bell.

Her stomach was full of those proverbial butterflies. Was she doing the right thing? Was this a totally misguided course of action? Hadn't she already been through all this interior debate before leaving her house?

One thing she no longer believed she had to worry about was waking Charlotte Davis. A glance up to the second floor showed that plenty of lights were on in the kitchen area. Surely Charlotte wouldn't have gone up to bed without switching off those lights.

She walked up the driveway and stood at the front door.

Just ring the bell. You're not going to turn back now.

She put her finger to the button, and pushed.

Maybe the doorbell sounded, but Anna did not hear it. It was drowned out, at that very moment, by a much louder noise.

A woman's scream.

A shrill, chilling scream that went through Anna like an icy wind, causing her to shudder.

It would have made sense for Anna to run, to get back into her car as quickly as possible, lock the doors, and call for the police. But Anna would have been the first to understand that people did not always do what made sense in emergencies.

Sometimes, they acted solely on instinct.

And Anna's instinct was to help. She had dedicated her *life* to helping.

She immediately tried the door, in case it was unlocked.

It was.

Anna pushed the door open with such force that it went as far as it could on its hinges, hit the wall, and bounced back. She launched herself into the house and was about to fly up the stairs but had to stop.

Someone was coming down.

Now it was Anna's turn to scream.

Sixty-Four

"W e can work this out," Charlotte said pleadingly. "We can solve this. I know we can."

"I don't see how," Gabriella said. She glanced at her son, who took a step closer to Charlotte.

"You can—Leonard here, he's big and strong—can get Bill out of here. Dump him someplace far away! No one knows Bill came to see me tonight!"

"Where's his car?"

"Up the street. You could take it! I'll give you the keys. They're upstairs, in his pants. You get rid of the car and him." An idea struck her. "I could help! I can drive the car! Whatever you need, I can do it."

"And you'll never tell a soul," Gabriella said.

Charlotte brightened. "Yes!"

Gabriella motioned to the table where the typewriter sat. "Sit. Let's talk."

Charlotte was eager to oblige. She pulled out a chair, sat down. Gabriella sat down at an angle to her.

"Why would I tell anyone?" Charlotte said. "I did—I admit this—I did a bad thing. Very bad. If I ever told anyone about what happened here tonight, all that would come out. So I have to keep quiet. Not just to protect you, but to protect myself."

Gabriella nodded slowly. "I did a bad thing, too. When I slit the throats of those two women. But my motivation was pure. It was just. Those women had slept with my husband. They had mocked the sanctity of marriage. What I did was teach them a lesson. That was why I wanted those apologies. In *writing*. I had the law of morality on my side. Oh, I know not everyone would see it that way. You might argue that my husband was no better. But he was *my* husband. I'd taken a vow, as had he. For better or for worse. And he did redeem himself."

Charlotte said nothing.

"And while both of us have done bad things, I think you and I are very different. What you did was so very selfish, so self-centered. You plotted to kill your husband so you could be with that man." She shook her head disapprovingly. "Your bad deeds have been in the service of mocking the institution of marriage. Mine were in its defense."

Any hope one might have seen in Charlotte's eyes was fading. "I know what you're saying, I do. But—"

Gabriella raised a silencing hand. "I don't think you're someone I can trust."

"I am! I—"

"Where's the bathroom?" Len said.

Their eyes turned to Leonard, who was standing at one end of the kitchen island.

He shrugged. "I have to go."

Charlotte sprang to her feet. "I can show you where it is," she said with forced hospitality. She started across the room, pointing. Her path was taking her close to the top of the stairs that led to the front door.

"No!" Gabriella said. The order was meant for both Charlotte and her son.

As she neared the top of the staircase, Charlotte bolted.

"Leonard!"

Despite his size and lumbering nature, Leonard was quick. He turned on his heels and went after Charlotte.

He reached out and managed to grab her by the hair, yanking her back like a puppet on a string. As she was snapped back, he used her momentum against her, propelling her into the wall where he'd first pinned her by the neck.

Charlotte screamed.

Gabriella cocked her head to one side. Was that the doorbell she heard? It was hard to tell with all the other racket. She pushed back her chair and moved toward the struggle.

Leonard grabbed Charlotte by her right arm and flung her toward the steps like a bear flinging a rag doll. Charlotte sailed out into the stairwell, airborne. She didn't land until seven steps down, her head connecting first with a wooden riser, making a sound like the crack of a bat hitting a ball.

Leonard and his mother ran to the top of the stairs and watched Charlotte's lifeless body tumble down the remaining steps.

And the door at the bottom was flung open.

Anna White took two swift steps into the house, froze momentarily as she saw the body hurtling toward her, then screamed.

"Good God," Gabriella said.

Anna's gaze went higher. Saw Leonard and Gabriella looming over her like two vindictive gods.

She backed out of the house and ran.

"Stop her!" Gabriella said to her son.

Leonard ran down the stairs, leaping over the dead woman. Gabriella followed, but it took her longer to navigate around Charlotte. By the time she was outside and could take in what was happening, Anna had reached the end of the driveway, Leonard only a step behind her.

Anna tripped on the curb and went down in the middle of the deserted street. Her purse fell off her shoulder and hit the pavement, spilling car keys and a cell phone. She tried to scramble to her feet, but Leonard was on her, viciously kicking her upper thigh. She shrieked with pain, fell back, and clutched at her leg.

Now Gabriella was at her son's side, struggling to catch her breath.

"Who the hell is she?" she asked, shaking her head furiously with frustration.

"I don't know," her son replied. "What should I do?"

Gabriella took a quick look up and down the street and was relieved to see it was deserted.

"Kill her," she said.

At which point there was a strange sound. A *whoosh*. Something cutting through the air at considerable speed.

Behind them.

And then a loud *whomp*.

Leonard staggered, nearly stepping on Anna.

Gabriella whirled around and said, "What the—"

Another *whoosh*, followed by a *whomp*.

Frank White swung the head of the club—a driver, more specifically, a one-wood—into Gabriella's temple.

The woman went down instantly, her legs crumpling beneath her.

Leonard was clutching the back of his head as he stumbled a few more steps. Blood was seeping through his fingers. He managed to stop pitching forward, stood a moment to regain his balance, then turned to see what had hit him.

Frank, standing there in his striped pajamas, could see that he didn't have much time.

He swung the club back over his shoulder, then came out with it a third time, putting everything he had into the swing. His arms, molded from hundreds of hours on his rowing machine, were pistons.

Leonard went to raise an arm defensively, but he was too slow.

The club caught him in his upper left cheek, just below the eye. That whole side of his face was instantly transformed into a bloody, pulpy mess.

Leonard went down.

Frank stood there, wild-eyed and frozen, panting, holding the driver like a bat, waiting to see whether he was going to need it again. When Gabriella and Leonard hadn't moved for fifteen seconds, Frank knelt down next to Anna, dropped the club onto the street and reached out, tentatively, to stroke her hair.

"Are you okay, Joanie?" he asked.

"Yes," Anna said, struggling to hold back tears. "I'm good." She reached an arm up and cupped her father's bristly, unshaven chin.

"I've never been better."

Sixty-Five

Detective Joe Arnwright: Are you okay now, Mr. Hoffman? Can we continue?

Kenneth Hoffman: Yes, yes, I think so. I needed a minute.

Arnwright: Of course. I'm very sorry.

Hoffman: It's all my fault. All of it. When you follow everything back to the beginning, it's the decisions I made that set the wheels in motion. Did the doctors have anything more to say about Leonard?

Arnwright: He's still in a coma. He's in the Milford Hospital.

Hoffman: So he has no idea his mother is dead.

Arnwright: No.

Hoffman: That son of a bitch. He didn't have to do that to them. I hope he spends whatever years he has left in jail.

Arnwright: They were going to kill his daughter, Mr. Hoffman. He won't be charged. Mr. White saved her life. And he's an old man, to boot. He'd fallen asleep in the back of her SUV. Thought they were going to visit his late wife.

Hoffman: God, this is so . . . Maybe it'd be better if Leonard never wakes up. He'll face so much trouble if he does.

Arnwright: I don't know what to say to that, Mr. Hoffman.

Hoffman: Gabriella never should have involved him. Not this time, and not that night. At heart, he's a true innocent. All he ever wanted to do was make his mother happy.

Arnwright: I understand, Mr. Hoffman, that while he didn't kill those two women, he was culpable. He helped your wife put them in the chairs and tied them up after she'd drugged them. And he did kill Paul Davis. And he killed Bill Myers. And Charlotte Davis. I don't know that I'd call someone like that innocent.

Hoffman: He wouldn't have done any of this without her telling him to do it. He loved his mother so much. He always wanted to please her. At heart, he's a gentle boy. That was why they hired him for the ice cream job. It was the perfect thing for him. And he was a good driver. He never had so much as a fender bender. I know that it's hard to believe, but before all this, I can't think of any time that he ever hurt anyone. And God knows, he'd have been entitled. The way the other kids used to tease him when he was little. Always a little slower than the others. They mocked him, called him stupid, but he isn't really. He's not *book* smart, not *school* smart, but he's smart enough. He manages. Well, up to now.

Arnwright: You were close with your son?

Hoffman: Yes, I mean, I loved him very much. I still do. It's why I did what I did.

Arnwright: Confessing.

Hoffman: That's right. Sure, I ended up protecting Gabriella. But it was never her I was concerned about. It was Leonard. He'd never have stood up to a police interrogation. I had to confess right away before it came to that. And my God, I certainly know now that the boy could never have survived prison. Can you imagine it? What they'd have done to him if he ever went inside? A boy like him? Sure, he's big and strong, but he'd be a toy for every sadistic bastard in there. I couldn't let that happen. It really would be for the best if he doesn't wake up. Prison would be worse than death for him. You have no idea what it's like in there.

Arnwright: You've tried to take your own life since you began your sentence.

Hoffman: I'll probably keep trying till I get it right.

Arnwright: Was there no way you could have blamed Gabriella and left your son out of it? She could have been the noble one. It didn't have to be you.

Hoffman: There was the blood, you see.

Arnwright: Tell me about the blood.

Hoffman: Jill bit him.

Arnwright: Jill Foster bit your son.

Hoffman: Gabriella thought Jill was unconscious. She'd kind of drifted off after she'd typed the note Gabriella demanded she write. Gabriella asked Leonard to double-check, and when he reached out, to touch her chin, Jill woke up. All of a sudden. She lunged out and grabbed Leonard's hand with her teeth. Bit hard into the heel of his hand. He pulled back quickly, and his hand landed on the type-writer, and it really started to bleed.

Arnwright: Why don't you take us back to that night.

Hoffman: I came home, saw what Gabriella, with Leonard's help, had done. She'd figured out I'd been seeing both Catherine and Jill. She'd confronted me about it, earlier. I tried to deny things, but I knew she didn't believe me. I couldn't have imagined, not in a million years, what she would do. Inviting those women over, drug-ging them. Making them apologize to her in writing, actually mak-ing them type the words. Gabriella always had a strong belief in the written word, that oral contracts and promises were not worth much. And once they'd typed what she wanted, she killed them. But it was me she wanted to punish. She was doing this to me as much as she was doing it to those women. I got home right after she'd done it. Gabriella, she was almost in a state of catatonia. Leonard, if you can believe it, was eating a sandwich. After he'd bandaged his hand, of course. But Gabriella, she seemed to be in a dream. I don't know how else to describe it. But pleased with herself, too. She was . . . she was a strange woman. Cold. I'm not making excuses for why I cheated, but she was a cold woman.

Arnwright: Right.

Hoffman: So I'd been looking for love elsewhere, for a long time. But I guess I'd always been that way. Not like Paul. He was a good man. A loyal man. I wish, looking back, I could have been more like him.

Arnwright: And yet, look where it got him.

Hoffman: True enough. Have you figured out what his wife actually did?

Arnwright: We're still putting it together. We found a phone, and one of the available ringtones on it was the sound of a typewriter. And we found more sample notes, written on that typewriter, at Bill Myers's townhouse.

Hoffman: Wow.

Arnwright: Yeah. But back to that night.

Hoffman: Yeah, anyway, I came home and saw what she had done. I told her I could fix it. I'd help her cover it up. I got the bodies into the car, the typewriter, too, because it had so much of Leonard's blood on it. If they ever found that, and ran a DNA test, well, that would have been the end of him, wouldn't it? So I got everything into the car and told my wife I'd clean up the house when I got back.

Arnwright: But you didn't get back.

Hoffman: No. I managed to get rid of the typewriter, but the police caught me with the bodies. And with Paul, of course. I'd really thought, if I could have gotten rid of Catherine and Jill, and Paul, too, that we could move on. Be a real family again. I'd change my ways. I'd be a good husband and father. But then I saw the flashing lights, the officer heading my way. I had seconds to call Gabriella on my phone. I said to her, I've been caught. I'm going to tell them it was me. Just me. Talk to Leonard. Tell them you were out driving all evening, helping Leonard practice for his new job.

Arnwright: So you confessed.

Hoffman: Yes. You see, when you look at the big picture, I *was* guilty. It was my behavior that set all these things into motion. I deserved prison.

Arnwright: So you played the part of the murderer. All this time.

Hoffman: Yes. I must be the first accused killer in history to be grateful not to have an alibi. I'd spent the evening alone in my office on campus. I'm in one of the older buildings. No surveillance cameras, regular keys instead of cards. No one had seen me, I'd talked to no one. No witnesses to come to my defense.

Arnwright: What did you think when Paul Davis showed up at prison with those letters?

Hoffman: Right. The letters . . . they were troubling, I admit. I don't believe in the supernatural, but they gave me pause. They *had* to be bullshit. And yet, I couldn't stop thinking that maybe, somehow, Paul had the actual typewriter. And if the police got hold of it, if they checked that blood, found out it was Leonard's, mixed in with the blood of those women, then all of this would have been for nothing.

Arnwright: You told Gabriella to get it back.

Hoffman: Yes. I just . . . I didn't know it would turn out the way it did. I know I tried to kill Paul that night, but all these months after . . . I never wanted Paul to die. I liked Paul. He was a good man. Bill Myers, I didn't know him. Charlotte I had met once. But Paul . . . I feel badly about Paul. I was something of a mentor to him when he came to West Haven. Did you know that?

Arnwright: Yes.

Hoffman: Maybe Bill and Charlotte got what was coming to them.

Arnwright: If you're looking for a silver lining, I guess there's that.

Hoffman: What happens now? Do you think I'll be exonerated? I mean, I didn't really kill those two women. And what I did to Paul, that was a spur-of-the-moment thing. There was nothing premeditated about it.

Arnwright: Are you saying you're an innocent man?

Hoffman: I guess I wouldn't go that far.

Arnwright: Neither would I.

Sixty-Six

I like this place," Frank White told Anna. "I do."

They'd been given a private tour of the seniors' residence. They'd seen the dining hall and the recreation center and the exercise room, and the last stop was what might end up being his room. It was spacious enough. There was a bed, and a big cushy chair, and a television.

"And I can put my rowing machine right there," he said. "Look out the window. You can see the water."

"I don't know, Dad," Anna said. She'd been trying hard not to limp throughout the tour. Leonard had nearly broken a bone when he'd kicked her. She was going for physical therapy twice a week.

Her father had seemed remarkably lucid ever since that night. While he'd believed, at one point, that he was saving his wife and not his daughter, since then, he'd shown considerable understanding of what had happened.

He knew he'd killed someone, and put someone else into a coma. And he'd had not a moment's regret.

"You do what you have to do," he said.

But he did see it as a turning point. He'd insisted it was time for him to become independent, at least from Anna. They'd been arguing about it for days.

Now, standing in this oversize bedroom with a flat-screen and a view of the sound, she stated her feelings once more.

"I don't want you to go."

"I've lived with you for as long as I did for a reason," he said. "And now we know what it was. It was to be there that night."

"You don't believe in that kind of thing," Anna said. "You think that's a load of shit, that our lives are somehow preordained."

"You'd be surprised what I believe in."

And that was when he told her.

"The night your mother died, I was sound asleep. And then . . ." He struggled a moment to find the words. "And then she spoke to me, like in a dream, and said I should get to the hospital as quick as I could."

Anna said nothing.

Frank sat on the edge of the bed, ran his palms across the bedspread. "And I didn't pay a goddamn bit of attention, because I didn't believe in that sort of thing. And you know what happened. She passed that night. I should have believed. I should have listened."

Anna, softly, said, "Why have you never told me that story?"

Frank shrugged. "I didn't want to upset you. I didn't want you to know I had a chance to say good-bye and didn't take it."

Anna sat down in the easy chair and looked away. Outside, a cloudless sky made the sound a deep blue.

"Anyway, I bring that up now," her father said, "because your mother spoke to me again."

Anna looked back, blinked away tears, tried to get her father into focus. "When did she do that?"

"After what happened with those people who tried to kill you. Couple of nights later, I guess it was."

Anna wasn't sure she could bring herself to ask. But she had to know. "What did she say?"

Now it was her father's turn to gather his strength.

"Joanie said to me, she said, 'Frank, you saved her life. The only thing more you can do is *give* her her life.' And that was it."

Anna stared at her father. He reached out a hand to her and she took it.

"I guess you think that's a bunch of horseshit," he said.

She shook her head from side to side.

"You believe it?"

Anna stopped moving her head and swallowed.

"I do."

Acknowledgments

At HarperCollins and William Morrow, thanks to everyone for getting *A Noise Downstairs* ready, with a special nod to Liate Stehlik, and my terrific editor, Jennifer Brehl, who kept pushing when I thought we were done. We weren't.

In the UK, I am grateful to David Shelley, Katie Espiner, Harriet Bourton, Emad Akhtar, Ben Willis, and the entire Orion team.

As always, thank you to my amazing agent, Helen Heller.

For all manner of support, current and past, thanks go out to Robert MacLeod, Bill Taylor, Douglas Gibson, and Stephen King.

And once again, a huge shout-out to booksellers. Thank you for everything you do to get writers' works into readers' hands.

Finally, I'm long overdue in recognizing two people who are no longer with us, but to whom I remain immensely grateful all these years later for their encouragement, guidance, and friendship: Margaret Laurence and Kenneth Millar.